Lost River Anthology

Lost River Anthology

Short Stories and Tall Tales

Harold Raley

LITERARY PRESS
LAMAR UNIVERSITY

ISBN: 978-1-942956-37-2
Library of Congress Control Number: 2017940916

Book Design: Theresa Ener
Manufactured in the United States

Lamar University Literary Press
Beaumont, Texas

To the memory of Dr. Julián Marías—Mentor, Friend, and Champion of Truth

Fiction by Lamar University Literary Press

Acknowledgments

I much appreciate all the admired teachers who instructed me in literary theory and admirable storytellers who taught by example.

Other Fiction by Harold Raley

That Lowdown Rascal (2008)
Swapping Places (2009)
Louisiana Rogue (2013)
Barefoot on a Frosty Morn (2016)
The Prodigal (2016)

CONTENTS

Preface

Preface

Most of the stories selected for this anthology are set in the mythical Deep-South town of Lost River. The remaining tales are scattered over vast areas of America: Tennessee, Indiana, Texas, Kansas, and Nebraska. All are linked in ways evident to the reader but not always to the people themselves. The connections are not intended to "novelize" the stories, which are stand-alone tales. Instead they reflect patterns of expansion that built a nation but often severed personal and family ties.

Shorter versions of some of the stories appeared in my earlier books. While always respecting the originals, in this volume I invoke authorial privilege to extend and deepen some of them.

Except for a few words, I chose not to write the stories in regional dialect and to standardize versions authored several years ago. Though it is gratifying to repeat the ancestral language I learned as a child, my experience as a reader taught me—the Thomas Hardy novels, for example—how hard it is to slog through the rough syntax and antique vocabulary of other times and places. But having made this decision, I cadenced the words to suggest, so I hope, the older phrasing without repeating it.

1.

That Lowdown Rascal

"Hey, boy, what's that noise I hear under the ground? Sounds like water running down there. The folks around here operating a mine or something?"

The barefoot boy, who looked to be about thirteen, continued to scrape pigeon droppings from founder Colonel Abner Stokesbury's statue with his pocket knife and did not answer or look at the young man mounted on a droopy-eared old mule.

"Hey, boy, don't you have any manners? I'm talking to you. What's your name?"

The boy wiped the blade on the concrete, snapped it shut, and put it in his pocket. "Johnny," he said finally without looking up.

"Johnny what?" the man asked in an irritated tone as he dismounted.

"Johnny, that's all."

"Well, damned if you aren't a big talker. But tell me, do you know a man around here that does have more than one name, Henry Patterson?"

"I ain't heard."

"You live here, don't you, Johnny?"

"No."

"Then where do you live?"

"Up yonder."

"Up yonder where?"

"Up on the mountain," Johnny said with a vague sweep of his hand.

A two-horse wagon clattered down the dirt street and stopped at the crossroads. Short, red-bearded, and squint-eyed Hubert Pirkle braced himself on the iron rim and sideboard and jumped down.

"Johnny, get your lazy ass in the wagon and quit wasting this man's time and mine. We need to get on home so you can get started gathering the rest of that corn, nubbins and all. I'll need it all. I told you to finish yesterday, but you're so damned lazy it takes you two days to pick your nose. Mister," he said, turning to tall, curly-headed young man, "I hope he wasn't giving you any trouble."

"No, sir. I was asking him if he knew where Henry Patterson lives, and about that sound I can hear under the ground. But I couldn't get much out of him."

"That's because he's as dumb as a post. I doubt if he could tell you what day of the week it is. Anyway, I can tell you about Mr. Patterson. If you take this same road on through Lost River and go about two miles west, his place is on the right. Big white house and his name is on the mailbox."

"I thought this town was called Stokesbury."

"Well, it used to be and I guess that name is still on maps, named after that old fart in the statue there with the bird crap on his head. But it's been Lost River for as long as I've lived here."

"What about that sound I hear? Is it a mine of some kind?"

"No, not a mine, mister. Old timers call it the Lost River and say it runs underground from the mountain back up where I live. I've heard that way back in Indian times it used to run above ground. You can still see the dry bed down there a ways. But then about the time this country was settled there was an earthquake, I guess they call it, somewhere north of here, and the river above ground dried up. Right around town here is the only place you can hear the sound it makes. I imagine there must be a waterfall or something like that down there to make the noise."

"Anybody ever dig down to see?"

"They claim one man with a crew tried a long time ago, but he fell down the shaft and they couldn't get him out. So they filled it up and let that be his grave. But I wouldn't swear that any of it is so or not. Some of the biggest liars I ever met live around here."

"Just curious, does the river come back above ground somewhere?"

"Not around here. Some say it runs underground to one of the big rivers up north, but I don't know that, and I'm pretty sure nobody else does either. No telling where it goes. Well, mister, we'd best be going. I need to get some work out of this lazy kid. Dammit, Johnny, didn't I tell you to get in the wagon? And move that sack of corn to the middle of the wagon bed and don't let any more seed spill out."

The young man got back on his old mule and rode west. Hubert rapped his mule team smartly with the reins and headed off the other way toward the mountain. When he wasn't looking, Johnny slipped corn grains out of a rip in the sack and tossed them to the birds.

Lloyd Patterson, 24, showed up later that early March morning in 1878 at his Uncle Henry Patterson's place. Tall, curly headed, and lusty as a barnyard rooster, Lloyd was so devilishly good-looking that girls got butterflies in their stomach just looking at him. Folks who knew him said he was so lucky he could fall in a muddy creek and come up with a fish in his back pocket.

Talk soon got out in Lost River that he was on the run from some kind of woman trouble back in Georgia. That's where the Pattersons had come from after General Sherman and his Yankees pranced and burned their way through that country. Not that anybody could ever get the straight of his troubles from Lloyd. He was smoother than oil and could come up with more convincing lies than hounds have fleas. But judging from what he stirred up in Lost River, nobody doubted that he left plenty of ruffled feathers amongst the Georgia womenfolk too.

In no time at all, so they say, Lloyd had his way with certain accommodating wives around Lost River, and Lord knows how many single girls he relieved of their virtue with heart-melting promises to march them to the marriage altar. But because it's human nature to prefer the preferable, the minute he saw her, Lloyd set his sights on pretty Nellie Stokesbury, the young Tennessee-born wife of old Homer Stokesbury, the grandson of city founder Colonel Abner Stokesbury.

Behind his back, neighbors made nasty jokes about Homer and his young wife, especially about whether he still had enough "nature"—as folks alluded to manhood back then—to be a proper husband to pretty Nellie. But at the same time they respected the money he had in the local bank and his three hundred acres of prime Valley land.

Folks who had known old Homer personally said he was a hurtful sight to behold. Blind in one eye from a Yankee bullet at Shiloh and fearsomely disfigured after botched surgery by a Confederate doctor, he caused young children to run from him in terror and their parents to lower their eyes to keep from staring at his disfigurement.

But with just one eye Homer was sharp-sighted when it came to money. And even though he was foolish to a fault about sweet little Nellie, he kept business matters strictly to himself.

Ole Lloyd saw his chance at a Sunday singing and dinner on the ground at Lost River Holiness Church. With all the confidence in the world he sidled up to Miss Nellie, who was serving cake.

"You can give me a piece if you please, Miss Nellie."

"Big piece or little?" she asked with a trace of a smile, as aware as ole Lloyd of the double meaning of his words.

"I like big pieces, ma'am," he said with a sly grin.

It looked like he had a bird nest on the ground: a young, pretty woman married to an ugly old goat who wouldn't or couldn't give her the affection her prime womanly nature surely needed.

But for once and in what looked like the most promising of circumstances, ole Lloyd failed in his romantic quest. After most of the church folk had dispersed and they could speak privately, Miss Nellie laughed in his face. For unbeknownst to Homer, Lloyd, and folks in the Lost River community, Miss Nellie, though ignorant of schooling, had learned a lot in other ways. As the daughter of a Memphis pleasure woman, she had been baited, hooked, and tossed back into the muddy stream of life by some of the slickest riverboat Romeos from Memphis to New Orleans. Country lovers like Lloyd couldn't pull any trick on her she hadn't already seen. She came right out and said it: she was sticking with old Homer for as long as it took her to get her hands on his bank account and three hundred acres of prime Valley land.

Then came the crowning insult. She ended their conversation by telling him that, yes, boy, he could have what he wanted from her provided he could cross her palm with a hundred dollars in cold cash money. She laughed again when she said it, suspecting from the looks of him that ole Lloyd didn't have a spare dime to his name.

Well, her humiliating putdown was like a hornet sting to his pride. Lloyd's cocky assurance turned to anger, and he started racking his brain for a way to get even with Miss Nellie for her insult. A day or two later he had the makings of a plan.

Ole Lloyd approached Homer, taking care not to come up on his blind side, to ask if he could rent the McClellan place Homer had recently foreclosed on. As always—except in Nellie's case, of course—Lloyd was convincing. He explained that although his Uncle Henry was good to him and treated him like a son, it was time to put his rambling days behind him and think about marrying and settling down. He hinted that a certain girl over in the Evergreen community west of Lost River had caught his eye. It was true, she had—like nearly every girl—from Evergreen to Fairview out east of Lost River.

The longer Lloyd talked, the more persuaded Homer was to help this earnest and honest young man get a start in life. Though twice married, Homer had no children of his own, and Lloyd's respectful lies and polite manner must have struck a dormant paternal chord in the old man. Like everybody around Lost River, he had heard talk about Lloyd's escapades. "But hell," he remembered with an ugly grin, "I sowed a few wild oats in my day, too." Homer was heard to say on occasion that "Men that don't have any juice young won't be worth a fart old."

They struck a deal for Lloyd to rent the farm. But then he brought up another problem. He had no money to start spring planting. He explained that he needed to buy a mule team and wagon, plows, tools, seed, and have some ready money for fertilizer and other necessities. His Uncle Henry and Aunt Becky would give him maybe a table, chair, and a few dishes to set up housekeeping, but right now they didn't see how they could help out with any money, not with Aunt Becky always ailing and needing medicine and doctoring.

Despite his natural caution, Homer was convinced that Lloyd was a good risk and agreed to make him a loan of two hundred dollars at three percent interest payable come fall. He also agreed to add the price—at the going rate—of seed corn and cottonseed to his account. In return and according to sharecropping rules, come fall gathering time Lloyd would be obliged to turn over to Homer a third of the corn and a fourth of the cotton. Homer asked Lloyd to accompany him in his buggy to the Lost River Bank—of which he was the principal shareholder—to draw up the papers to be signed, notarized, and filed. This done, Homer withdrew two hundred dollars from his account and carefully counted out the bills in bank president Charlie Bunker's office, squinting with his good eye at each one. Then after giving Lloyd a ride and a year's worth of unwanted advice, Homer dropped him off at his Uncle Henry's and both men went on about their business.

Homer's dealings went on at their usual profitable pace, but Lloyd's monkey business was even brisker. Under their several solemn pledges of secrecy, Lloyd told his Valley girlfriends about his new farm and promised each one that she was to be the mistress of his household and his life as soon as he had a proper chance to speak man to man with her father. With this assurance they loosened up with their favors. It had taken some expert doing for Lloyd to kindle their little fires, but once ablaze the flames were just about more than even he could handle.

But the real object of all his shenanigans was, of course, high and mighty Miss Nellie. The following Friday, the day old Homer went in his buggy several miles out in Stokesbury Valley to inspect his farms, Lloyd showed up at Nellie's house riding Uncle Henry's smart little mule with a sack of cottonseed slung across its back. Naturally, Homer had said nothing to her about his dealings with Lloyd, so she was surprised when he tied the mule to the gate, set the cottonseed on the porch, and reminding her of the price she had quoted him for her favors, put a hundred dollars in her hand.

Though she never expected to, Miss Nellie honored her word without the usual pouts and delays that womanly modesty normally requires. And in the natural run of things, it seems reasonable to think that handsome Lloyd was a pleasurable alternative to the pawing and gasping of old Homer. In fact, at the conclusion of their feisty frolic, she purred that she would welcome further visits and that the price paid for the first would cover others to follow.

Ole Lloyd promised an early repeat of their energetic tryst. In fact, he was so pleased that he placed an extra dollar on her pillow, "just to show you my true love," as he put it. But now, he reminded her, he must be on his way before Homer happened to come home sooner than expected.

There was just one more little matter: the sack of cottonseed on the porch. If she wouldn't mind writing her name or making her mark on a paper he pulled out of his pocket, it would show that he had come on legitimate business to deliver the cottonseed, in case he met Homer down the road. Besides, Homer liked to have everything on paper.

Without hesitation, the contented lady made her mark in receipt of the cottonseed. Then Lloyd trotted away on Uncle Henry's smart little mule, whistling loud enough to startle the birds into silence. Down the road a piece he stopped, and moistening a stubby little pencil with his tongue and working hard to make the letters as the little mule flicked flies with her tail and chomped on the grass, he wrote next to her mark, "and one hundred and one dollars paid on my debt to Mr. Homer Stokesbury."

Imagine Miss Nellie's surprise and anxiety when the very next morning ole Lloyd rode up as big as life on that same little mule, this time with a sack of corn slung across its back. Homer, though, was glad to see him and curious to know why he had brought back the cottonseed and now some of the corn.

"Well, Mr. Homer," Lloyd said in his polite Georgia accent, "same reason why yesterday I brought back that hundred and one dollars of the money you loaned me. The other day Uncle Henry saw his way clear to help me with some money and seed corn and cottonseed. He's a fine man, Uncle Henry is, goodhearted as can be. It's just that he and Aunt Becky have had some hard times lately. But that's the reason, Mr. Homer, I left the money and cottonseed with Mrs. Stokesbury. I didn't want to have any more debt than I had to. And knowing how you like to keep regular accounts, I asked Mrs. Stokesbury to kindly put her mark on this paper, as you can see. I hated to put her to the trouble and do appreciate her being so kind and obliging. Now I didn't know how to figure the interest money, but I thought a dollar might cover the time it was in my use. You tell me if I need to give you more and I'll do it."

Homer was steamed with Nellie. "Woman, you didn't tell me about the money? Where is it? Fetch it! You hear?"

"Lordy mercy," she answered, her face a cherry red, "I'll get it right away. I put it away and forgot all about it. You know how bad I am to forget things, honeybunch. I depend on you for business things and never trouble my head, knowing how smart you are in stuff like that."

Miss Nellie produced the money, all tied up in a dainty little pink handkerchief. Homer counted it, squinting and pressing the bills. Then satisfied with the count, he allowed as how Lloyd showed good judgment by paying off as much as he could on the debt and predicted he would do well in life if he stayed on that sensible pathway.

"Well, Mr. Homer, I can't tell you how obliged I am for the kindly way you speak of me, and that's why I truly regret now to have to tell you what's happened to me and my good intentions just since yesterday."

With this admission, ole Lloyd hung his head and for a moment it looked like he was about to cry.

"Why, what is it, boy?" Homer asked, moved by the young man's troubles.

"Well, sir," Lloyd answered, getting a grip on his emotions, "you see, it's like this, two nights ago Uncle Henry and I talked and he told me he had figured out how he could help me with money so that I wouldn't have to carry so much debt. Then yesterday about the time I left the money and cottonseed with Mrs. Stokesbury, Aunt Becky took sick again. Uncle Henry had to send up to Tylerville for Dr. Cunningham, I believe his name is, to come out and doctor her. The Doctor's afraid she's truly bad off this time, and now Uncle Henry can't spare me the money he meant to. He'll need all he's got and then some for poor Aunt Becky. But he can still give me some seed corn and cottonseed. So that's why I brought these two sacks back to you. But as I was saying, sir, I reckon that's all he can do for me. So, Mr. Homer, I was wondering . . ."

"Wondering what, boy?"

"Well, sir, wondering if you could see your way clear to let me have the money back, just like it was when I signed the papers at the bank. I hate to put you to so much trouble, but like I said, it's something we didn't see coming."

Homer thought for a moment, then reached over and laid a hand on ole Lloyd's shoulder, looking into his eyes with his one good one.

"Why, young man, of course you can have the money back, same conditions as before. As far as that goes, nothing has changed about our agreement. The papers are still down in the bank just the way we left them. But there is one other thing I'll hold you to."

"Whatever you say, Mr. Homer," Lloyd said in a humble voice. "You just tell me and I'll do it."

"Son, I know you think a lot of your Uncle Henry and Aunt Becky and want to help them all you can. They're good people. Nobody's disputing that, and I'm real sorry to hear about your Aunt Becky's ailments. I truly am. But here's what I have to ask you to do, that is to say, not to do. Don't you spend this money on them, no matter what. This money is for you to make the crop on and get a start in life. Do you understand what I'm telling you, son?"

"Yes sir, I do, Mr. Homer, and I give you my word that I'll not spend a penny of this money on them, even though it hurts me to see them up against it like they've been since Aunt Becky's health went bad."

"I know it's hard for you, son, but it truly is for your own good."

And so the deal was done anew. Homer handed Lloyd one hundred one dollars under his solemn promise to use the money only for his own purposes.

Meanwhile, behind Homer's back but in plain sight of ole Lloyd, Miss Nellie was silently shaping with her pretty red lips every last one of the cussing words she could think of—and she had a good supply—to describe Lloyd's sorry canine ancestry and his barking, four-legged mother. But to all ole Lloyd smiled sweetly. Then thanking Homer for his help with a handshake and bowing politely to Mrs. Stokesbury, he took his leave, mounted Uncle Henry's high-stepping little mule, and trotted briskly down the road. He had not gone far before he started whistling so loud that the birds made not a peep.

And from what people said later, he didn't stop, not even to pick up his clothes at Uncle Henry's or swap mules. He must have known things were closing in on him. In fact, only a couple of hours later, Mr. John Thomas Hunter showed up at Uncle Henry's place with his shotgun and announced that he was looking for "That lowdown nephew of yours" and promising to shoot him on sight when he found him.

By that time, though, with Georgia already behind him, Lost River soon to be, a good head start on Uncle Henry's smart little mule, and Homer's two hundred dollars in his pocket—plus fifty more Uncle Henry had lent him to help make the crop—chances were looking better all the time that instead of raising cotton in Stokesbury Valley, ole Lloyd would soon be raising Cain in Texas.

Privately, old Homer took it hard when he found out how Lloyd had tricked him. And loyal little Nellie supported her husband with angry outbursts of her own every time they talked about it. But for fear of stirring up more gossip, Homer had little to say publicly about the swindle. Anyway, he was pleasantly distracted a few months later when Nellie gave birth to a strapping baby boy, who was Homer's pride and joy in his declining years.

Folks respected old Homer's manhood after he became a father, even though certain suspicious neighbors noticed that little Leon didn't look a bit like Homer. But proper minded folks called them loose-tongued, pointing out that it was hard to say what Homer's features had once been before his war wounds and all.

Sweet Nellie simmered down in time and stopped obsessing over ole Lloyd. Besides, she had her hands full trying to raise tall, curly-headed Leon who nearly drove her crazy with his womanizing and hell-raising ways. But she kept things in perspective through it all, consoling herself with the idea that one day old Homer would pass on and she would finally get her hands on his bank account and three hundred acres of prime Valley land.

But life has a way of playing its little tricks. She died in 1899, a year before old Homer, and Leon inherited everything.

2.

Johnny

In March of 1876, two days after he talked to the man in Lost River, Johnny, 13, came back to his house to find it empty and his family gone. There was a letter on the fireplace mantle. It was as hard for him to read as it was for his mother to write:

Son

I reckin Huberts movin us to Texas. He's been talkin about it fer a good while cause we aint doin no good here. They say the lands real good out there. His brother claims the cottin land will make two bales to the acer and hell hep us get settled. Hubert says if we leeve now we can still git there for spring plantin. I hate that he won't brang you with us. It breaks my heart to leeve you but you know Hubert ain't never gonna acept you as a son. He'd just beat you more if you was with us and I cant stand that no more. I have to go do for your litle brother and sisters. I left you all the clothes I could but Hubert told me to take the good pare o shoes for Jimmy. Hes growin like a weed and can ware them by fall. The girls cried when they found out Hubert was leevin you here but theyre to litle to understand thangs. I cooked ye some beans and left a pone of cornbread and the ol skillet with the broke handle sos you can cook yourself some thangs. I wush you could go to my kinfoks up in east tenessee but I cant tell you how to get there and my brother Jeff cant abide the idear o havin you there but I know momma would like to see you and some of my cousins mite let you stay with them. Theys still a few taters in the shed and the onyins in the gardin look good but the greens aint no good this year for some reason. We took all the chikens we could cetch sos we could eat on the way to Texas but theys some that got loose in the woods so ye mite find some aigs. I love you son and I'll pray for the good lord to look after you. That's all I can do. Miss Hardin mite spare you some milk if ye ast her and you thank her kindly if she does.

Momma

Confused and scared, Johnny ran through the two-room log house to see for himself. It was true. They were gone—people, beds, chairs, kitchen table, dishes, clothes, quilts, guns, everything. The only things left were some of his clothes in the back room, a pot of beans by the fireplace, a pone of cornbread on a folded tablecloth beside it, and an old iron skillet with half a handle, propped against the wall. He ran outside and saw that the wagon and mule team were gone. The place had never been so quiet and he had never felt so alone. He missed the happy chatter of his little sisters.

The panic of abandonment overcame him. Without thinking, he ran down the road after them until he was out of breath. He didn't know the way to Texas or how far it was, but there was only one way out to the main road to Lost River. Maybe he could still catch them. But when he got to the high curve and could see across the mountain in all directions, there was no movement or sound except for three crows hopping from limb to limb in the trees below him and cawing warnings of his presence.

He stopped and put his hands on his knees, panting and trying to make sense of things. He had worked all day cutting cornstalks and sprouts in the south field as Hubert had ordered him. If they left in the morning they would be miles away by now. And which direction once off the mountain would they have taken? He had never been past Lost River.

But why would he want to be with them? He was angry with himself for even considering it. His mother was right: Hubert would just whip him again if he showed up. But he loved his sisters and did not want to lose them. But for them he might have run away already.

Johnny walked back to the house, still conflicted in his feelings. Every now and then he would turn to listen or catch sight of anything on the road. But now the sun was setting. The crows had flown away. A whippoorwill began its mournful evening call.

The problem was that Johnny was not Hubert's son.

Furloughed in May of 1862 for their wounds at the battle of Shiloh, Confederate soldiers Homer Stokes and Gordon Drake brought word to young Lois Pirkle that her husband Hubert was listed among the dead. She mourned for him and returned to her father's home in East Tennessee. A man comforted the young widow in her loneliness, and when Hubert turned up in October of the same year, she was pregnant with Johnny. He threatened to kill her and her lover. The man fled when he heard that Hubert was coming after him with a gun. Lois pleaded circumstances and begged for her life. Hubert agreed to take her back provided that as soon as her bastard was weaned she would send it to her father, Milford Sullins, to raise.

But when Johnny was four months old, Milford died of a stroke and his semi-invalid widow, Mildred, went to live with her son, Jeff Sullins. Jeff angrily declared that under no circumstances would he raise his sister's bastard. He had enough mouths to feed already, making sure his mother heard him.

So Johnny lived under Hubert's roof and his wrath. He beat the child savagely and refused to call him by his name, addressing him as "bastard" when it was necessary to speak to him at all. Johnny ran away once when he was eight, but hunger brought him back after two days. As punishment, Hubert gave him a ferocious beating that fractured Johnny's left arm. It healed but was permanently crooked because of improper setting. Lois's pleas for Johnny only made matters worse, for Hubert took them to mean that she secretly preferred Johnny's father. The more she denied it, the more convinced he was that she missed the other man. She gritted her teeth and said nothing when the beatings started. But in spite of her submissiveness, Hubert sometimes whipped her, too, calling her "slut" and "loose woman."

Johnny's usefulness as a field hand saved his life. Hubert worked the boy like an animal, sending him to the fields at daybreak and allowing him back in the house only at sundown. At midday his mother or sisters, Chloe and Sarah, would bring him fresh water, a piece of buttered cornbread, and onions and tomatoes if they were in season.

His mother was right: the girls were too young to understand their father's hatred. Despite Hubert's angry disapproval, they loved Johnny. On the other hand, if their brother Jimmy did not fully understand Hubert's hatred himself, he bullied his older half-brother as much as he pleased. For many years Johnny knew better than to lay a hand on him.

During the three weeks Johnny's broken arm was healing, Hubert let Lois send him down to the Lost River School with his sisters and brother. In that short time Johnny learned to read simple words, but writing and arithmetic were harder for him and his progress was minimal. In any case, Hubert ordered him back to the fields as soon as the arm looked strong enough. Jimmy and the girls finished out the school year. Remembering his brief attendance and the children he met there, Johnny would pause in his field work to look down in the Valley at the school. He practiced his letters sometimes by tracing them in the dirt with his hoe and trying to remember what his teacher had said. But the school memories and friendships faded in time.

Scrawny, underfed, and overworked all his life, Johnny suddenly started to grow and fill out at thirteen. And he was changing in other ways. A month before the family moved, Johnny's temper overcame his fear and for the first time he reacted to Jimmy's bullying by shoving him to the ground. His shocked half-brother ran to tell his father, who came toward Johnny with a thick board in his hand and rage in his voice.

"I've told you I don't know how many times not ever to lay a hand on my boy if you know what's good for you! And when I get through with you this time, bastard, you won't ever forget again! I promise you that!"

Always before, Johnny had submitted without a word to the beatings, but lately his feelings were changing and he was growing stronger by the day. The pent-up anger and humiliation of many years suddenly broke like a dam, and words that neither of them had ever heard came out of Johnny's mouth.

"Jimmy's the one that needs a whipping! If you take that board to me, all I can tell you is there'll come a day when I'll get even! You beat me all these years for no reason while I was a little boy, but one of these days I'll be a man and I'll be coming for you, Hubert!"

Hubert stopped in his tracks, not believing what he was hearing. "What did you call me, bastard?"

"I called you 'Hubert.' That's your name."

"You call me 'sir'! You show respect!"

"I'll never call you 'sir' again," Johnny said defiantly. "You're not my daddy! You're nothing to me!"

"We'll see about that, you little bastard!" he said, waving the board.

Hubert came at Johnnie in a red rage. Johnny fought back as best he could but had the worst of it against the much stronger man. When finally Hubert stopped hitting and stomping from pure exhaustion, Johnny's face and arms looked like bloody sausage. But Hubert had a few bruises himself and blood was dripping from his nose.

For Johnny it was another beating, but with a difference. Always before, Hubert had simply whipped a helpless child. For the first time, Johnny had fought back with a man's spirit, though not with a man's strength. Hubert won the fight but Johnny gained the victory. Both of them knew that he would no longer live in fear of Hubert, and neither of them would forget this day. The next morning Johnny could barely move, but he had never felt better about himself.

Jimmy was awed by the way Johnny fought back against Hubert. From then on he held his tongue and kept his distance.

As for Hubert, he tried but could not forget Johnny's ominous promise: "One of these days I'll be a man and I'll be coming for you." And seeing how big and strong Johnny was getting, Hubert realized that day was not far off. As he saw it, he had two choices: either he could shoot Johnny and risk hanging for his murder, or move to Texas as he had been considering and leave him behind. He chose the second option. "Let the bastard starve to death like a mangy dog," he muttered to himself.

As Johnny scooped beans out of the pot with a piece of cornbread—Lois had not left any utensils—he took stock of his resources and his chances. He was thirteen and field tough, able to do just about any work a man could. But his only working tools were his pocketknife and the hoe he had been using that day. It was too dark now to see if Hubert had overlooked anything useful around the house and outbuildings. He guessed he had taken all the traps and tools for spite if not for need.

The cornbread and beans gave him a two or three-day margin of food at most. The onions looked promising but winter had been hard on the greens. There were still the few potatoes his mother had mentioned, but he knew most of them were rotten and the others soon would be unless he ate them first. Maybe he could catch one of the maverick chickens or find their eggs, as his mother said, but then he realized that even if he could, he had no way of starting a fire to cook them.

He brought straw from the barn and made a place to sleep next to the fireplace. The March nights were still chilly on the mountain, but there was enough straw to warm him if he slept with his clothes on and piled the others on top. His head was in turmoil with conflicting emotions and his dreams were no different.

Most of all, he was scared. Since the fight with Hubert, he had fancied himself almost a man. That night, alone on the mountain, he realized he was still just a boy with a boy's limitations. Maybe he would end up like some unwanted puppies Hubert had thrown out of the wagon the year before on a trip down to Lost River. The next day they were still whimpering by the side of the road, but that night raccoons or foxes killed them.

By morning light he confirmed his bleak prospects. Just as he feared, Hubert had taken all the tools, nails, metal traps, and implements. And without a hammer or saw he had no way to build wooden traps for rabbits and possums as he first hoped. He ran to a chop block behind the barn where recently he had tossed a pole axe, but it was gone too.

He emptied the sack of potatoes and sorted out five sound ones. The others stank like carrion and he pitched them over the pasture fence. Green flies buzzed in and covered them. He would save and rinse the sack for future use. The well bucket and rope were gone, but there was water in a nearby spring in the pasture.

He looked in the corncrib, but except for shucks and a few loose grains, it was empty. He put the kernels in his pocket and regretted not stuffing more when he had the chance that day in the wagon.

He checked the garden. The onions looked delicious, and he calculated they would last him two or three weeks. He pulled one up, dusted it off on his pant leg and devoured it dirt and all. The greens were sparse and good for no more than two meals at best. Maybe some tomatoes would come up volunteer from last year's seed, but even if they did, it would be months before they produced. He needed food now.

He remembered seeing a few corn nubbins on the stalks he had cut the day before. Luckily he had disobeyed Hubert's orders to gather them. He washed the smelly sack downstream from the spring and ran to retrieve the corn before crows and deer ate it. He found half a dozen ears. That would keep him from starving for a few days, provided he could find a way to start a fire and parch the grains.

He remembered what his mother said about the chickens. Three had wandered back to the barn, but he hoped others were still out in the woods. Later he would search for any stragglers and their eggs.

He sat on the edge of the porch and ate a helping of beans and cornbread, taking note of what was left. Maybe he could stretch them to last two more days. With the beans, cornbread, and the onion in his stomach he felt better. With luck maybe he could make it. Maybe he wouldn't end up like the puppies Hubert had dropped by the side of the road.

His mother had left him an extra pair of pants and shirt, along with the old pair of shoes, but he had outgrown all his clothes, especially the shoes. He needed to slit the leather to give his feet more room. They were still too small, but he could wear them on freezing days. Otherwise he went barefoot the rest of the year.

It took him a long time to make a hole in the right shoe with his pocketknife. Then he widened it, first with the smaller blade and then with the bigger one. He repeated the process more expertly with the left shoe and set them aside.

He searched around the house, but another of his first fears was confirmed: his folks had left no matches, and the fireplace fire had gone out before he thought to save it. He knew of no way to start a fire. He had heard stories about how the Indians used to make fires with sticks, but he had tried it before as a game without any luck.

Maybe Widow Arvalee Hardin, the nearest neighbor, would give him some matches. And his mother had mentioned that she might have some milk to spare, too. He didn't like to talk to people. But this was no time for shyness. He went down the mountain to her Valley home.

"Why, you're Johnny, aren't you?" she said in surprise as she came to the door. "You've grown so much, I didn't know you at first. But, son, your folks left, I'm told. For Texas, they say, or somewhere way off. Why aren't you with them?"

"I stayed here."

"You stayed? But, Johnny, you're just a boy! Ye can't be by yourself up on that mountain. They say there're still panthers and wildcats up there. Johnny, did you run away from your family?"

"No. But I need some matches, and Momma said you might have some milk."

"Well, I reckon I can let you have a few matches, and I sure can give a growing boy some milk. You just come on in the house and sit while I get it ready. And then we'll talk about all this."

She wrapped half a dozen matches in an oil paper "to keep them dry," she explained, and brought a half gallon jar of rich milk.

"You can just take the jar with you. And keep it if ye need it. I'll have no more use for it."

"My momma said to thank you kindly."

"Well, you're more than welcome. But Johnny, I don't know what to say about the other. I don't think you should be by yourself up there on that mountain. You say you didn't run away. Then how is it that your folks left you behind?"

"Hubert don't like me, so he left me."

"Left you by yourself?"

"Yeah, they were gone when I got back from the field yesterday."

"Well, if that doesn't beat all! What will you do? How old are you, anyway?"

"Thirteen, my momma says."

"Thirteen. And they just left you on your own. Didn't your mother have any say in the matter? Surely she wouldn't just leave you."

"Momma's got no say. She's scared of Hubert. He beats her sometimes, and used to whip me all the time."

"Well, I had heard some talk. But that just isn't right that he would treat you that way. I just don't know what to say. Son, did they leave you anything in the way of food and such?"

"Not much, beans and cornbread. Worst thing is, I don't have any tools, except my knife and the hoe I was using when they left. I could make some traps for rabbits and possums if I had a hammer and handsaw. I know how."

"Well, now, I reckon Mr. Hardin left a hammer and some things when he passed on last year. I don't rightly know what's down there in the shed. He used to work there a lot, but now I don't ever go down there myself. I tell you what, you go and see. And you just take what ye need. I won't be using any of that stuff anymore. My children are moving me out of this house next week. They've sold the place to Mr. Homer Stokes, so I reckon I'll be living in Tylerville from now on."

"Is that as far away as Texas?"

Mrs. Hardin laughed. "Lord no! It's not far at all. I guess it's about fifteen miles north of Lost River. I've been there several times. It's the county seat."

Johnny didn't understand what she meant by "county seat," but he decided not to ask. In the shed he found a hammer, handsaw, nails, file, and a double-bladed axe. He showed them to Mrs. Hardin.

"These things are what I need. I don't have any money to pay you."

"Why, son, I don't need your money. You just take them and make good use of them."

"I will," he said, turning to go.

"Johnny, wait a minute."

She went to her kitchen and came back with a sack of food.

"Here, you take this with you. You're going to get hungry up there on that mountain by yourself. And, Johnny?"

"Yeah?"

"Come April you might try finding work down here in the Valley. You could talk to Mr. Homer Stokes. He lives over past Lost River. He farms a lot of land. They say he's going to plant nearly a hundred acres of cotton this year, including part of this place. The thing is he'll be needing hands to hoe and chop cotton. That way you can make some money and buy yourself clothes and things ye need. And if he doesn't need field hands, ask other folks down here in the Valley. There'll be some that can use you."

"How far is his house past Lost River?"

"About three miles past."

"I've never been that far, but I'll find it."

Johnnie went back up on the mountain weighted down by the cumbersome tools and food. But it was a good weight that lifted his spirits. Maybe it would have been right to thank her kindly for the tools too, he thought to himself. Some things didn't come naturally to him.

Back at the house he drank some of the milk then put the jar in the cool spring to keep it from turning blinky. It should last me another day, he thought. Mrs. Hardin had given him half a dozen sausages, with as many biscuits, butter, nearly a whole pone of cornbread, a sack of uncooked black eyed peas, and a salt shaker. Best of all, she had included a slice of apple pie, which he meant to eat a little at a time. But it was delicious and he was so hungry that he finished it at the first sitting. He wrapped the remaining food as best he could and secured it on the fireplace hook along with the precious matches. He would have to guard it closely or raccoons would steal it right from under his nose.

Things were looking better for him, especially in the bright sunlight, and his fears faded for the moment.

Then he got busy building traps for rabbits and possums. He knocked wide boards loose from the shed and sawed them to the right dimensions. By late afternoon he finished his first trap, complete with triggering mechanism that would spring the door as soon as an animal tried to eat the bait. He used several nails but replenished his supply by extracting old ones from the boards he had wrenched loose. The shed was half demolished when he finished, but he had no further use for it anyway. He tested the trap a few times, made some adjustments, and pronounced it fit to set. He knew that rabbits came out of the woods in late afternoon to hop around the edge of the field. He would bait it with corn and greens and place the first trap there.

He wondered if his folks had made it to Texas. He missed his sisters.

He set the trap and then built a fire with pine kindling and wood from a dead tree that the wind had blown down the year before. He hated to see the sun go down. The night would be chilly but the firelight would dispel some of the gloom.

He slept better that night.

The next morning he drank the rest of the milk and ate most of the beans his mother had prepared. They were turning sour and he would have to finish them that day. But with what Mrs. Hardin had given him he had enough food to last several days.

The trap was sprung but nothing was inside. Johnny wondered if there was something wrong with it. It seemed fine when he tested it, so he reset it and started on the second trap.

He looked up when he heard a rooster crow and saw the three hens scratching around behind him near the barn. Maybe he could have chased them down, but it was better to let the hens and rooster live to produce eggs and chicks, provided hawks and foxes did not kill them first.

He set the second trap in the woods on the north slope of the mountain. Surely, he thought, I'll catch something. Looking around at what was left of the shed, he believed he could make one more trap, but he might have to use a board or two from the barn. That would be all right. Without mules or cows, he had no use for the barn either.

Glory be! There was a rabbit in the second trap when he checked the next day. But in his carefulness to grab it by the ears, it slipped through his grasp and escaped. He was angry with himself. "Next time I won't treat it so kindly," he muttered.

The first trap was still empty.

Two days later he caught a possum in the same trap and impaled it with a sharp stick. It died hard and was still wiggling when he cut its head off with the axe. It was a bloody mess to skin and gut, but it was meat, and his food was running low.

He had never cooked. At first he tried to use his mother's skillet, but without flour or lard he discovered it was easier to roast the meat over the fire on a stick. Possum was not his favorite meat, but well-cooked and sprinkled with a little salt, it tasted delicious.

The next day he found a rabbit in the first trap, and this time it did not escape. He was feeling good about his chances.

But then, out of the blue—or more exactly, out of the Valley—the unexpected happened and everything changed. He was working on the third trap when he heard a buggy drive up and the ugliest man he had ever seen came walking toward him. Johnny rose and stared at his one eye and disfigured face.

"Who're you, boy?" he asked, looking at Johnny and then at the boards and demolished shed.

"Johnny."

"Johnny who?"

"Just Johnny, I reckon."

"What're you doing here, boy?"

"I live here."

"No you don't. I'm Homer Stokesbury and this is my property. I bought this place from Hubert Pirkle."

"Hubert and my momma and brother and sisters went to Texas. I stayed."

"How come you didn't go with them?"

"Hubert don't like me, so he left me here. He's not my daddy."

"Well, you can't stay here. I've rented this place to Rayford Wilhite. They'll be moving in pretty soon."

"I was going to go see you."

"You were coming to see me? What for?"

"Miss Hardin said you might give me some work, hoeing work."

Homer looked him up and down, squinting with his good eye.

"You're a good worker?"

"Yeah, I'm a real good hoe hand."

"You like to brag on yourself a little, do you?"

"No."

"Who tore up the shed?"

"I did."

"Why? You've made a mess of my property."

"I needed the boards to make traps. Didn't have anything else to use."

Homer rubbed the stubble on his chin.

"Well, Johnny, you're going to have to pay me for the damage you've done here."

"I don't have any money."

"You can work it out. You come to my house tomorrow and I'll put you to work. But there're two things I'll hold you to."

Johnny said nothing, so Homer continued: "You work till I say so to pay for the damage you've done here, and as soon as Rayford gets here, you get out of his way. You understand me, boy?"

"I don't have anywhere to go."

"That's not my problem. I don't want any trouble with Rayford."

Homer inspected the barn and house and walked back to his buggy, shaking his head. As he was turning to leave, he called out to Johnny, "Be at my house at daylight. You know where I live?"

"Miss Hardin said about three miles past Lost River."

"On the left. There's a big iron gate in front of the house. But don't knock on the door. My wife's delicate lately and she needs her rest. You just wait by the gate till I come for you."

The sun was up when Homer found Johnny waiting by the gate.

"What are you doing with that hoe?"

"I came to hoe."

"It's not hoeing time yet, boy. Don't you know anything?"

Johnny did not answer.

"You don't say much, do you, boy?"

"What I have to."

"You know how to plow?"

"Yeah."

"Leave the hoe here by the gate. I want you to turn this field. I aim to plant some early corn in a week or two, as soon as it warms up a bit."

Johnny had plowed since he was nine or ten, and the lush Valley land was easier than the rocky fields up on the mountain. The team was young and brisk, and he kept them moving. By the middle of the afternoon he was finished.

"You finished turning that field already?" Homer said in surprise as Johnny brought the team to the gate and started scraping the red dirt off the plow point.

"Yeah, what else you want me to do?"

"Nothing today. You can leave the hoe here, but be back early tomorrow. I'll put you to turning the big field across the creek. I'll give you half wages till you pay me back for that damage done to my property."

When Johnny got back to the mountain he found a wagon loaded with furniture. Rayford Wilhite came out to confront him.

"You that boy Homer Stokesbury was telling me about?"

"Yeah."

"That your stuff I found in the house?"

"Yeah."

"Well, I fed the meat and stuff to my dogs. Now you take the rest and get off my place."

"I'll get my tools."

"No, you won't. Everything left is for my use. That's my agreement with Mr. Stokesbury."

"The tools are not his. Miss Hardin said I could keep them."

"Well, boy, that's what you say. You might be lying."

"I had some clothes."

"Ye can take them. Just rags anyway. Now you skedaddle, you hear?"

Johnny took his clothes and matches, which luckily Rayford had overlooked. He started toward his second trap. It had another rabbit. This time in his anger he grabbed it and dashed its life out against a tree. At least he would eat again.

But where?

Once or twice he had climbed around the bluffs called Buzzard Roost nearly two miles from the house. He remembered a natural shelter under the bluffs. As good a place as I can find, he thought. It was getting dark when he found the shelter. He had just enough time to gather kindling and wood.

By the firelight he skinned and tore the rabbit apart with his hands. A year ago, I couldn't have done it, Johnny noted with satisfaction. Tomorrow evening I have to bring my traps over here close by before Rayford finds them. And I have to find water. I think there's a spring below these bluffs.

It was different sleeping in the open with all the night sounds of the forest. He remembered what Mrs. Hardin said about panthers and wildcats. But the fire will keep them away, he thought. I'll just have to keep it burning all night. I'll be all right. I just have to be careful.

The more Johnny worked for Homer Stokesbury, the more he came to appreciate the boy. He turned the big field quicker than anybody ever had.

"Where'd you end up staying, boy?" he asked him at quitting time a few days later.

"I found me a place up on the mountain."

"You got yourself a house, have you?"

"No, just staying in the bluffs."

"You sleeping under the bluffs?"

"Yeah."

"What's that you're gnawing on?"

"Rabbit."

"Where'd you get it? You got a gun?"

"Naw. Made me some traps. The ones I told you about."

That night Homer told Nellie about the boy. Ordinarily he didn't tell her anything about his doings, but this boy was different somehow. Not that he was stirred by any thought of generosity. The way Lloyd Patterson had betrayed his trust had soured him on helping people.

"Well, Homer, don't mistreat the boy because of what Lloyd Patterson did. You're a good man with money and business but so tight with a dollar that I can almost hear ole George Washington yelling in pain. I don't meant to pry into your business, but I would ask you not to work that boy into the ground without paying him a little something. The idea of a boy living in the woods like a wild animal by night and working like a slave by day makes me so sad. And you tell me his folks just moved off and left him up there. Why don't you bring him down here and let him sleep in the barn? At least he'll be warm there, and we can feed him something."

"Now, Nellie, we can't afford to feed and house every vagrant that wanders down the road," Homer complained.

"Homer, from what you tell me, the boy's no vagrant, just a victim of some of the meanest people I ever heard of. I've watched him out there in the field. He works hard. You said yourself that he's about the best worker you've ever had. The whole thing troubles me. I don't know what it is, but lately things I never thought much about bother me. My feelings are so tender these days that I'm wondering if . . ."

"If what?"

"If I might be in a family way."

Homer's eye got big and his twisted face looked like somebody had hit him with a two by four.

"In a family way, you mean with child?"

"I believe I am, honeybunch," she smiled sweetly.

"But I don't see how that . . . I mean I don't understand how you could be, not with my little problem. We haven't . . . lately, you know, been together like that."

"Well, of course you would say that because you don't remember, do you, honeybunch? You were sound asleep last time. All I can say is that I woke up and you were all over me."

"I was?"

"Yes, you were, honeybunch, and such manhood! Like nothing I'd ever had before. I'll never forget that day, that night I mean. And I think that's when it happened."

"Well, glory be. While I was asleep?"

"That's right, honeybunch, sound asleep. I didn't hear you say a word the whole time."

"Well, I'll be doggone."

Homer's disposition improved drastically when the stunning news was confirmed. And several people benefitted, including Johnny. Homer allowed him to sleep in the barn and eat food from their table. It was the best Johnny had ever tasted. Regardless of her dubious moral qualities, Nellie was an excellent cook, and for once Homer did not protest the expense of an improved larder.

"Nothing but the best food for my honeydew and the little man on the way," he repeated.

When the time came to chop and hoe the cotton, Johnny got to know other people, especially Idois Alvis, who was a year older, and Asa Henson, 15, who already claimed her as his future wife. Both had a vague recollection of Johnny from his brief school attendance. Idois took it on herself, as they worked, to review his letters and arithmetic and to talk to him about the Bible and Christian faith. Asa was not happy with the attention she paid Johnny but did not think of him as a rival. Johnny looked like a scarecrow. His clothes were too small and in tatters, and his dark hair was down to his neck. It never occurred to him to take a bath.

"Johnny, I hate to be the one to tell you," Idois said one day, "but you need to take yourself a bath. And now that Mr. Homer is paying you some, maybe you could get a haircut and buy yourself some clothes and shoes. I wish you would because I want you to start going to church with us. Reverend Burl

Yates, the new minister of Lost River Holiness Church, is a real good preacher. He knows the Bible and can tell you things about it that I can't begin to explain. And the singing is so pretty. Do you like singing, Johnny?"

"I don't know, I've never done any singing."

Johnny didn't know anything about the Bible things Idois was talking about. But he trusted her and believed everything she said. Late that day he took an old saddle blanket down to the creek in Homer's pasture and washed off in the chilly water. The next Saturday, after a rain kept them out of the fields, he walked to Lost River with seven dollars in his pocket, the first money he had ever had.

"I need to buy these clothes," he told the storekeeper as he handed him a pair of pants and a shirt that seemed to be about his size. "And some shoes."

"You have money, boy?" Mr. Miller asked.

"Yeah. Seven dollars."

"How did you come by it?"

"I worked for it. For Mr. Homer Stokesbury."

A man who was inspecting items in the back of the store looked up and became interested in the conversation.

"What's your name?"

"Johnny."

"Johnny who? You look like a wild boy with those rags and hair down to your shoulders. I make it a point to know who children are and who they belong to when they come into my store to buy. You don't look like anybody I know. Who do you belong to?"

"Nobody."

"What's your last name?"

Johnny stood silent, uncertain about what to do next.

"It's all right, Mr. Miller," said the man who had been listening. "You can take his money. I know his father. I'll vouch for him."

Johnny paid for the clothes and shoes and followed the man out of the store.

"You know my daddy?" he asked the stranger. "They always told me I didn't have a daddy."

"Well, the people that told you that were wrong. I know your father. He's my father, too."

"You're my brother? But you're so much older than me."

"Son, we all have the same father. And he loves us all as his children. God is the Father of us all, and we are all his children. You are a child of God, a son, and from what I've seen and heard about you, a good son. You work for Mr. Stokesbury, don't you?"

"Yeah."

"Idois Alvis has told me a lot about you."

"You know Idois?"

"Yes, I do. Idois has prayed long and hard for you. And I've prayed with her ever since she told me about you. I'm Burl Yates, Minister at Lost River Holiness Church. Nothing would please us more than to have you join us at our church service Sunday. We'll talk about your Father and how much he loves you. That's what church is all about. There's a lot we'd like to tell you. Johnny, you don't have to be alone anymore. You have a church family. We are your brothers and sisters."

Johnny had not cried in years, but all of a sudden he began sobbing as Reverend Yates put his arms around him.

After a while Reverend Yates took Johnny to the barbershop where, tense and frightened, he endured the scissors and clippers. Men laughed at the pile of hair on the floor, comparing it to the shearing of a sheep.

Johnny went to church that Sunday and nearly every Sunday for the rest of his life. He gave himself the surname Goodson because of the remark Reverend Yates had made. By his life he caused the name to be honored and respected in Lost River country.

Years passed and as a grown man he made a trip to Texas, not to settle accounts with Hubert, as he once threatened, but to reconnect with his sisters and to offer forgiveness to the others. But that story deserves its own telling.

Later he met Miss Jenny Kilpatrick who was to be his wife and mother of his three children. Johnny and Idois were lifelong friends, and eventually he was able to repay some of her early kindnesses. He was a moderating influence in young Leon's turbulent life, and in gratitude old Homer helped him become an established farmer. Throughout his life people knew Johnny to be a dependable, generous man, though never much of a talker—or a singer. Whenever he needed to think through a problem or have time to himself, he would return to the mountain where he had suffered but survived as a boy. He always remembered a verse Idois taught him from the Psalms: "I will lift up mine eyes unto the hills. From whence cometh my help?"

3.
The Kidnapping of Mary Beth Hunter

A. The Abduction

On a Saturday in mid-June, 1878, a week before she was to marry Titus Vance at Lost River Holiness Church, somebody kidnapped Miss Mary Beth Hunter.

Mary Beth's cousins Lester and Levitus Clark were the closest to being eyewitnesses to her abduction. But they were not much help late that day when Mary Beth failed to come home and her anxious parents asked them for information.

"I figure that man in the buggy grabbed her, Uncle John Thomas," said slow-talking Lester as he expertly sent a long stream of snuff juice into the fireplace ashes and wiped his chin with the back of his hand. "We were hoeing cotton out yonder by the Lost River Road like you told us to do, and we saw him go by. It was a little while after we saw Mary Beth carrying that mess of okra and tomatoes over to Miss Gertie Flowers's house."

"Yeah," added fidgety Levitus, "that's right, that's sure enough right, Uncle John Thomas. I bet you money it was that fellow all right! We didn't know the man. Fact is, we never saw him before in our life, did we Lester? But, aw, he was big man. Lester and me, we both waved a polite howdy to him, like we do to every passing soul, but that man didn't even return the greeting. He was laying leather to that horse like he was in an awful hurry. Yes, sir, he was gone before you could bat an eye. We didn't see anything else out of the ordinary. But on the way home close to sundown we found Mary Beth's bonnet and that mess of okra and tomatoes in the middle of the road. I guess she dropped them when that man grabbed her. That's her bonnet you're holding, Aunt Florence, and we set the okra and tomatoes in yonder on the kitchen table. They got a little dirt on them, but they'll still be fit to eat."

"Lord in Heaven, I wish you boys could've helped your cousin!" Aunt Florence lamented as she pressed the bonnet to her bosom as tears ran down her cheeks. "Why did that awful man take my darling daughter?"

"Look here, boys," said Mr. John Thomas Hunter, as he sighted down the barrel of his shotgun. "I need for you to describe the man as best you can recollect so that I can sic the law and everybody else on him. That is, if I don't shoot him first. Tell me what he looked like."

"It was a young fellow, Uncle John Thomas, in a buggy, like I said," Lester offered.

"That's right, that's sure enough right, Uncle John Thomas," added Levitus. "It was a young fellow and big, in a buggy. Like we said, we were hoeing cotton out there close to Lost River Road and we saw him when he passed. We've been hoeing that stretch for the last two days, and I figure it'll take us about another day to finish up. Grass is real bad. It was a couple of hours after Buck McCoy brought you that load of hay. Big load, too much for that wagon, in my judgment. Sideboards were too low. We talked to him a little bit, and I told him he was about to lose part of his load. He said he was hauling it from his brother Filmore's house, you know, about a mile on past the creek."

Mr. John Thomas Hunter's patience was running out as he filled his pockets with shotgun shells. "Well, dadblame it, boys, I know it was a big man in a buggy that must have grabbed Mary Beth. And I know about Buck and the hay. Now tell me something I don't know, like how tall the man stood and the kind of horse he had. You sure you never saw him before?"

"Can't rightly say as I have, Uncle John Thomas. You, Levitus?"

"Can't say as I have either. Come to think of it, though, he looked a little like that Wynn boy that used to live over yonder in the Evergreen Community. You remember, his Uncle Cletus used to work some for Mr. Homer Stokesbury. Course it couldn't been him. That boy up and died last summer, wasn't it, Lester?"

"I believe it was last summer, around July's a year ago, or it could have been August. I don't recollect exactly, but it was about the same time that Aunt Sadie Parker passed away. Wasn't it?"

"I believe it was. Of course Aunt Sadie died of consumption, so they said, but that Wynn boy had fits and such. They said he'd foam at the mouth just like a mad dog. They buried him in the Evergreen graveyard. You remember when we went over there for Decoration Day and the graves were all covered with flowers."

"Yeah, there's a bunch of McCoys in that community," Lester added, as he raised a little cloud in the ashes with another long sluice of snuff juice.

Mr. John Thomas sighed, spread his arms, and looked toward the ceiling in a gesture of futility and frustration. Getting Lester and Levitus to tell things in a straight way was like trying to herd drunk ducks in the dark.

"And which way did you say he was heading?"

"Who?"

"Dadblame it, Lester, that man you saw, that's who!" Mr. John Thomas said in exasperation.

"Well, yeah, Uncle John Thomas, it looked to me like he could've been heading for the mountain, 'cause he wasn't going the other way. But I guess he could've circled around on the Barkley Road. That's what he could've done."

"That's right, that's sure enough right, Uncle John Thomas," Levitus agreed. "Or he could've swung around past Evergreen and come back that way. Course he could've headed on up the mountain, like Lester said. But whichever way, he was a laying leather to that big ole horse of his and in a hurry to get there."

"What else can you tell me boys? What about the horse and buggy? What did they look like?"

"Couldn't tell you much, Uncle John Thomas," said Lester, "except it was a big red horse that looked a little like that young horse Emmit Turner traded for over at Murphy's mule barn the other day, except it was bigger. Couldn't see much else for the dust."

"That's right, that's right," added Levitus. "Dust everywhere, Uncle John Thomas. And if it doesn't rain pretty soon, crops are going to dry up. Hasn't been this dry since we lived on the Jones place, four seasons back. Corn's already turning yellow. You recollect how dry it got that year, Lester?"

"Sure do, just like it was yesterday," Lester answered thoughtfully as he wiped the snuff juice off his chin. "We lost most of our corn that year, and we didn't make half a bale of cotton to the acre. Hard times, mighty hard times, and if we don't get some rain, we'll see hard times again."

"God d—!" Uncle John Thomas started to say in pure frustration with his nephews, but caught himself just short of full profanity.

But Aunt Florence suddenly squalled out in pure sorrow at the image of her daughter in the hands of the awful kidnapper. "Oh, dear Lord, my precious little girl at the mercy of that fiendish man! Oh, I just can't stand the thought of it!"

"Well, Florence, I've got my shotgun ready, and I've sent Henry to get the Sheriff! We'll catch that sorry son of a b—! And when we do there won't be enough of him left to feed the buzzards!"

"Oh, Lordy, will our baby be all right?" Florence wailed. "Please tell them to find her and fetch her back home safe! Please tell them that! Please help us, Lord Jesus, in this hour of trial and tribulation and bring our little girl home safe!"

"We'll find her, Florence. Don't you worry, we'll find her. And when we do, that lowdown son of a b— will wish he had never been born, not when we get through stomping his sorry you-know-what into the ground!"

Since he repented and started living right ten years earlier, Uncle John Thomas Hunter had been a church-going man who tried manfully to keep from swearing and cussing, especially around womenfolk and preachers. Usually he managed, but a lifetime of profanity dies hard and sometimes things still got under his skin so bad that he would just about burst wide open if he couldn't let loose with a little cussing. And this was one of those times. Just the thought of the kidnapper with his innocent daughter made his blood boil and his hands tremble with anger.

Mary Beth was their third child, after brothers Henry and Edgar, and the oldest of three sisters. She had always been the apple of her father's eye. But Lord God in Heaven, he said to himself, it was enough to put a man in his grave to have to keep a protective watch over a trio of pretty daughters, and especially Mary Beth, who was as headstrong and opinionated as she was beautiful. And Ruth Ann and Inez were not far behind her.

Sometimes Uncle John Thomas wondered if Mary Beth was touched in the head. She had crazy notions that included womenfolk voting, working at public jobs, and getting more education than he thought proper for a woman.

But the main feature of her character was determination. As her father said, shaking his head, "When Mary Beth gets it in her head to do something, you better just get out of her way, because she'll do it one way or another." Because of the girls' good looks and his money, second in Lost River only to Homer Stokesbury's fortune, men buzzed around like bees around a beehive. Both Ruth Ann and Inez had solid marriage prospects with Hardin brothers Buell and Ray. But at twenty-three Mary Beth looked to be on the verge of becoming an old maid. As much as he doted on her, for she was more like him in character than his other children, John Thomas confided to Florence that he was ready to turn her over to a husband and have a little peace and quiet in his life.

But now peace and quiet were the farthest things from his reach. He had not been so agitated or set back so far in his Christian life since that lowdown rascal Lloyd Patterson toyed with her feelings and left her broken-hearted two years earlier. John Thomas might have shot him the morning he took his shotgun and went looking for the scoundrel at Henry Patterson's house. But by the time he got there, Lloyd Patterson was already on the run with a good head start.

Mary Beth fell hard for Lloyd, and for the longest time insisted that he would come back for her. Time eroded her confidence, and as months passed without any sign or word of him, she became listless and spent so much time sleeping or looking out the window that Florence started worrying about her. Then two letters came a month apart from her Cousin Roberta Hunter down in Hattiesburg, Mississippi. Mary Beth perked up and seemed more like her old self. When family members asked what was so special about Roberta's letters, she gave only vague answers and refused to let anybody read them. And to make sure her sisters didn't do so on the sly, she scandalized everybody by burning the letters. The very idea of not letting her own family, especially her sisters, read a cousin's letters caused John Thomas to shake his head. Not that it did any good to argue with her about it. You didn't win arguments with Mary Beth; you only hoped you could survive them. And regardless of how right you might be, she always had the last word even if she had to put it in edgewise.

John Thomas was worn down from a proud man to a nervous frazzle. But at least after the Lloyd Patterson scandal Mary Beth still had her "virtue," so she confided to her mother. John Thomas calmed down when Florence told him. He reasoned that in time Mary Beth, who swore she would never love another man, would change her mind and accept another suitor. Titus Vance was that man, or for a few weeks seemed to be.

If any man took Mary Beth's disappearance and its implications nearly as hard as Mr. John Thomas Hunter, it had to be Titus. He was not an unpleasant looking man, but he appealed to her not in the least. It had taken him weeks of trying to persuade indifferent Mary Beth to let him court her just to get a sigh-filled "I reckon so" out of her. Even so, she held him at arm's length with no more than a peck on the cheek for his efforts. Though he kept it hidden, Titus relished the idea of consummating their marriage to show her who was boss. He promised himself he would get even for all her haughty rebuffs.

Of course Titus knew all about Lloyd Patterson, and despite her denials, he suspected that Mary Beth secretly still yearned for him. He wondered how far Patterson had gotten with her, suspected the worst, but was anxious to get her married and under his control. Titus came from a family "too hard up to pay interest on the air they breathed," as one sarcastic neighbor put it. Titus knew that a poor man didn't often get this kind of chance to better himself, and he was not about to let the opportunity slip out of his grasp.

Now, damn it all, just when things were finally going his way and the Hunter money and land were so close he could almost smell them, this kidnapping business had to happen. Titus was doubly frustrated and conflicted. Not that he shared John Thomas Hunter's reluctance to lace his feelings with profanity. He let loose a blue streak of cussing every time he thought about the dilemma her kidnapping posed for him. Not only was Mary Beth the prettiest girl in Stokesbury Valley but also future heiress to a fortune. But on the other hand, how could he take her as his wife if another man had possessed her first? Why didn't I court one of her sisters? They'll get as much money as Mary Beth and are just about as pretty. To be fair about it, he realized that it would not be Mary Beth's fault if the kidnapper abused her. But that would not change the way people would judge the matter. The possibility that the kidnapper had had his way with her was enough to damage her name for ever. Pure or not when they found her, assuming they would, people would gossip and suppose the worst regardless of what she said. Men would look on Titus with a mixture of pity and contempt. Besides, he knew that many men believed all women were just waiting for a chance to deceive their men folk. As dirty-minded old Silas Burney put it, "You turn your head for just a minute and a woman'll put a set of horns on it." Titus didn't understand the expression but he got the meaning. People would talk behind his back. He might be poor as dirt but he had his pride just like any man.

First though, they had to find Mary Beth and then he would have to figure out what would be in his best interest to do. I could still be talked into taking Mary Beth off his hands, he thought, if Mr. Hunter would agree to deed me that sixty-acre tract of his best bottomland. I'll have to work on that in case I need to do things that way, he said to himself. Sixty acres of good bottomland would outweigh a lot of aggravations. That pleasant thought lifted his spirits considerably every time all the dreary possibilities depressed him.

Soon John Thomas and sons, Henry and Edgar, along with Titus, men from Lost River, and lawmen from Stokesbury County and surrounding jurisdictions were scouring the roads and woods for any sign of Mary Beth. But despite an all-night search they found no trace of her. In the sobering daylight there was more concern than ever about her very life, and hushed speculation—never voiced in Mr. John Thomas's presence—that the kidnapper might have taken advantage of her.

Distraught Florence had a spell of "the vapors," as people back then called them, and took to her bed to keep from fainting. Inez, Ruth Ann, and neighbor women sat with her. Meanwhile, John Thomas rode over the countryside with his shotgun asking everybody he saw for the umpteenth time if they had heard or seen anything. And for the umpteenth time they shook their head and sympathized.

Even though they were the only ones who may have seen the kidnapper, Lester and Levitus couldn't tell him more than they had already. However, they were more than a little scandalized that Aunt Florence and her daughters were about to let the okra and tomatoes go to ruin.

"That's a good mess of okra and tomatoes," observed Lester disapprovingly.

"Yeah, yeah, real good mess," added Levitus, shaking his head. "But they'll go to ruin if they don't eat them real soon."

That Sunday morning Henry noticed an unstamped letter in their mailbox. How it got there was a mystery, but soon anxious neighbors scrouged into the house to ponder its chilling message.

B. The Ransom Letters

The letter left no doubt about its meaning and threat:

Mr. John Thomas Hunter,

Suh, if you ever want to see yuah daughtah again leeve five thousand dollahs in a Place I will tell you. But if you try to befuddle or trick me or bring the law in on it you wont never see this purty girl agin except to bury huh body. She is awright so fah and will stay that way if you do just what I say do.

There was no signature and no clue about the kidnapper's identity, but when word got out about the letter, the Lost River community was abuzz with gossip. In the first place, five thousand dollars was an unimaginable sum of money for most people thereabouts. Probably only Homer Stokesbury and John Thomas Hunter could readily come up with so much cash. In fact, the very thought that these men could have so much money stirred up scads of envy and wonderment.

Then there was excited speculation over the identity of the kidnapper. People pored over the language. The misspellings pointed to a poorly educated man, and words like "yuah daughtah," "huh," and "fah" seemed strange for the English of the north end of the state and hinted of someone from a deeper South.

"People talk that way down in south Georgia where I used to work," Sylvester Sandlin allowed, "like they got a mouthful of mush."

"Yeah, or full of sh—" , his grinning brother Pete started to say before he spotted his Aunt Gertie Flowers in the gathering. "What I meant to say is that white and black people both talk that way down there, not the regular way we do around here."

It was generally agreed, based on this linguistic conjecture, that the kidnapper was not from the upper part of the state or from the north but a semiliterate vagrant wandering up from the far South. But it was a mystery how he could have known about Mary Beth and her family. And nobody could recall seeing anybody in the area who spoke that way.

"Only man I can recollect that talked that way," said Newt Pierce, "was that ole Patterson boy from Georgia that ran off two or three years ago with Homer Stokesbury's money and his Uncle Henry's best mule. But I doubt he'd be fool enough to show his face in this country again. Course Henry Patterson talks like that, being from South Georgia, but Henry's so easy going he would try to make peace with a rattlesnake that was fixing to bite him."

"Yeah, it wouldn't be that worthless nephew of his, not unless he wants a load of buckshot in his behind," observed Jim Malone. "There're still some men around here that would shoot that devil on sight."

People looked knowingly at one another, aware that Jim himself was probably one of them because of how the rascal had lied to his daughter Velma.

The minute Florence read the message she squalled out in terror and collapsed a sobbing wreck on the bed, pleading with John Thomas to get the money and have it ready.

"Oh, John Thomas, did you read what that man threatened to do to Mary Beth if we don't do what he says? Oh, Lord God in Heaven, just get the money before he does something to our precious daughter! We can get along without the money but not without our child, not our darling Mary Beth!"

John Thomas agreed, even though he would sooner have his jaw teeth pulled out than turn loose that much money. As for Henry and Edgar, they were almost shaking with rage and frustration as they could see their weak-willed father letting sentimentality erode the clever arguments they had given him to favor them over their sisters when it came to the inheritance. "The girls will have husbands to look after them. But we promise to take care of them, if for some reason there is ever a need."

Just as Henry and Edgar feared, paternal love prevailed, and by Monday afternoon after a visit to Lost River Bank, John Thomas had five thousand dollars ready to ransom Mary Beth.

Then another letter addressed to John Thomas showed up in Sylvester Sandlin's mailbox a quarter mile from the Hunter household. Sylvester delivered it breathless and wide-eyed. Like the first, it had no stamp or postmark and contained a frightening message:

Mr. John Thomas Hunter

Suh,

this lettah went to Sylvester Sandlins in case the laws watchin yuah house. Now heah is what you do. you leeve the money in a tow sack on yuah front poach an you git everybody two mile away from the house tomorrah night all night you can come to the house at daylight to check but the family has to stay away till dark now if the law or anybody else is there or the money aint right yuah daughtuhs a dead girl she is tied up in a wild place where nobody can find huh an if anything goes wrong or somebody steals my money she will die a cruel death an if anybody shows up before the times I say my men will shoot them dead they can see you but you cant see them.

To the terrified wailing of Aunt Florence and the subdued mood of the Lost River community, who took the last comment to mean that the kidnapper had accomplices, John Thomas did exactly as ordered. They waited at Andrew Burleson's house as the night hours ticked slowly by. At sunup John Thomas saddled his horse and raced home. The money was gone but Mary Beth was still missing. Then began a second wait for her return.

C. The Return of Mary Beth

The day passed as John Thomas, Henry and Edgar, Titus, and the Lost River men patrolled the roads for any sign of Mary Beth. Finally, when they returned at sundown with fear and failing spirits to the empty house, there sat pretty Mary Beth on the front porch.

The reunion was joyous, but Mary Beth's description of her ordeal was vague on details.

"Daddy, all I know is that a man grabbed me, tied my hands, and put a blindfold on me. I screamed as loud as I could and fought him as long as I was able. But it was by the woods on the way to Aunt Gertie's house and the man was too stout. I know he took me somewhere up on the mountain. It seemed like we rode a long way in a buggy, and when we stopped I couldn't hear anything but katydids and owls off in the woods. Not a human sound anywhere. I couldn't see anything either, but I could tell it was dark and wild. Later on he took the blindfold off and it was pitch black."

"But what did he look like, Mary Beth?" her father asked. "Was he that man Lester and Levitus saw pass by? You reckon it was him? They said he was big and looked to be young."

"It could've been, Daddy, yes, I guess it was. It was a buggy and he was big and dark-bearded, and ugly, real ugly and mean looking."

"Oh, my darling girl," Florence wailed in retrospective horror at the thought.

"Did he . . . hurt you, daughter?" John Thomas asked carefully, dreading to hear the wrong answer.

"Well, he bruised my arm a little bit, tying up my hands. Because I tussled some with him. I wasn't just going to sit there like a scared chicken. You know me. And once when I told him off for his sorry ways, he poured a bucket of water on my head. Just ruined my hair. Every now and then out of nature's need he'd untie my hands and let me walk into the bushes. But no, Daddy, he didn't hurt me, not in the way you're thinking. And if he had tried it, I would've clawed his eyes out."

After things calmed down and Titus and the neighbors went home, Mary Beth postponed the wedding indefinitely—forever in her own mind, but she didn't say it. What she did say was that the ordeal of her abduction and the prospect of getting married both coming at the same time was more than she could handle.

"I need some time to get over all this and sort everything out," she explained.

Titus fretted and privately cursed up a blue streak when he found out, but there was nothing he could do but agree to it. He was relieved that Mary Beth was unhurt but regretted at the same time that he had lost any leverage he could have had with John Thomas's sixty acres of good bottom land.

The very next day Mary Beth said that a trip was what she needed to clear her head of bad memories. Cousin Roberta of Hattiesburg had invited her for a visit, and now she was ready to take her up on the offer. A few weeks in Mississippi with new things and people to distract her was just what she needed to put all the unpleasantness behind her. What she didn't say was that Titus was part of what she wanted to forget.

John Thomas and Florence hesitated to let her go so far from home. But after all, Mary Beth was now a grown woman, legally speaking. Besides, she was right; a trip could do her a world of good after what she had been through. At first Inez begged to accompany her, for she had just had a spat with Buell Hardin. But while her parents were thinking about it, she and Buell made up.

Meanwhile, Mary Beth insisted on packing her trunks herself, even though her mother and sisters offered to help. To top off her odd behavior, Mary Beth asked her father to give her a small handgun for her purse. John Thomas thought it was a strange request, but he understood her nervousness that coincided with his own concern for her safety. He gave her a derringer that had belonged to his mother.

So it was that with elaborately wrapped gifts for Roberta and her Aunt Flora Hunter, the derringer in her purse, heavy trunks with more clothes than she could wear in a month of Sundays, and a goodly sum of money from her father, Mary Beth said goodbye to her teary-eyed mother and sisters, choked-up father, and stone-faced brothers. And leaving Titus and troubles behind, she turned her thoughts to Mississippi where she had a certain person and other matters to straighten out.

D. The Last Word

Cousin Roberta and her fiancé, Bill Smalley, were waiting for Mary Beth at the Hattiesburg train station. She hugged plump little Roberta, whom she had not seen in six years, and shook hands with Bill. At the first opportunity she pulled Roberta aside and whispered in her ear.

"Is he really here in Hattiesburg, Roberta?"

"Not just in Hattiesburg, Mary Beth, but right here at the station. I told him you were coming. Oh my Lord, look! Here he comes now!"

"Howdy, Roberta" said Lloyd. "Mary Beth, it's been a long time, way too long. How are you?"

Although her heart was pounding, Mary Beth took her time before answering. Instead she looked Lloyd Patterson up and down. She reckoned he looked about the same as she remembered him: still good looking enough to stir butterflies in her stomach, but maybe a little thinner and a trifle weather beaten around the edges. He made a move toward her.

"I'm fine, Lloyd," she finally answered, "but you keep your distance. We have some talking to do."

With this cue, Roberta excused herself and motioned for Bill to follow her outside the station, leaving Mary Beth and Lloyd alone.

"Mary Beth, sweetheart, I can't tell you how glad I am to see you. I reckon it's been close on to two years, but you're just as pretty as ever, no, prettier than ev—"

"Come with me over to the benches away from the travelers," she said, cutting off his flattery. "We can sit there and talk."

"Mary Beth, did you get my letters? Roberta said she sent them. Now I just want to tell you, sweetheart, that I love you—"

Mary Beth held up her hand to silence him again.

"Lloyd, you did your talking way back yonder when you told me all those lies and then left me. Now it's my time," she said as she pulled out the derringer and aimed it at Lloyd's midsection.

Lloyd turned as pale as death and his eyes got as big as half-dollars.

"Now, let's get some things straight this time around. If you ever try to pull that trick on me again, Lloyd Patterson, my daddy won't have to go after you with his shotgun. I'll shoot you myself. I mean every last word I say, so you will not want to put me to the test, will you?"

"No siree, Mary Beth. I promise I will never do that again."

"You say you love me. Is that true, or are you lying to me again."

"Mary Beth," he said, raising his eyes from the derringer to hers, "that's the one thing I never lied to you about. My love for you is true, even though I wasn't man enough at the time to live up to it."

"Say it again."

"Mary Beth Hunter, my love for you is true. Always was, always will be. I was in the habit back then of running away from things, good and bad. I couldn't go back to Lost River for you once I realized what a mistake I had made. That's when I looked up your cousin Roberta. You remember you told me she had moved down here to Hattiesburg. I missed you so much, darling Mary Beth, thought about you twenty times a day. I thought I would go crazy when she told me you were thinking about marrying that Titus fellow."

Mary Beth stared at him for the longest time, reading every flicker of emotion in his handsome features. Then she blinked back a tear, put the derringer back in her purse, laid it aside, and with a beautiful smile, held out her arms to him.

"Lloyd, I guess I ought to shoot you on general principles, and if not for myself, for all those other girls you lied to and left so grievous. But I love you despite all and I want you for my husband, you worthless thing you!"

"And I want you for my wife, you pretty thing you," Lloyd answered as he enfolded her in his arms to the curious glances and smiles of travelers watching them from the far benches. There was relief in his voice but also some quivering misgivings that Mary Beth sensed.

"What is it, Lloyd? If you're thinking of two-timing me again, just keep foremost what I said about shooting you. I love you, indeed I do, but I meant every word I said. Hear me well: you will not live to humiliate me twice."

"I know you mean it, darling Mary Beth. No, it's nothing like that. I'm through with that way of living and lying. It's just that I don't anything to offer you. Things have been going sour for me lately."

"Probably because of your tomcatting around. It's a wonder some woman's husband or father hasn't shot you for your rotten ways. But you don't have to worry about the money and things like that. I have enough for us. You see, Lloyd, I took matters into my own hands and got my inheritance early. Knowing my scheming brothers, if something ever happened to Daddy and Momma, they would cut me and my sisters off without a dime. So you and I will be just fine, Lloyd, as long as you are a good husband to me. But the day I find out that you've slid back into your old ways, that's the day your mortal life will be forfeit."

It was getting late, so Mary Beth went on with Roberta and Bill to her house. She still wasn't entirely convinced of Lloyd's change of heart and his feelings for her, but she was sure he would stick close by, now that she had told him she had money.

On the other hand, there was no doubt about the genuine affection her Aunt Flora and Uncle George Thomas Hunter showed their favorite niece. They talked happily long into the night.

The next day she described to Lloyd how she had arranged her "kidnapping." First, on her way to Aunt Gertie Flowers's house she tossed the basket of okra and tomatoes in the road and left her bonnet to make people think somebody had grabbed her. Then she ran through the woods and fields back to the one location where no one would think of looking for her: her daddy's own barn loft filled with soft hay, where she had left food and water for herself.

"I wrote ransom letters, making them sound like somebody from way down south. That was just to throw them off, but if you had wandered through about that time with your South Georgia accent, they probably would have strung you up from the nearest tree. And I would have been tempted to help them do it."

"Mary Beth, I have to say I am surprised at you. I declare that was some trick to play on your folks and friends. I couldn't have thought of a better one myself."

"Well, you remember I took lessons from a lowdown rascal," she laughed, pinching him on the cheek.

Later, in a more serious tone, they talked about where they would go and how they would live once they were married. Mary Beth was curious.

"Lloyd, the talk was that you were probably running off to Texas. Is that where you went?"

"No, darling Mary Beth, I never did make it to Texas. I gambled away my money in Mississippi and here I stayed, making do the best I could and worse off than I ever was in my life."

"You mean Mr. Stokesbury's money, don't you?" she said teasingly.

"Well, yes, no reason now to deny it," he confessed with a grin. "But it didn't do me a bit of good. It just ran through my hands like water. In fact, that was one thing that caused me to start thinking about changing my ways."

47

"Lloyd, you still want to go to Texas?"

"I would like to see it, maybe get me a fresh start out there and make something better of my life. I've already wasted a heap of years."

"Us, Lloyd, us," she corrected him, "get us a fresh start. Well, here's what we'll do. First, we get married. Then I'll write a letter to my parents telling them about it. After that we'll head out for Texas and buy us a nice place. What do you say to that?"

"If that's what you want, darling Mary Beth, then we'll do it. I'm burned out on wrongdoing and ready for us to get that new start!"

"Well, Lloyd, it is what I want, so that's what we'll do. All this took me a long time and a lot of doing, but like Daddy says, I always get the last word!"

4.
Angel

One Monday morning in May of 1896, as she was hoeing and singing in her garden, Idois Henson heard a noise behind her. Turning and raising her old, faded bonnet, she saw standing before her a little blond boy, naked as a jaybird, smiling and holding out his arms for her to pick him up. From his size, she guessed he was about fifteen months old.

"Lord have mercy on my soul! Where in the world did you come from, little fellow, and whose baby are you?" she asked, looking around for his folks as she dropped her hoe and took him in her arms.

There was nobody else in sight. But that can't be right, she thought. His folks must be around here somewhere, probably hiding out yonder behind my hedgerow and playing a trick on me. She looked carefully at the smiling little boy, now snuggled up against her bosom, but couldn't recognize his features. None of the young mothers at Lost River Holiness Church had a child this size, and her only nephew in Tylerville was nearly four. She looked all around the house and the hedgerow, but besides a pair of bluebirds bickering in her grapevine, the only living things in sight were her chickens scratching and clucking around the barn and her old dog Buck asleep on the porch. Funny, she thought, that he didn't bark at the boy. Guess he's getting too old to rouse up like he used to.

"You must've wandered over from Johnny and Jenny Goodson's house," she said aloud, giving the little boy a kiss. "I imagine that's what you've done. Most likely you belong to some of their folks. I better take you back, little fellow. They're probably worried to death about you."

She wrapped him in an old blanket that had belonged to her daughter

Betty and walked the quarter mile to the Goodson home. But Jenny didn't know any more about the child than Idois did.

"No, he's not one of ours, Idois," Jenny told her, peering over her spectacles at the boy. "But now isn't he just the cutest thing you ever saw! Cutchy, cutchy, cutchy, you cute little thing! But if he's not ours or yours, then who is he and where'd he come from? You don't think somebody just dropped him by the side of the road, do you?"

"Not likely or I'd have seen them," Idois answered as she handed the child to Jenny to rest her arms. "Far as I know, there hasn't been a wagon or rider by my house for the better part of a week. You know me; I'm outside working in my garden or my rose beds about all the daylight hours when the weather's good. Helps me pass the time and keep my mind off my lonesomeness."

"Well, you surely been through some sorrowful times, Idois. I wish there were something we could do to help you. But a body just doesn't have ready words for what you've been through."

"Jenny, you and Johnny have helped me more than you know just by being good neighbors and letting me live in that little house and giving me old Betsy for a milk cow. But right now, I'm concerned about this little baby. What do you reckon I ought to do, Jenny?"

"Lordy, Idois, I just don't know, to tell you the truth. Pray of course, and I know you do that. Maybe if you just keep him a while, his folks will turn up. Don't you think? Surely they will. I mean, how could anybody just leave a little baby out in the elements? Just pretty as a picture, too. Cutchy, cutchy, cutchy!"

On the way back home, Idois was thinking about how she could feed and clothe the little boy until his people showed up to claim him. I still have some of Audrey's diapers, she thought, and some of her clothes packed away in Grandma's old trunk, though they'll be a little big for him. But they'll have to do till we can get you back to your folks, little fellow. Don't have any shoes for you, but the weather's warm, so that's not a problem. As for the feeding, I reckon you're big enough to eat table food, if I pick it out and cut it into little pieces. And Ole Betsy's still giving some milk and probably won't go dry for another month or two. "Lord willing, I reckon we can manage, can't we, little fellow?" she said aloud. "Now if you could just tell me your name, but of course you're too little yet to talk, aren't you?"

The thought of being able to take care of the baby gave her a good feeling, the best she had felt since the tragic happenings of recent years. She was afraid people would be waiting for the toddler when she got home and was relieved when she saw no one. That afternoon she hummed a hymn as she dug out Audrey's old clothes and stacked pillows to make a sleeping space for the toddler on the other bed. Clinging to Betty's blanket, he watched her from his pallet on the floor and smiled when she went over to cuddle and comfort him. It was strange, she thought, that he had not cried at all.

Stranger still was that he never cried, then or later, despite bruises and bumps from playing around the house and yard. At church he held on to Betty's old blanket and endured hours of sermonizing and singing without a whimper. While young mothers were busy carrying their squalling children in and out of church as Preacher Yates struggled to make his sermon heard over their wailing, the little boy was quiet. Except, to hear Idois tell it, when he made little noises as though he wanted to join in the singing. Folks laughed and pointed out that the boy was much too young for such things. Nevertheless, everybody was impressed by his happy behavior.

"Why, Idois, I've never seen a child so good," Aunt Gertie Flowers said the next Sunday after church. "He's just like a little angel."

Idois took to the idea and started calling him "my little angel" and then just "Angel." Angel Henson, she thought, but then shook her head. That's not a proper name for a child, and he's not really my child anyway. I have to remember that.

But she didn't for long.

Nobody knew what to make of the little boy. But as some folks will when in doubt, there were those who thought the worst.

"Why, I'll bet you money she stole that baby and made up that crazy story," Mary Blevins speculated to anybody in earshot. "The very idea of a child just appearing out of thin air, to hear Idois tell it, why it doesn't make sense. I tell you, there's something strange about that woman."

"You're right about that," others agreed.

"I think somebody ought to go get the sheriff," Mary added, encouraged by the response. "That child's momma's surely grieving herself to death."

Word did get to the sheriff, and a day or two later Deputy Bluford Jones rode out to Idois's place.

Bluford asked Idois some questions, she asked him some, and they speculated about the child together. But since neither had any answers, he decided to leave the boy with Idois for the time being.

"Nothing else I know to do right now, Mrs. Henson," he said as he drained a dipperful of cool well water Idois offered him. "There hasn't been any word of missing children, and I can't take that little baby back up to Tylerville with me. We've got nowhere to keep it, and the baby needs a woman's care. So I'm leaving it with you for the time being, Mrs. Henson. I can see, ma'am, that you're caring for the child just like it was your own. But now I have to tell you something, just so you'll understand. The county judge may decide to place the child somewhere else, so the best advice I can give you is to keep that fact in mind and not get your feelings too wrapped up. In case later on the law says we have to come and get the little fellow. You understand what I'm saying, don't you, Mrs. Henson?"

Idois heard Bluford's words with her ears but ignored them in her heart. At first she had repeated the same advice to herself, but Angel's coming released a flood of feelings she had tried many months to control and reconcile. Now she could no more hold them back than she could keep the sun from rising in the morning.

Having more pressing matters to pursue, the county judge took no further notice of the unexplained child. As for Idois, motherhood began anew for her just when she thought it was over forever.

The Henson family tragedy of 1895 had been the talk of Lost River. Married in 1881, by 1887 Asa and Idois had already buried three children. And as their children died, each spouse reacted in different ways to the loss. Asa, once a staunch believer and pillar of Lost River Holiness Church, turned bitter after their surviving child, little Elbert, died of pneumonia. He threw his Bible to the floor, called it a pack of lies, blasphemed against God, and took to drinking.

Idois stayed the course of her faith. Not that her grief was less. She understood nothing and knew only the aching, endless pain of their loss. But in some way she could not explain—not even to herself—she knew only that to turn against God now would be to betray the love she had for her departed children. And in the end that love proved to be stronger than her bereavement. By lamplight she read her Bible, endured Asa's curses and drunken taunts with a gentle spirit, and often lay awake praying for long hours as he snored beside her in an alcoholic stupor.

Little Betty's birth in June of 1893 was a resurrection of hope, and the sound of singing and childish laughter was finally heard again in the Henson household. Even Asa relented, and though he would never go back to church with Idois, he cut back on his drinking and paid more attention to his farming.

But by then whiskey had a strong grip on him, and it was too late to make up for wasted time or to recover the borrowed money spent on liquor. Late in December of 1893, Homer Stokesbury showed up with Deputy Bluford to serve foreclosure papers on their farm on the Lost River Road. People said that old Homer, always hard when it came to money, had gotten even stingier with age. Once he was willing to give people a little time to pay off their loans. Now he cut them no slack, none, least of all to a man who had wasted good money on liquor. Homer didn't drink, and he had no respect for men who did, regardless of their reasons.

Asa took it hard. The land had been in his family for three generations. But instead of setting his life straight, he drank more. Idois's uncle Roy Alvis let them move into a little shack on the Barkley Road near Rock Creek. When he was sober, Asa hired out some to other farmers while Idois, an excellent seamstress, made a few dollars sewing and stitching for neighbors. Her garden kept them in vegetables, and Roy and his wife helped them out when they could.

They managed until 1898. As bad as things were, they still had little Betty. And then tragedy struck again.

One day Idois walked over to Claire Hardin's house to cut out a dress for her daughter Irene, leaving Betty with her father. Ordinarily she took Betty with her on such visits, for she was pretty and well-behaved. But Claire's mother was sick—folks suspected with consumption—and she did not want to expose the child. At the same time she had misgivings about leaving her in Asa's keeping, but they needed the half dollar she could make.

Asa took Betty down to Rock Creek to do a little fishing—and drinking. Bill Raley spoke to him on his way into town, saw that he was half drunk, and tried to get him to go home. He said he was worried about little Betty playing on the creek bank and warned Asa that it was slippery and she could fall in.

What happened later was a matter of speculation, for there were no known eyewitnesses. Most folks figured that little Betty slipped and fell in the creek, just as Bill Raley had warned, and that Asa jumped in to rescue her. But too drunk to save her—or himself—both drowned.

Idois fainted dead to the world when she found out, and folks wondered how she could bear this tragedy on top of all she had been through in recent years. But when she regained consciousness, she was strangely and unexpectedly at peace. And she explained why.

"I was just coming to my senses when somebody touched my shoulder and a voice said—and I mean said as clear as anything I ever heard in my life—'Betty and Asa are all right. They are here with me. They are happy with the other children. They say not to worry about them.'"

"Well now, Idois, we were all here," Gertie Flowers said, "but nobody touched you that I recollect. And we didn't hear anything but what we were whispering amongst ourselves."

"What do you think it means, Idois?" Bill Raley's wife, Rebecca, asked.

"I *know* what it means, Becky. That was the Lord speaking to me to comfort me in my sorrow. I know it better than anything I ever knew in my whole life. And I know as surely as I know my own name that Betty and Asa and my other children are with him up Heaven. I'll miss them and I'll do some natural grieving because of my lonesomeness down here, but I know they're in better hands than mine and happier and safer than they could ever be in this old hard world. Someday I'll see them again. So all I can say is Hallelujah and praise the Lord!"

Idois's epiphany was the talk of the community. At the request of Preacher Yates, she agreed to give a testimony of the experience. Some folks believed it outright and called it a miracle. Most wanted to believe her, though they found it hard. Behind her back, others wondered, maliciously or sympathetically, if her mind had snapped.

Angel's unexplained appearance fueled more gossip about Idois, and speculation about his origin continued for years. Maybe all the talk would have died down if Angel had been an ordinary child, but as the years passed, nothing about him deserved that description. He played with other children, who loved him dearly, yet Idois said she sometimes felt he played only to please them and to give her the pleasure of watching him play. He learned easily what she taught him, yet at times she had hints that he knew far more than she did. He spoke and sang words like everybody else, yet there was a resonance, a tone, a musicality in his voice that seemed finer than the speech of other people. With a word or a look he could dispel anger, and in school even the roughest boys were gentle in his presence. With a touch of his cool hand, Idois's headaches vanished. He was unquestioningly obedient in everything Idois told him to do, yet often he would point out to her better ways of doing things.

"I learn more from him than he learns from me," she confided to Jenny. "His teacher says he seems to know things he's never studied, things she doesn't know either."

Years passed, the century turned, and in 1911 Idois's stout heart began to fail. Angel stayed by her side, comforted her with his soothing words, and read to her from the same Bible Asa had once thrown on the floor in a blasphemous rage. Toward the end he would not leave her bedside, even though Jenny and the other women begged him to get some rest.

And then another mystery occurred. Folks swore that the minute Idois died, Angel disappeared. One minute he was there and the next time they looked up, he was gone. Not only that, but all his clothes and possessions had vanished also. The only thing of his they found was a piece of Betty's blue blanket worn threadbare over the years. Maybe the story grew some with time and telling, but it is a matter of record that when old Deputy Bluford Jones, now stove up with rheumatism, came out to look into the matter, he could find no physical trace of Angel. Everybody remembered, of course, that for years he had attended Lost River School and went with Idois to the Holiness Church, yet where his name and picture had once been now there was only a blank space.

Other people said there was no mystery at all about Angel. Old Mary Blevins, for one, claimed that somebody told her that some lawmen took him away the very night Idois died. His real mother finally came forward, so Mary said, and confessed to the new County Judge that she and her married boyfriend left him by the side of the road near Idois's house. Years later, her conscience bothered her so much that she couldn't keep it secret any longer.

But either way nobody ever saw hair or hide of Angel again.

Was he a real boy or some kind of higher being sent to comfort Idois in her sorrow? Who can say? Nobody actually saw the mysterious lawmen that Mary mentioned, and there was no official announcement or gossip about it in Tylerville.

"Mary Blevins makes up tales," said Aunt Gertie Flowers. "You can't believe anything that woman says. On the other hand, I never knew anybody more honest and truthful than Idois Henson. I'll just leave it at that."

Most people agreed with Aunt Gertie, yet no one ever knew for sure where Angel came from in the first place. The whole thing was a puzzle no matter how you looked at it.

As for me, all I can say is that I have told you what I know about it. You'll have to make up your own mind about what really happened.

5.
The Lady of Shiloh

The sharpshooters from Tennessee and Kentucky were generally acknowledged as the best riflemen in the Confederate armies. But even they had to admit grudgingly that the First Indiana Rangers were their equals. Many of the future Rangers, including Stokesbury twins Hiram and Hamilton, were the sons of resettled Southerners. When the Stokesbury clan broke up in East Tennessee, their father went north and resettled in Indiana, while his brothers and cousins moved west and south.

Hiram and Hamilton honed their skills not only hunting in the forests of lower Indiana but also in friendly but spirited competitions across the Ohio River with their Kentucky and Tennessee cousins. When the war came, the elites of both sides often knew one another by name and blood kinship and though deadly in battle, admired the skill of their adversaries and praised them as worthy foes when they fell.

To hear his men tell it, no Rebel and only his twin brother Hamilton could match Hiram Stokesbury shot for shot. If it had been possible, they claimed, in a contest they would put their money on the Stokesbury brothers against the best marksmen the Confederates could field.

Meanwhile, General Buell and his army, thirty thousand strong, were impatient to reach Shiloh. The boats were maddeningly slow with breakdowns and conflicting orders. They had waited for months to battle the Confederates, and now the urgency grew by the hour. It was no secret to anyone on board that there was a good chance—or a bad one—that they would arrive too late to save General Grant's forces from a major defeat. No one doubted the valor of the outnumbered Rebels. Nor was it lost on the Union generals that a Confederate victory would strengthen the rebel cause in the West and could persuade populous and prosperous Missouri to join the Confederacy.

But high policy and grand battle plans quickly break down into the private hell of each soldier who loses sight of the bigger battle. He sees only the smoke and dust, and hears the screams of dying men around him. The lines break, men charge and fall, run and regroup, and all sense of order and plan is lost in the mayhem. At close quarters friend and foe are not always distinguishable and a man may die at the hands of either.

Hiram's unleashed Rangers charged twice up the slope, but Rebel fire withered their resolve and they had to fall back, leaving fifteen of their two hundred men dead or wounded on the hillside.

"Drink and reload, men," he panted. "Then on my count of ten we go at 'em again, and this time all the way!"

But at the high count of ten, nearly twenty of the men froze, including Hamilton.

"Wait, Hiram," he yelled, "not yet! Don't fire!"

Hiram turned to his brother and the wavering men. "Wait for what? In God's name, it's now or never!"

"Hiram, wait, there's a lady up there on the slope right in front of us! See her? She's wearing a white dress. We can't shoot! We might hit her! I don't hold with shooting a woman, Rebel or not!"

"What woman? I don't see a woman! Come on, we've got our orders, and I'm giving you mine. We have to take out that Rebel nest! So move!"

"We see her, too, Lieutenant!" said several of the men holding back with Hamilton. By quick count he estimated seventeen or eighteen.

Hiram cursed for one of the few times in his life, as much in shock as in disgust with his reluctant Rangers, especially Hamilton. His brother had never faltered before. What had gotten into him and the others? A woman that nobody could see? Was it a cover for cowardice? Whatever it was, he couldn't let it contaminate the whole company.

"I'll count again. We go on ten, and those that don't will be subject to summary court-martial!"

Reluctantly, they fell in with the others and the charge began. This time, with heavy casualties, it carried over the Confederate trenches and in hand to hand fighting they took the hill. Sergeant Bob Jones reported that they lost eighteen men.

A young Confederate, gasping for breath as his blood poured out on the ground, looked plaintively at Hiram. "Lieutenant, I didn't think you would come up the hill with that woman our boys said was standing out there in the line of fire. Did you kill her too?"

"No, soldier, we didn't shoot her. We don't kill women, and I'm sorry we had to nearly kill you. Did you see the woman?"

"No, sir, but several of our men did, the ones that got killed."

"What's your name?"

"Homer Stokesbury, Lieutenant."

Damn all war, Hiram thought to himself. I believe that boy's my cousin. So young. He's lost an eye and half of his face and may not survive either. What a waste of life all this is.

"Jones," Hiram called out as the soldier lapsed into unconsciousness. "Where's Second Lieutenant Stokesbury?"

The Sergeant hung his head. "Sir, I'm sorry, he . . . he's wounded real bad."

They all saw the woman, or whatever it was, Hiram said under his breath. It must have been a signal that they were going to die. I've heard of such things. I guess that must mean the young Rebel will survive.

"Sir? I didn't catch what you said."

"Nothing. Take me to Hamilton."

Hamilton was on a stretcher, and two men were treating him. But Hiram saw at once that his wounds were mortal. In a detached, military space in his mind, he saw and accepted that Hamilton was dying, another casualty. But then the military veneer vanished and he was simply Hiram staring at his twin brother so like him, so constant, so close, so much a part of himself.

"Hamilton, I can't let you go unless I go too. We were born into this world together, we have to leave it together."

"No, Hiram, you have to stay here and live for both of us. You were always the leader, but this one time I'll take the lead and wait for you on the other side. I know you'll have a family and a good life, and you'll do it for both of us. But now I have to go. I can see people I recognize gathering to welcome me. I love you, Hiram. We'll meet again over there."

He rattled a last deep breath and was gone.

"And I love you, Hamilton," Hiram said as tears flooded his eyes. After a while, and back in his military role, he called Sergeant Jones.

"Yes sir?"

"See to it that my brother and our other men have a proper burial. The Rebel lying there is still alive and may live. I'll see if the Major will allow us to turn him over to the Confederates under a flag of truce."

"Sir?"

"Is there a problem, Sergeant?"

"No sir, I just thought that being a Rebel and all, you wouldn't want to bother . . ."

"Sergeant, someday when we've finished with the killing and the dying, we'll have to get back to the living and respecting one another again. Just think of this as a small step in that direction."

"Yes sir," Jones said with a puzzled frown, wondering to himself if the Lieutenant was about to break down on them.

Hiram fought on till the end of the war, taking part in a dozen major engagements and winning many commendations and medals for valor. And when finally the guns went silent at Appomattox, he hung up his guns and vowed never to fire another weapon. But later his resolve would be tested.

6.
Duel in Abilene

Nobody in Abilene, Kansas, knew much about Hiram Stokesbury. Despite the best efforts of town gossips, all they managed to discover about him was that he was from Indiana and had fought in the Civil War before homesteading a little north of Abilene in 1874. From land records he filed, they learned that he was thirty-seven and that his full name was Hiram Homer Stokesbury.

His two children were almost as tightlipped as their father, but daughter, Betsy, 16, confided to her new friend Kathy Schultz, 17, that their mother had died of typhus a year earlier in Indiana. And at a Thanksgiving turkey shoot in Abilene, his son, Daniel, 15, boasted to Kathy's twin brother, Bernard, that if he could be talked into it, his father could outshoot any man in Abilene, or for that matter, the whole state of Kansas.

But Daniel's claim would have to remain unproven: Hiram refused to fire any sort of weapon, including a sidearm he possessed but kept locked away. When pressed on this peculiarity, all Hiram would say was that he "had seen enough killing to make him sick to his stomach for a lifetime." He vowed never to shoot another gun.

Maybe it was destiny's decree that Hiram's resolve would be tested by the Wingates. Big Bill Wingate, 42, cattle buyer and father of a numerous clan, was a huge muscular man who on election days and other liquor-flowing occasions customarily challenged all men present to enter a circle he traced on the ground. Any man still standing after five minutes inside the ten-foot radius could earn twenty-five dollars. If he lost, he forfeited the five-dollar entry fee. At first many men accepted Big Bill's challenge and all lost. Later, few dared to face his ham hock sized fists. Bill was simply too strong for ordinary men.

Rumors circulated that he had beaten at least one man to death in an Omaha saloon brawl.

Bill's sons Vester, 21, Jack, 19, and Graham, 17, strutted in the glow of their father's reputation. As tall as Big Bill and already nearly as strong, they beat up the other Abilene boys and bullied the townspeople, insulting men and women alike with gross profanity. And the two Wingate daughters, Tressie, 16, and Florence, 14, were as arrogant as their brothers.

Privately, merchants and other townspeople complained to the sheriff and his deputies, who found it convenient to look the other way where the Wingates were concerned. For Bill and his sons were not only dangerous with their fists but also quick to draw their sidearms. They laughed at a new city ordinance forbidding the wearing of pistols inside the town. Finally their behavior became so flagrant, however, that Sheriff Norwood McGraw, hat in hand, appealed to Bill to control his sons.

"I know they're good boys at heart," he said, nervously twisting his hat brim, "but sometimes maybe they get a bit too feisty. You know, just like fun-loving boys will do. So I would appreciate it, Mr. Wingate, if . . ."

"Don't you bother my boys," Bill interrupted with a frown and a thud of his mighty fist on the table. "I'll take care of my folks. And don't let me hear about any of your deputies mistreating them."

"Oh, no sir; you have my word on that. My men are always respectful of our Abilene people. It's just that . . ."

"Well see to it that it stays that way. So you just be on your way and remind them of their civic duty and I'll see to my boys. Understand?"

"Yes sir, I sure do. So I'll not take any more of your time and I wish you a good day."

Bill spat contemptuously as McGraw closed the door.

On Election Day in November, Big Bill drew his customary circle and issued his usual challenge, but the only taker was a drifter half Bill's size and down on his luck. Driven by desperation, he proved to be surprisingly gritty and agile. Bill was embarrassed by the sweat he had to work up on a cold day trying to catch him. Finally, just before the five minutes expired, he caught his tiring victim with a crunching left hook to the chin. The drifter collapsed like a sack of rocks and lay motionless for several minutes as Bill calmly wiped away the sweat with a towel and collected the five dollars from crony Fergus Hanley. Some wondered if the man's neck might be broken, but finally he moaned, rolled over, and sat up, shaking his head.

"Mister," he pleaded to Bill as he staggered to his feet, "that was the last money I had in the world. Could you see your way clear to let me have a dollar back to eat on? I'm trying to make it on out to Colorado."

"You think we run a charity ward here?" Bill sneered. "Give you a dollar back? I'll tell you what I will give you if you don't get your scrawny ass out of Abilene. I'll beat you into sausage meat."

The drifter headed for his horse, head down. Hiram Stokesbury stopped him and handed him a dollar.

"Take this and stay out of trouble. There are better ways to live than getting your brains knocked out."

"Thanks, mister. I'm obliged," he mumbled, massaging his swollen chin.

"Hey! Hey! What the hell is going on?" bellowed Big Bill, elbowing his way toward Hiram. "I thought I made it clear that the drifter gets nothing!"

"I heard what you said," Hiram said calmly, "and that's your business. Helping him a little is mine."

"What I said, sodbuster, goes for everybody around here."

"The name is Hiram, Hiram Stokesbury, Mr. Wingate. And I make my own decisions."

"Hiram-skiram!" Bill thundered. "I don't give a rat's ass what your name is! If you don't want to end up like the drifter you'll take back that dollar!"

"As I said, Mr. Wingate, I make my own decisions, and this one's been made. He keeps the dollar."

The veins bulged on Big Bill's neck. "Step inside my circle, pilgrim, no charge for this one, and you'll learn what it means to cross Bill Wingate!"

"That's not my way. I have things to do, so I'll be going."

"You talk big for a little man, but I'm thinking it's all bluff. Here and now I'm calling you out for what you are, an outright coward afraid to fight."

"Call me what you will, Wingate, but I'll not get in that circle with you."

"I don't have to beat you like a drum to show everybody what a coward you are, clodhopper. If you won't fight with your fists, do you know one end of a sidearm from the other? I'll give you the choice, fists or firearms, if you're man enough to face me."

"I see no reason to accept either option. I have no quarrel with you or anybody, much less a reason to hurt or kill a man over a dollar. Good day to you."

And with that he walked away to the jeers and taunts of Big Bill and his crowd.

The next day Daniel came home from school with one eye swollen shut and his face bruised and bleeding.

"Paw, it was Graham Wingate," Daniel confessed to Hiram's questions. "He insulted you and I couldn't let him do that. But he's a lot bigger than me and . . ."

"Daniel, I appreciate your spirit, but I've told you before not to get involved in fights. I don't need you to defend me. I can take care of myself."

"But, Paw, he said some awfully insulting things about you."

"I imagine he did. He picked them up from his father. But you stay clear of the Wingate boys until things quieten down. You hear me, son?"

"Yes sir," Daniel said through swollen lips, secretly beginning to wonder if his father really was afraid to defend his name and honor.

Daniel stayed clear of the Wingate boys for the next few days, but Betsy was not so lucky. Two days later she came home from school in tears, barefoot and with her best dress ripped down the back.

"Daddy," she wailed, "Tressie Wingate knocked me down and her brother, the one they call Jack, threw my shoes in Schultz's pond! Then she and that nasty little sister of hers tore my dress! My best dress, too! Now I don't have anything decent to wear to church! And I was supposed to sing in the choir."

Hiram was silent for a moment, then sighed, got up, and knocked the ashes from his pipe into the fireplace. "You'll be all right, Betsy; as soon as I can, I'll see to it that you get a new dress and shoes for church."

"But, Daddy, the Wingates have got it in for us. The next time they see me or Daniel, it'll happen all over again. They've told us both we had better not come back to school if we know what's good for us."

"Well, you're not quitting school. So put that idea out of your head. I'm going into town now to settle the matter. You get supper ready for you and Daniel. I'll be home in a couple of hours."

"But what are you going to do, Daddy? You can't fight the Wingates. They're too strong."

"You leave that to me, honey. I'll take care of things," he reassured her as he opened his gun case.

Betsy's eyes widened in surprise when she saw what he was doing. She ran to tell Daniel.

Big Bill was holding forth as usual with his cronies in Eastland's saloon when Hiram walked in with his .44 strapped to his side. A hush came over the drinkers, and no one was more surprised than Bill.

"I came to speak to you, Mr. Wingate, more to the point, to accept your challenge unless we can come to an agreement. I can deal with insults about me, but I can't let you or your family mistreat my children. Now if you'll issue an apology for the events of recent days and give me your word it won't happen again, I'll go my way in peace. What say you, sir?"

Big Bill knocked over several chairs getting up from the table, his face turning purple with rage.

"Apologize? Me apologize to a sorry excuse of a man like you? Hell will freeze over before Bill Wingate apologizes for anything. What I'm going to do is break some bones and teach you some manners. So clear the tables, boys, and let the lesson begin!"

"You misunderstand, Wingate, I came here to accept an apology or to challenge you to a duel. You do recall, don't you, that you gave me the option of fists or guns. I choose guns."

A faint trace of uncertainty crossed Bill's broad face. "Guns? What do you know about guns, sodbuster?"

"Enough."

"You did give him that choice, Bill," Fergus Hanley reminded him. "We all heard you."

Bill hesitated for an instant before pounding the table with his fist. "I know damn well what I said, Fergus, and Bill Wingate stands by his word. Guns it is. You pick the time and place. We can do it right now, if you're man enough to face me."

"Not now, Wingate, I have more pressing things to do first. Let's make it a week from now, next Monday morning at 7 a.m. at the cemetery. That satisfactory with you?"

"Suits me fine, sodbuster, that way they won't have to carry your sorry carcass far to your grave," he chortled.

Subdued laughter ran through the group. The men were puzzled and some noted that Hiram's gun belt was worn smooth and his .44 nicked as though by long use. What they didn't know but some were beginning to guess was that Hiram was a keen judge of character honed by his years of leadership on the battlefield. He knew that a week was a long time for a man like Wingate, long enough for doubts to eat away at his bluster.

"All right then. Pistols at twenty paces, one shot each. Now let me give you two things to think about in the meantime: first, we can avoid this confrontation if you decide to apologize; and second, it may interest you to know that in the war I served as Captain of the 1st Indiana Ranger Battalion, Indiana's crack marksmen. By my count I have killed upwards of a hundred men, many in close combat. Killing men was my business and I'm good at it."

With that he turned and walked out of the saloon.

It took Big Bill a few minutes to regain his swagger, but by the end of the evening and fortified by a dozen drinks he was promising quick death and destruction to Hiram. But his companions were not so confident. Several of them had heard of the 1st Indiana Rangers, said to be as good as the best Kentucky and Tennessee sharpshooters on the Rebel side.

"I don't know, Bill," Fergus said shaking his head, "if that man's who he says he is, he's may be as dangerous as they come. If you noticed, that pistol and gun belt of his looked like they had seen a considerable amount of use."

Bill responded by kicking Fergus's chair from under him, sending him sprawling.

"Don't any of you ever doubt Bill Wingate! Sharpshooter or not, that was a long time ago if what that sodbuster says is true to start with. He could be the biggest liar and worst shot in Kansas."

"Or the best," Luther Foreman whispered.

"What did you say, Luther?"

"Me? Nothing, nothing at all."

Rumors circulated fast and furious in Abilene that week. Soon people were saying in bug-eyed excitement that Hiram Stokesbury had killed close to two hundred men in single-hand combat. Others recalled or invented stories of his legendary bravery, and most of the townspeople were secretly hoping that Hiram could take down Big Bill and end the Wingate oppression.

For all his public blustering and boasting about what he would do to Hiram, Big Bill could not shake a gnawing fear. By midweek it was keeping him awake at night. Damn! Why did he give Stokesbury an option? Why didn't he just beat the hell out of him inside or outside the circle and be done with it? Why was he dumb enough to give the runt a chance? And Stokesbury just might be as good at killing as he said. But try as he might, he could not think of a way to get out of the duel, and the clock was ticking toward the fateful hour. He considered ambushing Hiram, or burning his house at night, or hiring a gunman to kill him. But no, everybody would guess immediately it was his doing and his reputation would be tarnished, and if proven guilty, his life could be at risk. In Kansas murder was a hanging offense. Bill still remembered but never talked about the trouble he got into in Omaha.

By Sunday Bill could no longer hide his nervousness. His eyes were red from sleeplessness and the unbelievable quantities of whiskey he had drunk. Meanwhile Hiram's reputation continued to grow. Now the gossips were claiming he could shoot out a candle at forty paces, or a match at twenty. By now the men he had personally dispatched were counted not in dozens but hundreds.

Early on Monday, fortified by a fresh pint of bourbon, Bill rode out to the cemetery with a half dozen of his followers. There was scant comfort in whiskey or cronies, but at least they momentarily deadened the fear tying his stomach in knots. The only real comfort was a risky strategy he had worked out with Fergus.

Hiram was waiting when Bill rode up and dismounted.

"You still have time to save your hide, sodbuster," he said to Hiram.

"And you still have time to apologize and settle this matter like civilized men," Hiram answered.

"When hell freezes over, sodbuster, when hell freezes over."

"Then let's get it over with. These are the rules as I understand them.

See if you agree: we stand back to back, step off twenty paces to Fergus' count. From that point, we turn and fire once."

Bill looked at Fergus. "That's right, Mr. Stokesbury. Bill's .45 has one bullet. What about yours?"

"Mine conforms to the rules. Only one shell in the chamber. You can check it if you like."

Fergus shook his head. "Mr. Wingate will take your word for it. Now if you men will line up, I'll count off twenty steps."

Fergus began the count as Bill and Hiram began their march. But after "eighteen" he skipped nineteen and called out "twenty."

Bill turned and fired as Hiram was turning. Hiram went down and Bill threw up his arms and shouted gleefully.

"I told you I'd take him down! Didn't I tell you? Didn't I? Huh? Huh?"

But Hiram was not dead. As Bill was bragging, Hiram got to his feet; his left shirtsleeve was red with blood. His .44 came out and with practiced, steady ease lined up with Bill's ample torso. Bill panicked and screamed at Fergus.

"Fergus, give me another bullet, quick! I need one more shot to finish him off!"

Fergus shook his head. "No more, Bill. You had your chance. I broke the rules once for you, but I won't do it again. You're on your own now."

Hiram took a step toward Bill, his .44 steady, lethal, the weapon that had killed a hundred men, maybe more. Bill turned away to avert the menace, then he took a step backwards, then another. Dropping his weapon, he fell to his knees and began to plead for his life.

"Don't kill me, Mr. Stokesbury! Please don't kill me! I have a family! I apologize for what they did to your children! But let me live! Please don't kill me!"

"Wingate, I'll spare your life on one condition: that you leave Abilene before the sun sets today and never come back. What you and Fergus did here today dishonors you both. And these men with you will tell everybody. You are both finished in this town. Nobody here will ever respect you again. If you stay you'll be the laughingstock of Abilene. And remember that by the rules of dueling I still have the right to take my shot when and if I choose to. What say you?"

"We'll be gone by sundown, Mr. Stokesbury."

"And you, Fergus, what do you have to say for yourself?"

"My apologies to you, sir, for my part in this trickery. I should have never listened to Bill. If you'll spare me, you won't ever see me again in Abilene."

The townspeople were jubilant as the three Wingate wagons lumbered

63

away westward in late afternoon. Fergus had slunk out of town much earlier. Word quickly spread about Bill's cowardice and Fergus' complicity in the treachery. Everybody wanted to shake Hiram's hand and ask him to replace irresolute Sheriff Norwood McGraw. A grateful merchant saw to it that Betsy got her new dress and shoes.

As for Hiram himself, he wanted no part of being sheriff, and all the public adulation was an embarrassment. As soon as he could slip away to his farm, he took off a curiously padded vest that had slowed or stopped more than one bullet. Then cleansed his flesh wound and treated it, as he had treated others, his own and those of his Rangers, with a strong, burning ointment of his own making. Most of all he wanted to put away his .44, this time forever. The weight and feel of it had brought back old memories of gore and death. Daniel and Betsy watched as he doubled the thickly padded vest and stuffed it deep in a trunk.

"Daddy, what kind of vest was that you were wearing? I've never seen it before."

"One I made back in the War. It won't stop a direct hit, but it will absorb a lot of the force and maybe keep it from being a killing shot. It saved my life a couple of times."

"And today, too."

"No, Wingate's bullet grazed my arm. He was too shaky to shoot straight. It was no worse than a hornet's sting."

Hiram removed the shell from his weapon and doubled up the belt. Something caught Daniel's eye.

"Daddy, can I see the bullet?"

"You can keep it if you like, son."

Daniel gasped when he saw the empty shell. "Daddy, this is a shell casing. Where's the live ammunition?"

"There wasn't any, son. I told both of you and your mother I never intended to fire another weapon, and I kept my word. Not that I was dumb enough to face Wingate without any kind of protection. There's no rule that says you can't be smart even with an empty weapon. I figured Wingate for treachery but also counted on his cowardice that had him so rattled he couldn't think or shoot straight. But most of all, children, don't ever give your word lightly and never for things that aren't worth it. But once you do, always keep it. A man's word, or a woman's, is a pledge of honor, and if you break it, you dishonor yourself and God. And let me just say here and now, Daniel and Betsy, in case I haven't told you before, that you two are the most precious things in my life."

Daniel kept that empty shell casing all his life to remind himself of his father's courage and example.

7.
A Dollar Short

Back in 1905 everybody around Nacogdoches, Texas, knew that Myrtle Hendricks was "feeble-minded," as folks used to describe the mentally challenged before the age of political correctness.

After Myrtle's parents, Ben and Lois, died of influenza in 1900, her only remaining kinfolk that anyone knew about were two male cousins on her mother's side up in Longview. But they were ashamed of their simple-minded relative and would have nothing to do with her. And since the only asset she inherited from her parents was a ramshackle frame house down by the railroad siding, it fell to the Nacogdoches townspeople in general and the congregation of Full Gospel Church in particular to look after her. The church ladies gave her food and clothing and saw to it that she was reasonably clean and decently dressed. For their part, the men of the church made the necessary repairs to her house, paid the property tax, and in winter brought wood for her fireplace.

There were those who worried about Myrtle, now in her early twenties, but they did not include Myrtle herself. Her parents, themselves staunch believers, had taught her to attend church and to trust wholeheartedly in the Lord. Even though she never mastered reading and writing, and was barely able to count to twenty, Myrtle learned her religious lessons better than most. With an unshakeable simplicity of faith, she had an absolute certainty that God would provide whatever she needed. Thus with absolute peace of mind she wandered in and around Nacogdoches, singing, playing with dogs, birds, squirrels—and children when they would let her—and collecting wondrous amounts of junk, which she hauled about the streets in a little red wagon outfitted with homemade sideboards. Her doll, Molly, minus her right eye and a chunk of her nose, rode on a cushioned seat wedged between two boards. Like a caring mother, Myrtle cuddled Molly, told her stories, and always kept her dry and warm, just as Lois had done for her before she went to live in Heaven.

There were folks who wanted to institutionalize Myrtle in a state asylum, claiming that she could be a threat to herself or others. But most people, especially those who knew her best, opposed the idea. She was a happy, innocent soul and a threat to nobody. To lock her away would be like putting a bright flower in a dark room and leaving it to wilt without light, water, or nourishment.

On weekdays when the weather allowed it, Myrtle always followed a regular route around Nacogdoches. First, she would go by the church so that the ladies could feed her, check her clothing, and comb her hair. Then, unless it was raining, it was on to Lost River Ranch, the Lloyd and Mary Beth Patterson Ranch nearly three miles north of town. It was a long way to pull her wagon, especially in winter cold or summer heat, but unless Mrs. Mary Beth Patterson was gone from home—more frequently lately because of her husband's prosperous businesses—the trip was always worth it. There was food, tea, and cookies, often a slice of cake, fresh vegetables from Uncle Albert Patterson just down the road, and sometimes hand-me-down clothing from the Patterson daughters or the widowed Mrs. Florence Hunter, who now lived at her daughter's. Myrtle was shy around Mr. Lloyd Patterson, who, though kind to her, teased her sometimes about boys and things she didn't understand or care about. But she felt safe and loved by Mary Beth and her children and Mrs. Hunter.

Myrtle was always on the lookout for discarded or lost items of modest value in the streets or along the railroad tracks. She could exchange them for a few coins at Horace Simmons' Second-Hand Store. Her money did not last long, for she had a sweet tooth for peppermint candy. As soon as she had pennies in hand she would run to Tucker's General Store for her peppermint treat, her wagon clattering on the town square cobblestones. As soon as beefy old Thurston Tucker heard the approaching commotion, he would grin, emerge from his back store office, and, peppermint sticks in hand, position his considerable bulk at the entrance to greet Myrtle.

"I tell you the truth," he was heard to say, "it gladdens my old hard heart to see the look on Myrtle's face when I hand her the peppermint sticks. Man alive, if I could just enjoy life with the simple pleasure she does! No concerns about overhead, taxes, or profits or losses, no worries about tomorrow or remorse over yesterday. Maybe that's what Jesus meant when he said we must become like little children."

But one Sunday Myrtle had a crisis in her life. Pastor Melvin Skinner preached a sermon on Christian charity and highlighted his message with a gruesome story of Christian families starving in a severe African drought. He called on the congregation to give generously.

"For just fifteen dollars a month," he pleaded, "you could keep an entire village from starving and have enough left over to provide some clothing for the children. So please give generously as your circumstances permit. We may have hard times here in Nacogdoches, but it's nothing compared to what Christians are going through over there across the waters in Africa."

Myrtle understood the message, especially the part about hunger. For despite the generosity of the church and town folks and the Patterson family, there were days when everybody was busy with other matters and she went hungry. She wanted to help but at the moment she had no money. The day before she had spent her last few pennies for peppermint at Tucker's Store.

But there was always God, and she knew He would not fail her. So she prayed and after the service went up to speak to Pastor Skinner.

"I can give fifteen dollars for the hungry people over yonder somewhere across the waters that you talked about," she informed the surprised minister.

"In Africa. You can? Are you sure, Myrtle? How can you come by that much money?"

"I asked God for it," she replied matter-of-factly, "so you can count on it. God can do anything."

"Well, yes he can, Myrtle, but I was asking people with jobs and means, not—"

"You can count on it," she interrupted him. "I asked God for it. God can do anything."

Pastor Skinner was tied in an emotional knot about Myrtle when he said down for lunch with his wife, Helen.

"Helen, there's no way on God's earth that Myrtle can come up with fifteen dollars once, much less several times. I guess I'm sorry she heard the sermon. Just the thought of her pure, childlike faith being disappointed breaks my heart. But I don't know what can be done to prevent it."

"Why don't you do something yourself? After all, don't you preach that the church is the body of Christ? Can't you begin to do what Christ would do?"

"Helen, that's heresy! I'm not Christ! I can't work miracles!"

"Have you ever tried?"

"What do you mean?"

"I mean you start by giving a little something yourself, open your own purse strings, then ask others to chip in, and see what happens. It's a little like the story of the loaves and fishes in the Bible. I've heard you preach about how Christ multiplied the little boy's loaves and fishes and fed thousands of people. But they started with something very small."

"But Helen, this is different," he protested.

"Everything is always different, husband dear. It looks like you're the one who's having a test of faith."

Pastor Skinner was stung by his wife's attitude, which seemed unreasonable to him, but unable to come up with a better idea, he took her advice. He chipped in a dollar, Thurston Tucker contributed two, and others combined for eight more. By the next Sunday he had collected a total of fourteen dollars, which he showed to Myrtle.

She was not in the least surprised, but after laboriously counting it, she whispered to Pastor Skinner, "Maybe you better watch the people counting the money. Somebody kept some of God's money. It's a dollar short of what God gave."

"Uh, yes, Myrtle, thank you. We can't be too careful in money matters, can we?"

"But don't you worry about it. I'll pray for God to send another dollar.

And next month he'll see to it that you get all the money you need to help the people as long as they're hungry in that place over yonder across the waters. God can do anything."

When word got out about Myrtle's faith and what it had started, other congregations joined in the African effort and contributions multiplied many times over. Lloyd and Mary Beth Patterson gave two hundred dollars. Some people, Pastor Skinner among them, likened it to a miracle.

Myrtle didn't look at it in exactly the same way. She was happy about the money for the hungry people in that place over yonder across the waters, but as her parents always taught her, she knew it was God just doing what He does.

Of course, they also taught Myrtle that you shouldn't bother God about things you can do for yourself, or do without, and Myrtle still minded her daddy and mommy, just as she did before they went to live in Heaven. Still, though, sometimes she couldn't help thinking that if there was some way God would help her get her hands on a few more sticks of peppermint candy, now that would really be something special.

8.
Wearing the Pants

In 1852, Jeff Hargrove, 21, and his new bride, Mary Stokesbury Hargrove, 20, along with a dozen other families, moved down from East Tennessee to unsettled territory in north central Florida. Jeff and neighbors felled trees, burned stumps, limbs, and underbrush, and helped one another erect log cabins on their homesteads. They named the settlement Providence and built a small church, Providence Church, on the Jacksonville Road, just north of the community. South of their settlement stretched primitive pine forests that gradually merged with the tropical vegetation of lower Florida. War bands of young native warriors still ranged north of their customary hunting grounds in the southern swamps to forage and steal from the white frontier settlements. The screams of panthers were common at night, and Jeff and his neighbors kept shotguns loaded and ready to protect families, mules, cows, pigs, and chickens from both human and animal predators.

If Tennessee summers were hot, Florida's were sweltering, but Jeff and Mary adjusted and survived. The "crackers," as they came to be called later, were hardy and fiercely independent. In occasional letters to her sister Katherine in Cordele, Georgia, Mary told of the bears, panthers, and other animals that roamed the forest, but boasted that the Florida winters were usually like perpetual springs. Though she could do without the snakes and spiders.

Their son, Henry, was born in March 1853, and in April of 1855 daughter, Agnes. Mary was a tall, strong woman who delivered without undue labor or distress. Old Hattie Philpott, the community midwife, said admiringly of Mary, "She could drop a half dozen more babies with no trouble at all." Mary's strength was a good thing, which was more than could be said of some women in Providence. The nearest physician, Dr. Hansford Humphry, was sixty miles away in Jacksonville, much too far to save Sally James, wife of Arnold James, from fatal childbirth hemorrhaging. Their child, Tom, survived on goat's milk and Myrtle Simmons' loving care. Devastated by Sally's death, Arnold moved back to Georgia, leaving little Tom with the widow Hardin, who renamed him Tom Simmons and raised him as her own. Some years later Arnold moved west, and as far as anyone knew, never saw his son again.

With the secession of Florida and other Southern States from the Union in 1861, the Hargroves had a decision to make. Jeff and Mary discussed it after the children were asleep.

"Mary," Jeff said, taking Mary's hands in his, "I feel it's my duty to fight for my country, but I can't rightly leave you and the children here all by yourselves. So I was thinking that I'll take you back up to your sister's in Georgia. That way you'll have people to help and look after you. But if you're not of a mind to do that, then I'm not going."

Mary withdrew her hands and placed them firmly on his shoulders. "Jeff, I have just two things to say about it. First, I would be ashamed to be the wife of a man who wouldn't fight for his country. And second, this is my home now, not Katherine's house, and this is where I mean to stay. You go on and do your duty like the brave man you are, and I'll stay here and do mine. We didn't move down here to turn back the first time things got tough."

"But I'll be worried about you and the children here all by yourselves."

"And I, dear husband, will be worried about you. We'll pray to the Good Lord that He will guard and protect you and bring you safely back to us. And don't you worry about the children and me. We have neighbors I can call on if things get rough. Just leave me the mule team, the shotgun, and plenty of shells, and we'll be just fine. I'll educate Henry and Agnes as best I can. All I have is God and the Bible, but with them we are strong enough to face any enemy. The children are smart, so I'm sure they will learn quickly all I can teach them. When will you leave?"

"This Saturday, I reckon," he said with a faraway look in his eyes. "A couple of the men here, Jeb Bennett and Levi Stevens, were saying they'd walk over to Jacksonville and join up there. I'm hoping I'll get assigned to my brother-in-law's company. But I don't know where they're liable to send us. But

I don't think this war will last long, and I'm hoping to be back by spring. And this I promise you, Mary, I will come back."

"I believe you will. I'll fix up some food and water for you to take on the road."

"But what about the crops, Mary? That's a worrisome matter. The corn will need gathering in two months and the potatoes will be ready about the same time. It's a lot of work for a woman."

"And a lot for man, too, Jeff. You always told me I was a strong woman. I guess it's time to find out just how much truth there was in your words. Remember, Jeff, I won't be alone. Henry is strong for his age and works like a little man, and he'll try all that much harder while you're gone. And Agnes can already cook and clean just about as well as I can. Besides, we've all worked shoulder to shoulder in the fields, and I know just about as much about farming as you do. We'll get it done."

Jeff's eyes were aglow with admiration for his Mary. And a lump formed in his throat when he thought how lucky he was to have a wife like her.

Two days later, in June of 1862, he left.

Jeff was wrong about the war. At first his occasional letters were cheerful, but by 1863 Mary could sense his fatigue and discouragement. Levi Stevens, he told her, died in Tennessee and Jeb Bennett was missing in action on a Confederate raid across the Ohio River into Indiana. Of his original Florida platoon, the two men left were reassigned to a Georgia company. From comments he made about tobacco fields, she guessed he was now in North Carolina or maybe Virginia. In his last letter he mentioned the Tennessee River and the Smoky Mountains. That's Tennessee, she thought. At least he's a little closer to home.

Things did not go all that well for Mary either. A few weeks after Jeff left, she discovered she was pregnant. Now we're in a pickle, she thought. Harvest time was upon her, and she had to take extra care of herself to protect the life of her unborn child. She did not dare tell Jeff, even if her letters reached him. If he found out, he might desert and rush home, and the roving "home guard" of Northern Florida, as it was called, had a reputation for hanging or shooting renegades and Confederate deserters. Anyway, she was sure she could work until the corn and potatoes were gathered, but her dresses were already becoming too tight and restrictive. A big baby, she thought, with joy and worry, probably another boy who would be tall like his brother, Henry.

Then an idea occurred to her. Digging into Jeff's clothes, she found one of his old shirts and a serviceable pair of pants. Since she was nearly as tall as Jeff, they fit fairly well and much more comfortably than her dresses. Although she had washed them before she put his clothes away, she imagined they still had his aroma. It was a comfort to her.

But her solution did not last long unchallenged. One Sunday afternoon she was surprised to see half a dozen neighbors standing at her front door when she opened it to a loud knock.

"Good evening, Mrs. Hargrove," said Matthew Henson, a short graying man in his fifties who did the preaching. "We thought we'd all come over and see how things were coming along for you."

Mary was surprised by the formality of his greeting. The Hensons had been their nearest neighbors since moving to Providence five years earlier.

"Why, doing just fine, Matthew. You all come on in. I don't have chairs enough for everybody in the fireplace room, but you are welcome to sit on the bed or take a seat at the kitchen table. Agnes, run and fetch a glass of water for everybody. It's hot out there today."

They talked about the war, crops, illnesses, and other matters, but it was obvious to Mary that they really had other things on their mind. She was a patient woman and knew that eventually they would get around to the real purpose of their visit. After a while Matthew did.

"Mrs. Hargrove," he said with obvious nervousness, "some of us have noticed lately that you've been working in the field wearing men's clothing."

"Why, that's right, Matthew, Jeff's old clothes. I imagine most of you know that I'm . . . in a family way, and dresses are just not suited for that kind of heavy . . ."

"You know, don't you, Mrs. Hargrove," Henson interrupted her, "that women aren't supposed to dress like a man. The Bible speaks against it."

Mary was stunned and angered as the meaning of his words sank in. After a pause, she responded.

"Well, I tell you what, Mr. Henson and you other men, if you'll agree to come down here and do the plowing and field work that has to be done, I'll be happy to wear a dress and take my ease out yonder under that oak tree."

"We meant no offense, Mrs. Hargrove, and you have no call to speak harshly to us. Our intention is to be a God-fearing community," Matthew offered, hastily getting to his feet. "The Scriptures teach that a sharp tongue spawns many evils."

"In that case, Reverend Henson, I'll keep my words short. We won't be back to your church. Now I bid you all a good day."

Some of the embarrassed women mumbled offers of sympathy and help as they left, but Mary made no response. Still smarting from Mary's rebuke, none of men offered to help her with the fieldwork.

Not that she needed help until it came time for her to give birth. Henry, growing stronger by the day, gathered most of corn, and she and Agnes managed to harvest the potatoes and vegetables. The rains held off until the most demanding work was done, and for every fair day, Mary gave thanks. At night they prayed for God's help and Jeff's safety.

Then one morning in late March of 1863 her contractions began.

"Henry, you run over to Miss Hattie's house and see if she can come. And hurry, son! You know where she lives, don't you?"

"Yes, ma'am, I pass by her house when I go fishing in the Santa Fe fork. She always asks me about you when she sees me."

Henry ran all the way, and within an hour Hattie was there. And a good thing, too. For the delivery was harder than the earlier ones. And for a good reason: twin boys.

"Twins, Miss Hattie? I knew I was bigger this time and the thought occurred to me, especially one night when I guess both were kicking. I thought to myself, this boy is going to be born half grown."

"No, but they're full term, judging by their eyelashes. Both look fine, and they're identical, like two peas in a pod. You think you'll have milk enough for the pair? If not, maybe we can get some goat's milk from Myrtle Hardin's old nannies."

"I usually have plenty for one baby. We'll just have to see about two, specially two boys."

Agnes hovered over the twins like a guardian angel, which freed Mary, on her feet after a couple of days, to attend to urgent farm matters. Henry was now measurably stronger and fiercely committed to being the man of the house. Mary was convinced that with his help they could get the planting done on time.

And so they did. The 1863 crop was good, and Mary's milk held out until the twins, Daniel and David, were able to begin eating table food.

But on another front, Mary was troubled as the weeks and months passed without word from Jeff. By the winter of 1864, she had not heard from him in over a year. Word reached Providence of heavy casualties as the tide of war turned against the Confederacy. Was Jeff among them? He had promised to return, and she refused to let go of the assurance. You promised me, Jeff, and I'm holding you to that promise, she told herself as she wept almost nightly on her pillow.

Worms, drought, and parasites took a heavy toll on the 1864 corn crop. The potatoes did better, but then another calamity happened. By the winter of 1865, Mary had used up all her shotgun shells and she had no way of getting more. Hawks and foxes made off with most of their chickens and thus their supply of eggs. Mary sensed it was the beginning of the end for them on the homestead. In spite of her oft-repeated assurance that Jeff would return, her sense of realism was eroding her confidence. But where would they go if they had to leave? Georgia did not seem to be an option, and as far as anyone in Providence knew, it might not even exist. Sherman's army had destroyed

Atlanta and cut a wide swath of destruction through Georgia. I have folks that settled farther west, in Lost River. I don't think the war has affected that part of the country that much, but it's a long way off and I really don't know them.

Henry and especially Agnes were beginning to forget their father. They asked their mother about him, where he was, the kind of man he was, and when he would come home. She did all she could to keep his memory alive for them, even sketching a picture of him that Henry hung over the fireplace. The actual likeness to his features was casual, but affection made up for the artistic deficiencies.

Then word came that the war was officially over, and not long afterwards the weary Confederate survivors began to straggle home. Jeff was not among them. Nobody could tell Mary anything about him. Yes, one remembered a man by that name in Tennessee, another thought he was sent to Virginia, and still another said that he was lost defending Atlanta.

Summer passed and fall was upon them. The harvest was better, but Mary's situation was increasingly stark. The twins were healthy, but always hungry. Henry and Agnes were outgrowing their clothes and no new ones were to be had. Mary began cutting and redesigning her old dresses for Agnes and re-stitching Jeff's remaining garments for Henry. They were running low on food. Since that fateful day when the church delegation came to reproach her, with the happy exception of Miss Hattie, Mary had little contact with her neighbors, most of whom, persuaded by Matthew Henson's sermons, now warily regarded her as a heretic.

One afternoon Mary and her children were sitting under the oak tree. Mary was thinking about what she had to do—and soon. The twins squealed as they chased each other around the yard. Henry was jumping to reach a low branch of the oak, happy that he was able to touch it. Soon a man, he said to himself, and then I'll reach it for sure. Agnes was placing strips of cloth together in a pattern on the lush grass. It won't look too bad, she thought, if I can get the right thread. Maybe Miss Hattie has some I could use.

Suddenly Henry stopped his jumping. "Momma, look yonder. Who's that man coming down the road?"

"Why I don't know, son. I can't make his features out from this distance."

Agnes abandoned her cloth strips and turned to look.

All at once, Mary jumped to her feet so swiftly that her children were alarmed. Even little Daniel and David stopped running for a moment and looked at her in puzzlement.

"What is it, Momma? Do you know the man?" Henry asked.

"I'm not sure, son, but there's something about him . . . I don't know, but I think . . ."

Mary usually kept her feelings under control. But all at once she screamed, "It's him! It's him! Children, it's your father! He said he would come back! And he has! Oh, children, it's your father! Your father!" she cried as they ran to meet him, all that is but the twins, puzzled by the affair.

"Oh, Jeff, it's you! It's really you! You said you would come back, and you did!"

"Not all of me, Mary, just what's left of me," he said wearily as he slumped down in a chair. "Lost my left arm at the end of the fighting to a Yankee cannon south of Atlanta and messed up my right leg. A doctor at the Macon hospital where they took me told me the only way they could save my life was to amputate the bad leg. I told him no, that I would need that leg for farming. He shook his head and said I would never make it back to Florida. I told him I would, told him I had to, because I had promised you I would. I just asked him to clean and dress the wound, soak it in alcohol if he had any, push me out into the sunshine maybe to die of gangrene or live by the grace of God, and tend to men worse off than I was. I lay there for nearly two months. Then one day I felt better and the next, better still. A week ago I got up from that bed as shaky as a newborn calf, and a couple of days later started wobbling my way towards Florida. So here I am. But, Mary, tell me, who are these young people, this big stout boy and this girl as pretty as a picture? Are these Henry and Agnes? I can't believe they've grown so much."

"They are, Jeff, these are your children and better ones than these you won't find anywhere. I couldn't have made it without them. Children, come and hug your daddy."

They did, a little unsure how to behave with a man they barely remembered, especially Agnes. Henry hugged him, then shook hands, too.

"But Mary, I see two little ones standing off over there like little deer, twins by the looks of them. Who are they?"

"Our boys, Jeff, our twin boys, Daniel and David. They were born in March of 1863. Do the arithmetic, if you have any doubts."

"Arithmetic?" Agnes asked. "What are you talking about, Momma?"

Jeff laughed. "Nothing, darling, just something that grown people worry about sometimes. Bring the boys to me, Agnes, if you can catch them. They don't know me from Adam. But, Mary, you never told me about them in your letters. Why not?" he asked as Agnes chased them down and brought them squirming and protesting for Jeff to hug.

"Because you had enough to worry about with the fighting. I didn't want you running home and risk meeting up with the Home Guard."

"Yeah, I heard about that pack. I respected the Yankees. They fought like men and a lot of them died too, but not these cowards and murderers. Our fighting may not be over until we rid Florida of that vermin. But tell me, Mary, what shape are we in as far as the farm is concerned?" he said as he released the squealing, twisting twins.

"I'm sorry to say that things are not in good shape. We managed to plant and harvest every year you were gone. But last fall I ran out of shotgun shells and the foxes, hawks, and panthers killed off our chickens and so our egg supply, and made off with all but one of our pigs. These last few months I have to say I wasn't sure what we would do next."

She thought it best to keep the matter with Matthew Henson and the church to herself for the time being.

"Well, I'm afraid a one-armed man is not going to be that much help."

"Daddy, I can plow and work like a man in the fields," Henry offered.

"And I can take care of the twins," said Agnes. "I just love them to death. And I can cook and do other chores Momma taught me, and work in the field too if I have to."

"Jeff, you may have just one arm," Mary broke in, "but it's the strongest one in this family. I have two, Henry has two more as strong as mine, if not stronger now, and Agnes can do nearly everything I can. And now that we're all together again, now that we have our husband and father with us, I'd say we make a considerable work force, able to take on just about any problem that comes our way. What say you to that, Jeff?"

Jeff hugged Mary with his good right arm. "Children, I say your mother's right. Come tomorrow, we get started working on whatever it is we're facing. But today let's just be happy and thankful to the Good Lord that we still have all that is dearest to our hearts. And one more thing, Mary, something really important."

"What's that, Jeff? Mary asked with a worried expression.

Jeff laughed and rubbed his stomach. "Is there anything left to eat around here? I'm about half starved!"

"Not much left, Jeff, to be honest about it, but I think I can still fix something fit for our family hero!"

"Man, I can't tell you how glad I am to hear it! I have missed your cooking like you can't believe. But you're wrong about that hero business. Children, let me tell you right now, the real hero of the family is this lady named Mary Hargrove, and you two are right up there with her."

"Well, we could argue the point, Mr. Hargrove," she said, planting a kiss on his forehead, "but I can tell you ahead of time that you'd lose. If you don't know it yet, I imagine folks will tell you soon enough that I wear the pants in this family."

Henry leaped higher than he ever had before and finally brought down the limb.

9.
The Cordele Ghosts

Mr. Albert Patterson, our great uncle on our father's side, used to tell us many stories about his life back in Georgia. He repeated them so often that my sisters and I knew them all by heart. They differed from what our Daddy remembered about Georgia, but out of affection and respect for Uncle Albert, we hardly ever questioned his versions or reminded him that he had told them many times over. One of his favorites and ours was the story of "the Cordele Ghosts." Only he didn't call them "ghosts" but "haints."

Uncle Albert never married, and when his last kin died in Georgia, he moved to Lost River to be close to his brother Henry Patterson. Then when Uncle Henry and Aunt Becky passed on only a few years later, he came on out to Texas to be next to us, his nephew Lloyd Patterson's family in Nacogdoches, Texas. Daddy set him up in a little frame house with a sizable garden plot—Uncle Albert loved to grow flowers and vegetables—and we children would help him clean the rows, gather the vegetables, and listen to his stories. He was happy with us, but the farther he got from Georgia, the more he relived his glory days back in old Cordele.

"Did you ever see the haints yourself, Uncle Albert?" we children would ask him as we rested after noonday dinner, taking care not to crowd him too closely and get splattered by his chewing tobacco spit.

"Why, I could tell you young'uns about a lot of queer things back in the old days in Cordele. Why if I was of a mind to, I could tell you things you wouldn't believe if you saw them with your own two eyes. But as for spirits and such like, why the colored folks always said there were haints aplenty up in Boney Hill Graveyard by the burned-down ruins of the old Hampshire Plantation. Generally speaking, we white boys didn't go up there ourselves, you understand, unless we were drinking a bit or daring one another to do mean things, the way boys will. That was the colored graveyard that'd been there since way back in slave times. We respected it, just like the colored folks respected our white graveyard."

"What did they see, Uncle Albert?" we asked, crowding in a little closer and risking the tobacco juice.

"Why, the colored folks would tell how they saw the haints a running and prancing around in white sheets, little ones, big ones, all sizes so they said. But the scariest thing was the lights and the chains a rattling and other commotion. Their eyes'd get big as saucers when they told us about it, so we reckoned they surely had seen something terrifying up there at Boney Hill Graveyard."

"Do you believe there really are haints, Uncle Albert," our brother

Henry asked, "or were they just imagining things?"

Uncle Albert gave Henry a withering look, as if he had uttered a blasphemy.

"Why, child, of course there are haints. All the old folks in olden times knew about them. Haints, witches, spells, evil eye, and all such things as that. The old people knew a lot more than modern folks do about things like that."

Uncle Albert always talked of going back to old Cordele, but even though he lived to a good old age, he never got the chance. I thought of him when I chanced to drive through Cordele once many years later. I didn't see any "haints"—nor the truth be told not much of anything else. Maybe it was better he never went back, I thought to myself. Some places welcome us only once in life.

But if most of what Uncle Albert remembered about Cordele existed only in his memories, "The Cordele Ghosts" were more real than he knew. Now hear the other half of the story as Dr. Leland Hampshire of Tyler, Texas, told it to me a few years later after Uncle Albert had passed away.

Colonel Saunders Hampshire and his two older sons, Wadsworth and Geoffrey, died in the battle for Atlanta, leaving Mrs. Katherine Wadsworth Hampshire with a ruined plantation and three younger children to care for: daughters Mary Hope, 16, and Alice Beatrice, 14; and son, Leland Wadsworth, 12.

Food was not the only problem facing Mrs. Hampshire. With the advance of the Union forces and the fading Confederate resistance near the end of the War Between the States, the hitherto loyal Hampshire slaves either fled or were forced to flee, taking with them most of the remaining food, animals, carriages, and implements. In the end Mrs. Hampshire was reduced to one old farm wagon and a half-starved mule team.

Worst of all, word came that some ex-slaves had formed themselves into a marauding band sworn to rob and kill their erstwhile masters and families. There had already been atrocities in east Georgia, so it was rumored. The matter was desperate. Mrs. Hampshire was alone and unarmed, but she was no weakling. If she had held things together in good days, she would do her best, with God's help, to do so in bad times. But what could she do to save her remaining family? Then pushed to the limit she hit on an ingenious strategy. She called Leland to her side.

"Son, I need for you to hitch the team to the wagon. Can you do that while the girls and I are getting things ready?"

"Yes, Ma'am, but what are we going to do?"

"I'll tell you later. You just hitch the team as quickly as you can."

As Leland hitched the team to the old wagon, she and the girls packed all the clothing and everything of value, ripped up the remaining bed sheets, and gathered all the candles and lanterns they could find. At dusk, ever fearful of the vengeful marauders, they headed for Boney Hill Graveyard. The girls were frightened, and Leland, though trying to make a manly show of courage, was shaken.

"Why the colored graveyard, Mommy?" whispered trembling Alice Beatrice. "I'm afraid of that place."

"And so are a lot of other people, Alice Beatrice, including the servants. Right now it's the safest place for us. Now here's what I want you all to do. Are you listening to me, Leland and Mary Hope? When we get to the cemetery, you take these sheets and . . ."

When the Black riders arrived at the Hampshire plantation all was dark and deserted, and hardly anything of value was left. Infuriated, they torched the mansion and outbuildings, then rode on, the lurid crimson of the burning buildings casting giant, eerie shadows behind them. But as they came within sight of Boney Hill Graveyard they saw an even grislier sight: ghosts marching in white sheets, with bobbing candles and lanterns, while another rapped a chain on the grave markers. Behind came a taller figure in white with arms uplifted that cast distorted shadows in the flickering light. All screamed weird cries.

The riders panicked in superstitious terror and raced away. Some said it put an end to their lawlessness. What is certain is that the next day and for days thereafter no one dared go near the "haints" of Boney Hill Graveyard, which was time enough for Mrs. Hampshire and her children to make good their escape from Georgia and, after many hardships, eventually to a new life in Texas.

"They said that when they finally reached Texas that genteel lady's hands were as calloused and rough as a plowman's from handling the reins for all those weeks. God knows what hardships and privations she faced. But she saved her family. I don't know if they still make women like her today."

Then Dr. Leland Wadsworth Hampshire IV chuckled as he ended his story. "Mr. Patterson was right about the Cordele ghosts. But they were more real than he knew. And thank God for them. Without them and my great-grandmother Katherine's courage and determination—along with a clever plan—I wouldn't be here today."

10.

Memories of Ann Guilmore

I cannot tell you how many times over the past twenty years I have tried to write a sensible account of a woman named Ann Guilmore, and the same number of times I have failed. Although her story could be nothing more than a misunderstood series of events with some inexplicable twists—or perhaps gaps in my mind—it lingers as the most unsettling experience of my life.

I am haunted by what may have been a strange displacement of time, which baffles me each time I try to write the story. Because of these repeated failures, I started to imagine that from wherever she is—or was—Ann was displeased by the direction my narrative always took and in some unknowable way saw to it that those earlier versions never materialized. She seemed to be reminding me that, no matter how involved I was, it was after all primarily her story, not mine, and that I was not free to take it in any direction I pleased.

Yet the compulsion I felt to write her story never left me. Indeed, the urgency increased as the years passed. So now after more than twenty years, I have decided to give it one last try, dispensing with any literary finesse and simply letting the few facts I remember about her speak for themselves. Make of them what you will; for my part, I have given up trying to explain them. Here is what happened as I recall it.

As a graduate student at the University of Missouri from the fall of 1961 through the spring semester of 1964, I made several trips back and forth between Columbia and Lost River down south where I grew up. Usually I went through Kansas City and then south through Eastern Missouri, sometimes choosing instead to cut through Kentucky or Tennessee. Some of the roads were two-lane affairs in those times, but the rural stretches and forests had a soothing effect on me and there were a few scenes I even thought about painting if ever I found the time to resume my amateurish hobby.

But this was not one of those balmy days given to vague aesthetic stirrings. The weekend before had deteriorated into an angry telephone dispute with my sister, and I was still smarting from her unreasonable accusations and much in need of soothing distractions.

It was unusually warm for Thanksgiving, but in the rear view mirror I could see the lightning flashes of a predicted cold front that was rapidly gaining on me. Twenty miles south of Cape Girardeau the clouds suddenly darkened so much that I switched on the headlights. Huge raindrops splattered on the windshield and soon turned into a windblown downpour. The temperature began a sharp drop. In a few minutes it was raining so hard that I could barely see the road. As I rounded a curve, violating both speed limit and good sense given the conditions, a gigantic bolt of lightning struck close to ground zero and an ear-splitting peal of thunder rang my ears and shook my car like a toy. Suddenly a pinkish aura limned the trees and fences, and in its surreal illumination I saw an old woman trudging along the highway. She was wearing a military green surplus overcoat and a frayed gray scarf that covered most of her head and face. Her body was so bent against the wind and rain that the oversized coat touched the ground with every step she took. As best she could she shielded a paper bag filled with what I supposed were food items.

In those days there were few houses along this stretch of road. The strange aura persisted and the rain was rapidly changing into sleet, which clattered ominously against the windshield. I slowed the car to a crawl and on a sudden impulse pulled over and offered the old woman a ride. I repeat, on impulse, because my rule was never to pick up hitchhikers or strangers on the road. But what harm could an old woman do? And God knows what might happen to her in the deteriorating weather.

"Thank you, young man," she said as she settled in with a heavy sigh of relief, the hem of her coat dripping water on my nice clean mats. "It's turned nasty out there. I've never seen lightning like this. I guess it's supercharged the air in some funny way. Looks like everything's ablaze, like a Christmas candle. Strange, really strange. Oh, but I'm forgetting my manners. My name's Ann, Ann Guilmore."

"Pleased to meet you," I answered, shaking her rough, calloused hand. "My name's Jim. Where you headed, ma'am?"

"Why about ten miles or so on down the road to my house. I had to go up to the store where I do my trading to buy these things, and I was hoping I could beat the storm home. But I guess I missed the mark, didn't I?"

I nodded and smiled at her. The nearest store I remembered was five miles or so back up the road toward Cape Girardeau. "You walked all that way in this weather?"

"Well, Jim, sometimes you have to get out and about, bad weather or not. I barely had any food left in my old house and had to go get a few things. And a good thing too. This sleet could ice over and last for days."

We rode on in silence for a few minutes. The sleet was already beginning to stick in spots, and I had to slow down and concentrate on my driving.

"Nice old car you've got," she said after a bit, running her fingers along the window trim. "A classic I believe they call them, don't they? You must be real proud of it. It's so clean and new looking for its age."

"Well, ma'am, it's not all that old, '58 Chevrolet. Needs a little work on the front end. Chevies always do, it seems, but it has to do me for the time being."

"A '58 Chevrolet! That's pretty old to my way of thinking! Not as old as me of course," she added with a chuckle.

I was puzzled by her comment. "Well, I'd get a new one if I could afford it. But I have to get through school first."

"You're a student, then?"

"Yes, ma'am, at the University of Missouri."

"I was a student there once," she said in a wistful tone, "a long time ago."

"I imagine things have changed a lot since you were there. They've done a lot of building lately. When were you there, if I may ask?"

"Oh, I'm sure there've been lots of changes; I haven't been back there in more years than I can remember. I enrolled there in the fall of '62, not long after this nice old car of yours was made."

'Uh oh!' I thought as alarms went off in my head. 'She's lost a screw or two from her brain and has lost track of time.' "But this is sixty-," I started to say when she cut me off.

"The University was a lot smaller way back then with only ten or twelve thousand students. The campus was mostly just the central area and a half dozen other buildings, as I remember. Last time I was there it was much bigger and spread out, and the stadium was much bigger. But that was several years ago. Everything must be even bigger now."

"What did you study?" I asked, hoping to distract her until I could drop her off, wishing I had not picked her up in the first place. You never know what mentally warped people are going to do.

"Oh, just the general stuff freshmen take: English, history, algebra, stuff like that. You know, core courses they called them back then. I don't know what the term is these days."

"What was your major?"

"Oh, I never got around to picking one. I only went a year and then had to drop out when my parents died."

"I'm sorry."

"No reason to be, young man. That's life for you. If I could have stayed in school I probably would have majored in history. I remember this fabulous young history teacher I had. His name was Jim, too, like you. In fact, you remind me of him. He had a big impact on my life," she said softly, "and not just in history." After a pause, she added, "And what are you studying?"

"Wouldn't you know it, history."

"Small world, as the saying goes. Are you going into teaching?"

"In a way I already have. I'm a teaching assistant finishing my Master's degree. I teach required courses in American history, along with several other TA's."

"Well, a lot of history has happened since I was a student. Back then we still talked about Korea, and even World War II. Then there was Castro, and the Berlin Wall. And Vietnam was just beginning to heat up. Since then it's been more than I can keep up with: there was the Cuban missile crisis, Kennedy's assassination, going to the moon, Watergate, the Twin Towers tragedy, the Mars fiasco, five or six wars in the Middle East—I've lost count—and martial law and insurrection in our own country, just to name a few. I'm glad I live here in the backwoods without Speedplus, Plasmoporting, immortality protocols, and all those other things. I don't even own an old-fashioned cell telephone."

I was more convinced than ever that her mind was adrift in another universe. Assassination? Wars that never happened? And what was Speedplus, Plasmoporting, and immortality protocols? But so far she seemed harmless enough, even though I wondered if she might have a weapon concealed in her overcoat.

At that moment a vehicle, the likes of which I had never seen, seemed to materialize suddenly behind me. Its headlights covered nearly the whole front of the car and their exceptional brilliance, magnified and distorted by the accumulating sleet, almost blinded me. I pulled off on the shoulder to avoid it as it whizzed past without a sound, then it abruptly vanished from sight even though I could see a few hundred yards down the road.

"Good God! Did you see that? What was it?"

"Why I believe that was probably Lois Shelby's vehicle just switching back to subplasma drive. She's a neighbor of mine down the way," she commented in a tone much calmer than mine. "She goes to her sister's up in Cape Girardeau two or three times a week. She's a good woman but not the nicest neighbor anymore. She won't give me a ride if she passes me on the road. Oh, there's my house just up ahead on the left."

By now the sleet had covered the road and the trees with an icy glaze. Everything still had a pinkish tint. I pulled off the highway and drove the hundred yards or so up to her house.

"Why, Jim, you didn't have to do that. I can walk."

"The ground's too slick, ma'am, and by now your front steps may be frozen over. I'll help you inside with your things," I offered as I opened the door.

"No, Jim, thank you, but I can manage," she insisted as she quickly opened the door and swiveled out of the car. She had made it to the second step when it happened.

She slipped, and before I could reach her she fell backward, striking her head with a sickening thud on the icy sandstone and sending her groceries flying down the incline. I ran to her, but she was unconscious. Blood trickled from her scalp, staining the scarf and running down her neck into the thick overcoat. In a panic but taking care not to fall myself, I carried her into the old farmhouse and laid her carefully on a bed near the fireplace. I noticed the old house had no electrical service. There was a kerosene lantern on a table, but I had no way of lighting it.

God in heaven, I thought, what am I going to do? Here I am with an old woman, a complete stranger, maybe badly hurt, and nobody to help her. For a merest second the thought occurred to me that I could get in my car and drive away like a bad Samaritan. No one would know; nobody could identify me, and even if they could, the accident was not my fault. But no, no, that wouldn't do. I would know. My conscience already had several stains on it, some put there in recent days by my boorish behavior toward my sister, but abandoning old Ann was one I would not be able to live with.

Her breathing seemed a bit steadier now, and she was beginning to move and make moaning noises, though not yet conscious. I found a towel and placed it under her head to absorb some of the blood. Then remembering her spilled groceries, I went outside to gather them before it got completely dark. I located two cans of pinto beans, a strangely shaped loaf of bread, a cabbage head, a bag of lettuce, and a thin rasher of bacon. Whatever else she may have had in the bag would have to wait for morning light. If there were perishable items, the cold would keep them overnight, unless animals found them first. There were more serious matters anyway.

By pure luck I came upon a box of matches and managed to light the antique kerosene lantern. By its weak yellow glow, I saw a scene of stark poverty: the sagging iron bedstead with a worn straw mattress on which Ann lay, a wood-burning stove whose flue had been inexpertly and dangerously rerouted into the chimney midway up the wall, a side box with a few sticks of stove wood, a rickety table bare of tablecloth on which sat an oaken water bucket with a dented metal dipper, a cupboard containing a bowl and two plates, a single straight back hickory chair, and two orange crates draped with worn, colorless blankets which, I supposed, served as extra chairs. On the opposite wall hung a faded, early-day ancestral photograph of an elderly farm couple.

Holding the lantern before me, I explored the three remaining rooms of the house. They contained no furniture at all. In one, newspapers and old clothes were strewn helter-skelter. In another, a long abandoned leather horse harness was piled in a corner. The last room was bare but wet from sleet and rain entering through a gaping hole in the roof.

The temperature was still dropping and I was concerned that old Ann might wake only to go into shock from the cold. I knew almost nothing about caring for the sick and injured, but I piled the blankets and some of the old clothes on her. Probably she needed water, but I was afraid she might strangle if I tried to give it to her in her condition. At least a fire might help. I stuffed old papers in the fireplace, selected the smallest pieces of wood I could find and hoped they would ignite. They didn't at first, but a few unburned remnants of previous fires did and before long the new sticks started to blaze.

Looking around I saw that Ann had opened her eyes and was looking at me.

"Hey, you've come to, Mrs. Guilmore. You had me worried there. How do you feel?"

"You look so much like him," she whispered, ignoring my question. "If I didn't know better . . ." Then she added, "I'm not so good, Jim, not so good. I'm sorry. I've caused you a lot of trouble."

"Not at all. But you had me worried there for a while. I was just starting a fire to warm this place a little. The temperature's dropping pretty fast. Oh, would you like some water?"

"Yes, I would. I'm so thirsty."

I held the dipper to her lips and she gulped down the water. "More?"

"No, I'm fine for the moment, thank you."

"I have to go find help for you. Do you have family around here, or neighbors I can contact?"

"No, no family. They're all gone now. Mrs. Shelby, the woman I told you about, lives about a mile down the road. She used to check on me sometimes, but I haven't seen her in a long time except when she passes me on the road."

"Well, you just rest until I get back. I'll get help and you'll be fine."

"Thank you, Jim, you're a kind person. I've been such a bother to you. I'm sorry. I know you have better things to do."

"I'm just glad I can help. Now, ma'am, don't you try to get up. I'll be back soon."

"Before you go, Jim, there is something I want you to do."

"Yes, ma'am?"

"Reach under the bed and hand me that old shoebox, please."

The lid slid off as I placed it beside her. I saw a jumble of old letters and photographs.

"Here, Jim, I want you to have this," she said as she held up between outstretched fingers an intricately worked necklace with a tiny gold cross. "You're going to meet a girl one of these days—maybe you have already—and I want you to give it to her. It's my gift for your kindness."

"Oh, no ma'am, I can't take it. It looks like a family keepsake."

"But I want you to have it. I don't have any family left, and it deserves to be worn by a pretty young woman. It's all right. Here, take it."

Hesitantly, not knowing what else to do, I accepted it, thinking that I would return it to her when she felt better. I started to say something but Ann had fallen asleep. Quietly I went to my car and drove to the first house I saw.

The storm had passed and the weird pink aura on trees and fences had almost faded.

"Yes, I'm Mrs. Shelby," the woman who looked to be about forty-five said guardedly behind the partially closed door. "What do you want?"

"Ma'am, it's about your elderly neighbor, Mrs. Guilmore. I gave her a ride, but her porch steps were icy and she fell. I'm trying to get help for her."

"Is that what she told you, that she's Ann Guilmore?"

"Yes, ma'am. She's hurt and needs help. Can you go with me up to her house?"

"No sir, no way! And I'd advise you not to go back up there either. You're the second person this week who's come here with the same story about Ann Guilmore."

"But she's hurt."

"No sir, she's more than hurt, she's dead. Has been for decades. And she wasn't old when she committed suicide, but a young woman, probably not more than twenty-one or two at most."

"There must be some mistake. This woman is at least seventy, maybe older. Maybe the girl was her relative, although she told me she didn't have any family left."

"Well, she told you the truth, young man. That girl was the last Guilmore that ever lived around here. If you talked to anybody around that old house, it was to a ghost. And if I were you, I'd get in my car and get away from that place. I tell myself there're no such things as ghosts and spirits, but wild horses couldn't drag me up to there again. I went up there once after that girl killed herself, and what I saw and heard was more than enough to convince me never to go back."

"What did you see and hear, if I may ask?"

"I don't talk about it, don't want to remember it. All I can tell you is that there is something unnatural about that place. Things there are not the way they're supposed to be, not in the world of the living. And that's all I'll tell you, young man. Just take my advice and don't go back to that place."

With that she closed the door in my face. As I walked back to my car, I noticed a Ford older than my Chevy parked in the back yard. So much for the super model car Ann had mentioned. Not knowing what else to do, I drove back to the old house. Maybe Ann was better, I thought hopefully.

Meanwhile, warm Gulf air had stalled the front and pushed it back, ending the lightning, and the sleet, which was quickly melting.

When I got back to the old house, there was no lantern, no fire, no furniture, and no Ann. The house had the musty smell of prolonged abandonment. I called out in the darkness but all was silent. The hair on the nape of my neck stood on end. This couldn't be. Then with a rush of relief, I decided I had gone to the wrong house. I started the car, turned on the headlights, and backed off into the grass to get a better look. It was the same house for I could make out my fresh tire prints. What were Mrs. Shelby's words? "Just take my advice and don't go back to that place."

I took her advice and headed down the highway as fast as a bad road and a shimmying Chevy would let me. It would be months before I drove up that highway again.

I decided the whole episode with Ann Guilmore had been some sort of hallucination, but that argument was greatly weakened when I reached in my shirt pocket that night and found the necklace she had given me. Something had happened that I could not explain or understand. So I made up my mind to forget it as best I could.

But that was not the end of the Ann Guilmore story. And the second part was much more personal and infinitely sadder than the first. Here's the rest of the account.

I felt the impact of Ann Baxter's charm and beauty the first day of class in the fall of 1962. Seated in the front row, blonde with perfect features, Ann Baxter seemed to hang on to my every word as I called roll, explained the attendance requirements, number of tests, term paper, and the grading system. After class she came up to ask me some trivial questions and walk out into the hallway with me. The buzz I felt next to her made me realize immediately that she was danger, a beautiful, alluring danger I had to be on guard against. Fraternization with students was strongly discouraged and dating was strictly forbidden. Predatory professors might break the rule and get away with it with nothing more than a reprimand, but teaching assistants could be summarily dismissed from the program for violations.

It was a hard semester for me. I was powerfully attracted to Ann, and it soon became obvious that she felt the same about me. The other students noticed it and gossip reached the Chairman of History who called me in to ask about it. It did not help my case that Ann had excellent grades, but I reassured the Chairman that she was a dedicated student whose grades were earned and that there had been no dating, nor would there be so long as she was my student. Although he appeared convinced and obviously relieved that he did not have to deal with an ugly problem, he recited the possible penalties for violation of the policy.

The spring semester was different. Ann enrolled in another TA's class and we began dating more or less covertly early in 1963. The policy against student/professor dating was still viable, though less stringent if there was no direct classroom contact. Our romance progressed rapidly and we began to talk about a more serious commitment. It did not bother me that she talked very little about her family and background. I talked enough for both, and was excited by the thought of her as my wife. I remembered what old Ann Guilmore had said about my meeting a young woman. Without telling her how it came into my hands, I gave my young Ann her necklace in a sort of symbolic engagement. But instead of being pleased by my gesture, she seemed disturbed and nervous and refused to touch the necklace.

"It's a prelude to a ring," I assured her.

"Keep it, Jim. I want you, but not that necklace. It gives me the willies. I don't know why."

Then one day she came to me in tears with terrible news.

"Jim," she said between sobs, "I just got word that my parents were killed late yesterday near our home place down close to Cape Girardeau. The police had trouble locating me and just got word to me this morning. Here's the article that came out today in the newspaper."

Mr. Jerome Guilmore, 51, and his wife, Claudie, 49, from Scot County near the Sikeston community were killed yesterday, apparent victims of a drunken driver. The driver of the other vehicle, whose name has not been released, is in extremely critical condition and is not expected to survive. The Guilmores are survived by their only child, Ann Guilmore Baxter, a student at the University of Missouri.

I was stunned on several levels by the news.

"Ann, I am so sorry for your loss. I never met your parents, but I know you were very close to them. But Ann, I always thought your surname was Baxter. Is it Baxter or Guilmore? Are you a stepchild?"

"No, Jim, it-it's something I've been working up the courage to tell you. My maiden name was Guilmore. I was married in high school, in the eleventh grade, to my classmate Billy Baxter. It was a mistake for both of us and lasted only a few weeks. We divorced and he joined the Air Force. He's been gone from my life for a long time. I've talked to a lawyer about dropping Baxter and taking back my maiden name."

"You didn't trust me enough to tell me the truth? Is that why you haven't talked much about your family and your past?"

She nodded tearfully. "I'm sorry, Jim. Please forgive me."

I attended the funeral with her and tried to be patient and understanding. But my nightmarish experience with the other Ann Guilmore came rushing back when we drove out to the old farmhouse her great-grandparents had homesteaded. Terrifying thoughts ran through my mind. Was this Ann in some way also the other Ann in an impossible time displacement? Did the storm have something to do with it? Had I known her briefly as an old woman in an unreal future before I fell in love with her as a girl in her past?

None of what I was conjecturing could happen in any rational universe, yet the thought tormented me. I could not look at beautiful young Ann without seeing the old woman she might be or could become, knowing the tragic life that lay ahead of her. It was too much for me. I realized our love was impossible, for me at least. I was not into sacrificial heroics for anybody at that point in my life, as my sister reminded me in our bitter quarrel. I was unwilling—and at that point unable—to deal with my conflicted visions of who Ann really was. And beyond all my frantic reasoning, I was terrified by the implications.

Ann never knew the real reason I broke off our engagement and left her. I was haunted by the thought that she committed suicide thinking I could not forgive her for keeping the secret about her marriage. But none of that, whether confessed or not, would have mattered once I discovered who she was, or imagined who she was. I mourned her death when I learned of it later and tried unsuccessfully to console myself with the idea that it was a greater kindness to let her think my motives had to do with her secrecy about her high school marriage. At least those were normal, petty, human reasons. The twisted, terrifying truth I suspected was not something I could tell any sane person, least of all Ann. But maybe she foresaw more than I assumed. Perhaps she had a premonition of the life that lay ahead of her and chose to end it rather than endure it. Except that maybe suicide is not the end of anything but the beginning of something else, maybe something worse.

I have told her story but not the mystery of her life, which I am no closer to understanding than I was over twenty years ago. It is normal enough to ask who Ann was, or is, but that suggests a deeper implication that disturbs me as much, if not more. Have I strayed from my own time and wandered into a time-warped alien world? I may never know for sure. How can I know for sure? I live with a subdued dread that everything I think is normal and rational could melt away at any moment, leaving me to confront a world that is not rational at all and which I suspect at times is the real world behind this false front we mistake for it.

11.

Sam and Synchronicity

Synchronicity (noun): The experience of two or more events that seem causally unrelated and unlikely to occur together by chance, yet coincide in a meaningful but inexplicable manner.

It was strange that Dr. Sam Narrimore and I did not meet earlier. We grew up not more than a dozen miles apart in Lost River Valley, and although we went to different high schools, we roamed the same back-country roads and enjoyed the same entertainments, legal or otherwise. Yet Sam and I did not meet until we began teaching as Assistant Professors the same year in Nebraska. It was almost spooky the number of things we had in common. Even physically there was a resemblance, and in comparing our genealogies we realized that we were distantly related.

But despite our physical similarities, academic achievements, and Southern heritage, we were different in other ways. I never wavered in my determination to make a career of university teaching, but Sam soon tired of the academic grind as a professor of psychology and made plans to leave the University to concentrate on an esoteric project he refused to describe. At the end of our first year in Nebraska, his grandparents died, leaving him a small farm and a modest amount of money. Whereupon he announced his resignation and his intention to go back to Lost River to begin research on his secretive project.

I jumped all over him for dropping out.

"You'll go to seed back there in Lost River and your ideas will dry up," I told him. "We both have some great memories of country life and wouldn't trade the experience for any other. The Southern experience marks a person like no other in America, but all that is history, Sam. Now you need to stay at the University, this one or some other, where there's intellectual stimulation and a small tribe of writers to bounce your stuff off of. Those are the kind of people you need to be around to be stimulated and challenged."

"I respect some of my colleagues, even you a little, cousin. But for the kind of work I'll be doing, I don't need mentors or busybodies looking over my shoulder and critiquing my work. That would be more of a hindrance than a help. I don't need to be challenged or stimulated. I know what I'm going to write."

"And just what kind of writing are you planning to do, Shakespeare, the Great American Novel? I've never understood why American writers are so secretive about their writing. You'd think they were doing something perverse like—"

"I'll tell you what I'm doing," he said, cutting me off sharply, "and it has nothing to do with fiction—and very little with traditional psychology, for that matter. But better than telling you, I'll show you a sample. Here read this."

"What is it?"

"A summary, or précis, of a story based on Jungian psychology, specifically on the theme of synchronicity."

"Now that is squirrelly, Sam—Viennese perspectives against a backdrop of Lost River mountains, cotton fields, blue-tick hounds, dirt roads, junk cars, and freckle-faced country girls. Classic European thinking in Lost River. It's hard to think of the two worlds in the same context. But hey, I'm sure our ole country buddies down there will be beating down the doors to buy your books. Why pretty soon every house in Lost River and thereabouts will have three books—the Bible, a Sears Catalog, and Dr. Sam Narrimore's sensational tome of Jungian literature."

"You're getting to be awfully damned sarcastic being around these fools in the English Department. You know the airheads I'm talking about. But as for you, under the skin you're still just a backwoods goober. You've picked a little cotton yourself, worked on old cars jacked up under a shade tree, drunk moonshine whiskey, and run after those freckle-faced girls, maybe some of the same ones I did—though being the freak you are, I doubt you ever caught one, or if you did, you wouldn't have known what to do with her. But yes, cousin, these are the ideas I want to develop and I need country quiet to do it in. So that's why I'm going back home. My dear old grandparents didn't have much money to leave me, but enough to get by."

"What about books? I don't remember a Jungian library in our part of the world. Maybe our town has gotten more cosmopolitan since we've been gone."

"Real funny, Ed. I'll collect my own library. I don't need many books, just a few key ones. And some of those I have already. Anyway, the ideas are forming here, not in books," he added, tapping his forehead.

A few days later I picked up Sam's "Summary" and read it without any real interest. To be honest about it, there was something about Sam's writing that disturbed me.

Synchronicity (Précis)

"The assassins murder him on the second try, but they do so as manipulated agents of an unknown malevolent force, not as instigators acting on their own volition. By coincidence as people call it, but a case of synchronicity in reality, just before the fatal attack the victim had returned an old English murder novel to its place in the bookcase. On page 379 of the book he had underlined three names in red ink. These turn out to be the names of the murderous trio in the novel, but also the same names associated with an actual unsolved murder a century and a half earlier in Yorkshire, England. The deputy absently picks up the old murder novel at the crime scene. It falls open at page 379 and he sees the three names underlined in red ink. To his surprise they are also the names of local delinquents who have had run-ins with the law. Without first telling the Sheriff, he investigates the three on his own and discovers incriminating evidence against them. He then goes to the Sheriff who orders him to drop the investigation, pointing out that these are the sons of prominent families. The deputy protests and intends to present his findings to higher authorities but dies under unexplained circumstances before he can do so. The case remains unsolved. These incidents repeat in essential details the plot of the old English novel and echo the earlier crime in Yorkshire."

I dismissed Sam's summary as drivel, an unlikely series of coincidences too far-fetched for the criteria of contemporary realistic literature. I felt bad for Sam. A week later he left for Lost River.

At first I missed him, but despite promising to stay in touch, we knew we wouldn't and we didn't. As for me, I plodded along in my career. My dissertation was accepted and published by a university press. Probably the members of my doctoral committee and a few specialists were the only people who read my opus: "Metaphorical Categories in Selected Works of Dryden: The Sequencing of Serial Tropes." But who cared? It was enough to get me started toward tenure. I thought how Sam would hoot sarcastically about my 240-page, footnote-laden study, which he would surely dismiss as an exercise in pedantic stultification. But I noticed that he had published nothing, at least nothing I knew of. Well, Sam, I thought, so much for your country solitude and Jungian psychology. My dissertation may not amount to much in the grand scheme of things, but at least it's more than you've done. Didn't I tell you your ideas would die on the vine out there in the backwoods? I felt sorry and superior at the same time. I wanted better things for Sam.

Ten years passed before I saw Sam again. I remained in Nebraska and climbed the academic ranks to Full Professor, published a couple of books in my field, and having just been named Department Chair, was feeling pretty full of myself. So when the University of Mississippi invited me to take part in a seminar on Restoration Literature, I arranged a couple of free days afterwards. It seemed an ideal time to look up family and friends in my old stomping ground, and Sam was at the head of the list.

"Sam Narrimore? Dr. Sam Narrimore, you say? I didn't know he was a medical doctor," the storekeeper said, craning his head and adjusting his glasses to look up at me from different angles. "Yeah, mister, I know who he is. He lives about a mile and a half over yonder off the Lost River Road close to the old Henry Patterson place. And I remember you too. You used to come around here way back when you were a boy, didn't you?"

"Yes, I did. Do you know if Sam's married or how he's doing?"

"Married? God no! No right-minded woman could live with that man! Now, Ed, I don't mean to speak ill of your friends and I knew his grandparents, but just so you'll know, people around here won't have much to do with him. And as far as I know, he's never done any doctoring around here."

"He's not that kind of a doctor. But why is it that people won't have much to do with him? Why is that?"

"Because he doesn't want to have much to do with any of us, that's why. He just stays shut up in that old house reading those books and writing stuff. Got a house full of books they tell me. Here a while back he took a shotgun to some boys that were swimming in the creek behind his place."

"You don't mean he shot them?"

"No, he didn't shoot them, just scared the hell out of them and warned them that if they came back he would shoot them next time. So you be careful around him, Ed. Some people sour with age. I don't know if you'll be safe around that man, since I gather from what you say you haven't seen him in a while. Whenever I see him here lately he seems to be in a kind of daze or something, addled you might say. Too much reading of the wrong stuff can do that to a man, you know. By the way, if he's not a medical doctor, what kind is he, a vet maybe?"

"No, sir. He's one of those university types, a professor, the kind that don't make a lot of money."

By the time I got to Sam's house in the woods a mile off the Lost River Road, I was having doubts about him myself, and the longer he took to answer my knock the more I thought about his shotgun. Maybe he really has gone off the deep end, I thought, living out here like a hermit. Finally I heard his voice.

"Yes? Who is it and what do you want?"

"Sam, it's Ed, Edward Harbison. I've come to see you. Open the door."

He did after a long pause. There was no shotgun, but plainly he was not happy to see me.

"So you've come, Ed," he sighed, turning his back and ignoring my outstretched hand. I thought you would, but hoped you wouldn't, at least not yet. But so be it. You're here, and it's too late for anything else. So come on in."

At first I thought his rudeness was a way of covering the failure of his grandiose project. But it would soon become clear that he was totally absorbed and fearful of something far different. Still, I was annoyed that he was completely indifferent to my comfort. Not so much as a glass of water on a hot day, and not a single question about how I was doing. But I decided not to be offended by his reaction and tried to reconnect with him by reviving memories of our days at the University. He cut me off.

"Ed, I look back on that experience as an almost total waste of my time."

"How can you say that, Sam? Wasn't that where you came up with the Jungian project"? And by the way, what became of your fascination with Jung and the synchronicity thing?"

"Jung was a fool, an intellectual primitive," he said disgustedly, "only slightly more enlightened than a lot of misguided people at the University. The man had no idea what he was dealing with when he wrote about synchronicity."

"And you do?" I responded, thinking that Sam had become an insufferable ass. Or maybe he always had been and I was just now finding out his real character. His attitude was getting on my nerves and it took an effort not to lose patience with his dismissive haughtiness. But maybe it's a defense, I thought, to cover his lack of accomplishment: putting others down because he hasn't done anything himself. I knew the type.

"I know a little of what he failed to understand at all. He and others like Arthur Koestler stumbled on a doorway but never looked inside to see what was really there."

"And you have? By the way, how about a glass of water? It's hot out there."

"Look in that old fridge. It's well water but good. There's a clean glass somewhere up on the shelf behind you. What were you saying?"

"I asked what you've found out behind the doorway you mentioned."

"I have gone in just far enough to be in awe of what I have seen and to keep silent about it with most people."

"Is that why you haven't written anything? At least I haven't seen anything you've published. Have you?"

"No, and now I probably never will, Ed. It depends on how soon and accurately I can interpret enough of the secrets hidden behind that doorway."

"That big, are they?"

"Bigger than you can imagine. And that brings me to the point of your visit. You've come earlier than my calculations showed. I'm still learning, still just a neophyte. But now that you're here I see that my time is short, very short."

"Sam, what the hell do you mean by that remark?" I asked, setting the glass harder than I intended on the table. "What have I got to do with anything? I haven't seen you in ten years and have no idea what you're talking about."

"You have everything to do with it. But calm down, Ed, and I'll explain as best I can what's going on. You deserve to know some of what little I know. And, by the way, if you're hungry, there's some food in the fridge. It hasn't given me food poisoning, so it probably won't kill you. You see, Ed, I knew you were coming. I just wasn't sure when. It could have been next week or as late as next year, but it was today. As I said, I'm not able to calculate things exactly. And after ten years I've barely made a beginning."

"Beginning of what?"

"Ed, what Jung, Koestler, and others called 'synchronicity' is much more than they ever dreamed. What they wrote about—mysterious connections detectable between seemingly unrelated events—is just the kindergarten stage in understanding the sequencing channels that events must fit into in order to happen at all. They are glimpses of what a philosopher might call 'existential modes'—if philosophers had any inkling of what I'm talking about. To a certain degree they are comparable to the subatomic structures with their binding and repellent forces. But in other ways they are quite different. The *I Ching,* Tarot, tea leaves, even various shamanistic hallucinogens are different ways of getting at the same modes. You can think of it as a kind of transcendental physics. Behind this first level of modes or sequencing channels there is an ascending spiral of mathematical elegance and perfection that culminates in a system, or science, of predictive events that to us seem random but which are linked beyond our perceptive limits. Then at a higher level and in even more elegant and beautiful perfection occurs the knowledge to control them. This is the level, I believe, where the events we call 'miracles' occur, the level that only a few great masters can attain."

"So, Sam, how high have you gotten in this transcendental spiral of yours?"

"I'm still at the beginning, at level 101, so to speak. What I have been able to learn in ten years boils down to two things: first, a set of procedures that enable one to foresee and, within varying limits, to predict events. But since I have not come near to mastering the process, I can do so only in an approximate, inexact way. Second, I am convinced by what I have discovered that each ascending level is a square root multiple of the power and scope of the one below it."

"Are there higher levels than those of prediction and control of events?"

"I have glimpses, Ed, little more than a vague prescience at this stage, of at least one more level and a shadowy suspicion of another above it. There may be still higher ones, and probably are. But you understand of course that my vision of them does not extend that far. It's like an ant trying to comprehend the vastness of the woods you can see out that window."

"And how would you describe them?" I asked, skeptical of Sam's hypothesis but intrigued by his conviction. "What happens on the third level?"

"I don't know for sure, but I suspect it is the creation level. I would call it the 'God level' if it didn't sound so heretical. I still have rudiments of my Christian faith, which I understand and interpret in my own way."

"Creation level? What do you mean by that?"

"Just what it says: the level where realities come into being, assume form and consistency. From there—if you can call it a 'there'—they cascade down into our plane as happenings, material things, life itself. If you can conceive of events and realities as embryos, then the creation level is where things germinate, gestate, and emerge into existence and persons, into life, which is a very different form of being."

"Sam, you're beginning to sound more like a rogue theologian than a researcher. Aren't you close to blaspheming the faith you profess?"

"Maybe, but doesn't practically every truth start out as forbidden knowledge, as a trespass on somebody's orthodoxy? What is the old saying, the demons of today become the gods of tomorrow? Humans have to fight for truth, to strip it from the gods, so to speak.

"This is as good a place as any to tell you, Ed, if you don't know it already, that you need to know also that there are immensely powerful entities that work to keep us from the truth and sunk in ignorance and powerlessness."

"You mentioned the possibility of a fourth level. What's it all about?"

"I can't tell what it's all about. I told you it's only a suspicion I have. Logic, which is all I have to go on beyond a certain level, tells me it would be the realm of finality, or as we might think of it from our biblical vantage point, the dissolution of worlds, realities, beings, life, in short, the Apocalyptic blowup we read about in *Revelation*, or the destructive task of Shiva in the Hindu religion. It is the opposite of the Big Bang, or from another perspective, its mirror image. The Big Bang may have been the end an elder creation and the birth of ours. But from our point of view, we can sum it up in two words: universal death."

"Then are you saying that after these grand, elegant creative spirals everything ultimately ends in destruction and futility, in the cosmic entropy that the modern physicists predict and our poets and pessimists describe?"

"Don't be so quick to put labels on what I'm telling you. These higher levels may not exist at all, or they could be totally different from what I think at this point. I just don't know. All I can say as pure conjecture is that if the fourth level is the consummation of all that is or can be in this universe, a *terminus a quem* in Latin, can't we also think of it as a *terminus a quo*, as the precondition of a new cycle of creation? In Hinduism, Shiva is not only the god of destruction but also of re-creation. Can't we think of it as the start of a new creative spiral, a new universe with different laws, structures and forms of happening, new forms of intelligence and happiness? In an odd way, Shiva is also the liberator who frees man from his existential prison, what the Western philosophers call the great chain of being. Isn't that what death is, a liberation, a rebirth in another realm? Isn't that what the Bible teaches?"

"Sam," I said, laying my hand on his arm, "I think you're telling me, not

95

asking, with these questions."

Sam smiled for the first time. "Ed, I don't talk about these things with people. I've been silent for years. Pardon me for gushing about them now. But these are things you need to know."

"Yeah, okay, Sam, if you say so. What did you mean when you said there are forces that would keep these things from us and are determined to keep us in ignorance and powerlessness? What forces are you talking about?"

"We have no names for them in secular and scientific language for the simple reason that secularly and scientifically we cannot even conceive of or admit their existence. They just don't fit into our concept of the universe. The very idea of them is illogical, and if illogical untrue, and if untrue then unreal. But in sacred languages these entities have an ancient pedigree and we describe them with the traditional adjectives we learned in church—wicked, demonic, satanic—you know them as well as I do. Simply put, they refer to our adversaries, the enemies of humankind. And they are real, very real. This I do know for certain."

"Why?"

"Why what?"

"Why our enemies? Why are they out to get us? What did we do to earn their hostility?"

Sam laughed for the first time. "Ed, I can't believe you're asking me to explain evil. Minds much greater than mine have wrestled with that problem. But since you asked, the way I see it evil is illogical, which is why logical minds cannot fully comprehend it. It makes no sense because it has no sense. All I can really say about it with any degree of conviction is that there are divine entities that do not wish us well, that work to prevent us from realizing our destiny."

"Why do you call them divine if their intention is to harm us? And what is our destiny? Sam, you're making me wade in deep water with all this."

"Divinity is no guarantee of goodness. As for our destiny—our teleology, as Aristotle called it—it is not to remain natural creatures, so I think, not to live as savages, goobers, slaves, overlords, or fools, in short, not to be the victims of fate but its masters, its shapers. It is to become the supernatural beings God created us to be. Ed, I believe our destiny is to rise above nature to the supernatural level, to acquire knowledge and power as yet undreamed of, to become beings able to foresee, control, and create events and material things. We are a species in transition to a higher state of consciousness, as Teilhard de Chardin wrote, and though too slow to notice in a single lifetime, the transformation is exceedingly rapid when seen from a geological perspective. What we call wicked, demonic, satanic entities are those supernatural beings that do not want us to reach the higher domain. Who can say why? Is it because they are afraid of us, afraid of what we may become, afraid that we may surpass them in power and knowledge? After all, the Bible tells us we were created in the image of God the Creator, the greatest mind and power of all. And we are like him, or at least we have the potential to be like him. If I were a devil I think I, too, would be afraid of humans. At least that part makes sense to me."

"What does this mean to you and for you? Where do you go from here?"

"To my liberation and to my death, Ed. And probably soon. That much I see as inevitable. My work has put me in the crosshairs of these same malevolent entities, me and everybody else who tries to break the cycle of ignorance and powerlessness that restricts humanity. And that's where you come in, Ed."

"Hey, hold on, Sam. All this is interesting, but I'm not involved and don't intend to get involved. This is your baby, not mine."

"But you are involved, Ed, whether you like it or not. Have you ever wondered, seriously wondered I mean, why you and I have an uncommon number of things in common. Our lives have been intertwined in strange, puzzling ways since we were boys, before we even met. Both of us were born into a cycle of synchronicity."

"I prefer to think of it as simple coincidence, Sam. Occam's Razor, isn't it, the simplest explanation is the best? Despite what you believe, I think some things are just that: coincidences. And if we seemed to be joined, or disjoined, at the hip in our early years, for the last ten we have gone our separate ways. The synchronicity has played out."

"No it hasn't, Ed, it's just beginning to come to fruition. But we won't argue the point. We've talked long enough. Come with me. I need to show you something."

"What?"

"You'll see."

He picked up a shovel from a shed and led me down a narrow pathway toward the creek, then stopped at a head-high sandstone bluff twenty yards from the water. He shoveled away dirt and pebbles under the overhang until a shiny steel container appeared.

"What's that?"

"That, Ed, is where my essential papers will be stored. Some are there already, and the others soon will be. When you get word of my death you must come to retrieve them. My work will be finished. Well, not finished but as far along as I can take it. And yours will be ready to start. You must continue where I leave off. The boys I drove off a month ago are poised to make their second attempt on my life, and this time they will no doubt succeed. They may burn the house as an act of simple vandalism, though I don't think they will, but obeying a deeper, diabolic motive they will destroy all my papers. But I don't think they will find these."

"Are you talking about the boys you drove off with a shotgun? The storekeeper told me about them. He said all they were doing was swimming in the creek here. They don't sound like would-be murderers to me."

"Ed, that's Horse Pond Branch down there. Look at it. It's too shallow for swimming. It doesn't have a foot of water in it. The boys weren't swimming; they were planning to kill me. But the time wasn't right. They came too soon. This time it will be different."

"If you know them and know they intend to harm you, why can't you stop them? Call the law. Keep that shotgun handy. Get the Sheriff's office or the police to watch them."

Sam shook his head. "Do you remember the story summary I gave you years ago?"

"Only vaguely, to be honest about it. But what does it have to do with this?"

"In the story the sheriff stops the investigation because the murderers are the sons of prominent families. And if you recall, the deputy who wants to pursue the case dies under unexplained circumstances. It will probably happen here the same way this time. I wish I could change the sequence completely but I'm not there yet, and it would be reckless, maybe even dangerous, to try. I'm dealing with powers I still don't understand. Yet there is one all-important difference between this case and all the similar ones of past centuries. And there are many more cases that were never reported."

"What is the difference?"

"You, Ed. You, or a person like you, weren't in the previous stories. You are unique to this event. A new actor has entered the ancient recurring drama. The sequence has been altered, and that can only mean, as I see it, that some progress has been made. I'd like to think my work has altered the sequencing in a slight but significant way. Of course that may be wishful thinking on my part, but if it is true, then my efforts have not been in vain. In all the other events the death of the researcher sent everything back to square one. This time there appears to be a chance, a real chance, to advance the cause."

"If your papers are so important, why not make copies—or maybe you have—and give me a set now?"

"No, Ed, and for a prime reason: the minute the papers are in your hands, you also become a target. Your work could end before it ever begins. You understand what I'm saying, don't you? Think back to our early years. The reason we never met when we were growing up, so I believe, was to keep you safe, to keep you from being contaminated with my personal pathway, my karma, or dharma, so to speak. Ed, you were saved for a work, and that work is about to begin."

"Well, I don't think so. With your permission, or without it, I think I'll decline the work and get back to the University and my work there. The stuff you're talking about is enough to make my hair stand on end."

"Then go, but be ready to come back as soon as you hear about my death. I'll see that you get word. The papers will be here."

"How will you get word to me? You don't even have my address, and I don't see a phone anywhere around here."

"Oh, I have your address, Ed, and your phone number. I've kept an eye on you over the years. I know all about your academic successes, your books—I've even read parts of them—and your new job as department chair, everything."

I drove away disturbed and concerned for Sam. At the same time I resented the nonsense he had told me, for try as I might to forget all he had said, it wouldn't go away. The story he had told me was preposterous, impossible, the twisted thinking of a recluse, but it was Sam, still my friend, still my cousin. And he was waging a lonely, personal crusade, at least in his own mind. Maybe he was jousting at windmills, mistaking them for giants, but to him they were real. I tried hard to convince myself that I owed him nothing, that I must forget him and get on with my own busy life, but it was a fragile, failing argument. I could not abandon him, and although I did not know how to help him, I knew I must try.

A few weeks later I knew what I must do.

Sam's letter, almost cryptic in its brevity, arrived May 12th:

"Ed, the extra time was more than I thought, enough for me to refine my predictive grid. The 'liberation' and all I described will occur between May 23rd and 25th. I cannot be more specific. Come as soon as prudent thereafter to begin your work. Protect yourself; you will be vulnerable."

There was no signature.

By May 17th I had turned in my class grades and hurriedly cleared my desk. The two journal articles I had promised had looming deadlines but they would have to wait. Ordinarily I preferred the winding rural roads to Lost River, but this time I took the speedy Interstates whenever possible. Sam could be off in his calculations and I had to get there in time to prevent his "liberation" if I could.

Sam was pale and disheveled when I pulled up to his old farmhouse on the 18th after an all-night drive. I suspected he had not slept in days.

"Ed, what are you doing here?" he stammered. "You're not supposed to be here till . . ."

"I know, until after the 'event.' Well, Sam, I'm here to tell you we're revising the script."

"But we can't. Everything must happen as it must."

"Says who? Sam, you've talked yourself into becoming a fatalist. Just because the sequence has always been the same is no reason why we can't alter it. Ever hear of free will? You said yourself that I am a new actor in the drama, a new element in a very old story. Look, I'm not at all convinced that what you've been working on all these years makes any sense. But you're my friend and my cousin, maybe a squirrelly, quixotic friend and cousin, but crazy or not—pardon my bluntness—I'm here to stand with you. And I haven't forgotten how to shoot. I have Daddy's old double barrel 12-gauge shotgun in the car and enough buckshot to scatter a small army if need be. It was probably not legal to haul it across state lines, but as they say, you gotta do what you gotta do. We're going to rewrite this story and give it a better ending if we can."

A gleam came into Sam's tired eyes. "You really think we can alter the sequence? You really think so, Ed? Maybe . . ."

"Sam, you're the expert on timing and predictions, but I have one I can make with confidence."

"What's that?"

"I predict that a load of double-oo-buckshot in a bully's butt can turn him into a screaming coward in no time at all. So get your shotgun and shells, Sam. We're going to do us some shooting just as we did in our old rabbit-hunting days. If these boys show up, as you say they will, we're going to give them a surprise they won't soon forget."

And we did. On the night of the 24th, three boys drove up the dirt road and parked their pickup a hundred yards from Sam's house. As I had every night since arriving, I waited in the dense bushes as they got out of the automobile with a gasoline can and swaggered toward the house. In gibbous moonlight I caught a glimpse of at least two pump shotguns. The tallest of the three fired two shotgun blasts at the door that splintered and collapsed to one hinge. Then he yelled out as they approached the house.

"Come on out here, you freaking son of a bitch! We'll see how brave you are this time!" Then in a lower voice, "Hand me that gas can, Fred."

"Hey, Bennie, look! There's a car over there by the house. I thought this f—kin' bastard didn't have a car!"

But Sam was not in the house. He had circled around the other end of the house and now stood profiled with his shotgun behind a corner. At that instant, just as Sam and I gained the advantage over the delinquents, something happened that defied explanation. I had a sudden, hypnotic urge to shoot him. A force much stronger than my will took control of my arms and hands. In horrified fascination I watched as though with a will of its own my shotgun raised and lined up with his body. In desperation I struggled against the urge. In horror, I realized suddenly that I was in the grip of the malevolent ones Sam had described, I was a part of the destructive force.

From somewhere deep in my memory there appeared the opening line of the Lord's Prayer, now a plea, so remote in my past as to belong to another lifetime: "Our Father who art in Heaven . . ." I recalled no more, but repeated the words over and over: "Our Father who art in Heaven." Then as my finger tightened involuntarily on the trigger, it took all the power I had left to jerk the gun slightly to the left. The gun fired but most of the shot went wide and knocked a few rotting boards off the old house. Only a couple grazed Sam's arm. Bennie wheeled at the blast, and spotting Sam, was about to fire, but Sam shot first, hitting Bennie in the side and leg and sprinkling the other two with pellets. Bennie's gun discharged harmlessly into the grass.

Bennie screamed, dropped the can and shotgun, and the three delinquents ran, bellowing and cursing, for their truck. At that, I snapped out of my stupor and shot out the left front tire with my remaining shell. One of the trio had the presence of mind to fire his handgun in my direction, but by then I was safely back behind the trees and the bullet went harmlessly wide of the mark.

"Goddamn, they've shot out one of the front tires! There's two of the sonsabitches! Maybe three! Run! Let's get outta here!"

"Hell, I'm bleeding! I'm hurt! I can't run! Help me! I've got to stop!"

"Well, dammit to hell, Bennie!" Bill yelled back. "I'm not staying here and let the bastards shoot me too! They're crazy! This is not the way you told us it would be! You lied to us, said it would be easy!"

"I'm with you! Let's get out of here before they shoot us too!" yelled Fred.

And away they ran, while Bennie yelled for them to stop and help him.

The shooting was a huge scandal in Lost River and Stokesbury County. Just as it was in ancient versions of the story, the three men had the familiar names, Bennie (Benjamin), Fred (Frederick), and Bill (William), which by a strange coincidence, deputy sheriff Matt Hogan confided privately, he had seen underscored in an old English novel that fell open at page 379 when he randomly picked it up at Sam's house during the investigation. But unlike the earlier sequences, the persistent deputy overcame the sheriff's stonewalling efforts, informed state officials, and by doing so convinced a reluctant but subdued District Attorney that he must bring the case to trial. Best of all, he survived a botched ambush by a party or parties unknown. Once the case was in court, local family prominence was not enough to save the boys from several months of jail time and a lengthy probation. The sharpest lawyers in the county succeeded only in getting reduced sentences for the trio. Not even they could argue away the abandoned gasoline can and shotguns with fingerprints, the blasted doorway, their abandoned pickup, the pellet marks on Sam's arm, and most of all bleeding Bennie, who though far from being seriously wounded cravenly confessed everything and implicated his friends. Oddly enough, the stray pellets from my gun that struck Sam's arm helped strengthen the case against the three by proving their malicious intent. Wasn't it biblical that things meant for evil could serve good?

All three swore vehemently that none of them fired at Sam, but by that point in the trial nobody believed anything they said, and I saw no reason to contradict the official version of what happened. As for Sam, no self-respecting person in fiercely independent Lost River was going to deny a man—no matter how eccentric he might be—the right to defend himself and his property with a gun. Sam was puzzled about the mysterious shotgun blast but decided that everything happened so quickly in the darkness and confusion that nobody could have a clear idea of what transpired.

Sam was euphoric when the trial ended in late summer. As for me, after I had time to reflect on what happened, I was amazed at the whole affair, especially at chances I had taken.

"My God, Sam, my whole career could have gone up in smoke, gun smoke, that is."

"But that didn't happen, Ed. You know I'll always be grateful to you for what you did."

"We did it together, Sam."

"No, you were the catalyst that changed things. Without you, Ed, it would have been a dreary repeat of the old synchronicity, the same dead end result, the same regression to ground zero. Until now it has been like running in place, a perpetual *déjà vu*."

"What happens now? What will you do?"

"Why continue my research, of course. I've made real progress in the past few weeks. I thought you would be my successor and continue with the work, but now I see that my part in it is not finished. How far I can go and what turns it will take, who can say? When we talked months ago, I was obsessed with the hostile powers that wish us ill and work us woe. It was the fatalistic mood I was in. Without realizing it, I was becoming part of the age-old repeating scheme. This experience has released me from that trap. Who knows for how long? Eternal vigilance we say, but eternal gullibility is what we do. But now, at least for now, I dwell more on the greater power that wishes us well, and my outlook is much happier. There are only one or two more things I want to point out to you, Ed, things that have been on my mind for a while and need to be said."

"What's that?"

"You are astonished at what you did. But remember, Ed, I once said you were saved for a work. And you were. Everything prepared you to do what you had to do when you had to do it. We are all more than we know, and if we are lucky, sooner or later we may discover who we really are."

"You have a point, Sam. But back to earth and the nitty-gritty details. I would think it would be uncomfortable and unwise for you to stay here any longer. You've burned some bridges and there are people around here who will bear grudges. Have you thought about that?"

"Yes, I have. And this is the other thing on my mind. To paraphrase the Boatman's line in Hesse's *Siddharta*, 'I have been the Boatman long enough.' I thought my life and my work were over and I was resigned to it. Now I wonder if they aren't just beginning. So will you help me pack up my good junk and get rid of the rest? I'm ready to sell this place and leave."

"You bet. What say we start with your shotgun?"

I could never tell Sam—or anyone else until now—how close I came to killing him. I still don't know for sure if all—or any—of the things he told me about synchronicity are real or not. I still have a healthy skepticism about it. But I have to admit the horrifying moment when something alien took over my will is chillingly persuasive, because it means that I was already under its control without knowing it. Probably Sam would interpret that bizarre event as an effort by the malevolent entities to maintain the recurring cycle of human ignorance and futility. And most likely it—they—would have succeeded had I not remembered—just barely—the opening verse of the Lord's Prayer. That said, no one should be surprised that thanks to Sam and his work on synchronicity I have returned to my childhood faith. Once I thought I was too smart to believe; now at least I know enough not to doubt.

12.
The Plough Line

Early one Thursday in October of 1931, while resting from squirrel hunting with his dog, Ole Jake, at the foot of Morgan Mountain, Ben Stokesbury saw a car pull out of Cove Road two hundred yards below him. As it bounced and swayed while crossing the shallow ditch that separated the roads, a piece of rope slid off the top and fell in the dusty rut. Ben took a good look at the car and its driver, and after it chugged away north over the mountain toward Stokesbury Valley, he picked up his 12-gauge shotgun, called Ole Jake, and went down to see what he could find.

"Hm-mm-mm," he hummed as he inspected the three-foot section of rope. (Ben always hummed.) "I reckon I'll just take that home with me. Hm-mm-mm. Might come in handy for something."

He smelled the rope. (Ben always smelled the things he found, for his nose was nearly as good as his eyes.) Ole Jake looked up at him, wagging his tail in hopes that food was involved.

"Brand new plough line; no mule sweat on it, but there's some kind of sweet stink about it. Don't know what it might be. Hm-mm-mm. Wonder why that fellow left it on top of that motor car. Forgot it, no doubt," he said as he wound the rope and put it in the back pocket of his overalls.

Not that finding things on the road was anything new for Ben, or any of his six brothers for that matter. They all had eyes like a hawk and the soul of scavengers. If they failed to find items, it was only because they hadn't been lost yet. As soon as things dropped and the Stokesbury brothers happened along, they would pick up coins, pocket knives—with or without blades—keys, washers, cans, bottles, twine, nuts, bolts, nails, horseshoes, spoons, spools, sticks, boards, pencils, buttons, tinfoil, knobs, clothes, shoes, chains, tools, rubber, leather, stoppers, toys, tow sacks, chair legs, baling wire, and anything else that had fallen through the cracks of civilization. The Stokesburys jumped on junk like buzzards on a dead mule.

Any self-respecting Stokesbury was bound to have a pile of odds and ends in the yard or the barn for which he had not yet found a use. Other items, though, might be nailed or wired up in creative ways to cover roof holes or replace broken latches and windowpanes. The Stokesburys practiced modern art long before sophisticated folks in New York and places discovered the aesthetics of junk and gave it a name. They could have taught Andy Warhol a thing or two. In fact, some of their creations probably would have been the envy of art departments and museums.

Showy items, like a smashed watch or shiny ball bearings, they preferred to carry in their pocket so as to display them to brothers and kin, explaining with understated manly pride where and how they found them and how many people had walked by without seeing them. It was a poor day, indeed, and almost a cause for embarrassment if a Stokesbury came home without significant trash to show for it. Even half of a pair of pliers or a broken currycomb was enough to save their sharp-eyed reputation.

The Stokesbury brothers were distant kin to old Homer Stokesbury and assorted relatives down in the Lost River region, but a century earlier a family feud divided the clan not long after they left the Tennessee Appalachians and settled in Stokesbury Valley. Colonel Abner's side of the family became land-rich and powerful, but his Brother Elmer's bunch preserved the mountain ways and independence of their old Tennessee homeland, preferring the mountains south of Lost River where they lived as squirrel hunters, trappers, occasional farmers, and whiskey makers. Both sides acknowledged their kinship if pressed on the matter, but neither was proud of it.

Later that day Ben showed the rope to his brother Earl.

"That man just left it on top of his motor car, I reckon. And it's a brand new rope, too. Never been used, as best I can tell, hm-mm-mm."

"Aw, that little ole rope won't be any good," Earl said, eyeing it disdainfully as he sliced off a cud of Brown Mule Chewing Tobacco with a Barlow knife he had found in the road a year before. "Other day I found a whole trace chain over yonder on the Powell Road. Except the first two links, it's just like new. Got it out there in the barn. Come on, I'll show it to you."

Ben didn't care much about the trace chain but he went along anyway.

"Look at that back band I found, too" Earl said proudly. "It's ripped a little on one side, but a man could still get some good use out of it."

"I don't see that it's much account," said Ben. "It'll tear in two first time a mule bows up and starts pulling a load."

About that time their older brother Marvin walked up, crushing a cigarette butt with the toe of his brogan. "What are you all doing? You ought to be out yonder cutting yourselves some firewood afore winter gets here."

Since their daddy Charlie died, Marvin had taken on himself the fatherly job of preaching to his younger brothers what he hardly ever practiced himself.

"I was just showing Earl this piece of rope I found over yonder in the Cove."

"Let me see that," Marvin said, putting it up to his nose. "Smells like it's new, but it stinks kinda sweet too. How come it's cut off?"

"I couldn't tell you that. All I know is I saw it fall off a man's motor car down there by the Cove road, hm-mm-mm."

"What were you doing way down there?"

"Squirrel hunting."

"Kill anything?"

"Naw, saw a rabbit's about all."

"I've told you before, Ben. You keep that old dog of yours too fat. Don't you recollect what Pa always said: 'a fat dog won't hunt'?"

"I'll put ole Jake up against any squirrel dog around this country, any day of the week," Ben said defiantly.

Earl looked at Marvin and grinned. Marvin had a way of getting Ben's goat about his dogs.

"You all heard the big news?" Marvin asked as he pulled out a sack of Country Gentleman tobacco from the bib of his overalls and poured the makings in a cigarette paper.

"Yeah, but that's not news," Earl said. "They busted up the Sellars boys' whiskey still again. Last Friday, I reckon it was. Every year they go in there and chop up ole Calvin and Hiram's still, and every year they just start it up again."

"I'm not talking about a still," Marvin said, striking a match on his pant

105

leg and lighting his cigarette.

Grudgingly, Earl was forced to ask, "What are you talking about, then?"

Marvin inhaled and blew a ring of blue smoke at his brothers before answering.

"Somebody robbed the Evergreen Bank yesterday; got away with nearly three hundred dollars, they say."

"Three hundred dollars!" Ben exclaimed. "That's a right smart of money! Why I was just in the bank yesterday to pay off my note and I didn't see anything out of the way. Town was just as quiet as an old maid's bed. They catch the ones that robbed it?"

"I reckon not. Not yet. I found out that deputies were asking questions down in Lost River and Evergreen when I was over at Buddy Ballinger's house this morning. They said it happened after the bank closed. Tied up the president with a plough line and made off with the money. Just one man. Had a mask on, they said."

"What was the law doing in Lost River if it was the Evergreen bank?" Ben wondered.

"I reckon they're going all over the country trying to find evidence and clues, as they call it. That's the way lawmen work."

Word got out about Ben finding the plough line and seeing a car over in the Cove. The next morning two county deputies showed up at his house in a shiny Model-A Ford and asked to see it. He displayed it proudly.

"I don't think it's ever been used," he said proudly.

"That looks like the piece that was cut off," one of the deputies said knowingly to the other.

One of the deputies wrote down everything Ben could tell them about the "motor car" and its driver. Then they asked him to go with them over to the Cove and show them where he saw the car and found the plough line. The speed of the car, at times reaching twenty miles an hour, bothered Ben. He was sure they would run off the road or hit a tree at such a dizzying velocity.

"I just don't think folks ought to travel that fast," he told his wife, Gracie, after they brought him home. "Hm-mm-mm. It's plumb scary and I bet it's not healthy for a body either. Hm-mm-mm."

Ben and the deputies walked down the Cove road a quarter of a mile and came to the spot where the car had turned around. The deputies told Ben to wait as they searched the area. Finding nothing, they came back to the car.

"I reckon you don't want that little sack over yonder under that bush, do you?"

"A sack?" the driver asked. "I don't see any sack."

It was hard for Ben to hide his scorn.

"It's right under that bush in plain sight, a little gray sack. Don't you see it?"

The deputy spotted the bag and rushed over to retrieve it. It had Evergreen Bank written on it.

"You men going to keep it? If not, I could put it to some use," Ben said hopefully. "And what about my plough line?"

"We'll keep both," said the driver. "They're evidence."

"Doesn't seem fair," Ben complained later to Earl. "I was the one that found both of them. The deputies are about as blind as bats."

On the basis of the evidence gathered and Ben's testimony, Eddie Hargrove, who lived out on the Barkley Road, was arrested and charged with bank robbery. At the trial in Tylerville, Eddie's lawyer, Warren St. John, set out to demolish Ben's account. Eddie glared at Ben.

"Do you mean to tell this court, Mr. Stokesbury, that from a distance of more than two hundred yards you could read the license number of my client's car and even describe the wristwatch on his arm?"

"Yeah, I used to see a right smart better, but you know, don't you, Mr. St. John, that our sight fails a little as we get older. Leastwise, that's what my daddy always said. Now he had sharp eyes. I guess we all do because they say we have Cherokee blood. They say the Cherokee people—"

"Your Honor," said the exasperated attorney, "would you instruct the witness to answer a simple 'yes' or 'no' to the questions put to him?"

"Mr. Stokesbury, kindly restrict your answers to a 'yes' or 'no,'" said the obliging judge, trying not to smile at St. John's perplexity.

"Your Honor, I submit that the entire testimony of this witness is unreliable and ask that it be stricken from the record. By his own admission, he was in the Evergreen Bank the day before the alleged robbery took place. At which time he obviously saw my client in the bank conducting lawful business. There he had ample opportunity to observe his wristwatch and memorize the license plate of his automobile parked outside."

"Before I rule on your request, Mr. St. John, explain to this court what you mean by 'alleged robbery.' Are we not here to try your client precisely because a robbery took place?"

"Indeed, Your Honor. We do not deny that a robbery occurred, but we do strongly deny that my client had anything to do with it. In the course of proving his innocence, we shall demonstrate the likelihood that another person, at present unidentified, is responsible for the theft."

"Mr. Prosecutor, do you have anything to say before I rule on the admissibility of this witness's testimony?"

"We do, Your Honor. I propose that before the court rules on the motion put before it by the able defense attorney, we be allowed to demonstrate that the vision of the witness is, indeed, of the uncommon acuity and range implied in his testimony."

"The court will allow the demonstration provided it meets certain criteria, which you, the defense attorney, and I will discuss and agree. Come with me to my chambers. Court will recess until 2 p.m. this afternoon."

"Hm-mm-mm," Ben hummed. "I wonder what those men were talking about. I've never heard such words. That lawyer man seemed like he was mad at me about something. I don't know what, though. I've never laid eyes on him before in my life."

"You said the right word, Mr. Stokesbury," said the prosecutor's young assistant. "It's the eyes. If you can see like they say you can, then his whole defense will be shot down."

"You all are not planning on killing nobody, are you?" Ben asked with a worried look.

"No, Mr. Stokesbury," the young man laughed. "Nobody will be killed, provided you tell the truth."

"I always do, hm-mm-mm," Ben replied. "By the way, mister, is the judge sick or having stomach problems?"

"Why no, not that I know of. Why do you ask?"

"Well, he was talking about going to use his chambers and that it might take him till after dinner to get through. I just thought he must be constipated something terrible. We keep a chamber pot under the bed for night use when we don't want to go outdoors. Like when it's raining or cold. But I don't recollect ever hearing of a body needing more than one at a time. And it's peculiar that he wanted the men he talked with to be with him while he's doing his business. Using a chamber's something a body generally does by himself."

Ben could hear the young man howling with laughter out in the corridor. "Seems like a happy young man, hm-mm-mm," he said to no one in particular.

The prosecutor's office arranged for a car to drive by at approximately the same distance from Ben as the car in the Cove.

"What make of car do you see, Mr. Stokesbury?" asked the lawyer.

"Well, now that I couldn't tell you for certain. When it comes to motor cars, I can't tell them apart. It says F-O-R-D, if I recollect my letters, out there on the front. So I guess that's what kind it is."

"Tell us about the driver. Have you ever seen him before?"

"Why, sure have. It's that young man that works for you, I reckon. The one I was talking to before dinner. He's wearing that same wristwatch."

"Mr. Stover, can you tell this court the numbers on the license plate?"

"I guess you mean the tag, don't ye"

"That's right. Tell us the tag number."

"Well, it says 6-2-3."

"And what state, Mr. Stover?"

"Well, I can't tell you that. The letters are K-E-N-T-U-C-K-and Y, I think it reads. There's some mud or something on the last letter. But I disremember what they spell out."

"Kentucky, Mr. Stokesbury, the state of Kentucky!" the prosecutor said with enormous satisfaction.

"Objection, Your Honor," St. John said over the admiring murmur of the spectators. "The testimony was possibly tainted by the prior conversation the witness had with the attorney driving the vehicle."

"Objection sustained," Judge Holladay ruled. "Mr. Prosecutor, the demonstration is disallowed for the reason pointed out by the defense. You may, with the court's indulgence, repeat the experiment, but the court itself will conduct it to ensure impartiality."

The demonstration was repeated with a different car and driver but with equally impressive results. In light of Ben's astonishing eyewitness account, the follow-up testimony by banker Hannibal Jones was anticlimactic. But as he walked by Ben, the aroma of aftershave lotion triggered recognition of the scent.

"That's that sweet stink I smelled on the plough line!" he blurted out in surprise. "Mr. Jones' got that stuff smeared on his face!"

The spectators laughed as the Judge gaveled the court back to order.

Eddie was found guilty and sentenced to a year and a half in prison.

As for Ben, he never did get his plough line back. But it pleased him that folks talked a lot about his part in the conviction. Marvin and his brothers, however, were mightily unimpressed with it all.

"We all went down yonder to the Cove to look around for ourselves after you and the deputies had tromped around like a bunch of blind chickens," Marvin said as he rolled a cigarette. "You all missed a bunch of things that we brought back. Like that mask they talked about at the trial. They're out in the barn, if you want see all the stuff we found. Ben, you always did have the weakest eyes in the family. Pa used to say you couldn't see your ass if it crawled across your face. No wonder you don't kill much when you go squirrel hunting. Course that old dog of yours is not much help either. Too fat."

13.
Ole Jake's Last Hunt

Not much had gone right for Ben Stokesbury and his family these last few years. His forty acres up on the mountain south of Lost River was gullied and rocky. Even a good farmer in a prime year would have had trouble coaxing a respectable crop from its eighteen cultivated acres of thin, depleted soil. And Ben came nowhere near to qualifying for that title. To the despair of his wife, Gracie, he didn't even try. He farmed only when he had to, and the more she nagged him, the more he hunted. As he put it, squirrel hunting beat walking behind the mule's ugly rump any day of the week and twice on Sunday.

But if his neighbors and kinsmen looked down on Ben for his piddling farming habits, they looked up to him as a champion squirrel hunter. And back in the middle and late 1930s, no fair-minded squirrel hunter along the upper reaches of Rock Creek could deny Ben's claim that his dog, Ole Jake, was the best tree dog in the county and maybe in the whole state.

There were some, of course, who bragged that their dog was just as good, if not better than Ole Jake, but everybody—probably themselves included—knew they were just blowing smoke. For when it came to the number of squirrels treed and take-home kills, Ole Jake and Ben always came out the winners. And the nights that Ben decided to go possum or coon hunting, Ole Jake could switch tactics and scents without missing a beat. It helped that like all the Stokesburys, at least the mountain branch of the family, Ben was eagle-eyed and steady-handed when it came to a rifle or shotgun. But he rightly gave Ole Jake most of the credit for his success.

Twice one fall—it may have been in 1939—his fox-hunting cousins Vernon and Lemuel from Tennessee baited Ben into letting Ole Jake run with their fox hounds. Ben accepted the challenge, and Ole Jake outran the best of them. But Ben didn't think much of fox hunting to start with, and when Ole Jake limped home bruised and all but famished from an all-night run, Ben swore off.

"Ole Jake can outrun the whole mangy pack and everybody knows it, if I was of a mind to let him do it," Ben said in disgust. "But a year or two of running him all night like that, getting banged and maybe snakebit to boot, and what do you have? A dog too beaten down to gnaw a bone. No siree! Ole Jake's too good a squirrel dog to run him into the ground after some fool fox. And I've got better things to do myself than sit out there on that mountain freezing my hind end off. Drinking a little moonshine's not a bad thing, but I do get tired of listening to my dumb cousins telling lies about their dogs!"

Descended from the legendary Big Jake, Charlie Stokesbury's top squirrel dog for many years, and a Tennessee bitch said to be of such pure bloodlines that owner Bill Milligan "had papers on her," Ole Jake had an uncanny nose for squirrels and always seemed to know where they would be feeding and where they would run to hide when hunters showed up. Ben claimed that Ole Jake could think like a squirrel. That was probably taking things too far, but it was often true that as other, less experienced dogs stampeded in one direction, barking their fool heads off, wise Ole Jake would slip silently off in another, intently watching the feisty grays or bigger fox squirrels scurrying through the treetop fall foliage. Only when he had the squirrel really treed would Ole Jake let out his long, quavering signature bark that rose, wafted, and echoed for miles across the mountains, hills, and coves.

"That's Ole Jake! He's got him treed," Ben would say, "just like I told you he would! Didn't I tell you he would? Now didn't I?"

At those moments, Ben was proud enough to pop his buttons, while other hunters would shake their heads in grudging admiration of Ole Jake and embarrassment over their own clueless hounds.

But time hunts down even the best hunters, man and beast, and by 1942 Ole Jake was slowing down and his eyes were beginning to cloud. That fall he started to lose the scent and sight of squirrels, and when one day Ben and his friends found him barking up the wrong tree, it was obvious to all that Ole Jake's best days were behind him. It troubled Ben, especially when some of the other hunters snickered behind his back. And by the way he whined on the way home, Ole Jake also seemed to know that he had failed. His hunting days were over.

Gracie, though, was glad when she learned about Ole Jake's decline. She had never cared for dogs in the first place, and she particularly resented all the care and food Ben lavished on Ole Jake. Now that he was slipping, she thought hopefully, maybe I can get Ben to spend more time working this farm before we all starve to death. But it was all just wishful thinking on her part.

One Saturday not long after that sad day, Ben walked back from Evergreen proudly leading a splendid young hound, Big Red, to replace Ole Jake. The newcomer growled at Ole Jake, who was lying in his customary place by the front doorstep, as if to warn him that he was no longer the alpha dog and that he had come to take over.

Not that Ben allowed Ole Jake to be mistreated. To get him away from Gracie's wrath and Big Red's hostility, he built Ole Jake a pen and a warm bed at his mother's shack a long quarter of a mile across the field by the edge of the woods and extracted a promise from her that she would care for the old dog.

"Why, I reckon so, son," she said with a toothless grin. "It'll just be two old ones looking out for each other and for little Sadie."

Miss Ethel, as people called Charlie Stokesbury's widow, lived alone, although Ben's youngest daughter, Sadie, 5, spent more time at her grandmother's house than at her own. Her older sisters Meg, 15, and Peg, 13, were happy to have her out of the house and away from their things.

So even as his hunting exploits passed into local legend, Ole Jake resigned himself to spending his old age curled up by the kitchen door of Miss Ethel's shack, patiently enduring little Sadie's squealing games and scuffles.

But there was a sadness in his eyes. Since that last fateful hunt he did not raise his voice; no longer did his long, quavering, signature bark echo over the mountain and coves. To everybody's surprise, he never went near Ben's house. Only when Ben, sons Billy, 17, and Clarence, 16, and Big Red left for an early morning hunt did Ole Jake rouse up at all. He would stand whining and wagging his tail until they were out of sight. Then he would curl up again on his bed, put his head between his paws and close his eyes, his ears and legs soon twitching to dreams of hunts long ago.

Three years passed. Ben came over often to check on Ole Jake. With his practiced eye, he could see that the old dog was nearing the end. His eyes were cloudy and he could barely stand, not even to watch Ben, Billy, Clarence, and Big Red head for the woods. Ben thought of putting him down, but he didn't have the heart to take him away from Sadie.

Ben's farming ways had not improved, and around 1947 things suddenly got worse for everybody in the Lost River region. The recent winters had been warmer than usual, which allowed boll weevils from Texas and the Deep South to spread north and devastate the cotton. The consternation was general and many farmers were close to panic.

"Somebody told me that boll weevils live out in the woods," said Harvey Bolton. "So what we need to do is set the woods afire and burn up all the brush and stuff where they hide. That'll get rid of them. Folks used to burn the woods off every so often and we never had boll weevils back then."

"That's right," said Will Mayfair, nodding in thoughtful agreement.

"Well now, men, I don't see much good that'd do," said Henry Sandlin. "I don't care how many there are out in the woods. I need to get rid of the ones in my cotton field. I went out this morning and I bet there wasn't a third of the blooms you'd normally expect this time of year. And the ground's just covered with bolls that the weevils have bored into."

"Well, that just it, Henry," answered Harvey. They tell me they die off as soon as they bore into a boll and new one's come out of the woods to take their place. Birds and such eat them too, they say. So if we burn them out, we'll be shed of them in a few days and maybe save most of the cotton."

"I don't know about you all," observed Henry, "but I'm just about ready to try anything. It's going to be hard times for me if I don't get at least ten bales this year."

"That's pretty much the shape we'll all be in if we don't do something, and do it quick," said Will.

Ben didn't say anything, and nobody would have listened to him if he had. He didn't like the idea of burning the woods as dry as the spring had been. All that would drive off the squirrels and other creatures. He was concerned, of course, about losing the two or three bales of cotton he usually made. It didn't lighten his mood when he got home and found Gracie close to panic.

"Ben, what're we going to do? We just can't make it if we lose this cotton crop! Oh, Lord, how are we going to live? How can we feed these five kids? And we have your momma to think about too."

Ben didn't have an answer but he did have a reaction, which was to take his shotgun and head for the woods to get away from Gracie's anguish and doomsday talk that always turned into accusations. It wasn't squirrel season, but maybe, he thought, if I kill a rabbit or two she'll feel better.

Hours later on the way home with a brace of rabbits, Ben could see smoke rising off to the east. "I reckon those damn fools have started the burning," he said, shaking his head in disgust.

Later that night after the family had gone to bed, the wind shifted and the fire raced across the mountain toward them. Ole Jake was the first to become aware of the peril. Miss Ethel said later that he woke her up scratching and whining at the kitchen door. She bundled the sleeping Sadie in a quilt and hurried out of the house just as the flames burst out of the woods and engulfed the shack. Ben's house would be next.

But somehow, decrepit and half-blind Ole Jake summoned the heart and strength to outrun the racing flames across the field. Then as he neared Ben's house, he stopped and let loose for one final, heroic time his long, quavering, signature bark that so often had echoed and resonated across the mountains and coves in his prime. All across the mountain men roused from sleep at the sound.

In a flash Ben was awake, understood what was happening, and with Billy, Clarence, Meg, and Peg got Gracie and the barn animals to safety. Big Red seemed dazed by the fire and ran back and forth uncertain of what to do.

In less than an hour the old house and most of their material things were lost, but everything living was saved.

Except Ole Jake. As they gathered in the scorched field between where Miss Ethel's shack and Ben's house had stood, they found him, exhausted and breathing his last. Sadie cradled him in her arms and cried for him to live. And if it had been day, you would have seen a tear or two in Ben's eyes.

"Daddy, don't let him die!" she begged, hugging Ole Jake protectively. "Please don't let him die!"

"Sadie, darling," Ben said, putting his arms around her, "it's time for Ole Jake to go. He's lived his life, and saved the best for last. Now we have to let him go. He was a good dog. Best squirrel dog I ever had. I guess saving the family was his last hunt."

"But, Daddy, I want him to stay here with me, with us! I love him!"

"We all love him," Miss Ethel said, "but your Daddy's right, it's time to let him go."

"Will Ole Jake go to Heaven, Daddy, like good people do?"

"Of course not, Sadie," snapped Gracie. "He's a dog, and dogs don't go to Heaven. It's not in the Bible!"

Sadie cried bitterly as Ben tried to console her.

Early the next morning Ben buried Ole Jake at the edge of the woods as Clarence and the girls watched. Harvey Bolton waited in his truck to take them and the few things Gracie and Billy had pulled out of the ruins over to cousin Vernon's house. He was the only descendant in the Charlie Stokesbury line with a house big enough to take them all in. They would stay there until they figured out their next move.

"Grandma," said Sadie, staring at the grave, "is it really so that dogs don't go to Heaven like Momma said?"

"Well, child, I don't know. I guess none of us knows about things like that. We'll just have to wait and see, I reckon. You respect what your momma tells you, Sadie. But also think about this: the Bible tells about animals back yonder in the Garden of Eden. So if the Good Lord put animals in the First Paradise, why would he have anything against having Ole Jake in Heaven?"

"Amen, Momma," said Ben as he gave a gentle pat to Ole Jakes's little grave and then led Sadie and them all toward the truck. "I just have to believe Ole Jake will hunt again someday, and I hope to be there to help him."

14.
Reds and Purples

Jeff Woodward and wife, Jane, lived all fifty-odd years of married life in Lost River on a corner lot a hundred yards or so east of Colonel Abner Stokesbury's statue. In all that time they had only two disagreements. Jane loved her hydrangeas and all things lavender and purple, but Jeff preferred his red roses and everything crimson, including his pickup truck. Even his hair was a vivid red, though now fading into gray as the weight of seventy-three summers was beginning to bend his strong frame. At sixty-nine, Jane's hair was cotton white, though her face was still smooth and unlined.

Now that both were retired from teaching, Jeff in math and Jane in English, they spent much of their time working in their flowerbeds. Responding to the love and care the Woodwards lavished on them, flowers of all kinds were a mosaic of color in their yard. Jeff's red roses prevailed in the front yard and along Jordan Street that ran by it on the west side, but Jane's hydrangeas dominated along both sides of their four-room white frame house. People went out of their way to see the flowers and shake their heads in admiration and envy.

Their other disagreement was a sadder matter: Jeff did not believe in God. He was a logical man for whom religion and the Bible were fables and fairy tales. Despite Jane's pleadings, he would not attend church with her. The most he would do was drive her to Lost River Holiness Church on the other end of town and wait in his red pickup till the service was over.

"You know, don't you, Jane, that I wouldn't do this for anybody else, not even our children?" he said grumpily as they drove home. The service had been longer than usual and Jeff was hungry.

"Oh, Jeff, it breaks my heart to see you sitting out there by yourself under that oak tree while everybody else is inside worshiping God. Husband, can't you just loosen up a bit and at least come in and sit with me? It would please me, and I believe it would please God. You know the other families feel sorry for me sitting there all by myself."

"Woman, don't start that God stuff with me, and don't think you're going to get me inside that church by pushing my pity button. I don't give a hoot what other people think. You know what I believe and don't believe. I've felt this way all my life and I'm not about to change now. You're a sensible woman about everything else, but when it comes to religion you're just as dumb as all the rest of these fools around here."

"But Jeff, you're not young any more, and we're all mortal. Don't you think it's about time you gave some thought to the Hereafter? God's real, Jeff, and one of these days, no matter how long we live in this world, we'll go meet Jesus and face eternity with him or without him. Jeff Jr. and Pauline have grown up to be faithful Christians with beautiful families. My happiness would be complete if you . . ."

"Now, woman," Jeff interrupted her, his red face even redder in anger, "we've talked about that a thousand times. You had your way with our children, and I let you. But they know where I stand. And as for the Hereafter, is it God or Jesus that we're supposed to meet? Which one is which?"

"Jesus is God, Jeff. The Bible says they're the Father and the Son, and with the Holy Ghost they make up the Trinity, three persons in one, in the Godhead."

"That's the silliest thing I ever heard of. How can you be somebody else and still be yourself? No wonder the preachers and theologians can't explain how three Gods can be one. Any first-grader knows that three can't be one, or one three. It's hard to figure out because things that aren't real are always hard to understand."

"When you have faith, dear, a lot of things become clear, things our human minds can't figure out."

"Well, one thing I'm sure of is that when we die, that's it, the end of the line for us. Now you take old Harmon Jordan who died a few weeks ago. He lived his whole life down at the end of our street. It was named after him. Now there's his fresh grave you see out there in the cemetery. He was a religious man if ever there was one, but if you opened his casket, I'll bet you a thousand dollars Harmon, or what's left of him, would still be there. We live and we die, and that's all there is to it. If there was a Heaven and a better life after our time in this world, why folks would be happy when somebody dies, instead of moaning and groaning about it."

Jane sighed and looked out the truck window at Henry Hamilton's horses grazing peacefully in a pasture a quarter of a mile away. "Jeff, all I can do is pray that someday before it's too late your heart and mind will open up to the truth."

"I'll be happier if you can get some food on the table. I'm starving. It's nearly one o'clock. Every Sunday that fool preacher Williams, or whatever his name is, goes on a little longer."

"His name is Yates, John Wilcox Yates, the grandson of a minister who used to preach here back in the 1800s. And the younger Yates preached a good sermon today. I wish you could have heard it. It was about the loaves and fishes and how Jesus fed five thousand people."

"Pure fairy tales, all that Bible stuff. They probably scrounged up enough food for a few people that were following Jesus. Then the more they told the story the bigger it got. You know how people like to stretch the truth, and in nearly two thousand years you can be sure there's been a lot of stretching."

A few weeks later Jane complained of a sharp pain in her stomach. "Just indigestion," she said to Jeff's worried inquiries. "I'll be all right. It's nothing to worry about."

But days passed and the pain grew worse with each one of them. For several weeks Jeff had noticed that Jane was losing weight. She was a strong woman who had always stoically ignored her ailments, but now even she could not suppress an occasional groan. Finally, Jeff laid down the law.

"Jane, I'm taking you to the doctor."

"No, I don't want to go. I'll be all right."

"We're going and that's that." Then in a gentler voice he added, "I love you, Jane. You're my life and I want to take care of you. So now come on, we're going."

So they went to Dr. Walter Hathaway in Tylerville After an hour he came out and told Jeff that he wanted Jane to stay in the hospital for a couple of days.

"Doctor, what's wrong with her?"

"I don't want to get involved in hasty speculation, Mr. Woodward. We'll need to take X-rays and run some tests to find out what's causing her pain. Then we can treat her. Your wife is a gentle but resolute woman, and wants to go home and get back to her household duties. You must convince her to stay in the hospital until we can complete the tests. It's important that she do so."

"You suspect it's something serious, don't you, doctor?"

"As I said, I don't want to make a premature diagnosis. Let's run the tests and do the X-rays first. Then we'll have the facts we need."

Reluctantly, Jane stayed in the hospital and Jeff sat at her bedside when they were not doing tests. Dr. Hathaway gave her a sedative and she slept peacefully most of the first night, but the next morning the pain came back with such a vengeance that Jane could not hide it any longer.

"Oh, Jeff, it hurts really bad. What does the doctor say it is?"

Jeff held her hands, fighting hard not to let the tears come. "He hasn't yet, but soon they'll be finished with the tests and then we can get you well again."

Finally Dr. Hathaway came, gave Jane something for the pain, and as Jane closed her eyes after a few minutes, motioned for Jeff to step outside.

"Doctor, what is it? What's wrong with Jane?"

"I'm sorry to say I don't bring good news, Mr. Woodward. It's cancer, as I suspected, and in an advanced stage."

Jeff trembled uncontrollably. "But there are treatments. I read that advances in medicine are being made all the time."

"Yes they are, but to be honest with you, in Mrs. Woodward's case I can't be optimistic. The cancer has spread throughout her body, which removes surgery as an option. Radiation is not indicated for this kind of tumor, but we can begin chemotherapy. That may buy us some time."

"Time for what, doctor?" asked Jeff, his florid face drained for once of color.

"Time for us to plan other procedures and I assume for you to alert family and friends to her condition. And I need to ask you a delicate question, Mr. Woodward."

"What's that, Doctor?"

"Will you choose to tell your wife the truth about her condition?"

Jeff hunched over for a moment, then rubbed his eyes, and straightened himself to his full height and looked the physician in the eye. "Doctor Hathaway, Jane and I have been married for more than fifty years, and in all that time we have never kept secrets from each other. She will want to know the truth, and I'll not keep it from her, just as she would not keep anything like this from me."

"A courageous decision, Mr. Woodward. God bless you for making it. I think the patient should always know the truth, especially in cases like this, but not all family members—and not all doctors—agree with me."

"God has nothing to do with it. It's a matter of truth and trust, and Jane and I have always dealt in truth, and we've always trusted each other."

Jane took the news with Christian serenity and courageous acceptance. Within two weeks it was obvious to all but Jeff that chemotherapy had not worked and that she was close to death. Dr. Hathaway said they could do nothing else for her.

"When the doctor first told me, I knew in my heart that my time had come. Maybe I knew it even before," she said to teary-eyed Jeff. "I am not afraid to go, Jeff, but there are some things I need to say before I leave."

"Don't go, Jane!" he pleaded, his tears now flowing freely. "You are my life. What would I do without you?"

"Dear Jeff, you may not wish to hear these words, but they are true. Please listen and do not tempt divine patience any longer. Our time is in God's hands. We are here for a season and then we must go, some earlier, some later. My time is up in this world, but you still have things to do here. I know you will do them well."

She stopped in exhaustion as Jeff held her hands. "Maybe if we took you to Nashville," he offered hopefully, "to the big medical center with all the expert doctors . . ."

She shook her head. "No, Jeff. This part of our life together is over, but not ended. It will never end. I love you for being a good husband to me, a great father to Jeff and Pauline, and a wonderful grandfather to the grandchildren."

"I don't see how I could live without you, Jane. We've always done everything together."

"We'll be together again in a better world and a better life, Jeff. But first you must end your hostility toward God. Promise me you will, if you love me, promise you will. And God will honor your intention."

"Jane, I have never been a believer. I would do anything for you, but how can I make myself believe something I have always thought was based on fable and falsehood? How?"

"Just promise me you'll be open to God's sign. If you are, he'll respond and you'll know he's real."

"What sign?"

Jane smiled and closed her eyes for a few minutes. Jeff was afraid she was slipping away. But when she opened her eyes again, she seemed to have a renewal of strength.

"What sign? I don't know, Jeff. But I know a sign will come if you are willing to receive it. Are you willing, Jeff?"

"I'm willing. For your sake I'm willing. God, if you are real, give me a sign and I promise I will try to believe."

But in his heart and despite his grief he doubted.

"Thank you, Jeff. God has never failed me, and he will not fail you. Trust him. He always has the last word.

"Now some practical matters, Jeff. Remember I keep the plates and silverware in the top left counter drawers, not in the cabinet. That's where I keep the spices you like, over the shelf where you keep tools and stuff that I could never persuade you to leave in the shed. You will need to heat the food in the refrigerator and freezer. See that Pauline and Jessica sort through my clothes and belongings and donate any suitable to charity. Keep any things of mine you want, then let Pauline and Jeff Jr. take what they wish. And don't forget to water my hydrangeas."

That night with Jeff, Jeff Jr. and wife Jessica, Pauline and husband Arnold, and the two older grandchildren around her bed, Jane slipped peacefully away. They buried her two days later in the Lost River Holiness Church cemetery not far from Harmon Jordan's grave. Jeff thought momentarily of what he had said to Jane a few Sundays ago and wondered for an instant whether Harmon was really still in the grave. What if I have been wrong all this time and really will meet the God of the Christians? Doubts and regrets—and above all, the unhappiness he had caused Jane—flooded over him and he broke down in sobs and tears. Jeff Jr. and Pauline, both redheaded like their father, came and put their arms around him. They stayed with him for several hours after the funeral, but then he told them to go home, take care of the children, and get on with their lives.

"I'll be all right now," he assured them. "I have to work in the flowers. That way I'll feel closer to her. Your mother told me to be sure to water her hydrangeas. You know how she is— was—about them."

He managed a weak grin, but the more he thought about it, the more he rebelled against the idea that Jane was gone for good. It angered him to speak of Jane in the past tense. If she is still alive somehow, somewhere, he thought, then she *is* concerned about her hydrangeas. The language has it wrong. Even the Christians get that part wrong, he thought.

The next morning, church secretary Patti Townsend came in to the Reverend Yates's office to announce that Mr. Woodward wanted to see him.

"Mr. Woodward?" he asked quizzically. "Jane Woodward's husband?"

"Yes sir, the same. But I need to tell you he's really nervous or upset over something."

"Well, send him in, Patti, and we'll find out what it is."

Jeff came in squeezing the brim of his straw hat in both hands.

"Come in, Mr. Woodward. As I said at the funeral, I'm so sorry about Jane. She was one of the most faithful members of this congregation."

"*Is*, Reverend, *is*. She's still a faithful member. It's just that now she's up there, worshiping with the faithful in a different pew, so to speak, and in another way."

"You're right, Jeff, isn't that your name? Here, have a seat and tell me what's on your mind. Your wife spoke to me several times about you."

"I can imagine what she said, and I'm sorry. I regret all those Sundays I didn't come into church with her."

"What she said, Mr. Woodward, was that you were a good man, kind, honest, hardworking, and truthful."

"But not a believer."

Reverend Yates nodded. "Is there anything I can do to help you?"

"Yes, there is, Reverend. You can get me baptized and made a member of this congregation."

Reverend Yates came around his desk to shake Jeff's hand. "What a happy decision you have made, Jeff! Nothing could please me more. That's what Jane prayed for all the years I knew her. I'm sure God heard her prayers."

"No doubt, but it was something else that opened my eyes—and heart—as Jane always said."

"And what was that, if you don't mind telling me?"

"I'll tell you and everybody I see. You know how Jane loved her flowers, especially her hydrangeas. We both loved—love—flowers and worked together in our flowerbeds."

"So they tell me. I know you have the prettiest flowers in this part of the country. I've seen them myself."

"Well, I don't know about that. But we did have one difference of opinion. I preferred my red roses and the color red in general, but Jane loved lavender and purple hydrangeas. We never did settle the argument until now."

"Now? I'm afraid I don't understand, Jeff."

"I don't either. All I can tell you is what happened."

"What was that?"

"When I went out this morning to check on the flowers and water the ones that needed it, I saw a miracle, a real miracle! Jane's hydrangeas were purple as always, but, Reverend, so were my roses and every other flower around the house! Purple! Purple! It was the sign she said God would show me! I hoped she was right, but in my heart I doubted. But she was right! Everything was purple, the color of royalty and kingship! That was the sign and now I believe! She was right after all! I guess you could say she and God had the last word!"

After Jeff was baptized into the Christian faith and joined the congregation, Pauline and Jeff Jr. had a conversation about their father. Both were concerned, especially Pauline.

"Jeff, what are we going to do about Dad?"

"Yeah, I'm a little worried about him, too. But at least he's now a baptized Christian. That's what Momma and we always prayed for."

"I'm happy about that, but that business about the purple flowers. You've seen the flowerbeds. They're red, purple, and every other color, just like always."

"I know, sis, the flowers haven't changed, but he thinks, or thought, they had. Although he told me yesterday that some of them were returning to their original colors. You know what I think happened?"

"No, what?"

"Momma's passing was more than he could take in his normal rebellious frame of reference. They were so close to each other. And you know she had been working on him for all the years they were married, praying for him, setting a Christian example. I think he secretly wanted to believe, maybe believed in spite of himself, but you know about masculine pride and stubbornness. But under so much pressure, the dam finally broke and he saw purple. That was his way of accepting what she had been trying to convince him of for fifty years. Think of it as his personal miracle. Momma did say it would be a sign for him, not necessarily for everybody. And who really knows? Maybe the flowers really were purple for a while."

"You may be right. So you don't think Dad has gone over the edge?"

"I hope not. Just think, sis, it may be the best thing that could have happened to him now that Momma's gone. We'll keep an eye on him, but I have a feeling that even though he's alone now, in a way he's better off spiritually than he's ever been. Just imagine how much worse off he would be otherwise, without Momma and without God."

Jeff Jr. was right. His father lived another decade as a dedicated Christian, always retaining the fire and enthusiasm of a convert. His story, which he told over and over without tiring of it, made him an effective witness to many unbelievers, as he once was. His motto, based on his experience and what Jane always tried to tell him, was that God always has the last word.

15.
Double Take

Before World War II, Robert Spurgeon Vaughter had never traveled more than twenty miles from Lost River nor felt any reason why he should. Everything he wanted was close by. On November 16, 1941, his 20th birthday, he asked Betty Sue Wilson, 18, to marry him. She accepted, but on the condition imposed by her parents, that she first graduate from Lost River High School.

Exactly three weeks later the Japanese attacked Pearl Harbor, and Robert was among the first Stokesbury County boys drafted. The army sent him to Fort Hood, Texas, for basic training and then on to combat in the South Pacific. Robert and Betty Sue would have married before he left if calmer parental counsel had not prevailed. And so with kisses, tears, and promises of eternal love and fidelity, they parted for what all hoped would be a short absence and a joyous reunion.

But what man would join together, destiny often puts asunder.

Betty Sue's letters to Robert continued for a few months, but they got shorter and colder. Time ate away at her feelings and Robert soon became an old memory. Her last letter of barely a dozen lines and not a word of love reached him in early May. By then she had transferred her affections to Melvin Talley. She told Robert they were engaged and hoped that he would understand and forgive her. In June she married as promised, but Melvin was her groom.

Robert grieved in his private way over Betty Sue, but his pain, like her love, belonged to the Lost River world he had left behind and might never see again. In any case, he had no chance to be morbid about it. He saw too many broken bodies to dwell on a broken heart.

Nearly four years passed and the war ended. He survived the war years but his parents did not. Both died in 1944, his mother in January and his father in June. Robert was discharged in October of 1945. In November when he got off the Greyhound bus at Tylerville and walked the ten muddy miles to his home, he was thinking of a saying he had read or heard somewhere: "You can't go home again."

But of course that saying's not right, he thought to himself as he surveyed the deserted old home place. You can go back home, all right; it's just that home doesn't come back to you.

Neighbors and relatives tried to show him and the other veterans how much they appreciated what they had done. But after a few weeks, the novelty wore off and things settled into their old routine. The remaining excitement had to do with engagements and marriages as the veterans chose wives and started their families. But Robert was not a part of it.

People had trouble connecting the thin farm boy they had known before the war with the muscular, sun-bronzed man who returned to them. He seemed like a different man. Even his speech had changed, and it bothered some people.

Beatrice, his only sibling, took no interest in the old home place. Bea, as Robert called her, had her hands full in her Fairview home with four children and womanizing husband, Lemuel Stokesbury, one of Leon's sons and grandson of Homer Stokesbury. With her permission, for the past two years neighbor Enos Brown had planted cotton—rent free—on the twenty acres fronting the Barkley Road. But the back fields had lain fallow and weed infested since the elder Vaughter died.

Robert bought a '37 Chevrolet pickup, had the electricity turned on, and for the next few weeks repaired fences and buildings to get ready for spring planting. Without giving it much thought, he always meant to go back to farming when his military days were over. A possum had died in the well and he had to draw it dry several times before the water was drinkable again. Meanwhile, he hauled water from the spring over in the pasture.

He knew he was bound to see Betty Sue sooner or later, and even though he dreaded the moment, was relieved when it came. One Saturday he ran into them in Lost River Market. She was a little taller and heavier than he remembered but pretty as ever. That disappointed him; he expected—and maybe even hoped—that life would have been a little harder on her. He was surprised at how much pain was still there.

It was an awkward moment of silence that lasted too long and words said too quickly. Melvin, whose polio-shortened left leg kept him out of the service, offered his hand, which Robert shook. Betty Sue presented their two children: Brenda, 3, and Billy, 1. They could have been mine, he thought. It took an effort not to imagine Melvin and Betty Sue together.

He thought about things far into the night. The next morning he drove into Tylerville to get the power turned off. Then he came home and went over to see Enos.

"Enos, I'm leaving, and I'd appreciate it if you'd look after the place for me again."

"But, Rob, you just got back from all the years in the army. We thought you had come home to stay, maybe ready to find a wife and settle down. Where you heading to this time?"

"Well, I had this buddy in the service and he told me about a trucking job he could line up for me in California. I guess I'll head out that way and see if it's still open. If the old Chevy will make it."

"California! Man o man, that's a long ways from here, they tell me."

"Pretty far, but it sounds like a good thing. So can you see after the place for me? Farm as much of the land as you want and the same goes for the firewood. Cut what you need. And you may want to graze your stock in the pasture. The grass looks good, and you know the spring never goes dry in the summer. Now the well water's good, too. I got that mess with the possum all cleaned up."

"Well, now, Robert, I do appreciate your offer of the farm land, and you can count on me to take real good care of things till you come back. And we'll all be hoping that'll be real soon."

But it wasn't. The money in California was good for a couple of years, but he drank too much to save any and then the trucking company went out of business. Robert moved on to Oregon and logged for a year or so. Then he hired on in Portland as a sailor, making runs to Canada and Alaska. When that went stale, he ended up working for an American construction firm contracted by the American Military in Okinawa.

The work intervals became shorter with the years. At first he traveled to work; later he worked so he could travel and drift. And then he drifted farther. And still farther.

He saw again the blue paradise of the South Pacific with its soft breezes and brown-bodied women and thought how soon his great war was forgotten. The easy rhythm of island life enraptured some American expatriates and they stayed. Robert understood the attraction without sharing it. He was at ease with the world but not at peace with himself. He moved on to Australia, and India, and the Near East, and Africa, and Europe. Sometimes he had an urge to see America, but never for long. Faraway lands called him and he was off again, always preferring the roads traveled to the places reached. Until . . .

One beautiful day in the South of France it was over, the wanderlust was gone like a wound healed, and he knew it was time to go home—if there was still a home. Seventeen years had passed. Seventeen years! He felt betrayed by time. Did it have a right to rush by him so quickly? Was there anything left?

Two weeks later, in 1963, again he walked down the Tylerville Road toward his house. But it was no longer his house. Enos, now gray and bent, had paid the delinquent taxes and claimed the property for his own. But instead of acting defensive about it, he swelled up in anger.

"You told me you would come back, but you didn't. No sir, you just left it up to me to take care of that property for years on end. And not a word from you, out there running around all over the world. And Bea never showed interest in things here. So I paid the taxes, sure I did, and now the place is mine. If I hadn't, they would've auctioned it off. And if you don't think it's legal and all, then we'll just go to Tylerville and I'll show you it is."

"I believe you, Enos, and I don't hold it against you at all. So don't worry about it. I don't mean to cause you any trouble, and I'm sorry if I did."

"Well, if it's trouble you want, you can find it right here."

"Enos, I just told you that I'm not looking for trouble. So let's just drop the whole thing."

"I'll have you know I haven't cheated nobody. And I can stand up for what's rightfully mine, I don't care who it's against."

Robert shook his head, realizing that no good thing could come from trying to be reasonable with a fool like Enos. His arteries must be hardening, he thought to himself.

For the next week Enos went around proudly telling everybody how he had got the best of that Vaughter boy that used to live around here a long time ago.

"The smart aleck Rob Vaughter backed down like a yellow dog when I faced up to him. Never was much account to work. Just a born drifter, if you ask me. Never did think much of his bunch myself, and he's no improvement. But I guess I set him straight."

With the last of his money, Robert rented a little house in Lost River and, luckily, got a job as a delivery man. It paid next to nothing, but since he was used to nothing, it was more than enough. Within modest limits, Mr. Tucker, the franchise owner, agreed to let him use the company vehicle if he would pay for the gas.

Things went on without incident until one day he had an experience that shook him to the core. He made a delivery out to the Fairview Community out past the Barkley Road. He rang the doorbell— and he did a double take when Betty Sue opened the door.

Not the matronly Betty Sue of forty but the girl she was when he knew her.

"Betty Sue!" he said in astonishment.

The girl laughed and corrected him.

"No, sir. I'm Brenda Talley. Betty Sue's my mother. Folks say I look like her. Do you know her?"

"Well, I did once, a long time ago. I'm sorry, it was my mistake. You look so much like her that I thought . . . But I'm forgetting my business. Here, I have a package for you."

Brenda took the package and frowned.

"Is something wrong, Miss Talley? This is the right address, isn't it?"

"Yes, it's the right address, but I'm not sure I want to accept it."

"Well, if there's a mix up, I'll take it back."

"No, it's nothing that's your fault, or your company's. It's just a personal matter I'll have to take care of."

"In that case, I'll be on my way."

"You didn't tell me your name. Momma'll want to know about an old friend."

"Old is the right word, Brenda. My name is Robert Vaughter."

Brenda extended her hand and gave him a firm handshake.

"I didn't mean 'old' in that sense, Mr. Vaughter. I'm pleased to meet you, and I'll be sure to tell Momma about you. She's not here right now or you could talk to her."

Robert started to say something else about how much she resembled her mother but thought better and went on his way. Brenda was probably tired of hearing it anyway.

Before many weeks had passed, Mr. Tucker caught his office manager in a compromising situation with his married secretary and fired them both. From route driver one day, Robert was promoted to office manager the next with a good hike in pay.

With that lucky turn, Robert decided to make the most of his small world. As a boy he had attended Evergreen Methodist Church, but that was many years ago and he had not been to a service since. The next Sunday he rose early, bathed, shaved, and put on a new pair of dress pants and shirt. He had no coat or tie, but when he got to Lost River Holiness Church he saw that men his age didn't wear them anymore.

He had picked the church at random and knew nothing about the denomination and didn't really care. Any connection he made would link him eventually to all the people around town.

The church was full—to hear their new pastor, he found out later. Of all people, there were the Talleys, and before he could get away Brenda saw him and made room for him to sit with the family. He hesitated and then sat beside her, unable to think of a graceful way to decline. Older but otherwise recognizably the same, Betty Sue and Melvin smiled and welcomed him. Son Billy, or so he supposed he was, looked as though this was the last place he wanted to be. As for Robert, he felt as tense as a pig in a butcher shop.

The new pastor, Reverend Ralph Fincher, gave a rousing sermon and the singing was spirited. It was comforting to Robert—like meeting old friends again— to hear the biblical passages and sing the old hymns. Robert had not thought about his religious beliefs in a long time, but after the service he felt better.

"Momma tells me you've traveled a lot, Mr. Vaughter," Brenda said as they all headed for the parking lot. "I'd like to hear about it. I haven't done much traveling."

"Robert, after church we always go over to the Steak House Café, for dinner," Melvin said. "Why don't you come with us? We'd like to have you."

"No, I wouldn't want to intrude on a family thing."

"Not an intrusion at all," added Betty Sue. "It'll be our way of giving you a Christian welcome back home."

To Robert's surprise, scowling Billy turned out to be the decisive voice. "Aw, come on, Mr. Vaughter. If you don't, we'll have to listen to Daddy's dumb old stories again."

It was the first of several visits. For the Talleys seemed genuinely fascinated by Robert's accounts of his travels—those he selected as suitable for the family to hear. Some of the times he was down and out he kept to himself. Brenda, especially, hung on to every word. He wondered if she was just being polite, but if she was, he couldn't tell it. And from his reactions, it was plain that Billy was itching to get out into the world and see what he could stir up. One Sunday after their now customary lunch at the Steak House, Brenda stopped Robert as he was getting in the company pickup.

"I'll miss you and your travel stories, Robert. They have really brightened what could have been a dreary summer. Next Thursday it's back to Jackson State for the second summer session. I'll graduate in late August and it looks like they're going to hire me to teach at the middle school here. Keep your fingers crossed for me."

"I will, and congratulations, Brenda. Betty Sue tells me you've gone through college in just a little over three years. You're talking to an old boy who didn't make it past eleventh grade."

"You don't sound like a dropout. Your English is better than anybody's around here."

"All my traveling and reading, I guess, and a lot of Yankee friends. I've been away from Lost River for a long time," he said. "And what's next for you, Brenda? Must be somebody waiting for you down in Mississippi."

"Not anymore!" she said cheerfully. "Remember that package you brought me the day I met you? Well, it was from somebody I once thought I was waiting for. But I was wrong. Yesterday I finally gathered up all the things he sent me and did what I should have done a long time ago."

"And what was that, if you don't mind saying?"

"Sent them back to him and ended the whole thing."

"I'm sorry."

"I'm not."

"Brenda, we're leaving!" Betty Sue called out. "Bye, Robert! We'll see you next Sunday, Lord willing!"

"I have to go, Robert. I'll talk to you soon, tomorrow if I can!"

It was the first time Brenda had called him by his first name. Twice too. Like a broken record, her simple, ordinary words kept repeating in his mind and her face reappeared each time he tried to think about something else. Lately he had caught himself thinking a lot about her, and it made him feel like a dirty old man, like an uncle with incestuous thoughts.

She's just a girl, dummy, he told himself. And she's Betty Sue's daughter, for God's sake! She could even be my own daughter if Betty Sue and I had . . . I can't let myself think of her as a woman. What's the matter with me? Maybe a drink would help me get my mind off her, he thought. But then he shook his head. Since coming back to Lost River country he had been dry and it wouldn't help matters to start drinking again. And what did she mean by saying 'tomorrow, if I can'?

He found out. Late the next afternoon there was a knock on Robert's door. There stood Brenda.

"Hello, Robert, may I come in?"

"Brenda, what are you doing here? I didn't know you even knew where I lived. Are your parents in the car?"

"Not unless they're hiding in the trunk. I came here to talk to you. Alone"

"I don't understand."

"You will if you'll let me come in and not keep me standing here on the porch all afternoon."

"Well, sure, come on in, but I don't think you ought to be here."

"And I think I should. So here I am."

"Well, sit down, Brenda, if you can find a clean spot. Here, let me move those magazines out of your way. What's on your mind?"

"You."

"Me?"

"You."

"I don't understand."

"That's twice you've said that."

"And twice I told the truth. Because I really don't understand. Brenda, your family—you—all of you have been nice to me, and I appreciate it. And I don't want to do anything to cause trouble."

"Maybe that's your problem. Maybe you should cause trouble sometimes. Don't you think it's about time?"

"What do you mean?"

"Look, Robert, let's stop beating around the bush and do some plain talking. To start with, I know about you and Momma. I know she hurt you a long time ago and she's sorry about that. But I can tell you this: Momma and Daddy were meant to be together. Maybe she could have been happy with you. We'll never know. But what I do know is that they've been happy in their marriage and good, caring, Christian parents to Billy and me."

"Brenda, I don't doubt that for a minute. And I hope I haven't caused them or you any trouble. I wouldn't hurt you or your family for the world. If I have said or done anything like that, I didn't mean to."

"No, you haven't, and I know for a fact that Momma and Daddy are happy that the three of you have been able to put things behind you and build a new friendship. Because they always felt bad about what happened back then; it's been like a dark cloud over their marriage. You've let them clear it away."

"I'm glad."

"Me too. But that's not what I came to talk about. That was just to clear the air so we could get to more important things."

"Like what?"

"Like us, Robert, you and me."

"Brenda, I . . . if you've started down the road I think you have, I don't think you should go there. I'm old enough to be your father, could've been your father. We just talked about that."

"But you're not my daddy, thank goodness. And let's cut out the 'old man' crap, if you'll pardon my French. I've seen the way you look at me. I'm young but I'm a woman— full grown and husband high, as some of the old folks say around here—and you've noticed I'm a woman."

"Yes, Brenda. You are a woman, a beautiful woman, and I have noticed that you're 'full grown and husband high.' I'd be lying if I said otherwise. But the fact remains that I'm nearly twice your age and . . ."

"Robert Vaughter," she interrupted, "I'll cut to the chase and say what both of us need to say: I'm in love with you! Now, I've said it, and that entitles me to an answer from you. Robert, do you love me?"

"No, not like that. I love you like a daughter, or niece, or something like that. That's how I have to love you."

"You're not a very good liar, are you? I see the truth in your eyes. You do love me. I know it, I feel it, and you know it."

"But even if I did, I could never do anything about it."

"Then what will you do?"

"I don't know. All I can say is no, I can't be involved with you. I can't take advantage of you, no matter how tempting the idea is. What would your parents say?"

"Oh, they've said it already, that you're too old, that I'm too young, that there are some delicate points in your relationship to the family—everything that caring parents tell their children. Robert, I told them how I felt about you. Well, I told Momma first and she told Daddy. Then we talked about it together—without Billy of course."

"You talked and told them what? My God, I can't imagine what they must think of me! Melvin's probably on his way here now with his shotgun."

"No, love, I explained that you didn't know anything about my feelings and that you had always been a perfect gentleman with me. I don't hide things from them—well, not much anyway."

"And what did you all decide? I need to know, since I'm just a little involved, you know."

"You better believe you are. Well, I told you about their concerns, but at the end they just said they had raised me in a Christian way and that I needed to be careful and not end up with a broken heart. They want me to be happy."

"Well, we can all agree on that. I want you to be happy, too."

"If you really mean that, then listen to me. I have five more weeks of college. I'll be back here on the 25th of August with degree in hand if all goes well. And when I return, Mr. Robert Vaughter, you and I are going to start making our wedding plans. Now stop being so noble and kiss me to seal the deal!"

His willpower, already weakened by her nearness and beauty, and stunned by her resolve, wilted completely. Before he could regain control, he did as told, kissed her and confessed his love.

But in the weeks she was away in Mississippi, he regained his emotional balance and rebuilt the arguments against their love. He stayed away from church so he would not have to face the Talleys and left Brenda's letters unopened. On the 10th he announced to Mr. Tucker that he was quitting his job and leaving Lost River.

Suitcase at his feet, he waited on the highway in the early morning fog of the 24th for the Greyhound bus. By the 25th, the day of her return, he would be long gone.

Somebody tugged at his sleeve as the bus drove up. It was Brenda with her own suitcase.

"Going somewhere?" she asked innocently.

"Brenda, you're home early! You said the 25th."

"I lied. Forgive me, Lord. I knew you'd try to play this little trick."

"But how did you know I'd be here?"

"Mr. Tucker told me. He and I have been plotting by telephone all these weeks behind your back. He likes you, Robert. We both want you to stay."

"I'm surrounded by scheming people! But I still have to leave, Brenda."

"I know; we've been through all your reasons before."

"Well, they're good reasons, so you know why I have to go."

"No, not really, but if you're bound and determined to hit the road again, then I'm going with you. Here I am, all packed and ready."

"Are you crazy? You can't go with me!"

"I can if I have to. Tell me, Robert, did you ever find what you were looking for in your globetrotting days?"

"No, never did."

"Then, what makes you think you'll have any better luck this time?"

"I just don't want to hurt you and cause trouble."

"I can tell you this: you'll do both if you leave and I go with you instead of staying here and getting married as we planned."

"As you planned," he corrected her.

"A technicality. I was just saying what we both wanted."

"But what would people say? And people would talk. And how could I go up to Melvin, a man as old as I am, and tell him I want to marry his daughter?"

"Well, darling, you should be able to figure that out for yourself, but if you can't, here's what you say: 'Mr. Talley, I want to marry your daughter.' Simple as that. Can you remember, or should I write it down on a piece of paper for you?"

"Funny, funny. But seriously, people will talk."

"Did you ever see *Gone with the Wind*?"

"Yes, and . . . ?"

At that moment the bus driver announced departure.

"Sir, give us just a minute, will you?" Brenda pleaded.

"Okay, Miss, but then I'm closing the door."

"Robert, do you remember what Rhett Butler said to Scarlett?"

"'Frankly, my dear, I don't give a damn.' It was pretty strong language for a movie at the time."

"And that, my dear, in those well-chosen words is what I think about what gossipy people will say. But I do give a damn about us. So let the bus go and let's get on with the rest of our life. What do you say? Do we run from life together or do we stay here and let me make an honest man of you?"

"I left my job."

"Mr. Tucker's holding it for you. I told him you were coming back. Any more excuses?"

"Miss," said the driver, "I have to go. I'm closing the doors. Are you boarding or not?"

"That's the question, Robert, are we, or not?" Brenda asked Robert as she reached for her suitcase.

He thought for a moment, head down. Then he straightened, smiled, and hugging Brenda, announced to the driver: "Close your door, Mr. Driver, and take it on the road. We're staying. I don't know what I'm going to do with this beautiful, stubborn girl, or what she's going to do with me. But I'm going to stick around and find out!"

16.
Queen Zeenab

After their honeymoon in Panama City, Robert and Brenda Vaughter moved into their new residence, a red brick house close to the Fairview Road which they rented from her Uncle Claude ("Red") Wilson. It was convenient to Brenda's new teaching job at the middle school but too small to accommodate both the new furniture and all the things Brenda's parents had given her. So in her take-charge way, she tagged the items that had to go. They included some oddities that Robert had picked up in his travels.

"This thing, for example, darling. What is it anyway? It looks like it has a tiny statue inside."

"That little lady is Queen Zeenab. And she has to stay."

"Who? Queen Zanob?"

"Queen Zeenab. She's the other woman in my life. I bought her in Cairo, Egypt, about ten years ago and she's been with me ever since."

"If I find out there really *is* another woman after all the trouble it took me to get you, you won't be able to go back to work for Mr. Tucker, not unless you can hobble in on two broken legs."

Robert laughed and pulled her down to his lap.

"Tell you what. Let's take a break and I'll tell you her story, or read it. It's in this little booklet tied to the base."

"Okay, but kiss me first."

He did and then read.

There is a tale told by the Persian dervishes about a beautiful Kurdish girl named Zeenab whose father sent her as a gift to the mighty ruler of Persia. But instead of languishing like other women in the Shah's harem, lady Zeenab's beauty and grace so captivated the dread monarch's heart that he made her his new Shahbanou, or principal wife, thereby condemning her predecessor, the aging but still beautiful Khaadija, to humiliation and ridicule. Khaadija screamed in rage, and swearing vengeance on the "Kurdish slave," as she called Zeenab, hatched a plot to poison her young rival. But her murderous scheme was discovered, and in punishment for daring to harm the Shah's property, Khaadija, who once led the mighty ruler by the beard, was dismissed from her lush apartments, stripped of her jewels and finery, and sent to work as a mere palace menial. Only her former standing saved her from death. For her part, Zeenab gleefully heaped scorn on Khaadija.

The Shah loved Zeenab devotedly for several years, but as she aged without bearing him a male heir, he turned his affections to younger women. Fearful of suffering the same fate as the wretched Khaadija, Zeenab sought the aid of doctors and magicians so as to restore her fading youth. But their potions and talismans turned out to be mere chicanery, as worthless as they were costly.

In the midst of despair over her prospects, Zeenab received hopeful word that the great divine and miracle worker of that age, the saintly Abdul Hassan, rumored to be hundreds of years old, had descended from the Afghan mountains with his disciples and was even now passing through Teheran on a pilgrimage to Mecca.

At once Zeenab sent her faithful eunuch, Ali, with gold and precious gems to lavish on the holy man, receiving from him in turn the unusual courtesy of a private audience.

Their words were not recorded, but swayed by her pleas and pleased by her gifts, the saintly Abdul Hassan agreed to restore her youth, for despite his piety and powers, it was said that he was childishly fond of worldly baubles. Yet he warned her sternly of dreadful consequences should there be the slightest deviation from his instructions.

These were obeyed in every detail. At a precise hour of auspicious planetary angles and alignments, Zeenab swallowed a powerful potion that within minutes produced in her a swoon that imitated death in every visible particular. Ointments and talismans were then applied to her inert form. Ritual prayers were recited, and her loyal servants lowered her body into an oval casket of clear crystal where she was to remain sealed for four full days. Day and night they guarded her.

But such a portentous secret was too mighty to keep. Whispered rumors soon ran throughout the palace, eventually reaching the ears of old Khaadija, now a spent, ugly hag, yet still murderous in her hatred of Zeenab.

Then occurred the worst. Despite the vigilance of Zeenab's most trusted servants, Khaadija cunningly slipped past the drowsy guards and opened the casket after only three days. Inside, Zeenab's doll-sized figure stirred and realizing her doom, screamed in a tiny despairing voice, "Too soon! Too soon!" At the sound the servants subdued Khaadija, who dangled the writhing Zeenab by the hair and squealed in evil glee. Then they watched in horrified fascination as Zeenab raced in panic about the shrinking oval until her form commenced to slow. In mid step she turned to stone, unable to speak and imprisoned in the crystal egg. Only her eyes remained pleadingly alert.

Ali hurried after the great Abdul Hassan, who having resumed his journey, was now several leagues removed from Teheran. Informed of the tragedy, the holy man cried out and fell to the ground. "For her folly and my misuse of gifts, she shall remain entombed in living death and her woeful story shall be told as a warning to mortals. May Allah in time or in eternity free her and forgive me. Now I go to face his judgment for my temerity. For he alone holds the key to life and death."

So saying he breathed his last and died with the burden of his sin.

Heed well, o mortals, the story of beautiful Zeenab and what it can teach us about the pride of life.

"Oh, Robert," Brenda said, staring at the tiny figure inside the crystal oval, "it gives me goose bumps just thinking about her. Do you think all that really happened and that she's real, maybe even . . . alive?"

"I don't know. The man who sold it to me swore it was a true story. But he probably said that to all the tourists. He also told me that if you're mean to me, she'll get out of her case and come after you!"

"Have I been mean to you?"

"No, I'll have to say you've been on the plus side of wonderful, and I've never been this happy in my whole life."

"Me too. Do you think Queen Zeenab will be jealous if I kiss you?"

"Maybe, so just to be on the safe side, here, I'll turn her face to the wall."

17.
Buried Treasure

If everybody in Lost River could agree on anything back around 1920, it was that Buddy Ballinger, 21, was the laziest man that ever drew breath. Old Doc Humphrey said he was as worthless as a clock without hands, and storekeeper Edgar Laney added he was so lazy he leaned against a wall to spit. But if Buddy had no stomach for work, he seemed to have two when it came to eating and drinking.

He came from stock that had once been prosperous, but he was living proof of an old adage about the generational rise and fall of families:

The grandfather works and builds;

The father wheels and deals;

The grandson lies and steals.

By the time Buddy's father Henry died in 1922, he had gambled and drunk away nearly all the family's assets. In 1921 young Leon Stokesbury exercised a lien his family held on most of their property, and what few holdings Henry did not squander in his lifetime, Buddy ran through as soon as he took over. In the end only the old ramshackle house and barn and fifteen acres of the poorest farmland remained.

I forgot to mention one dissenting opinion about Buddy. His mother, Ethel Mae, thought Buddy was a perfect son who could do no wrong. Never mind that he would not work, that he lied to everybody, that he stole from neighbors, that he drank and caroused, and that he sassed her. As Ethel Mae saw things, other people were to blame for his low fortunes. She believed that prosperity was his birthright. He was a Ballinger, descended from the Georgia Ballingers, and to her way of thinking, that entitled him to a higher station in life than the common riffraff of Lost River. What other people thought were defects in Buddy's character, she saw as marks of superiority. They were just too low class to recognize them.

"Son," she explained to Buddy, "they can't expect you to work like a common day laborer. Why, the very idea! Your daddy never did field work, and you shouldn't either. That's for hired hands and dirt farmers. We're educated people, and back before the War Between the States, we owned plantations and money and were one of the finer families of the Old South. It pains me to hear you talking like all these low class people around here. That comes from associating with uncouth folks. Your daddy was well-spoken and a pleasant sight to behold, Buddy, a real Southern gentleman always dressed up in fine clothes and tipping his hat to the ladies. And you'll be just like him. Your day will come. Just you wait and see. And then all these low-class people around Lost River will have to eat their hateful words."

Buddy's grandmother, 75-year-old Effie Wedgeworth, shared the old house with her daughter and grandson, but not Ethel Mae's adoring opinion of Buddy and the Ballingers. Miss Effie, as everybody around Lost River called her, saw him for what he was: the worthless son of worthless Henry—God rest his soul. To Ethel Mae's great displeasure and embarrassment, Miss Effie went around telling anyone in the community who cared to listen to her that only a miracle would keep the three of them from ending up in the poorhouse.

Ethel Mae's plan to restore Buddy—and herself—to the economic ease and graceful living of their glory days back in Georgia was to marry him into money and property, namely, to Miss Magnolia Martin, whose daddy, Carl, owned the best land and cattle in the Evergreen community. For once, lazy ole Buddy objected with real energy.

"But, Momma, Magnolia's uglier than a cross-eyed billy goat! For God's sake, I don't know how you could expect me to marry something like that! I'm sick of going over there to see her! She makes me want to puke!"

"Now, Buddy, you just calm down and think about it. It's true, it's true, I'll admit it. Magnolia's not the prettiest girl around. But she's clean and decent, and with good clothes and some rouge and paint and done up hair, why any woman's already half pretty. And who else are you going to find around here with her kind of money and land? If you had acted better, you might have had a chance with Buell Hardin's daughter. Now she's as pretty as they come, and the Hardins have money. But you ruined your chances with her by showing up intoxicated at her party. If we lived in a decent community, like where I was born in Georgia, you could have your pick of girls with good dowries, but people around here are too low class to offer what you deserve."

"Lordy, I don't know why any girl, ugly or not, would want to marry anybody as sorry as Buddy," Miss Effie mused out loud to herself, "any more than I ever understood what you saw in that worthless Henry—God rest his lazy soul."

She and Ethel Mae didn't argue about Buddy—or Henry—anymore.

They had agreed years earlier that neither would ever persuade the other to change her mind.

Buddy grumbled and fumed, but since he knew his mother was right about Magnolia, he saddled old Red that evening and, putting himself in a sacrificial mood, rode off again down Lost River Road toward Evergreen and Miss Magnolia.

His visits to Magnolia were always short, just long enough to eat a hearty meal and chat a bit with Mr. Martin about crops and the weather, the two things besides Magnolia that Buddy cared least about in the whole world. Just the thought of planting and plowing made him tired. To Magnolia's shy invitation for him to stay longer, Buddy explained that he had a lot of things to do tomorrow. (Buddy always talked about his busy tomorrows that always turned out to be idle todays.) He hinted broadly that he was settling some business matters so that he could make big changes in his life. Delighted by the insinuation, which she translated into dreams of marital bliss, Magnolia accompanied him out to the porch. There she blushingly told Buddy that since her daddy had accepted him as her suitor, now it would be all right for him to kiss her. Buddy declined the favor, explaining that her folks might be watching them out the window and he wanted to show the proper respect.

To wash the bad taste of the evening out of his mouth, he stopped on the way home to do some drinking with the Sellars brothers, Calvin and Hiram. Buddy made it over to Evergreen as seldom as he could, but he went several times a week to drink with Calvin and Hiram in a shack at the foot of the mountain. Being of the higher class himself, Buddy secretly looked down on the brothers, but he put up with their disrespectful ways, including their jokes about his forced romance with Magnolia, because of the good whiskey they made.

That night the vision of Magnolia was particularly mortifying, especially after what his mother had said. It was close to midnight when Buddy staggered out to Red with more than a pint of Sellars moonshine whiskey sloshing around in his stomach.

He had not gone far when Red shied away from something out in the woods and almost threw Buddy off. He caught sight of something out of the corner of his eye, but when he looked straight it was gone. It happened again and Red refused to go any further. Cursing, Buddy dismounted and pulled on the bridle reins, but the horse planted its feet and would not budge. Then suddenly Red neighed, jerked the reins from Buddy's grip, and galloped away down the road toward Lost River. That's when Buddy saw plainly what had frightened it.

A young woman was standing at the edge of the road beside a big oak tree, with her arms outstretched to Buddy. Even in his drunken haze, he could see an unnatural luminous glow around her, and his first thought was that he was seeing something that human eyes were not meant to see. The apparition came nearer, but not with any apparent physical motion. Somehow she was just closer now. Buddy could feel the hair standing up on his neck. The woods on both sides of the road were as still as a tomb. Even the crickets were silent.

"Who . . . who . . . are you?" he stammered in terror.

The young woman did not answer.

"What do you want?"

At first there was no sound. Then as though her voice came from inside his head, he heard her say, "My treasure, bring me my treasure!"

Despite his terror, the mention of treasure struck a chord in Buddy's besotted mind.

"Well, tell me, where is your treasure?"

At first there was no answer. Then he heard her repeat, "Bring me my treasure!"

The apparition then began to waver and fade, and as she did so, the trees around Buddy seemed to undergo a subtle change. Some were gone and others appeared in their place. Features appeared and shifted their shape. Everything seemed fluid, as though one reality were being superimposed on another. He realized he was seeing double. It's the whiskey, he thought with a sense of relief. But what about that woman?

"It was no woman, nothing," he said out loud. "Just me seeing things. I've been drinking too much lately, trying to forget all that ugly business with Magnolia. I need to ease off some. Damn horse! Some varmint must've spooked him, maybe a bobcat. Now I'll have to walk home!"

Red was waiting at the barn when Buddy trudged in more than an hour later.

He was so shaken by the strange experience and worn out by the two-mile walk that he stayed away from the Sellars brothers' whiskey for, oh, maybe two or three whole days. But then thirst overcame his resolve and, convinced that what he saw was nothing, that night he rode back to their shack to get drunk with Calvin and Hiram.

Since he had been dry so long, Buddy drank more than usual that night, all the while cursing his bad fortune as the disrespectful brothers hooted and made nasty jokes about his getting yoked up with Magnolia.

On the way home late that night, the luminous apparition confronted him again. Buddy was so drunk that he fell off when Red veered suddenly and ran away up the road toward home.

"Who are you? What do you want with me?" he mumbled, staggering to his feet.

There was no sound at first. The figure stood beside the same oak tree as the time before. Then he heard a voice inside his head.

"Bring me my treasure!" After a moment, as she faded away, he heard what sounded like an echo: "Bring me my treasure."

Buddy was cold sober and truly scared by the time he walked home. He was so shaken that he was awake and out of bed by noon the next day. It was not like Buddy to rise so early. Ethel Mae asked if he was sick.

"No, Momma, I'm not sick of body, just of things in general. And I can tell you this: I am not going back to Evergreen! I don't know if I'll ever go down that road again! Far as I'm concerned, Magnolia can stick her land and cattle you know where!"

"Buddy, don't talk like that. Did you have a quarrel with Magnolia?"

"No, it's got nothing to do with Magnolia!"

"Then why . . .?" she started to say.

Buddy walked away, refusing to tell worried Ethel Mae the reasons behind his decision. Instead he went out to where Miss Effie was digging in the garden, and even bent over to pull up a weed. She straightened up in surprise and leaned on her hoe.

"Lordy, Buddy, you might rupture yourself! You need to be careful about straining so much. You're not used to working."

"Grandma," he asked, staring at the weed and ignoring her sarcasm, "do you believe in ghosts, haints, some call the spirits around here?"

"Why, I don't know, haven't thought much about such things," she said, surprised and pleased that Buddy would say anything to her. "A lot of folks do though. But then a lot of folks are ignorant. Why do you ask?"

"I think I've seen one, Grandma. Twice now."

He told her about the apparition on the road to Evergreen.

"Well, Buddy," she said when he finished, "it could be that rotgut whiskey you've been drinking with Calvin and Hiram. And if it is and you don't put a stop to it, you'll be seeing things a lot worse. You need to stop keeping company with people like that."

"But what if it's not that? What if I really did see something'?"

"Well, then, if I were you, I'd consider two things. First, the old folks used to say that when a body gets close to the end of natural life in this world, supernatural things from the other side start appearing to him. So, it could mean that if you don't mend your ways, you won't be long for this world."

"And what's the other thing?" Buddy asked, tossing the weed out of the garden.

"They say that if a spirit, or ghost, or whatever you call it, asks you to do something, you need to do it, if you can. Otherwise, they'll keep pestering you. And if you don't help them, they can even do you harm. Spirits aren't very smart, they say, just obsessed with something that troubled them in this life. So

138

what I'd say, Buddy, is that if she comes to you again, you'd better do what she says."

"Well, I told you what it—the woman—said; something about a 'treasure.' But I don't know anything about a treasure. Have you ever heard anything like that around here?"

"Once I did, way back when I was new to this country, come to think of it. But it's been so long I've almost forgotten the story."

"Well, what was it? Was it about that—woman—I saw down out on the road?"

"Well, Buddy, I don't know that for a fact. But folks used to tell how late at night on close to where the Lost River Road and the Barkley Road fork, they would meet up with a young woman like you describe. But that was forty or fifty years ago before they cut the new road. I haven't heard any talk like that since. Back then some people claimed they recognized her and remembered when she was a living person."

"A living person? Then who was she—or is she?"

"Her name, so they told me, was Rebecca Day. They said she was about nineteen when she died. I don't know much more about her or her folks except that some of the Days were prosperous and there was a settlement somewhere over there named for them. It was called Day's Gap, before the War Between the States. Afterwards it died out and folks moved away. I think the Yankees and Confederates fought a battle there."

"What happened to her?"

"A lot of federal soldiers were wounded, but the Confederates were in such hot pursuit that the Yankees were forced to leave them behind. They provided for them as best they could with blankets, water, and a little food. But everybody knew they probably wouldn't survive. If their wounds or wild animals didn't finish them off, outlaw bands and Confederate sympathizers would. The lucky ones died on the battlefield."

"What's that got to do with the Day girl?"

"That's the real story, Buddy. The Day girl found one of the wounded Yankee soldiers and nursed him back to health. In the process, they fell in love and Rebecca had a child by him. There were no men folk around, just Rebecca and her mother, who died not long after. Her father and brother fled south with the Yankees. They say the Day family were Northern sympathizers, like many folks around this region.

"A year later, the Home Guard rode up from the south. They claimed to represent the Confederacy, but a lot of them were deserters, murderers, and thieves. When they found Rebecca living with a Yankee and mother to his child, they killed all three and looted and burned the house, or so I was told."

"You said the Days were prosperous. Do you think they had gold or money buried around the house somewhere? Maybe that's what the girl was trying to tell me."

"I said some of them were prosperous, Buddy. Maybe Rebecca's family was, but I don't see what good it would do her now."

"Does anybody know where the old house was located?"

"I don't know. I doubt it. Woods have probably covered it over. Maybe Calvin and Hiram would know something. It was down there somewhere close to them. But, Buddy, if you're thinking of doing what I think you are, you be careful. You're tampering with things better left alone. And another thing, you'd better stay away from that whiskey!"

Miss Effie was right in her suspicions. To Ethel Mae's surprise, the next day Buddy was up and about even earlier. He packed some food and a jug of water, tied a pick, shovel, and axe to Red's saddle, and headed off toward Evergreen. He was afraid of what of he might find, but more concerned about what he might miss if he did not search.

Buddy had no trouble finding the oak tree where the specter had appeared, but Calvin and Hiram knew nothing about an old home site. They found it hard to believe that Buddy rode off after only a few swigs.

"Now, I don't know what to make of that. Not like him at all," Calvin said. "And what do you reckon he's doing with the tools? And all his fool questions about some old house, what was that all about?"

"I don't know," Hiram responded. "Maybe there's something wrong with him. You know he's been drinking a lot here lately. Maybe it's affecting his mind. Or," he grinned, "maybe he's just planning to dig a hole to hide in so he won't have to marry Miss Magnolia."

The brothers had their best laugh of the day at the thought.

For two days Buddy rode or walked over half of the west end of the county before he found the scattered rocks of a demolished chimney close to what appeared to be an old road bed. He dug around in the leaves and roots and found enough glass and scraps of iron to convince him that a house had once stood on the spot.

Buddy tied Red to a hickory sapling and started digging in earnest for the treasure. His flabby muscles quivered with exhaustion, but his greed drove him on. After three days and aches in every joint, he had almost completed a ring of diggings around the house. It was late and he was about to quit for the day, when he saw the apparitions.

For this time there were two: the now familiar image of the woman and the taller shape of a man. Red neighed and rolled his big eyes in terror but did not break the reins.

As for Buddy, he felt calmer this time, and without the whiskey was able to think about what he was doing. There was a hush all around. The crickets and katydids were silent.

"I know who you are. What do you want me to do? Tell me and I'll help you." The apparitions said nothing but moved soundlessly at his words towards the old road. Buddy picked up the shovel and followed them. Maybe they're leading me to the treasure, he thought with an upsurge of greed.

The apparitions stopped and pointed to a small mound. Carefully Buddy dug into it. His shovel struck something—a rotten edge of a wooden container. It crumbled to dust on impact and a sliver of a bone fell out, then another. The apparitions glided closer as though anxious, waiting. Despite his repeated reassurances to himself that he was safe with them, the hair rose on the nape of his neck.

When he completed the digging, he had what he was sure were the scattered remains of a child's skeleton. He took his shirt off, placed all the bone fragments he could find in it, and turned to the hovering, glowing, anxious specters. They moved away and Buddy understood that he was to follow. They came to two mounds below the house site and stopped, and Buddy knew he was to rebury the child there. With them. For surely these were their graves.

He finished and the specters retreated. Only now there were three: the girl, a man, and a child. Finally, they were together again. As Buddy watched, they rose and faded from view, and Buddy knew he would not see them again. The crickets and katydids resumed their singing.

The next day some curious people found where Buddy had dug up the old house site, and gossip spread around Lost River and Evergreen that he had found a buried treasure. The size of it was exaggerated with every telling.

"Well, Buddy, what about it?" Miss Effie asked him late that afternoon. "Did you find the treasure, like people are saying?"

Buddy was still so tired and stiff he could barely move.

"Yeah, I found it, Grandma," he said softly.

"Well, what was it and where is it?"

"It's gone, Grandma. It was not mine to keep, only to give back."

"Then what was it and who has it?"

"It was better than gold. It was a lesson, and it's where it was always supposed to be."

Buddy never did tell Miss Effie or anyone everything he saw and learned. But in the coming weeks and months it was plain that whatever it was had changed his life. He drank no more of the Sellars brothers' whiskey, itself something of a minor marvel, and he broke off his engagement to Miss Magnolia.

But it was when he hitched Red to a rusty old turning plow and started farming his land that Lost River folks almost fainted from the shock. It was hard, but he battled back and saved the family from ruin. A couple of years later he was married—this time by his own wish—to Miss Thelma Thigpen of the Fairview community.

Ethel Mae had trouble adjusting to the laboring status Buddy had assumed, but she took some comfort in the fact that in time she was able to buy new shoes and dress more in keeping with a refined lady of her class. And as the grandchildren started coming, she got busy teaching them high class things, especially about the Ballingers and their glory days back in Georgia.

As for Miss Effie, she went around Lost River saying to anyone who cared to listen to her: "I always said it would take a miracle to keep us out of the poorhouse. Well, a miracle of some kind is exactly what happened to Buddy down there by the mountain."

18.
Swapping Places

As far as I know, old Bascomb Barker was the only man in our part of the state buried in two graves in two different counties. In 1910 he was interred in the Lost River Cemetery, and in 1925, I believe it was, the same man was laid to rest in the Evergreen Graveyard. But if there was confusion about the year and place of his passing, there was none about his birthday. He always said he was born in East Tennessee on July 8, 1840, and had an old family Bible to prove it.

Now everybody knows that it's impossible for a living person, and more so a dead one, to be in two places at the same time. And just in case you have already surmised that one of the graves must be empty, trustworthy witnesses swore to me years ago that both tombs contain a casket and a corpse. Let me tell you how it all came about.

After his wife, Hazel Stokesbury Barker, died childless in 1899, Bascomb sold his place in Evergreen and moved into a log hut up on the mountain south of town and for ten years or so lived as a virtual hermit, eating food that would make a possum puke. Except for some distant kinfolk in Tennessee with whom he had long since lost contact, his only relative was a nephew, Cletus Forsythe, who lived in Lost River with wife, Daisy.

One August day Bascomb drove his one-horse wagon twelve or fifteen miles to his nephew's house and told the startled Cletus that he was dying.

"I'm needing some help, son. I won't trouble you much for long. All I need is to make a few arrangements for my funeral."

(Bascomb always called Cletus "son," even though they were nearly the same age.)

Cletus gave Uncle Bascomb the customary false reassurance that he would live many more years. But the truth was that the last thing the stingy nephew wanted on his hands was the dead expense of supporting a live uncle. Still, under the circumstances he had no choice but to help Uncle Bascomb into the house and put him in the spare bed.

As soon as she found out, Daisy stormed in from hanging wet clothes on the clothesline and made her disapproval loud and clear.

"Cletus, just what in hell are you thinking about? Bascomb's nothing to us, and certainly nothing to me! I can't take care of a sick man. He claims he's dying, but he might just be lying to get us to take him in and wait on him hand and foot. Now you just get him out of my bed and put him back in that wagon. If he was well enough to drive down here, he can drive back to the mountain, or to hell for all I care!"

"Hush, woman, he might hear you raring and carrying on."

"Well, you know what, Cletus, I don't give a damn whether he hears me or not! That's what I said and that's what I mean. Times are hard enough without another aggravation like Bascomb. You don't owe that old goat anything. Some uncle he's been. What's he ever done for you, or your momma, his own sister, when she was alive and suffering?"

Cletus had no rebuttal to her arguments. Bascomb had always been stingy like everybody else in the family. Still he didn't have the heart to turn his uncle away.

For his part, Bascomb, who had listened to Daisy's rant, reassured his nephew that he was not long for this world.

"Son, my time's up. I feel it coming. It started out like a chill in my hands and feet and now it's working its way all over my body. You tell Daisy not to worry about having to take care of me, you hear?"

"Uncle Bascomb," Cletus replied, hanging his head, "I'm real sorry you heard all that, but you know when Daisy gets started with her raring and pitching, the only way to shut her up would be to shoot her, and I'm still just a little ways from being ready to do that."

"Aw, don't you worry about her fretting, son. Women are all like that. It's just that Daisy's more open about it than most. It's nothing personal with me. Fact is, at this point, I have just one or two little things that concern me, and if you'll promise to help me out, you and Daisy will be shed of me real soon."

"Well, Uncle Bascomb, you know you can count on me. Uh, what is it you want me to do?" Cletus asked, fearful that his request might involve some kind of out-of-pocket expense.

"Here's what I need from you, son, and it's not much. Hazel always had me a nice suit of clothes ready just in case the Lord called me—and probably hoping he would. But after she passed on, well, I guess I wore it out trying to catch me that Wilhite widow woman. And you know how that turned out for me. She ran off with that slick-talking Tennessee salesman and twenty-five dollars of my money. But here's the thing, Cletus. I got me five hundred dollars here in my pocketbook, all I got to my name, except a few sticks of furniture in my cabin and this old horse and wagon. And I reckon I'm leaving it all to you, son, if you'll help me out. What I want you to do is buy me a suit of clothes to be buried in. And I reckon you can bury me next to Hazel over yonder in Evergreen, though Lord knows she was a pure aggravation of a woman."

Cletus tried hard to keep a somber face, but the news that Bascomb had cash money brightened his spirits and he swore on his mother's honor that he would carry out his uncle's instructions to the letter.

"Lord strike me dead if I don't keep my promise to you."

The very next morning Bascomb was stiff as a board and Cletus could detect no breath or pulse in him. He was getting ready to go buy a suit at the general store when Daisy stopped him.

"Cletus, are you crazy? You're going to waste good money on a suit just so it can rot in the ground? Bascomb'll have no use for a suit where he's going, but we're going to need that money!"

"But I promised him I would," Cletus protested weakly.

"Well, that was just to comfort a dying man, but we're still in the land of the living, and the living have got to come first."

"What will folks say if we bury him in his old clothes?"

"Well, nobody knows about the promise you made, and Bascomb's not going to say anything to anybody. And we're sure not either. Now here's what we'll do: you still got that old suit you wore when your momma died. You and Bascomb are about the same size, so we'll bury him in it and save the money for better use. Lord knows we got more need for it than a dead man."

Her logic and their shared stinginess won out over Cletus's pious promises. Thus it came to pass that, laid out in Cletus' old suit, Bascomb was conveyed in his one-horse wagon to what was to be his final resting place next to Hazel in the Evergreen Cemetery.

Howard Blakely, his two half-grown sons, and Miles Adams, all of whom lived next to the cemetery and for a modest consideration customarily helped dig most of the graves and make the pine board caskets if need be, swore that what I am about to tell you is the truth.

The day was blistering hot and Daisy sat on a shaded bench fanning herself as Cletus, Howard, Miles, and the boys put ropes under the pine box casket and lowered it into the ground. Cletus, exhausted from the heat and the digging, was leaning on his shovel with his back to the grave. As Howard shoveled the first dirt on the casket, the clatter of the gravel together with

Bascomb's stout constitution roused him from his catatonic state induced by severe food poisoning brought on by a mess of tainted pork. The men gasped as the coffin lid popped open and the indignant Bascomb stood up and confronted his horrified nephew.

"Cletus, where's my new suit of clothes? You lied to me! You promised to buy me a new suit, and here you have buried me in these old rags!"

The sight of his resurrected and outraged uncle was too much for Cletus. His face turned beet-red; he tottered and croaked incoherently, then fell and rolled, shovel and all, into the grave. When the men rushed to pull him out, he was dead. Daisy came running, but Howard and his sons stopped her and led her back to the bench with consoling words. Meanwhile, Bascomb stepped over Cletus and with a hand from Miles clambered out of the grave and brushed the dirt from his face and hair. He was still groggy and indignant when Daisy came to explain things to him.

"I told him, Bascomb, that he was wrong to do what he schemed up. Lord forgive him. I told him as plain as day to go buy that suit just like he promised. You know me; I say things the way I see them. I had my doubts when you showed up at our house, claiming to be at death's door, and I don't hide my feelings as you know. But a solemn promise is one a body keeps, particularly to somebody that's dying, or appears to be."

"Well, at least I can still get my money back," Bascomb said as his anger subsided. "I guess it worked out all right for me. Didn't need the suit anyway as it turned out. But now we got Cletus on our hands. What are you going to do with him, Daisy?"

"Well, Bascomb, being that we, you and me, are his only living kin, I reckon it's up to us to decide."

"What you all want us to do with the grave?" asked Howard. "Want us to fill it back up?"

"That is a problem, but I'd say that since we have a dug grave and a dead man, we might as well go ahead and bury him in it. It's just a matter of swapping places with him. What do you think, Daisy?"

"Lordy mercy, it's just too much for me to think about in my grief," Daisy replied, putting her fan aside and wiping her face with her handkerchief. "Bascomb, you're the man of the family now, so you decide. Of course, if we don't bury him today, I reckon we'll have to come back tomorrow anyway and grieve twice over my dear sweet husband."

And so it was decided in the most expedient way. The men carried Cletus down into the woods so that he and Bascomb could change clothing. Bascomb was happy to find his pocketbook with the five hundred dollars. The task completed and a few Bible verses read, they lowered Cletus, dressed in his old suit, thereby condemning him to rest eternally next to nagging Hazel.

145

Better him than me, Bascomb thought, and it serves him right for what he meant to do.

Afterwards, Bascomb accompanied the grieving Daisy to her home and stayed a few days to comfort her. Being the strong woman that she was and relieved to learn that Bascomb had rescued his money, Daisy soon overcame her grief and, lacking other family members, became quite caring and solicitous of Bascomb. Indeed, their cordial bond grew into affection, and affection became such closeness that just as Cletus had taken his spot next to Hazel, so Bascomb took his place with Daisy, sharing her bed and board. He allowed that even though neither experience was anything special, at least Daisy's cooking was a shade better than what he had gotten used to up on the mountain.

There he remained until death called a second and final time in 1925, this time in Lost River. But even though they dug two graves in two different graveyards for Bascomb—and buried a body in both— he was destined never to have a new suit of clothes for either burial.

"Now I ask you," Daisy confided to her friend Lizzie Snodgrass, "what good would a new suit of clothes do a dead man? I know Bascomb wanted one, and I promised I'd get it for him. But that was just to comfort the dying. I'm still in the land of the living, and the living has to come first."

19.
The Resurrection of Theotis Marlow

For ten years or more in the 1920s and 30s, Theotis Marlow of Lost River studied his King James Bible verse by verse, inside and out, backwards and forwards. Wary of contamination by devilish modern teaching, Theotis read nothing but the Bible, consulted no scholarly commentaries, and listened to no seminary-trained preachers' exegesis of the Scriptures.

Then one July day in 1937, he closed his Bible, gathered his family and kin, and told them that the Lord had revealed to him the key to biblical prophecy and the time and sequence of end-time events.

By the strength of his convictions and the weakness of theirs, Theotis gathered around him a small group of believers in his teachings and founded the Bible Church of the Resurrection.

Not that there was anything strange about another Bible-based church in Southern Appalachia. Nearly every church around claimed to be nothing less and nothing more. The difference was that Theotis not only gave specific dates for end-time events but revealed that, as a sign to the flock and the doubting world, he himself would die and return to life in three days.

Never mind that several of his predictions did not come to pass on time—earthquakes, pestilences, the appearance of the Beast and the Four Horsemen of the Apocalypse—discrepancies which Theotis said could be accounted for by tweaking his biblical arithmetic. But he hit on a few—war in Europe, storms and floods in America, and most of all, the rebirth of Israel in 1948. It was enough to establish his reputation as a prophet, and in prophecy, one hit will cause folks to overlook a dozen misses.

By the end of World War II his flock had grown to seventy-something families, and would have exceeded a hundred if some believers had not questioned his teachings and gotten themselves disfellowshipped for heresy.

Israel was his most convincing prophecy and led to a surge in church membership. By 1949 the congregation had grown to nearly three hundred families and a tripling of revenues. And Theotis and his family prospered apace with church growth. Whereas in earlier years he drove the family to church in a two-horse wagon and preached in his overalls, now he wore a suit and tie and drove a new chrome-laden black Buick. His wife, Thelma, who quickly forgot the floursack dresses and barefoot days of the Depression, now bought her clothes in Knoxville and Chattanooga. She often cast a longing eye on fine jewelry, but Theotis taught that such adornments were an abomination and forbade them in his house and church.

But no such prohibition applied to food. In earlier times Thelma was lucky if she could scrounge up a meager fare of cornbread and turnip greens, but now her larder bulged with the most select hams, eggs, roasts, desserts, and bakery breads that money could buy. Lean to the point of gauntness in their years of poverty, Theotis and Thelma expanded in girth as their income grew. There was some grumbling from the congregation that their children, Matthew, 18, and Mildred, 16, were beginning to run wild with money and cars of their own. For their part, however, Theotis and Thelma believed they had more important things to do than look after their offspring, and nobody had the courage to call their hand in the matter.

Then in the midst of their spiraling prosperity, calamity struck. Although Theotis believed he could prophesy the end of time and history, he did not foresee his own demise. One day his overworked heart failed and on his deathbed he repeated his oldest prophecy.

"Three days after you bury me," he told his weeping family and followers, "you'll see me sitting out yonder on that bench by the graveyard where I always like to sit and pray. And I'll be eating the food and drinking the water that I'll ask you to put there for me. For just like the Lord ate real food to show the Disciples that he was flesh and blood and not just a spirit or ghost, so you'll see me doing the same. But don't you get too close. You remember how the Lord told Mary Magdalene not to touch him. You'll be in the presence of miracle-working power, and it's not something to play around with."

"Will you come back then to stay with us?" asked one of the deacons.

"Maybe just for a little bit, for the Lord is calling me to his work in Heaven. But you'll see me and it will do away with any doubts. And one of these days you'll follow me in the Resurrection if you keep the faith as I've been telling you all this time."

Shortly thereafter Theotis breathed his last, and the family and flock wept and mourned as if he were gone forever and not just for three days.

Two days passed and on the third day, by coincidence a Sunday, many of the congregation hid in the bushes across from the graveyard. And lo and behold, as the darkness began to lift they saw a reclining figure on the bench suddenly sit up. "Theotis!" they whispered in awe. Then in hypnotic, terrified fascination they watched as he drank from the water jug and took food from the covered basket the women had left there for him. Woman fainted and men fell to their knees in prayer and praise.

At that moment, though, Thelma screamed out Theotis's name and ran across the graveyard towards him. Theotis looked up and with an incoherent yell, the meaning of which the deacons would debate theologically for many years afterward, disappeared into the bushes and was never seen again.

There are always doubters. Some suggested that after it got light enough to make features, the man didn't look exactly like Theotis. Old Judd Minter even came right out and said that the whole matter could be settled for sure by opening the grave to see if Theotis was there or not. But others reminded him that no judge would grant permission to exhume a body unless there were pressing legal reasons to do so. And Theotis always taught them to stay clear of the world's legal system. In any case, even if Theotis's mortal remains were still in the grave, which they doubted, a hundred eyewitnesses had seen his heavenly body and would swear to it on a stack of bibles a mile high.

Some members of the congregation held it against Thelma that she had done exactly what Theotis had warned them not to do. If she hadn't run screaming across the graveyard, maybe Theotis would have stayed a while to talk to them and offer guidance and comfort. But, after all, they reasoned, she was a grieving widow and eventually all forgave her impetuous act.

News of the resurrection spread far and wide, and people came from the hills miles around to swell the congregation and the coffers. Several small churches had to close because of it.

Since Theotis had told them that he would linger only briefly before going on to the hereafter, the deacons realized that something had to be done quickly about a preacher. As George Payne put it, "Men, we have to dig us up a preacher right away." Then realizing what he had said, he qualified it, "I didn't mean that the way it sounded, but somebody's got to take Theotis's place."

Two days later, following long discussions, a delegation of deacons finally found Matthew parked in his shiny Ford coupe with friendly Vera Murray. After saying howdy to Miss Vera and asking how her folks were, they explained to Matthew that they needed to talk him about some church business. Miss Vera took it as a signal and excused herself and went home while Matthew girded up is spiritual loins and accompanied the deacons to church to take on the Lord's business.

If Theotis was a good teacher, Matthew turned out to be a better preacher. The father sowed the seeds of prophecy but it was the son who reaped the truly bountiful harvest. Under his leadership, the Church of the Resurrection soon became the largest congregation in east Stokesbury County. On any Sunday morning cars and pickups—and a few remaining farm wagons—were parked all across church property and nearly a half mile along the sides of the dirt road leading to it.

Matthew referred at times to Theotis's successful prophecies and especially his miraculous reappearance, but he did not add any of his own. His exciting rhetoric and powerful metaphorical style so roused the enthusiastic congregation that Matthew expanded his ministry to radio and later to television. He became a household name, and the Bible Church of the Resurrection, which eventually outgrew its country origins, moved to Atlanta and became one of the largest megachurches in the South.

***

In the wee morning hours before the congregation came out to await and hopefully to witness the resurrection that Theotis had predicted, disreputable ole Sonny Miller was reeling along the road back toward Kentucky. Cold, hungry, hung over, and head throbbing from a three-day drunk, he happened to spot the cemetery bench on which—hot diggidy!—somebody had left a basket of food and a jug of water. Seizing the jug with shaking hands, Sonny gurgled down nearly a third of its contents, then devoured a thick slice of ham. A minute later his shriveled stomach rebelled and it almost came back up on him. He set the food and water aside and stretched out, shaking, on the bench. It was cold, but oh man, he just had to rest a while. Mercifully, in a minute he was asleep.

A couple of hours later something stirred in the bushes across the cemetery and woke him. Light was growing in the east. Sonny sat up and took another swig from the jug as he peered into the darkness to see what had roused him. He was about to eat more ham when a figure screamed and came running across the graveyard toward him. Behind it he spied other moving shapes. To his horror, he saw what must have been a hundred sets of eyes watching him. All Sonny could think of was a graveyard, ghosts and spirits, and one of them was coming to get him.

If ever there was a time to haul ass, Sonny thought in his terror, this was it. He yelled, dropped the ham, and ran for his life into the woods. The adrenaline flowed through his tired limbs, tree branches and bushes slapped him in the face, he stumbled and staggered, but ole Sonny did not stop till he had put all the distance he could between himself and the things he had seen in the graveyard.

Later, back home in Kentucky, he told his story to his drinking buddies.

"I'm telling you, boys, there really are ghosts and spirits. I've seen them up close. They're real. And I wouldn't go back to that graveyard for a case of the best sipping whiskey in Kentucky."

"Sonny," one of them laughed, "it's a wonder you're not seeing worse things than spirits in a graveyard, which I'm not believing in the first place, you understand. But you keep on drinking the way you have these last few months and you'll start having the tremens and seeing pink elephants and purple snakes coming out of the wall."

Despite the doubters, ole Sonny knew what he had seen with his own two eyes, and stuck to his story even if everybody laughed about what they considered to be his drunken delusions. If in time he learned better than to talk about it with skeptical people, he never forgot the experience. The memory of it made him start thinking seriously of mending his ways and making some changes in his life.

The last I heard of Sonny, he had curbed his drinking, gotten a steady job, and was trying to make something out of himself. How far all that went, I couldn't say for sure. I only hope he made it.

20.
Miracle in Meridian

Possessing a fabulous memory but a skeptical spirit, Barnabas B. Pritchard, 27, a native of Lost River, knew by heart every verse of the King James Bible and believed not a single one of them.

But despite his invincible skepticism, BB, as he was called, used his remarkable talent to support himself and his vices. For a few years in the late 1940s and 50s, he roamed through small towns across the South and Southwest, showing off his ability to Saturday crowds.

His style was dramatic. Striding briskly to the top of the courthouse steps or other public venue to address the milling crowds gathered to hear the iterant preacher of the day, he would hold up his Bible and thunder forth in his baritone voice.

"Brothers and sisters in Christ and all you unsaved, hear my words! My name is BB Pritchard and the Lord worked a miracle in my life by giving me the gift of memory! All my life from my earliest years I have been able to recite by heart each and every verse in this King James Bible! Yes, my doubting friends, by heart, from Genesis to Revelation I can instantly tell you any verse you ask me! Probably you doubt my words, for no one without God's help can remember the whole Bible. But test me, you brothers in Christ and unbelievers alike. Here, I'll ask this brother to hold my Bible while you test me so that you may come to believe in the power of the Holy Ghost!"

And test him they did. From the Old Testament's most obscure verses to the most complicated writings of the New, they tried their best—and worst—to trip and trick him. But BB prevailed in every test they put him to. Some suspected he was receiving a secret signal from a confederate in the crowd. So he let the skeptics blindfold him. The results, verified by those with Bibles, were the same: with infallible memory he recited every verse without missing a beat or stumbling over a word.

Most were convinced and marveled at his gift, while others, impressed but suspicious, murmured that the Old Devil himself had to be behind such a display. Still others rebuked them, asking how it would serve Hell's purposes to have the Word of God proclaimed publicly with inerrant accuracy. As they fell to bickering amongst themselves, BB asked the brother holding his Bible to pass a hat while the mood was still favorable. He had done all he could with the crowd. His gift, which most took to be a curiosity, could take him no further.

The collection was nearly always disappointingly small. His audiences were usually farmers or idlers with little cash in their pockets. A meal or two, a drink of whiskey now and then, a few unlucky rolls of the dice, a flower or gift of candy for a pretty girl, and the meager contributions were gone.

And so was BB, on to the next town and next crowd. A few times local churches asked him to give a sermon. But he could not organize and make sense of the passages that flooded his mind. He could remember them; he could not understand them. No church ever invited him again.

In June of 1955 after a particularly disappointing Saturday appearance in Bolivar, Tennessee, he was waiting at the bus station for the eastbound Greyhound when a man in a suit and tie approached him.

"Mr. Pritchard?" he asked in a Northern accent. "BB Pritchard, I believe? I was at the gathering down at the courthouse."

"Yeah, that's me," BB answered, wondering if the stranger would flash a badge at him for some infraction. "Something I can do for you?"

"The question, Mr. Pritchard, is what I can do for you. My name is

Lawrence Curtis, Larry, they call me back in Ohio," he said, flashing a toothy smile and shaking hands with the startled BB. "Where you headed?"

"Over towards Pulaski, I reckon, Mr. Curtis. After that, I'm not sure which way I'll head."

"Well, BB—and let's drop the misters—I saw your 'gift,' as you call it, and what you did with that crowd today. Let me say I was impressed, so impressed, in fact, that I just may have a business deal for you."

"What kind of a deal?" BB asked cautiously.

"Tell you what, I'm staying in Pulaski myself for a couple of days and you can ride over there with me in my car. Save yourself the bus fare, and if you want to, I'll even put you up in a nice place for the night. It didn't look like you did much good out there today."

"No, it was pretty bad. Been having a run of bad luck lately. Times are changing, I guess. Country people don't flock into town on Saturdays the way they used to. Getting to where everybody's got a car and can come and go whenever they take a notion."

"Well, you're right, things are changing. If you don't mind my saying so, BB, you've got a great gift, an amazing talent, but you need to change some things to keep up with the times, upgrade your act, as they say in show business, and I'm the one to help you do it. BB, we could be talking big money here. Interested?"

"I'll listen."

He did. By the time they got to Pulaski, BB was more than just interested, and after a good meal, a few drinks, and a night's lodging at Larry's expense, he was convinced.

"Here's the way we'll work it," Larry explained. "You've got the gift of memory, but that doesn't get you very far. What you need is something really special, something that will knock the socks off a crowd. BB, what you need is a miracle!"

"Hey, wait a minute, Larry. I don't know how in hell I could come up with one. I'm not a miracle worker, never claimed to be."

"You don't have to be. That's where I come in, or more exactly where my people come in."

"Your people? Who are they?"

"They're the people you're going to heal, that's who. BB, you're going to have a healing ministry!"

"Hey, hold on, Larry. I don't have a healing gift. I couldn't heal a dog of fleas. And I found out that I can't preach a lick. All I can do is recite verses of Scripture by heart, but I don't know what they mean a lot of times, and to be honest about it, I don't give a hoot what they mean."

"That's just it, BB. You don't need a healing gift. All you need is a crowd or congregation with enough plants in it to work the people into a religious lather—and a generous, giving mood. What I mean by 'plants' is people you'll 'cure' of different diseases by the laying on of hands: blindness, deafness, paralysis, cancer, TB, palsy, and the like. Except, BB, there's nothing wrong with them. It's all a show, a sham, as innocent as a cowboy movie where they kill off all the bad guys and then when it's over all the actors get up and have lunch and a beer together. But we won't overdo the healing; just a few at each service to tease the crowd and keep people coming back. As for the preaching, you have a good voice. All you need on that side of the ledger are a few stock sermons memorized and practiced. That shouldn't be hard for you. Besides, people will come primarily to see miracles, not listen to long-winded sermons."

"I expect you're right about that. As for remembering some sermons, if somebody writes them down, I can memorize anything in a few minutes and I never forget it."

"Amazing. Now here's the plan, BB. First off, no more BB. It's not dignified enough. And we need to get you some better clothes. By the way, what do the initials BB stand for?"

"Barnabas."

"And the other B?"

"Nothing, just B. My parents wanted me to have a middle name but they couldn't agree on one. So they just left me with a B instead of a name."

"No problem. From now on you'll be the Reverend Barnabas B. Pritchard. Okay?"

"Well, go easy on the 'reverend' stuff. I'm not an ordained preacher."

"You are now. I just ordained you," chuckled Larry, flashing his big smile. "Don't worry about it, man. Being a preacher is kind of like being a mechanic. If you call yourself one, you are one."

"If you think about it, I guess you're right. I know preachers that have no more education than I do, and half of them haven't been ordained. Anyway, one way or another, I guess it's all right with me if it'll bring in the money. I'm tired of living on pocket change."

"Trust me, Reverend Barnabas B. Pritchard, I've seen it happen. We'll start off in small towns in tent meetings and such, never staying too long in one place, no more than three or four nights at the most. Later, when I have time to recruit more people, train them to work the crowds, and you get your act down pat, we can move up to the big time. And that's when the big money will start to roll in.

"Up until a couple of months ago, we had a great operation going over in Arkansas and Southern Missouri, raking in money until one night our preacher shows up drunk—and in a dry county, if you can believe it. The sheriff scares the begeebies out of him and he confesses everything, even things he wasn't guilty of."

"What happened?"

"I think he spent a couple of days in jail—for the drinking, not the preaching and healing. Ended up with the sheriff having to protect him from the locals, mad as hell that he had fooled them."

"What about you and your people, as you call them? What happened to you all?"

"Listen, Reverend, I might as well tell you now, as a warning, to play straight and do it the way we set things up. Nothing happened to us. We were long gone when we heard the sheriff was coming. Our names may have been mentioned, but there was no way they could link anything illegal to us. And this is what you have to keep in mind. You screw up and it's you who'll have holy hell to pay. I'll play it straight with you, give you your share, take my cut—the bigger part, no use hiding that from you—and we'll all be rolling in cash. Think you can do it? I noticed that you don't turn down a drink. Is that a problem? I'm a little touchy on that subject, as you can understand."

"No problem. I can take it or leave it, just like gambling and girls. I'm no dummy, been around some myself. And you better believe I can play it like you set it up, provided I get my rightful cut."

"You will. Cheating won't work for any of us. But if we do it right, we—and especially you and me—can get rich."

It was the kind of music Reverend Pritchard liked to hear. He devoted himself full bore to becoming a miracle healer. Fred Sulligent and wife, Millodene, who had helped run the Arkansas-Missouri scam, wrote out a dozen sermons for BB to memorize. Fred claimed to have studied for a whole year in seminary before poverty and nagging Millodene eroded evangelical zeal and drove him to the crass pursuit of easier lucre. To the genuine amazement of Larry and the Sulligents, BB memorized the sermons in a matter of minutes.

The problem was his delivery. Unable to understand half of what he was spouting, at first BB emphasized the wrong sections. In passages requiring somberness and a dramatic lowering of his voice, he was more likely to go off in a shrill rant, and when a thundering rhetoric was called for, he lapsed into conversational mode.

"This is serious," Larry complained to Fred. "You and Millodene take him somewhere and coach him until he gets it right. I didn't believe him when he said he couldn't preach, but now I see he was right and worse than I thought possible."

"Leave him to us, Larry. Give us a week with him and we'll bring you back a first-rate preacher."

"Or he'll die trying," laughed Millodene.

It worked. They took BB to their isolated farmhouse up in the

Tennessee hills east of Nashville. There for six to eight hours a day, BB preached, Millodene listened and encouraged, and Fred critiqued and corrected. When they returned him to Larry a week later, the Reverend Barnabas B. Pritchard could deliver a sermon—a dozen of them—in the great Southern tradition of fire and brimstone homiletics. Now his style was a rhetorical delight of master cadence and sin-stomping effect. Larry, who meanwhile had reassembled four more members of his Arkansas-Missouri crew, listened to a sample sermon, applauded, and pronounced BB ready for the road.

"Okay, Reverend Pritchard, let's get going! The money's waiting for us out there! You ready to go get your share?"

"As ready as I'll ever be, I think," BB responded with a nervous hitch in his voice."

They started with small towns in middle Tennessee—Hickory Station, Mr. Moriah, Stella, Rockvale, Silverhill—spending only three days in each place. This gave them time to work out the kinks and polish his performance.

Hickory Station, their first stand, had its rough moments, but the second, Mt. Moriah, was a major triumph. The biblical citations were faultless as always, the sermon was smooth but fiery, and the healing service astounded the locals. Millodene, who claimed she had traveled over a hundred miles to have the famous healing Preacher Barnabas B. Pritchard "lay hands on her," was instantly cured of her phony blindness. A certain "Brother Sulligent," a paralytic who was brought in on a stretcher (none other than Fred), left shouting and jumping for righteous joy, announcing that he was as fit as a man could ever hope to be. There were no more miracles that night, but the outpouring of praise and money was gratifying in the extreme to Larry, BB, and the whole crew.

In the weeks that followed, the routine worked as smoothly as fine clockwork. But seeing his capital grow to a size he could only dream of in his old Saturday morning Bible stunt, BB began to chafe under the discipline Larry imposed.

"Larry," he whined after two months, "let's take a break and spend some of that money. I've been working hard, hell we all have, and I'm feeling a need to tie one on, have a little fun for a change. What say we take a few days off and tear loose somewhere where we're not going for a meeting later on?"

"Reverend, you want to kill the golden goose just when she's starting to lay the golden eggs. We're on a roll, man, and when you're hot, the worst thing you can do is break your momentum. You've gambled enough to know that. I know we've been going at it pretty hard, but didn't I tell you the big money would start rolling in? Tell you what, let's work two more towns in Tennessee, and then we'll take a few days off to kick up our heels and get ready for better things. Remember I told you about moving up to bigger things? Well, I'm lining us up in a five thousand-seat arena in Meridian, Mississippi. The money's going to pour down on us like rain in a cloudburst."

BB grumbled but agreed, and they played out the string in Middle Tennessee. Then it was fun time for BB in Nashville: the Grand Ole Opry, all he could eat and drink with some friendly girls, and a few unfriendly hands of poker. When it was all over and his head was clear again, his wallet was nearly as thin as it had been in the old days. He sighed, shook his head, and announced that he was ready for Meridian.

Meridian was a smashing success. Before at least three thousand people the first night, BB recited, preached, and healed. Official publicity was favorable enough, but word of mouth about the healing portion of the service was even better. By mid-week they were turning folks away from the overflowing arena. BB was at his grandiloquent best in each phase of the three-part performance. When it came to the healing session, a long line of people waited, some in wheelchairs or on stretchers. BB was disturbed. He had never dealt with so many people. Larry was nowhere to be seen, and the Sulligents were out of sight working the crowd with the rest of the crew. But what the hell, BB said to himself, let them come. Larry knows what he's doing.

And come the people did—the crippled, the blind, the deaf, and the diseased. BB laid hands on them all, and without exception they declared themselves healed. There was near pandemonium in the arena as people surged forward to receive a miracle. Word spread to those outside the arena and they pushed forward in a human wave, forcing the doors and trapping BB behind a sea of people.

Goddamn it, BB said to himself, that greedy Larry has overdone it this time. He said we'd just heal a few here and there. And where in hell did he get all these people? They're overdoing it and it's going to get out of hand. People could get killed in this crazy crowd. And they're liable to trample me to death too. Where in hell is Larry anyway?

Finally, the people began to disperse, although several hundred lingered to weep and shout for joy. There's no need for all this bullshit. They're supposed to shout out that they're cured and then get off stage and out of sight as soon as they can.

As the crowd thinned, BB spotted Larry coming on a run down one of the aisles. He had a look on his face that BB had never seen before.

"Larry, where in hell have you been? These fool people just about stomped me to death!"

"I was downtown, at the police station. I got back at the end of the service, but couldn't push my way through the crowd. But I know we have problems," he said, looking at BB in an odd way.

"What kind of problems?" BB asked with a con man's natural dread of the police. "You got us in trouble with the law? Dammit, Larry, you promised me you would play it straight."

"I am playing it straight. The problems I was referring to are not with the police. The arena manager made a miscalculation in his figures and thought we had snookered him. We got that cleared up right away. No, the problems are what happened here while I was gone."

"I'll say they are. You or somebody in the crew made a mistake in their figures, too. I must have had a thousand people, maybe more, come on stage for healing. I've had close to that many, and I don't want to again. You said we'd 'heal' a few each night, just enough to boil the pot and chum the water to keep the fish coming back. Wasn't that our agreement? And where in hell did you get so many plants to lather up the crowd?"

"BB, I've got news for you; most of those people weren't plants or phonies. The fact is we had nothing to do with most of them. They swamped our crew and they couldn't handle them."

"But they were running all over the stage, shouting that they were healed."

"BB, that's the thing: they were healed. That's what I'm trying to tell you. What happened here tonight was not our doing. There was a power at work here that I can't explain, none of us can—not in the normal run of things. BB, it looks like you really healed hundreds of truly sick and suffering people. Tonight you performed a miracle."

"What did you say, Larry?"

"I said these were genuine healings, miraculous cures that I can't explain any other way. Fred and Millodene told me just a few minutes ago that they had never seen anything like it. They're in one of the dressing rooms over there, white as sheets, both on their knees praying and asking forgiveness."

As Larry's words sank in, the shock all but took BB's breath away. He felt like a horse had kicked him in the stomach. His lifelong skepticism, his disbelief, and his contempt for sacred things now came crashing down around in an ugly ruin. In an instant he saw the awful error of his life, the terrible waste of his gift. Grief enveloped him like a consuming fire. He remembered everything far and near: the squandered days, the wasted years, the lies and blasphemy that had become his second nature. It was too much to bear. He fell to his knees and sobbed at the horror of his deception—to himself and others.

Larry quietly left him to his remorse and grief. A long time later after the maintenance crew told him they were closing the arena, he returned to his room a changed man. He was packing his things when Larry came by with the take, more money than they had dreamed of, but BB refused it.

"I'm through with all this, Larry. You keep the money. I don't want to see or touch it. I'm going home to start my life over."

"I thought that might be your intention, BB, and I understand. I won't try to stop you. I know for one thing that it wouldn't do any good, and for another, I almost wish I could do the same."

"Maybe you will . . . someday," BB said softly, putting his hand on Larry's shoulder. "I'll pray that you will."

There is nothing else I know to tell you about Larry and the rest of the crew. But Fred and Millodene returned to Tennessee, where Fred resumed his seminary studies for the ministry. Eventually, with Millodene's loyal support and despite some very lean times, he earned his degree and became a faithful pastor and witness to the miracle they had seen in Meridian.

The last I heard of BB, he was running a street mission for the homeless in Atlanta. People who saw him in later years said that after what happened to him in Meridian, his fabulous memory began to fade and in time he remembered and forgot like normal people. And his one-time healing power disappeared as well. But what was always fresh in his memory was the experience that led him to change his life. He never tired of telling the story of how for one glorious night God chose him to be an instrument of healing, how through him many were cured of their ailments, and how he—the sickest of them all—was freed from his sins.

21.
The Day Susan Stokesbury Shot Jack Logan

Grandpa Asa Stokesbury used to say that the Stokesburys and the Logans had been feuding ever since old Methuselah was a pup. That may be stretching the truth a little, but even so the feuding had been going on so long that nobody still in the land of the living could remember how or when it started. Grandpa Asa always said it was over a prize fattening hog the Logans stole and barbecued at a family reunion back in his great-grandfather's day. That was way back when their clans still lived in East Tennessee before moving to West Texas. But the Logans claimed it was because Obadiah Stokesbury, Asa's granddaddy, cussed out Miss Arizona Logan when she turned down his marriage proposal with the comment, "I'll bet every time your momma looks at you she's sorry she didn't stay a virgin." (They say Miss Arizona was a caution in her day and had a tongue sharper than a razor.)

Since I don't know the straight of what really happened way back then, I'll just tell you how things turned out when Susan and the younger generation of Stokesburys matched up against Jack Logan and his pack. Things had been peaceful between the two clans for more than a dozen years. Of course there were the usual cuss fights, slapouts, window panes shot out at one house or the other, and other minor differences to be expected, but no real ruckuses since 1880 when Rooster Logan and Arlon Stokesbury got into a humdinger of a fistfight and Rooster ended up chewing off a piece of Arlon's ear. When they sobered up, Arlon said he was considerably concerned with rabies and Rooster claimed he had a middling case of food poisoning.

But the peaceful times ended when Grandpa Asa and Grandpa Abe Logan had their little fracas in Looney's saloon over in the neighboring town of Rockbottom. For about the hundredth time, Grandpa Asa was holding forth about his heroic exploits in the Civil War when Grandpa Abe, about half way to the bottom of a bottle of bourbon, slammed his fist on the table and called him a liar. "If Asa Stokesbury's lips are moving, then you know he's lying! Everybody knows that when the Yankees topped that ridge at Shiloh, he ran off like a dog with its tail twixt its legs! It was the rest of us that held our ground and sent them blue devils skedaddling!"

Now Grandpa Asa took Abe's words to be a bit unkind, and since the topic of conversation had gone to the dogs anyway, it seemed a good time to remind Abe of his canine pedigree on his momma's side. Of course he regretted that he couldn't say much about Abe's daddy, since nobody knew for sure who the man might be. Leastwise, he thought it was a human critter, but come to think of it, it could have been some other kind of varmint.

Well, sir, Abe staggered to his feet with an anger terrible to behold, let loose some of the foulest cuss words you ever heard plus a few you haven't, and hit Asa upside the head with his whiskey bottle, spilling half a pint of good bourbon on the sawdust floor. Naturally Grandpa Asa was offended by Abe's impolite act, what with his honor being called into question and his head all bloody and such. So he pulled his sidearm and I guess he would have shot Abe if a deputy hadn't run in about that time and grabbed the .45 out of his hand. At that point all Grandpa Asa could do was shove Abe down on the red-hot potbellied stove over in the corner. There Abe sat befuddled for the merest instant before jumping up screaming like a stuck pig and clawing at his pants that were scorched and his backside starting to fry like a rasher of bacon. Then, drunk, lightly fried on one side, and his pants smoking, ole Abe stumbled out into the street yelling bloody murder, and after considerable mismanagement forked his horse, and rode off—standing up in the stirrups—to gather his kinfolks for war.

Grandpa Asa turned philosophical when he heard what happened to Abe on his way home. "No fault of mine if he fell off his horse up on the Kid Branch Road and nearly froze his fool self to death. I tell you, if brains were water, Abe Logan would die of thirst in a cloudburst."

Well, that set the two clans off and they went at it again, and even though nobody got killed this go-around that I know of, there were enough bullet wounds, stabbings, broken legs and arms, knocked out teeth, lost fingers and toes, and general mayhem to keep the womenfolk in both families tending to miseries day and night.

"I swear," said Grandma Sarah Stokesbury, "if these fool men don't stop trying to kill one another pretty soon and get back to work, we won't have enough cloth scraps and bedsheets left to bandage a sore toe and not enough food to keep a lizard alive. The next man that comes in here with a busted leg or broken arm, I may just take a stick to him and crack his head wide open myself! I'm just mortally aggravated at the whole lot! Not a lick of sense in either bunch!"

Even though Abe and Asa had rekindled the fires of conflict, both claimed too much "rheumatiz" and other assorted ailments to do much riding and fighting themselves. So the actual feuding fell to the younger men like Jack Logan and his brothers, cousins, and uncles. And if the chance presented itself, sometimes even to the young women like Susan Stokesbury, as I will tell you directly.

But first I need to talk a bit about the two. Let me just put it this way: if pretty were money, Susan Stokesbury would have been the richest woman in the Texas Panhandle. And if manliness were gold, then Jack Logan could have claimed Fort Knox.

Just about every single man in and around that side of the Texas Panhandle had tried to court Miss Susan, 20, but she had no patience with their pleas of love and sent them all packing. She was as strong willed as Miss Arizona Logan of earlier times, but Susan broke male hearts with a sweet voice and an icy rejection. The difference between her and Miss Arizona was the difference between a dagger and a sledgehammer. But both got the job done.

"I have considered your proposal, Mr. _____," she would say, "and, sir, I find nothing of interest in it or your person. I will thank you not to call on me again." (Miss Susan had five whole years of schooling down in Amarillo and it showed in her polite way of speaking.)

Jack Logan, 23, was about the only man Miss Susan had not sent back out to pasture, and that was only because he had never had any dealings with her to start with. Of course he would have had to be blind not to notice how pretty she was, but being a practical man, he also knew he would have the whole Stokesbury clan after him like a swarm of mad hornets if he tried to approach her. And as Jack always said, "Shooting Stokesburys is about the same as shooting coyotes, and I don't like wasting my bullets on either set of varmints."

He caused the hearts of Panhandle lasses to do a stutter step when he walked by, all six feet three of him. But asked what she thought of him, all Susan Stokesbury would say was, "I may have seen worse looking men on the outside, but he's a black-hearted Logan, and if I came across him drowning, I might just pour another bucket of water on him."

Jack did his part in the feud, sending Denk Stokesbury home with a bullet hole in his leg and Love Benefield, cousin to the Stokesburys, to his bed moaning with bloody contusions and a nose repositioned on his face after a knockdown drag-out fist fight over in Rockbottom.

Not that Susan intended to do any actual fighting. She spent most of her time helping Grandma Sarah bind up wounds and do the cooking. But once, she did draw a bead on Luke Logan, uncle to Jack, when she caught him trespassing on Stokesbury land. She might have shot him if Luke hadn't politely removed his hat and explained that he was rounding up strays that had wandered onto her property. Then he wheeled his horse and flew home like a buzzard late for lunch. She could have plugged him, for she was handy with her carbine, but Susan didn't think it was ladylike to shoot a man in the back, not even a lowdown Logan.

I suppose that for its own perverse amusement fate had already decided that one day Jack and Susan would meet face to face. As I said, Jack was a practical man, and when not feuding, did his best to keep the ranch running and food coming to the kitchen. The feuding families had cut the fences between the two ranches in several places and now the herds strayed back and forth, interbreeding and eventually dropping calves all over the place as if they knew nothing about boundary lines and feuds. Each family blamed the other for the promiscuous commingling of the herds, which each swore bastardized their prized bloodlines.

"I'll sue Abe Logan for every dollar he's got," Grandpa Asa ranted, "if I don't shoot him first!" And Grandpa Abe promised a similar horror for Asa and the Stokesburys.

One day in early summer, Jack was riding fence and doing what he could to sort out the confusion of the herds. Pondering the problem and possible solutions, he rode up a ridge in Stokesbury land to size up the herd spread out over the valley. Pausing, he took his hat off and wiped his face with his bandana. At that instant a shot rang out and he felt something tear through his left shoulder, knocking him out of the saddle and sending his hat spinning several yards away. He lay motionless, slowly inching his .45 into an accessible position.

Miss Susan rode up in near hysteria. She had meant to fire a warning shot in front of Jack, but just as she was pulling the trigger, a bobcat jumped out of the bushes and startled her palomino. Oh my Lord, she had shot Jack, maybe killed him! She jumped down to see and her worst fears were realized.

Jack lay motionless with his eyes closed and blood oozing through his shirt.

Jack opened his eyes and looked on the prettiest face—and eyes to boot—in the Texas Panhandle.

"Mr. Logan, I didn't mean to shoot you! I swear I didn't! A bobcat spooked my horse and he bolted and threw my aim off! I was only going to warn you that you were on our property! Oh, my Lord, what have I done?! What have I done?! I didn't mean to shoot you!"

"It's all right, Miss Susan, don't you fret none. We all have to go sometime, and I reckon my time has come."

"Oh, but you'll be all right, Mr. Logan. Here let me help you. We'll get you home and then send for Dr. Howard in Amarillo. Are you hit bad? Can you stand up?"

"It's all right, Miss Susan, it's all right. Don't try to move me. It wouldn't do any good. I can feel the end coming. Just let me lie here as my life drains away. I know you didn't mean to shoot me and I don't hold it against you. Just stay here with me, if you will, and hold my hand till it's over."

Now ole Jack was playing his part like a professional actor and Miss Susan was taking the bait like a catfish swallowing a grubworm on a hook.

"Is there anything I can do, Mr. Logan, to ease your pain and make you more comfortable?"

"Miss Susan, would you mind calling me Jack in my last mortal minutes? I was born into this world as Jack, not as Mr. Logan, and that's how I want to leave it. And, Miss Susan . . .?"

"Yes, Mr.—uh—Jack?"

"I've never seen a girl as pretty as you are, Miss Susan. I always thought it, but knew I couldn't tell you, not with our families being what they are. But now, would it be asking too much of you to give me a goodbye kiss, so I can meet my Maker with a last pleasurable memory of this life?"

"Why, I don't know, uh, Jack, I-I don't know what to say."

"I understand, Miss Susan. That's all right. It was too much to ask, so I'll just say goodbye to you and go on to the next life and ask the Good Lord to bless and keep you in this one."

It was too much for Susan. Tears came to her eyes and ran down her cheeks. She cradled Jack's head in her arms and gave him a long, lingering kiss well-watered by her tears.

Ole Jack, of course, was not quite dead. The minute she put her arms around his neck and their lips met, he embraced her with his good right arm that was so strong a mountain cougar could not have broken his grip. Susan screamed, struggled, and scratched until finally Jack laughed, relaxed his grip, and received her stinging slap. He said later that she hit him harder than Love Benefield in their fight.

Then in language she did not learn in the Amarillo school or her church, including some words she was not even aware she knew, she compared him to the vilest varmints of the forests, the ugliest vultures of the air, and the foulest fiends of the infernal regions. If words could kill, as they say, ole Jack would have died a dozen times over that day. In fact, the thought occurred to him as Miss Susan ran to her palomino that she might really take aim at him this time with her carbine. But instead she rode away still spewing verbal venom at him.

Jack got to his feet, sore and bloody around his left shoulder and lightheaded from loss of blood, but overall mighty pleased with himself and feeling at least ten feet off the ground because of the lingering sensation of her lips on his. What a girl! What a day! And as he rode back home he wondered, and what next? For Susan had bewitched him and he would have her or die trying.

Susan was livid, but what she didn't know at the moment was ole Cupid's amorous venom had seeped into her system as surely as it had infected Jack. That kiss had done them both in. The anger would pass, but Cupid's arrows were firmly embedded in both hearts.

Days passed and Susan continued to fume and sputter. She was mad as a hornet at Jack but also angry at herself for being so gullible. To Grandma Sarah's questions, all she would say was "those damned Logans." Grandma Sarah scolded her for such salty language. "Don't you let these crazy men and their fights drag you down to their level. You're a lady and you have to be ladylike through thick and thin. That's how we raised you since your momma and daddy died, and why we gave you all that education down yonder in Amarillo."

Then Susan's mood changed from anger to concern. Despite his trick, Jack really was wounded and plainly he had lost a good amount of blood. Was he healing? Had he made it home all right? She had heard nothing. What if the wound had become inflected? Did they get the bullet out? She had to know, and when Miss Susan made up her mind about something, a herd of buffalo could not change it. That Saturday morning she saddled her palomino, stuck her trusty carbine in the scabbard, and rode off without answering any of the family's questions.

Now some things are just contrary to the order of nature, and one of them has to be a Stokesbury showing up at the Logan household, or vice versa for that matter. But that's exactly what happened. I don't have the words to describe the surprise, the consternation, the disbelief, when Susan rode up, dismounted, and tied her palomino to the hitching rail. The Logan men down by the corral were slack jawed.

"Susan Stokesbury, Asa Stokesbury's granddaughter? No that can't be,"

Ma Logan said, shaking her head, as one of the youngsters ran in wide-eyed with the news. But rushing to the window, she saw that it really was Susan. Ma met her at the half-open door.

"Mrs. Logan, I'm Susan Stokesbury."

"I know who you are, girl. What I want to know is what your business is with us. You come here to finish killing my boy Jack?"

"No, ma'am, I'm here to find out how he's doing. The shooting was unintentional, and I'm sorry, but my concern is real."

"He's doing just fine, thank you. Now is there anything else you want to know?"

"May I talk to him? Just to offer my apology in a proper way, if he's well enough to hear it."

Ma stared at pretty Susan, then sighed wearily and opened the door to her. "Come on in, I reckon. Take a chair there and I'll go get Jack."

Jack lit up like a lantern when he saw Susan. He was bandaged up and sore but, he assured Susan, just about ready to get into working harness again. Susan apologized for the shooting. But it was apparent that both had other things they wanted to say, and since everybody in the house was trying to eavesdrop on their conversation, Jack invited her to go out to the shade tree swing. You never saw so much curiosity in your life, but every time the children or grownups edged too close, Jack shooed them away.

To tell exactly what they said would be pure guesswork on my part, but we can get the gist by what happened later. Susan came away from their handholding chat with a blush on her pretty cheeks and a smile she was having a hard time hiding as she rode out past the incredulous Logan menfolk. As for Jack, he made no bones about his feelings.

"Ma," he said, forgetting his sore shoulder and swinging her around the room, "Susan's the girl I'm going to marry! And you can't deny she's the prettiest girl in the Panhandle!"

Ma Logan was horrified. "Marry a Stokesbury girl? No, no, son! Now I grant you, she's a beauty, all right. Everybody knows that. But pretty or not, your daddy might shoot you himself if he hears such talk from you! And Asa Stokesbury is liable to if your pa doesn't! Half our family's laid up because of the Stokesburys, and here you come spouting off about marrying Susan Stokesbury! Lord help us! Why that'd be like marrying into the Old Devil's own family! You just better get that notion out of your head this very minute!"

"Now Momma, I've always minded Pa in everything when I was tending to his business as his son. But now I'm tending to mine as a man, and neither Pa nor anybody else is going to tell me who I can or can't marry. I've only got eyes for Susan!"

Jack stuck by his guns and Susan by hers. Asa and Abe ranted and raved like two banshees, and Asa threatened to lock Susan up until she came to her senses. It was easier for Jack. After all, he stood half a head taller and was twice as strong as any man among his kinsmen. In the last year or two he had become the natural leader of the family. He was goodhearted and easy going in ordinary business, but in matters of honor and principle men soon learned—some the hard way—that it was better not to cross him.

To pleas, threats, and arguments of every flavor from their families, the two sweethearts met nearly every evening out on the ridge where Susan shot Jack. It became their sacred spot. Their romance so distracted both families that they almost forgot about their feud.

Seeing that threats would not work on the pair, both Asa and Abe resorted to underhanded financial methods to derail their romance. Asa swallowed his pride and found an opportunity to offer Jack a thousand dollars if he would forget about his granddaughter. Surprisingly, after mulling over the offer for a couple of days, he accepted.

"That's exactly what I figured that lowdown snake would do," Asa declared.

Abe made a similar offer to Susan, although he could muster only five hundred dollars. She also accepted the money.

"She's just as underhanded as all the worthless Stokesburys," Abe groused with a grim satisfaction.

Both families thought the romance was over like a bad dream, but a month later the sweethearts rode in a buggy down to Amarillo where Reverend Herbert Copeland married them in the Baptist Church. After a few days and frantic searches for their whereabouts or, God forbid, their bodies, Jack drove the buggy back to the Logan ranch and with Susan seated beside him, proudly announced that they were now Mr. and Mrs. Logan.

"Now, Pa," he told Abe, "you and Ma and all the family have to understand that our feuding days are over. The Stokesburys and Logans are joined, and if the Lord blesses us with little ones someday we'll need two sets of grandpas and kinfolks to help us raise them. And another thing, Susan turned the money you gave her over to me, and with what her Grandpa Stokesbury gave me we bought the old Varner spread. You both meant to separate us with money, but we meant it for the good of both families. But now I want you to understand something: we aim to pay you both back as soon as we get able."

A similar conversation and transaction took place at the Stokesbury Ranch, and for the first time in his life, Grandpa Asa was speechless. His world had truly been turned upside down. For his part, Abe groused and sputtered for a few days, but in time both old men started thinking more and more about the possibility of the couple's offspring.

It took time for the reconciliation to take hold, but by the following spring when Susan was expecting her first child, the two families met in an awkward reunion at the Stokesbury Ranch. At first Abe and Asa glared at each other, but as liquor flowed and food was devoured, they began to recite the tales of olden days, and the two old enemies warmed, then glowed with friendship and sentimentality.

"You remember, Asa, when the Yankees, the Indiana Rangers it was, topped that ridge at Shiloh?"

"Lord help us," whispered Grandma Sarah to Ma Logan, "it's all about to blow up again. Those two don't have the gumption God gave a billy goat."

"Sure do, Abe, as I recollect, you boys in Company D gave them hell and a half."

"Yeah, I reckon, but the Yankees had us two ta one. We couldn't have held them back for long if you and your company hadn't circled around and got the angle on them. That's what we needed to drive the blue devils back!"

"Yeah, and we would've whipped them for good if it hadn't been for that woman that showed up. Did you ever see her?"

"Not me, but some of our boys did, and you know something, they were the ones that got killed."

"I heard it was the same on the Yankee side. Everybody that claimed they saw her—a woman dressed in a white dress—died out there on that ridge that day. Have you ever thought of what that meant?"

"Many a time, but I can't figure it out. Maybe it was some kind of sign from a higher power. You reckon?"

"You could be right. Yes sir, I'll have to say that you could be right about that."

"Glory be," Grandma Sarah said under her breath, "I wouldn't have believed it if I hadn't heard it with my own ears. Those two agreeing on something for a change."

"That's what comes from working together, Abe." Asa was silent for a moment, then he added, "Maybe that's the way we ought to do business now. Working together, I mean. Don't ye reckon?"

"Well, yeah, Asa, I can't argue with that. I guess it's about time, don't you think? Maybe we've battled each other long enough. Now that some people claim we're both getting a little long in the tooth we need to help each other, like way back yonder when we fought the Yankees. You understand what I'm saying, so we can show these young folks how it's done."

Jack slipped an arm around Susan's expanding waist and they smiled at each other as the two old men chattered on in their memories. At the end of the day, mellowed by food and rendered expansive by drink, Asa and Abe allowed that the proper thing to do with the rejected bribe money would be to call it a late wedding present. Jack and Susan could use all the money they could get, they agreed, to fix up the old Varner spread. As for stocking it with cattle, well, that would be a lot easier. The two herds had been dropping calves something furious ever since the fences came down and were running together.

But there were still some fractious moments. One day Asa and Abe were sitting out under the shade tree at Asa's house whittling and spitting tobacco juice when Abe had a pleasurable thought.

"It's going to be right pleasant having a little Abe running around the place."

"What do you mean, 'a little Abe'? Susan's my granddaughter and she's going to name him Asa, after me. You can mark that down for a fact."

"Well, Jack's my son and he'll have the final say-so. And you can bet he's not going to allow a son of his to have an ugly old name like 'Asa.'"

"Are you going to sit there and tell me that an old-timey Bible name like Asa is not fit for a Christian boy like little Asa's going to be? What are you, some kind of heathen?"

Their rising voices got Grandma Sarah's attention. "Lord have mercy! Those two old goats have gotten into it over something, probably fighting the Yankee war again," she said to Susan and Ma Logan, who were busy sewing baby clothes. "Sometimes I think we just ought to take them out yonder somewhere and leave them like two strays! First thing you know they'll have the menfolk stirred up and shooting one another again!"

But what Grandma Stokesbury feared didn't happen. The two old men didn't exactly settle their argument, but Susan did by giving birth to a beautiful little girl she named Madelaine Marie.

"Now what kind of name is 'Madelaine Marie'?" Asa wanted to know. "There's never been a girl I can remember by that name in my family."

"In mine either," added Abe, "though I recollect some on the male side of your clan that deserved some names I can't mention in front of decent company."

Asa was about to light in on Abe when Jack stood up to full height and raised a big hand for silence. "Pa, Ma, Mr. Asa, Mrs. Stokesbury, everybody, Susan tells me Madelaine Marie was the name of a brave, good girl she read about in one of her schoolbooks down in Amarillo. And if my Susan likes the name, then I like it just as much. So that's the name our little daughter's going to have. Everybody understand what I'm saying? Anybody got a problem with it?"

Everybody understood and nobody had a problem, especially when Jack got a certain look on his face. In fact, before long both Abe and Asa could not imagine a better name for Jack and Susan's darling little girl. And the old men were in complete agreement: Madelaine Marie was the prettiest girl with the prettiest name in the Texas Panhandle, or the whole state, for that matter, and they would fight any man who dared to say differently.

Jack and Susan had several other children and all the boys got "Abe" and "Asa" as a first or second name. But that part of their life is a longer story that the people of the Texas Panhandle still talk and argue about over a hundred years later.

22.

Uncle Homer's Umbrella

Back in 1910, folks in Schuyler, Nebraska, said they had never seen it so dry. Except for a sprinkle in January, it had not rained since December, and now in mid-May the corn was yellow and wilted and the wheat crop had already failed. Local streams had all but dried up and livestock gathered to drink around the stagnant pools full of desperate, dying fish. Some folks were already hauling water from the Platte River, its stream reduced by the drought to the volume of a modest creek.

Uncle Homer Milligan, 80, and the oldest man in the region, compared it to the legendary Indiana drought of 1860 when farmers lost their crops and many of them their farms to boot. He remembered vividly a line of wagons piled high with furniture and farm implements and the tearful farewells as his family and many neighbors began their trek along Henderson Road bound for Nebraska and other destinations in the west. Sally Stokesbury, Homer's sweetheart, was among those who stayed behind in Indiana. Usually Homer was a talkative, animated old man who gave detailed descriptions of the drought and the exodus as though they had happened only yesterday, but his face took on a somber cast and he grew silent whenever somebody or something reminded him of Sally. They had made their plans to marry, and Sally cried bitterly when she learned that Homer's family was moving away.

Homer lost more than just a crop that year. In Nebraska he and his father worked hard to survive in the new land. His driving passion was to get far enough ahead to go back for Sally. But then his father suddenly died the following spring and his mother developed an illness that consumed all his time and money until her death five years later. He and Sally corresponded as often as time and distance permitted, and both kept alive their hope of an eventual reunion and wedding. When the War started she told him of the many men who had gone to fight, including her Stokesbury twin uncles, Hiram and Hamilton.

But in the fourth year of separation, he got a letter from Sally, explaining that she was marrying another man. Homer's hands shook but he said nothing. Folks still talked about his sad love story when they ran out of other gossip, but by that time fifty years had passed and mostly they dismissed old bachelor Homer as a curiosity, a one-woman man whom practical folks in Schuyler could not understand. After all, they reasoned, there were other girls in the area that became Colfax County, and he could have married one of them like any normal man.

Homer kept his pain to himself, never complained about his life, and his faith in God never wavered. He would have been the last person to reproach Providence with the customary, accusing question of most mortals: why me, Lord?

By the end of May, people were hauling water for their families and livestock from the deeper wells in the Valley. At first their neighbors were generous, but as the water table lowered they became concerned and cut them off. Hard feelings ran high and anti-Christian accusations against those with water were heated. Old friendships suffered and families divided. Armed with his double-barreled shotgun, normally mild-mannered Purvis Maywood guarded his well at night against potential water thieves.

As the drought reached biblical proportions, it became a theological topic. Preachers told their congregations that it was the wrath of God unleashed on sinful humanity, as in the days of the Prophet Elijah, and that repentance and prayer were their only hope. Reduced to desperation, the churches suspended most of their usual dogmatic differences and agreed to come together as a community to pray for rain at Schuyler Lutheran Church, the largest in Colfax county. But since some denominations could not bring themselves to set foot in another church on Sunday, they decided to meet on a Thursday.

And so they did. It was the biggest gathering Schuyler residents could remember, exceeding even the crowds that came for county fairs or harvest festivals. Wagons overflowed the church grounds and stretched for a quarter of a mile up and down the road. Father Hans Mueller welcomed his neighbors and preached an opening sermon, describing the three-year drought in ancient Israel and telling how Elijah triumphed over the prophets of Baal.

"Now brothers and sisters," he concluded, "we must likewise call upon the same God who responded to Elijah and brought rain to the parched land. For God hears the pleas of his servants, and as the Scriptures say, the prayer of a righteous man availeth much."

"Amens" chorused throughout the church and prayers for rain began. Eloquent and mighty words resounded, first from the assembled preachers, then from the elders, finally from the overflowing congregations.

But no rain came. The sky was as spotlessly blue and cloudless as it had been when the meeting began. As noon passed and the afternoon wore on, a pall came over the assembly. What else could they say? What prayer had they not prayed? Had God turned a deaf ear to their pleas? The consternation of doubt began to overwhelm the people. Father Mueller and the other ministers conferred and decided to dismiss the people with the promise that the Lord had heard their prayers and would respond in his own way and time.

At that moment Uncle Homer rose and asked to say a word before the prayer of dismissal. It was out of character for him to speak, for though talkative outside the church, he seldom spoke inside it, preferring to listen and remember what he heard. Surprised by the unusual request, Father Mueller invited him to come forth. He did so, carrying his old umbrella, which in late years also served him as a walking cane.

"Friends," he began, "I just want to ask how many of you brought umbrellas today? Would you raise your hand?"

No one did. Most of the congregation probably thought it was a silly question, since there was not a cloud in the sky that Thursday. But the few sharp enough to catch the ironic implications of the question lowered their eyes sheepishly.

"Friends," Uncle Homer went on, "we came here to pray for rain, but if we pray in faith, shouldn't we have brought our umbrellas or raincoats?"

Then Uncle Homer said his last words. "Friends, let's all go home, feed the livestock, milk the cows, eat a bite, and come back here around suppertime. And this time bring your umbrellas and raincoats."

There was a moment of stunned silence. Then Father Mueller and several other ministers jumped to their feet with loud "Amens!" Before long the church fairly shook with renewed faith and excitement.

That night an even larger crowd gathered amidst a sea of umbrellas and raincoats. But Homer was not among them. "He doesn't see well at night," somebody explained. The prayers began anew and continued into the night. The moonless night was still and star spangled.

Then far off to the west there came a faint rumble of thunder, and an excited man reported flashes of lightning. A half-hour later the wind whipped up and enormous dust-laden raindrops started to fall. The windows rattled with the thunder, the wind rose, and lightning lit up the night. The rain came in driving sheets. The drought was broken.

And by a convergence of events, either coincidence or Providence, so was Uncle Homer's life. The next morning they found his body on the front porch, his clothes soaked with rain and his umbrella clutched in his gnarled hand. Among his few possessions—the deed to his farm, a few old letters, a Bible beside his bed, and an ancient, faded portrait of Sally in a small box—was a letter from Sally's granddaughter that apparently had arrived in the Thursday mail. It read as follows:

July 10, 1910

Mr. Homer Milligan
Rural Route 3
Schuyler, Nebraska

Dear Mr. Milligan:

It is my sorrowful duty to tell you that our Grandma Sally Stokesbury Walker passed away May 29. We buried her at New Bethel Church. I'm sorry I didn't write sooner, but since I'm the only member of the family that still lives around here, it was my job to sort out her things and settle her affairs.

I imagine it will seem strange that I am writing to you at all, since we've never met. I'm doing so because Grandma asked me to, and I promised her I would. I hope this is the right address for you.

As she got older, especially after our Grandpa Walker died, Grandma talked a lot about her girlhood and mentioned you along with other friends and family. She was a good Christian woman and the best mother and grandmother in the world. As she got older her mind would wander sometimes and she forgot, I think, that some of the people she talked about moved to Nebraska when your family did. In her last hours, though, her mind was as sharp as could be, and we even got our hopes up that she might get well. But her time had come and she passed away peacefully in her sleep.

Grandma told me to tell you this, Mr. Milligan. These are her exact words: "I didn't forget, Homer, but life had to go on." She said you would understand their meaning.

I close with respect and best wishes for your health and well-being.

Mrs. Irma Mae McGuire
Rural Route 1
Salem, Indiana

His neighbors had no way of knowing how Uncle Homer took the letter, but many thought Sally's passing was a sign that he was now free to go on himself. Maybe his personal drought was finally broken. Some even imagined it was Sally's call for him to join her. But that may be stretching things too far.

However, there was no mistaking the church members' feelings about his umbrella. Nothing would do but that it should be displayed prominently over the Narthex. If the church were Catholic, it would probably be an icon of sorts. It remained there until a new sanctuary replaced it. Somewhere in the transition someone removed it and the umbrella disappeared. But the legend lives on as a mighty testimony to unbreakable love and faith.

23.
Barefoot Odyssey

Sooner or later most of us discover that only a fine line separates the sublime from the ridiculous, and some of us—myself included—seem to have a knack for stepping over to the ridiculous side. Even when we pretend and say otherwise, we secretly take ourselves pretty seriously, and expect that same quality in Providence, Fate, or whatever you call it, that pulls our strings and pushes our buttons. After all, our modern religions and sciences are grim and humorless things, which makes us think that humor is a low-class act occurring only in men, monkeys, and other lower animals, not in the big powers up there somewhere who run things and wouldn't be caught dead laughing or having fun. Now, though, I'm ready to think that sometimes, if not all the time, the powers that be play with us, as though we were their toys or pets, and maybe we are. But instead of arguing the point, let me tell you my story to illustrate it.

Pardon me also for forgetting my manners and failing to introduce myself properly. My name is Wesley Wilson. I lived at the time—1977—with my widowed mother a couple of miles from Lost River at the foot of what we called "the Mountain," though people who live close to real mountains would probably laugh at us giving it such an imposing name. The events in this story took place when I was twenty-one, so that's the time and perspective from which I'll tell what happened, resuming as far as I can how I felt and saw things at that age.

I am tempted to deny right off the bat that I was responsible for things that went wrong, but then honesty forces me to admit that in another way it was all my fault, the fault of my built-in stupidity. Anyway, I crossed that fine line I mentioned and walked into a series of silly and bewildering experiences that I could never have imagined. When I say "walked," I mean it literally, and that's part of the story.

It started on a Saturday in May when ten former high school

classmates from Lost River decided to take a trip to Corinth, Mississippi, to visit the Shiloh battlefield a few miles north of the town on the Tennessee River. We went in two cars, and since my old truck was on life support with transmission problems, I rode with my sort-of girlfriend, Melba. I liked her a lot, but she ran hot and cold with me, mostly cold, to tell the truth. Her real interest was Jeffrey, driver of the other car, and that's part of the story, too.

It was a fine day and we lived and laughed it up on the way, eating chips and drinking cokes and waving to everybody we passed in that pre-historic age before cell phones, Twitter, Facebook and the rest of our electronic arsenal. At the park several of us boys left our billfolds, shoes, and personal effects in the car and waded under a sprinkler system behind the museum to cool off. The sign on the fence said "Keep off the grass," but we were slow readers and it took us a good while to obey. Everything was going great until Melba got into one of her nasty moods. The reason was obvious. Jeffrey had paired off with pert, cooperative little Margaret Miller instead of her. The pair got up from our picnic lunch close to the big cannons and locked in a tight embrace, as though both were injured and needed help walking, then they wandered out behind the trees on one of the battle pathways. When last seen, it seemed to us that Margaret was putting up far less resistance than the old Confederates and that victory was within Jeffrey's grasp. Jeffrey's friends decided to follow them down the pathway to laugh and jeer at the lovers.

That's when I got the idea of trying to lighten Melba's mood. She agreed to go walk a ways with me. But halfway down the slope where the Confederates had overrun and captured a Union brigade, she blew up when I tried to kiss her, slapped me, and ran back to the others. I was stunned and humiliated and took a long time to cool off. I had great plans for that day, but Melba had ruined it all for me. When we started out that day, I thought I was close to making things official with Melba, and the rejection hit me hard.

I took too long to get my head straight. When I got back to the parking lot, both cars were gone. The attendant told me the girl and several passengers had driven away about twenty minutes earlier. "She left a note, maybe for you" he said, looking at my bare feet. Then he added: "You were one of the boys walking on the grass under the sprinkler."

"What about the other car?" I asked, ignoring his disapproving comment.

"They drove away a little later, after they all came back out of the woods," he said with a grin. "Been gone for maybe ten minutes."

Melba's note read: "Ride with Jeffrey. I'm leaving."

The full horror of my situation then hit me. I was 120 miles from home, barefoot and without money or identification. What to do? After thinking it over, it seemed the only thing I could do was wait until somebody in the two cars realized I was missing. Surely they would stop together on the road somewhere, then one of them would come back for me. But then I remembered how bull-headed Melba could be when she got mad. I was not sure at all she would stop on the way.

Still, I waited under a big oak for several hours, watching the road. It was getting late and there was no more incoming traffic. Finally, embarrassed, I went in and told the attendant what had happened. He shook his head in disbelief, sympathized with me, but offered no help.

"Is there any way you can get me a pair of old shoes and maybe a couple of dollars. I'll be sure to get the money back to you."

"I'm sorry, buddy, we park people have strict orders about that. We get tramps and vagabonds that wander in here, and if word ever got out that we're doing handouts, we'd have a mess on our hands."

"What about some shoes?"

"Buddy, the only shoes around here go with these old Yank and Rebel uniforms. We can't let them out of course. Most of them are rotten, and from the size of your feet, they wouldn't be big enough anyway. You're in one hell of a mess, and I wish I could help you. But I can't, and you'll have to leave. We'll be closing in another thirty minutes and the gates will be locked overnight."

"Can you give me a ride down to Corinth?"

"Not going that way, buddy."

He was getting annoyed with me, so I left. Luckily for me, my feet were fairly tough from going barefoot a lot at home, but the asphalt was hot and I had to walk in the shoulder grass to keep from getting my feet scorched.

By dark I had made it down to Corinth and was headed east on Highway 72. A hundred miles to Lost River, I repeated in cadence with my steps until the words started repeating themselves in my head. I was already tired and starting to get hungry. What I mess, I thought, what a goddamned mess any way you cut it! I was never into profanity, but there are some situations that just cry out for a full-throated curse word. You know what I mean.

I'm guessing it was about midnight when I found a deserted hayshed near the highway and slipped in to rest. God knows what kind of snakes and varmints were my housemates, but I was too tired and hungry to care.

The next day, a Sunday, I drank as much water as I could from a nearby spring. It relieved the hunger pangs for a time, but as the sun rose, so did they with an aching vengeance. By midafternoon I made it to Iuka. I could have tried my luck hitchhiking, but barefoot, I was too embarrassed to try. I was momentarily elated to realize I was only six or seven miles from the state line. But soon food was all I could think about. I wondered if I could ask for a handout at a restaurant, but back in those Blue Law days most businesses were closed on Sunday. It would have to wait till Monday. I stopped at a derelict house a few miles past the Mississippi state line. Bugs scurried out of my way, and before I fell asleep from exhaustion I seemed to hear a beating of wings. Probably an owl, I thought. I just hope it doesn't have a nest here and takes it on itself to swoop down and peck me. The next morning I sensed something or someone looking at me and got the fright of my life when I looked up and saw a pair of big eyes staring at me through a broken window. A cow had discovered me and was probably wondering what a human was doing in her domain. Then a thought occurred to me: I wonder if she would let me milk her. I tried, but as I stepped around the corner of the house, she abandoned her placid ways and ran away, kicking and mooing as though to tell me, no free milk around here, mister. It would have been funny if things were not so awful.

I walked all day in a kind of stupor. To add to my several miseries, my face was sunburnt and painful. By Monday afternoon I came to the city limits of Tuscumbia. Fifty-five miles to go if I take all the shortcuts, I thought. But now there was another problem: my left foot was lacerated and both were scratched and sore. The night before I had stepped on a broken bottle and it cut me squarely on the ball of my foot, causing me to hobble like a cripple. But my hopes were rising. Surely in Tuscumbia I could find food and maybe, if I got lucky, a pair of shoes. The shoes didn't turn up, but an old blanket tossed by the roadside did. I tore it in two and wound the halves around my feet, tying them as tightly as I could. The improvement was enormous and immediate, but the blanket strips slipped out of position and had to be readjusted every half mile or so. Meanwhile, my head was pounding from the sun, sunburn, hunger, and probably caffeine deprivation. For I was heavily at the time into coffee.

Then ahead I saw a neon sign that flashed intermittently: *home cooking*. There were several parked cars and the place looked busy. Dressed as I was—or wasn't—I knew better than to go inside with my "blanket shoes" and get thrown out as a bum. Instead, I planned to search for food scraps in garbage cans behind the restaurant. I could already taste a half-eaten hamburger or hotdog, or maybe some left-over green beans. For an instant, I almost hated people with full stomachs.

Things looked promising. I found nearly a full serving of sweet potatoes, a slice of bread, and at least half a cut of sirloin. Too rare—I liked my meat cooked to a crisp—but how does the old saying go, "beggars can't be choosers"? I had never tasted anything so delicious. At the bottom of the can I even found a partially emptied—but also partially filled—bottle of coca cola. I gulped it down in one swallow, even though I spotted what appeared to be cigarette ashes at the bottom.

But just as I was about to start exploring the second can, I felt something hard and cold jabbing my back. I looked around into the twin barrels of a shotgun and the very angry face of a middle-aged, muscular man:

"Hey, feller, just what in hell do you think you're doing? Get your ass against the wall and raise your hands! You make one move I don't like and I'll let you have both barrels!"

"Sir, I apologize. I was hungry and just looking for a few scraps of food. I couldn't go inside and ask your permission, dressed this way. I'm sorry. I meant no harm."

"Well, we'll see about that. You just stand there still and quiet as a dead man, which you'll be if you try anything tricky with me."

Keeping the gun trained on my midriff, he opened the door and called to someone inside. A moment later, a young woman appeared.

"What is it, Daddy?"

"I caught the man that broke into our place and other businesses around here. I want you to call the police, and be quick about it. I don't want to have to shoot him. But if he runs, I will, and be within my rights to shoot him."

Even in my bewildering and frightening circumstances, I could not help noticing how beautiful she was. I was not used to brunette women with creamy complexions. Most of the girls I knew, including Melba, were big boned, fair-haired and freckled. This girl moved to a different cadence and with a grace I had not seen.

"What were you doing back here?" she asked.

"I was hungry."

"Do you always eat out of trash cans? We serve fresher food in the restaurant," she said with a smile and a twinkling flash in her blue eyes. "Oh," she added, noticing my strange footwear.

"Don't talk to him, Veronica. He'll tell you nothing but lies. Now go and call the police, like I told you."

She looked at me then disappeared into the restaurant.

A few minutes later a police car rolled up.

"Who've you got for us, Bill?" the lanky officer asked.

"This is the thief that's been breaking into places around here. I caught him going through the garbage cans. Caught him in the act."

"What've you got to say for yourself, fellow?" asked the officer. I saw the name Winthrop on his badge. "Let me see some identification. And where are your shoes?"

"I don't have any shoes and no identification on me. My name's Wesley Wilson and my story is complicated, but I'll explain if you'll let me."

Veronica and two waitresses had crowded around the door to look at me.

"Well, I think you'll need to come down to the station to do your explaining," said Winthrop. "Will you come willingly or do I need to use these?"

he added, jingling the handcuffs. "And take those wrappings off your feet."

"I'll go willingly, sir," as I sat down to remove the blanket strips from my feet, "but I really haven't done anything wrong. Just happened to be at the wrong place at the wrong time."

"So he says," Bill grunted. "I bet you money he's the one that's been doing the break-ins."

"We'll sort it out at the station."

Behind me I could hear the waitresses giggling as I got in the patrol car.

I spent that night in a jail cell while the Tuscumbia police supposedly checked out my story. Plainly, they didn't know what to do with me. My picture did not appear on any of their wanted posters, but Bill Thompson was pushing for my formal arrest on burglary charges. The only positive note in the whole business was that they fed me, and compared to the places where I had slept on the way from Corinth, the jail cot felt like what I imagined a luxury hotel bed would be like.

Then I had the first glimmering of good luck. The police caught the real burglar and let me go after I detailed information about myself, where I was from, and ways to contact me. The cut on my foot was healing and I knew I could make the final fifty miles home, food or no food, money or no money. Once there I would worry about the job I had probably lost by now and do what I could to settle things with Melba in a reasonable way. I was as dumb as a fence post about girls, which is why, I suppose, it took the Mississippi fiasco to get it through my thick skull that she and I were never meant to be together. As I walked still barefoot along Highway 72, I felt strangely glad and ready to get on with my life, whichever way it would turn.

A red Chevrolet pulled over and stopped ahead of me. It was Veronica Thompson.

"Hello, Wesley. Get in. I have something for you," she said, flashing her dazzling smile.

"For me? What?"

"A pair of shoes. Come on. Get in. I won't bite you."

I obeyed but was baffled. The shoes were fine and they came with two pairs of socks.

"They're the right size, Veronica. How did you know my size?"

"I looked at your feet the other day. Did I guess right?"

"You did. You have a good eye. I'm impressed, but I can't accept them."

"Oh, they're not from me, they're from Daddy. He was so embarrassed after all those accusations he made that he asked me to buy these for you—to make up for some of the problems we caused you."

"Well, it was the other way around. It was me that caused you the problems, Veronica. Your father was just doing what he thought was right. I don't hold anything against him. You tell him that for me, will you?

"Maybe you can tell him yourself one of these days."

I laughed and replied, "I'm sure Mr. Thompson is glad to be rid of me and would just as soon not see me again."

"We'll see about that. Now, where do you live?"

"Oh, a few miles from here."

"No, where exactly?"

"Well, to be exact, in Lost River, close to the mountain south of Tylerville."

"My goodness, that's a long way."

"But not as far as it was from Corinth, Mississippi, so I guess I'd better be on my way. Thank your father, as I thank you, and I wish you all the best if I don't see you again. And I'll just leave the shoes here so you can take them back to the store."

"Wesley, keep your seat and your shoes. I'm driving you home."

"No, Veronica. It's too far for you to drive by yourself, and you don't know me. I'll tell you the same thing your father would tell you. I can't let you drive off with a man you don't know."

"You're wrong, Wesley," she said as she pulled the Chevy back on the highway. "Even though I just met you, I do know you, just like I knew your shoe size. I'm a pretty good judge of people, so my mother tells me."

"Veronica, I don't approve. I don't feel right. It's got to be a hundred miles down there and back."

"I think you're worth a hundred miles, don't you? Two hundred, I'm not sure yet," she laughed. "And try on those shoes, to make sure they fit. And I can tie them for you, in case you Lost River people don't know how. I've heard people down that way are a little different."

Well, Veronica had her way. We found my poor mother frantic with worry. I can't count the times she thanked Veronica for bringing me home. We discovered she had done some walking herself—eight miles to Melba's house in Evergreen to find out what had happened to me. Melba pretended to be mortified when she learned the truth. But knowing how spiteful she could be, I believed not a word of it. Momma brought my things home.

After scolding Veronica again for coming all this way, I gave her instructions about getting back to the main highway. Momma prepared lunch for us and we talked so long that I had to remind Veronica that she needed to start back.

"Are you trying to get rid of me, Wesley?"

"No, but I am concerned for your safety. You be careful and take the shoes with you."

"Are we going to have that argument all over again? It's settled. The shoes stay here, and the next time I see you, I want you to be wearing them"

"A nice girl, son," Momma said as Veronica drove down our narrow lane.

"That she is, Momma, but we won't be seeing her again. She's a town girl."

"Hmmm, maybe, but very nice."

"That she is, Momma; that she is."

For the next few days Veronica's face was etched in my mind. Despite all my troubles in Corinth and Tuscumbia, her beauty and spirit made the experience, the interlude as I called it, something I would hold on to as a pleasant memory. Momma was right, but a little short on the accolade. Veronica was more than a nice girl; in my mind she had become truly exceptional. I would miss her. But some good things happen only once, I thought fatalistically.

But then again, some things even better happen again. So it was that the very next Saturday, I saw Veronica's red Chevy coming up the narrow road to our house. My heart pounded like a jackhammer, and this time it didn't occur to me to scold her for the long drive. We hugged spontaneously, and that was the start of the best part of my life.

Years later, our ten-year-old daughter, Jennifer, asked me how I met her mother.

"Well, darling, I was barefoot, exhausted, eating out of trash cans, and about to be arrested. It was the best day of my life."

"Momma, is Daddy teasing me?"

"No, dear, he's telling you the truth from his side," Veronica answered as she came from the kitchen. "From my side I saw four things about him right away: one, he had some of the biggest feet I had ever seen on a man; two, he was cute; three, he was honest; and four, I knew from his eating habits that he would be easy to cook for."

24.
Tom's Gold

Back around 1915 folks in the town of Muleshoe, Texas, shook their heads and predicted that no good would come of Tom James' marriage to Miss Mildred Stanton. Tom was around sixty at the time and hard living had so stunted and bent him in body and spirit that he resembled a wind-twisted West Texas oak.

It would be another marriage made in Hell, they said, just like his two previous unions. To hear him tell it, his first two wives, Ida and Rose, died of natural causes, but people who knew stingy ~~Herman~~ *Tom* said that he worked and starved the women into an early grave.

Although some years Tom would farm a bit on his hardscrabble land two miles north of Muleshoe, the truth was he hated the plow and held on to the land only because it had the best water well in the whole region. According to old Wilburn Blackwood, who homesteaded the place around 1885, the stream was an underground creek that he believed eventually fed into the headwaters of the Brazos River. True or not, in the worst droughts, which Tom saw as a blessing, he scandalized the whole community by charging neighbors for water. The very idea, they grumbled, selling water to folks instead of sharing it like a Christian!

Tom was deaf to their reproaches and made no pretense of being a religious man. He had left Florida early in life and drifted out to West Texas in search of his father, Arnold. Eventually he gave up the search and discovered that his real obsession was gold. He spent a good portion of his life prospecting for gold along the streams and mountain ranges of far West Texas, New Mexico, and Colorado, sometimes venturing as far as Wyoming. When the gold craze came over him, he would abandon the farm and disappear for months at a time, leaving his wife of the moment without food or money. The only way the women survived was by drawing water from the 100-foot-deep well to irrigate a garden.

Not that life improved for the women when he returned home. He kept his gold, money, and other valuables locked in a forty-pound iron reinforced cedar strongbox chained to his bedstead with the only key on a strip of rawhide tied around his waist. His Colt .45 was always at the ready under his pillow at night. Neither hunger nor spousal pleadings could persuade him to dip into his trove for any humane purpose, though sometimes after she was abed and under threats to keep her distance, his wife could hear the strongbox's creaking hinges as Tom opened it by kitchen lamplight to gloat over his treasure. On his prospecting treks he strapped the box to his mule, Sadie, the only living creature he really trusted.

Now widowed for the second time and worn out in his joints and back from walking and digging over half of the West, old Tom had limped back to Muleshoe either to mend his body, as he hoped, or to end his days, as folks expected. They suspected he had enough gold and money in his famous strongbox to live in fine style—if anybody could ever persuade him to part with any of it.

Miss Mildred was as different from Tom as honey is from vinegar. With nineteen springs to her credit, blonde, blue-eyed, shapely Mildred was the romantic dream and erotic fantasy of nearly every young bachelor in Muleshoe.

Imagine their general indignation when Calvin and Minnie Stanton let it be known that their daughter and only child would shortly become the third Mrs. Tom James. It would have been bad enough to lose Mildred to a young competitor, they grumbled, but the idea of her ending up in the bed of ugly old Tom enraged the young men. They took it as an offense to their manhood and talked of plugging him between the eyes or less mentionable parts of his anatomy with a .45.

But despite their threats, which came to nothing, on a Saturday in May, Miss Mildred and Tom said their vows and Pastor Delbert Yarborough pronounced them united in holy matrimony.

The question that nobody could answer but everybody asked was why Mildred agreed to such an unnatural union. But soon it came out from some close neighbors that at first she hadn't agreed at all and in fact had objected to the marriage at the top of her lungs.

"Momma, I am not going to marry that old coot!" she yelled at Minnie when her mother first mentioned Tom's talk with Calvin. "I don't care how much money and gold he's got in that nasty ole box of his! Just the thought of him coming close to me makes my skin crawl! Anyway, I told you, I love Jimmie Beckham, and he's the one I'm going to marry! You hear me, Momma? He's the one!""

"Now, now, Mildred, just simmer down," Minnie responded in a much calmer voice. "I know how you feel. I was a young girl once myself, in case you didn't know. But let's talk about it without flying off the handle and letting the whole settlement know about our business. Look at it this way. We all know ole Tom's got gold and money in that box, maybe enough to set up a young widow woman for the rest of her natural life."

"But I've told you a thousand times, Momma, I love Jimmie!"

"Honey, you want the truth? Jimmie doesn't have the means to pay for a pine box to be buried in, and never will have. And neither do the rest of these Muleshoe boys that are panting after you. Now here's the thing, honey. Tom's got no kin or kids, and Dr. Bailey down in Littlefield let it slip here a while back that he's been giving him pills for his heart. And I'm here to tell you, Mildred, that when heart trouble starts, a body's not long for this world. And when he's gone—and he will be soon—all that money and gold will be yours!"

"Momma, I wouldn't get in that old man's bed and let him . . . do that . . . to me for all the money in the world!"

"Aw, honey, it's not as bad as you think, and generally it's over before you know it happened, if you just don't think about it. It's just something we women have to put up with. Anyway, I doubt if he's even got enough nature left in him to bother you. . . . You understand me, don't you, Mildred? Maybe a little now and then, or maybe not, but pretty soon he won't bother you at all.

And if he tries, he'll die all the sooner. The thing is, Mildred, you just have to keep your mind on all that money that'll be yours just as soon as he's gone on to his reward. Then you can marry who you want to, Jimmie or anybody else. The world's full of Jimmies, but if they can't provide for you, they turn out to be a lot worse than ole Tom. Believe me, I know."

"But Momma, you don't know all that much about men, do you? You've only been with Daddy."

"Child, when you get older, you just know a lot of things without having to learn by doing."

Minnie was mighty persuasive when she wanted to be, and eventually Mildred came around to her way of thinking and married ole Tom.

There was only one problem that neither Mildred nor Minnie counted on: old Tom refused to die on time. One, two, nearly three years went by and instead of edging toward his grave, Tom seemed to be on the mend. He even started making plans to go prospecting again out in the Sangre de Cristo Mountains of New Mexico.

By this time pretty Mildred had gotten tired of waiting and found consolation in a nocturnal friendship with old beau Jimmie Beckham. He tried his best to get Mildred to run away with him, but she was thinking more and more like Minnie. The thought of running off with Jimmie to live on kisses and an empty stomach no longer held any appeal for her. And since Jimmie could not think any further ahead than their next romp in the hayloft, Mildred started making her own plans.

The only concession sweet Mildred had gotten out of Tom after nearly three years of marriage was enough trust for him to remove the chain from his precious box.

"It's a humiliation to me when I have company for them to see that chain on my bed. It's like you don't trust me or something. Tom, I'm your wife, for God's sake, and everything you have is safe with me," she lied.

Finally he relented. Maybe the euphoria of prospecting again had softened him. Now the box sat there by Tom's bed, still locked but enticing and unprotected. Every time Mildred eyed it, greed akin to Tom's gold fever came over her. The gold trove grew larger and larger in her imagination. She promised herself she was going to have that box! Tom's not going to carry it off with him this time. In the shape he's in, she thought, he could die out there in the mountains and his gold would end up with somebody else. No sir! That gold belongs to me! I've paid the price for it: giving away three of my best years to that old fool!

Both Tom and Mildred were more animated than usual. The idea of prospecting again had put a new spring in Tom's step. He had Varner McReath, the Muleshoe blacksmith, put new shoes on trusty Sadie, and that afternoon spent a long time poring over maps with curious markings that only he could decipher. He fancied himself restored to health and was ready this time for the big lode that had always eluded him.

As for Mildred, she was thinking a dozen thoughts all at once. She would need Jimmie's help to carry out her plan, and her main worry was whether he could keep his mouth shut. She suspected that he had bragged about their nightly meetings. Lately people looked at her in an odd way, and certain men had made sly, insinuating remarks to her. Jimmie swore he had said nothing, but she didn't believe him. Still and all, there are certain things I can't do by myself, she sighed, but he'd better do exactly what I tell him.

That night after Tom was finally asleep and snoring, much later than usual, she slipped out of bed, gathered Tom's strongbox in her arms, and staggered out under its weight to meet Jimmie, who hid it in the hayloft. He had the usual monkey business on his mind, but Mildred was not in the mood for foolishness. Instead she made him listen carefully to her instructions.

"You take Sadie across into New Mexico and shoot the ugly thing in some deserted place. Varmints will eat the carcass soon enough. Then you get back here as soon as you can. I'll take care of things from this end."

"Why do you want me to kill ole Sadie?"

"We want people to think Tom's gone off prospecting."

"But what about Tom? He'll still be here, won't he, even if ole Sadie's gone?"

"Not exactly. You let me worry about him. You just do what I tell you."

Everything might have gone a lot smoother if it had not been for Sadie. As Jimmie led her away to her doom, she brayed and snorted, waking Tom from his customary deep sleep, probably the only sound that could arouse him. He jumped up, and seeing his box was missing, grabbed his .45 and ran out to the barn in his long johns to discover that Sadie was gone too. Mildred was returning to the house when he overtook her at the door.

"Where's my box, woman? And Sadie?" he yelled and blocked her way. "And what're you doing out here anyway? I bet this is not the first time you've slipped out of the bed! You got some man out here? What you been up to, you little whore?"

"I have no idea what you're talking about, Tom. I'm not up to anything! Just been to the outhouse, that's all. Now you let me in the house! It's chilly out here!"

"You're not getting back in my house till you tell me about my box and ole Sadie! Where are they?"

With that he hurried inside and bolted the door against Mildred.

At first she was in panic, but then Mildred realized that Tom had just made things a lot easier for her.

"You want your ole box, Tom?" she yelled. "Well, you can have it! I'm sick of that box. It's always been a humiliation to me. I'm dropping it down the well! As for your mule, I don't care if the wolves kill the ugly thing! And that goes for you, too, you damn old fool, you!"

She picked up the biggest rock she could lift and heaved it down the well. A couple of seconds later there was a loud splash. Tom came running and got there just as it hit the water.

"You hear that, Tom?" she taunted him. "There's your precious box, at the bottom of the well!"

Tom cursed and waved his .45, threatening to shoot Mildred, who ran to the house. Then, simmering down a bit, he started thinking of how he would retrieve his strongbox from its watery grave. At first light he set the water bucket aside, tied ropes to the windlass and his waist as backup protection, and carefully began the 100-foot-descent to the stream, cautiously placing his feet in the slippery dugout steps on either side of the wall.

He had made it about halfway down when Mildred reappeared and dropped a big rock on him. It glanced off his shoulder but did not dislodge him. He looked up at his tormentor and the next one hit him squarely on the forehead. He dropped unconscious toward the water. The ropes caught just before he plunged into the stream. And there he swung to and fro, his head and feet indenting the muddy wall with each pass. Mildred went to the kitchen, got her butcher knife, and returning, cut the ropes. Old Tom dropped silently into the water and the ropes came tumbling after him. Mildred stared for a moment at the murky water, then tossed the .45 down the well, wiped her hands in a gesture of finality, and went back into the house.

Later that day Jimmie returned to report that he had shot Sadie in a deserted ravine.

"Uh, where's Tom?"

"He's gone."

"Gone where?"

"Just gone, as far as know. I guess he went off looking for his mule. Don't worry about him and don't ask me anything else about him. I hope he breaks his neck and the varmints get him. I don't want to hear his name again as long as I live!"

Meanwhile, Mildred had burned or buried most of the things Tom planned to take on his prospecting venture. With sledgehammer and hacksaw Jimmie opened the strongbox, and Mildred removed the gold and money for her safekeeping. She handed Jimmie a few dollars to keep him quiet and after he left, she dropped the strongbox down the well.

"You wanted your damn box, Tom. Well, here it is!"

The gold and money was less than she hoped but enough to assure her of some good living.

She had already decided that Jimmie had no place in her future. Besides being dumber than a post, he was becoming tiresome and too possessive. She was beginning to realize, as Minnie used to tell her, there were other Jimmies in this world.

So it was done. Everything had worked out almost perfectly. True, there were some inconveniences that tried her patience. Since she couldn't bring herself to drink from the well, she either had to collect rainwater or walk over to Minnie's to drink and bathe. Then there was all the waiting until she could have Tom declared legally dead and herself a widow. Finally, she had to string Jimmie along to keep him quiet, even though she was sick and tired of him.

"What's the matter with that nice water at your house, honey?" Minnie asked her.

"Some kind of varmint fell in the well. I nearly gagged when some of it came up in the bucket. It'll be a while before it's fit for human use again. And with Tom gone off to the mountains, I'm sure not going to clean up the mess myself."

Nearly nine months passed and no sign of Tom. He had never been gone this long. Folks around Muleshoe started speculating that he might be dead somewhere out in the mountains. At his age and in his condition, yeah, he was probably dead, they agreed.

About that same time forty-odd miles southeast of Muleshoe, Mancil Barton, 45, was fishing at his favorite spot in the Double Mountain Fork of the Brazos River. He felt a tug and the cork went under the muddy water. There was no movement, but he knew by the weight that he must have snagged a whopper of a fish, probably another big catfish like the one he had caught the year before at this spot. But when he wrestled it to the surface it was Tom, or what was left of him: a skeleton with a few strips of clothing and a piece of rope still clinging to the bones. Old Wilburn Blackwood was right after all about the underground creek and its connection to the Brazos River. It just took Tom a long time to make his way down it, and probably he fattened a few crawdads and catfish on the way.

Of course at first neither Mancil nor anybody in the community knew it was Tom. By asking around and posting the discovery in other towns, Sheriff Blake Tate was finally able to identify the skeleton by the strongbox key still tied around his waist. A gaping hole in his skull convinced him that he was dealing with a homicide.

After that, things started to unravel a bit for Mildred, and since she saw she could not lie her way out of it entirely, she turned on Jimmie. The sheriff arrested him on a charge of murder.

"I always had a feeling that something was wrong," Mildred said at Jimmie's trial, "and the longer Tom was gone, the more I felt it. This is real embarrassing for me to tell, Your Honor, but Jimmie had been pestering me for the longest. I tried to get him to leave me alone, told him I was a married woman and all. But he wouldn't stop it. He kept hinting he was going to do away with Tom. And I guess that's what he did, knocked my poor husband in the head and dropped him down that well."

"Why didn't you tell somebody what was going on?" District Attorney Harrison Brown asked her solicitously, aware of the tears welling up in her pretty blue eyes.

"Oh, sir, I was just too ashamed. A lady doesn't talk about such things. I just kept begging him to go away and leave me alone. I was just plain mortified and didn't know what to do."

"It was rumored that Mr. James kept his valuables in a strongbox. What can you tell us about it?"

"Why, I thought Tom carried the box off with him, like always. But now I guess Jimmie must have slipped it out of the house and made off with it. I don't know what it had in it. Tom never let me or anybody else see the contents."

Outraged, Jimmie protested his innocence, saying that Mildred planned the whole thing, kept the contents of the strongbox, and that, in fact, he didn't even know Tom had been killed. The only part he had in it was killing ole Sadie, but even that was on her orders, so he claimed.

Some folks believed him. His words had a truthful ring, and Jimmie was too dimwitted to fabricate a big lie. Even before Tom's death, there were doubts and gossip about Mildred. But when it came right down to it, being a woman and all, the law couldn't hang her, and certainly not a young woman as beautiful as Mildred. Jimmie was a more convenient culprit. After all, he had confessed to killing ole Sadie, and the Muleshoe jury was inclined to believe that any man who would shoot a good mule would probably kill a bad man. And there was a certain amount of damning evidence against him: folks had noticed that Jimmie, who most days didn't have two pennies to rub together in his pocket, had spent several whole dollars around the time of Tom's disappearance. It was enough to earn him a life sentence in the penitentiary. He narrowly missed a hanging noose because of lingering doubts Judge Clarence Ledlow had about Mildred's story.

As for Mildred, with all the gossip that kept circulating, she thought it best to leave Muleshoe and resettle in another city, far from the unpleasantness. She sold the farm at a fair price— mostly because of its prize well—and moved up to Amarillo. Once there she cautiously began to dip into Tom's limited hoard.

But as it turned out, she didn't have to depend on Tom's gold very long. A rich businessman, Leonard Thornton by name, fell in love with her and they were soon married. He kept his money, rumored to be plentiful, in a proper bank vault many times larger than Tom's grungy little strongbox, and her charms were the key that opened it at any time and for any whim. It is true that she had a rough stretch five or six years later when Mr. Thornton shot himself one morning for no good reason anybody could think of, least of all grieving Mildred who found the body. She mourned in a proper way and wore black for the better part of a year. But with Mr. Thornton's considerable estate falling to her, she recovered from her loss, moved on to Denver, married once or twice more, and as far as anybody in Muleshoe knew, made it just fine the rest of the way.

25.
Missing Elderly

1.Setup

Walter Patterson, 68, returned from his Corpus Christi fishing vacation that August Monday to discover that his accounts had been hacked and two million dollars, nearly a fifth of his liquid assets, was missing, transferred to God knows where.

After a moment of panicky disbelief and a burst of profanity-laced anger, he took a couple of deep breaths and calmed himself as best he could. He told no one, not his children, not even wife, Vivian. He wanted to get things under control before any of the family knew. Then he phoned investment broker Bill Osman. A female voice answered.

"Good morning, Mr. Patterson. This is Faye Monroe, Mr. Osman's Assistant. You may remember I've talked to you a couple of times."

"Yes, of course, how are you, Faye? I need to speak to Mr. Osman."

"I'm sorry to tell you, sir, that Mr. Osman is no longer handling your accounts. He had a stroke last week and is in the hospital. The latest word we have from his doctors at the medical center is, frankly, not all that optimistic. We don't expect him back any time soon."

"I'm really shocked and sorry to hear that, Faye. Give me the location and number and I'll make it a point to visit him. Bill and I go back a long way. But in the meantime, who is handling my accounts? It's urgent that I speak to that person at once."

"I'm not sure, Mr. Patterson. The accounts were divided up among several senior people, but's it's probably Vice President Gerald Costa. He took over several of the larger accounts. Yours was probably one of them. If you can hang on for a couple of minutes, I'll check. Or I can call you back."

"I'll wait, Faye. And remember to get me Bill's information."

"Yes, sir."

A couple of minutes later Faye gave him Costa's number and the information about Bill Osman. Walter knew Costa, had dealt with him before and intuitively disliked the man, but he had no reason to distrust him. Still, he thought, I need to get my account out of the hands of a man I don't feel comfortable with.

Josh Farley, Costa's young assistant, told Walter that Mr. Costa was tied up in a meeting and would contact him later. Two hours later and still no call or text from Costa, Walter could wait no longer. Though it would cost him a chunk of money, he decided he would close all his accounts with Osman Investments, move his money to other investment houses where he already had some small accounts, and load up on gold to buy time to get to the bottom of the scam. But when he tried, he got a series of chilling impersonal responses: "Denied. Unauthorized password and codes." A part of him was professionally impressed by the scheme the thief, or thieves, had set up to scam him. "Whoever it is has me in a box. It's somebody who knows how it's done."

He thought of a stopgap maneuver to stop the financial hemorrhaging temporarily. He flooded his accounts with transfer requests. All were denied, but on the last try the message he wanted popped up in red letters: "System lockdown."

"Ah, finally," he said, slamming his fist on the desk. "That will drive a stake up their ass for a while at least."

A few minutes later Costa called. "Mr. Patterson, sorry it took me a while to get back to you. You've heard about Bill's condition. That and the readjustments we've had to make while he gets back on his feet have got this place turned upside down. But I see you've been trying to move your accounts and the system has gone into lockdown. Can you tell me what's going on?"

"Sure, if you'll tell me what's happened to my missing two million dollars."

"Two million dollars missing? That's the first I've heard about it. I haven't had time to study your account. But when I looked it over briefly last Friday everything seemed to be in order. There was no money missing that I detected in my quick scan. It all checked with my figures. Everything was in order, codes, passwords, everything."

"Well, it's sure as hell gone today, and I demand to know where it went, to China, Russia, or some Caribbean offshore bank. I haven't authorized any transfers. I'll get right to the point. I'm smelling fraud. I want my money back and I want it now, or I'm contacting the authorities, and somebody—maybe you—will be looking at prison time for it."

"Whoa, stop right there, Mr. Patterson! I don't deserve your threats and don't take kindly to them. We do honest banking and investing at this bank. I was ready to discuss this calmly with you, but your words and tone tell me it's best to let the lawyers do the talking from now on. I have nothing more to say to you."

The line went dead.

"Damn it to hell!" Walter said, angry with everything and everybody, including himself for losing his cool. "He's right. As the old saying goes, when threats begin, lawyers come in. Now everything gets a lot more complicated."

At first he was convinced that Costa was the culprit. But on calmer reflection he decided that it didn't make sense for a guilty man to call in lawyers, unless he was in too deep for any other option. And it didn't seem likely that in the bare week or so since Bill Osman's stroke, Costa would have had time to set up and carry out an elaborate swindle, not with all the new assignments he had. But then it could be that he had been setting it up while Bill was still in charge. There must be other crooks at work, and until I find out who they are, everybody is suspect. I can't trust any of them—not even my family, not even Vivian—until I get to the bottom of this.

Then as his temper gave way to calmer reasoning, he asked himself, why Vivian or family members? If there's anybody I can trust, surely it's my family, and despite our problems lately, especially Vivian. No, it's got to be somebody at the bank. Costa? Bill himself? Who?

His lawyer, Henry Freeman of Freeman & Fitch, assured him that his office would get a court order authorizing experts to examine his account records at Osman Brothers. They would inform Costa at once of their intentions.

"The fact that we're getting a court order and making as much noise as we can about it should discourage any more attempts to tamper with your accounts. At least for the time being," Freeman informed him.

"But what happens if my money is in some foreign account or outlaw bank not answerable to U.S. courts? How can I get it back?"

"Walt, let's wait and find out some facts before we get bogged down in hypotheticals. I know that's easy for me to say, since it's not my money. But you pay us to think clearly and act with good judgment. And that's exactly what we'll do in this case."

The next day while Vivian was out, Walter opened the family safe and put nearly all the gold, cash, and bonds in his briefcase. He had been thinking of the move for several weeks and now he felt the time had come. Then he withdrew several hundred thousand dollars in gold, cash, and assets deposited in another bank, just in case the thieves might hit that account too. Luckily everything was undisturbed. After the documentation was signed and stamped and the gold sealed in a new oversized steel briefcase, bank president Norman Driver hovered nervously.

"Walter, do you intend to just walk out to your car with ten pounds of gold in the case?" he asked, worried by Walter's odd decision.

"Well, yes, Norm, I guess I am. I sure can't fly out to it, not with this stuff weighting me down, can I?"

The words were funny, but anger leached all humor from his voice.

"I don't like the idea of your carrying all this gold and cash on your person. We're losing your business, and I wish you would tell me why. But I still feel responsible for your personal safety. You need security guards to protect you. Won't you let us get them for you?"

"And who would protect me from the guards?" Walter quipped.

Norm shook his head. "May I at least ask where you're taking it?"

"To a safe place. That's all I can tell you."

"At least let Oscar, our senior in-house security person, follow you if your destination is close by. He's been with the bank for years and is as trustworthy and responsible as they come."

"Fine, if it makes you feel better."

Walter led Oscar to Merchant's First Bank and waited at the door until Oscar waved and drove off. A couple of minutes later he walked back to his car and drove to a car rental agency on the west side of town. He transferred the two cases to the trunk of a rental car and left his own vehicle in the parking lot. "No disrespect for Norm or Oscar," he said to himself, "but the fewer people who know my movements, the better. Now they can't tell what they don't know, even if they wanted to, only what they think they know."

An hour and half later he was in the Ardmore State Bank over seventy miles away, where by prior arrangement with old friend Eloise Hardaman, bank president and cousin to Evelyn, and the help of Vice President Ed Eddleman, they verified and deposited most of the gold and much of the cash from the briefcases. For contingencies, Walter kept a hundred fifty thousand dollars and some gold coins distributed in the two briefcases. Eloise worried about Walter's safety and the circumstances responsible for the abrupt changes in his finances. But she knew better than to ask him. Walter was a good person but secretive about his business.

Even though his account in Ardmore State Bank had been essentially dormant since Evelyn's death, Walter had not forgotten it but knew to the penny how much was in it. He had grown up in the cotton fields and piney woods of East Texas. The Pattersons had been wealthy and respected in former times, but with the Depression, his Great-Grandfather Lloyd's gambling binges and his Grandfather Henry's unwise investments, most of their money had vanished. By that time, Lloyd had died and age had forced Henry to step aside, leaving Malcolm to try his hand at preserving what little was left of the family fortunes. He was moderately successful, but the prolonged effort turned Malcolm into an ultra-cautious and secretive man, traits that he tried to instill in Walter. The day Walter left home at eighteen to take an assistant teller position in a Dallas bank, Malcolm gave him the best advice he could: "Son, I've never lived or worked anywhere but in these piney woods, and I reckon I'll finish out my days here as our people have for generations. I don't know a lot and never had big money. But I can give you what I believe is sound advice: never tell anybody all your business, not friends and not family. And try not to get yourself in a bind where you have to depend on them. Always have some money on you. It's a hard fact, son, but even people closest to you will let you down just when you need them most. And that goes double when it comes to money. It can twist folks into ugly shapes. They'll look down on you if you don't have any and hate you if you have a lot. That goes for the whole human tribe, Christians, kinfolks, and heathens."

Walter thanked Eloise and Ed and alerted them to be on the lookout for a possible future transfer. "Can you accommodate me on that, if things go as I hope?"

"You betcha, Walter," Eloise answered with a reassuring pat on the shoulder. "We don't know what's going on in your finances, and won't ask, but there won't be a problem from this end. We're all set up to receive the transfer anytime. We're delighted to have your business."

"Ditto for me, Mr. Patterson," added Ed.

Now I may be able to weather the storm, Walter thought as he walked out to the rental car. It was dark by the time he hid the remaining gold and money on a suburban property he owned, turned in the rental car, and drove home.

"Walter, where have you been all day?" Vivian asked him. "It's way past dinner time and your food's cold."

He knew a storm was brewing in her words. He would try to avoid it, but he had a feeling it was already too late.

"Oh, just out running some errands and taking care of a little business."

"What kind of business, the monkey kind? You've been gone the whole day," she said accusingly. "And what happened to the money and gold in the safe? I noticed today it was gone. What did you do with it?"

"Oh, I put it in the bank. Remember we talked about that. It's not a good idea having that much cash and gold around the house, not with all the crime these days. As for how I spent the day, it was not with anything else of any importance, just this, that, and the other. Things that popped up while I was in Corpus. Throw in a few conversations here and there, a cup or two of coffee with friends, and first thing you know the whole day's shot. I guess I lost track of time. I remind you that I am retired, Vivian, and not on schedule."

She pouted in her familiar way. "Walter, I know when you're keeping something from me. You've been up to something you don't want me to know about. And don't deny it. We both know I'm right. You've always been squirrelly about your business, but since you retired you've gotten a lot worse and forgetful. Are you feeling all right? I think you need to go to Dr. Morgan for a checkup. I've been telling you that for the longest."

"I'm fine, except when you start the FBI interrogation. You know I don't like having to account for every minute of my day. And you can write this down: I am not going to the doctor when I'm not sick."

Vivian whispered a profanity too faint for him to hear and opened a kitchen cupboard. "Did you remember to pick up the coffee I asked you to get?" she asked as she set a steaming cup before him

"I guess I forgot. Sorry."

"Walter, lately you seem to forget everything."

"But you," he snapped, "sure don't forget to remind me in spades of everything I forget."

"Your food's in the oven," she said, turning her back in a familiar angry movement and walking out. He knew she would not speak to him until the next day. He admitted to himself that his last remark was tacky. Would he never learn to keep his mouth shut in these situations?

Her prolonged silences were worse than her criticism. They married two years after his first wife, Evelyn, drowned in Lake Tahoe. Bob and Helen were worried about his choice.

"Dad, Bob and I want you to be happy," Helen said. "You were a good husband to Mom and a good dad to us. You have a right to redo your life, and Bob and I want you to. But, frankly, we're worried about the age difference with Vivian. You know she's only a year older than me. They say age doesn't matter, that it's a state of mind. But in real life we all know better. The years do count."

"Yeah, Dad," Bob added. "And I'm just three years younger than Vivian myself. Think about all the things you don't have in common: tastes in music, entertainments, friends, memories, maybe even political differences, all the shared experiences we take for granted with people our same generation."

Walter had heard his children but didn't listen to what they said. He was convinced it would work out with Vivian. She was devoted to him and told him every day how much she preferred a mature man who knew what he was doing, and how to do it. Her quick laughter and flirty ways lifted the gloom that had settled over his life after Evelyn's death. As for sharing things, she grew up back in the Oklahoma Panhandle, and even though things there had changed since his day, she knew a thing or two about the hardscrabble country life and the value of a dollar. Later, she earned her nursing degree, worked in a hospital for several years, and then landed a good-paying job as a specialized nurse in a Dallas forensics laboratory. She was good folks, he assured his children. He knew her kind because, when you got right down to it, he was one of them, despite more than half a lifetime in Dallas.

For a couple of years it seemed that Walter was right. Vivian reveled in her new social and financial status. They traveled to places she had only dreamed of, bought clothes at Nieman-Marcus, polished her rough country speech, and took to her new circles like a duck dropped in a big pond.

Then, abruptly, the wheels started falling off their marriage. After a couple of trips to Oklahoma and East Texas to impress both sets of kinfolks, she refused to make any more visits to her country relatives. She wanted to make trips to more exotic places.

"Why don't you retire?" she asked him almost daily. "That way we could do more fun things. I still haven't been to Italy, and you promised me we'd go."

Walter explained that it was too early, that he had too many things going to drop them without a prolonged phase-out. And besides, he liked what he was doing. She pouted and began her tactic of long silences when things did not go her way. In manly fashion, Walter wanted to repair what was obviously breaking down in their marriage, but also in usual male fashion was angry and frustrated that he didn't know where to begin. By the third year he was tempted to give up and give in to everything she wanted. "Not good, not good," he thought to himself. "Guys die from this kind of pressure." And he thought of two or three who had. But he stopped short of surrendering to her growing demands. Instead he took a gritty resolve from a defiant statement he always said to himself when things threatened to overwhelm him: "I'm not dead yet." He thought he was tough, but then he wondered whether he would have to keep telling himself that if he were really strong. Self-doubts were creeping up on him. Until now he was always proud of what he had accomplished. He had restored some of the old Patterson glitter and it felt good.

Finally, though, he made what he told himself was a rational decision and retired at 66. But in reality it was neither rational nor realistic and did not heal their rift. Instead the gap widened; the residual respect Vivian had shown him as a shrewd business man and investor vanished with his position. He sensed that to her he was now becoming just a crotchety old man and an emotional throwaway. Things were a mess; his children knew it, and he knew it. What he didn't know was what to do about it. Having lost Evelyn, he was doubly afraid of losing Vivian.

That night he slept on his study sofa. It would do no good to try to talk to Vivian before her anger ran its cycle. At least they agreed on one point: he was not handling retirement well. She had encouraged him to take the fishing vacation alone. It was nice, but the minute he got home the tension between them resumed. Things were falling apart. He was not dead yet, he repeated to himself for the hundredth time, but was he closer than he knew? Age had never been a concern before; now it was becoming an inevitability and dead ends in his life were popping up all over.

First thing next morning he went to see Bill Osman. Vivian, just emerging from her silence, made her excuses and went off to one of her clubs, explaining that she had to give a financial report. Sally Osman hugged and thanked Walter for his visit. Bill was sleeping and his breathing seemed peaceful, but Walter guessed he was sedated. Assorted tubes attached to his wrists and nose and flickering monitors by his bed were disconcerting. Bill was almost his age. Walter imagined himself lying there like Bill before mentally dismissing it with a slight shake of his head.

"Sally, I heard about Bill after I got back into town. Sorry I couldn't get here sooner. What can you tell me about his prognosis?"

"The doctors say his condition has stabilized. Bill's been resting comfortably for several hours. It's still too early to know anything definite about a recovery protocol, but Dr. Hansen seemed more optimistic this morning. You know how cautious doctors are."

Sally forced a smile, but her eyes were bloodshot and sunken from distress and sleeplessness.

"Bill's a strong guy, Sally. He'll pull through, and we'll all be praying that it happens soon. And you and the family will be in those prayers."

"Thank you, Walter. You don't know how much I appreciate your visit and your encouragement. Bill treasures your friendship."

"As I value his, Sally—and yours. You know, we all go back nearly forty years."

They talked quietly for a few more minutes, then Walter said goodbye with offers of help if Sally or the family needed anything. But just as he was leaving, Bill roused and opened his eyes. At first they were blank, then he smiled faintly at Sally and noticed Walter by the door. He moved his lips slightly as though he wanted to say something.

"Just rest, dear. Walter's here, Walter Patterson. He came by to see you."

"I'll be by again soon, Bill. When you're up and around, we still have that golf game we talked about. Meanwhile, you just get well. Sally says you're making progress."

Bill managed a weak hand motion in Walter's direction. Sally and Walter looked at each other. "Walter, I think he wants to tell you something."

"Bill, whatever it is can keep until you're up and around. We'll have a lot to talk over then. For now you just take care of yourself, old friend."

"Walter's right, dear. You must rest now."

Bill made one more unsuccessful effort to say something but was far too weak and sedated to speak.

That afternoon he had a call from Henry Freeman.

"Walter, I'm mad as hell with you!" Henry thundered in the deep baritone voice that had swayed so many juries.

"What are you talking about, Henry?" Walter asked, stunned by the vehemence in Freeman's tone.

"I'm talking about that goddamn court order we drew up! When we presented it all approved and signed, that guy Costa showed our young lawyer Nancy Steadman that your accounts are in proper order: no money missing and nothing wrong. Walter, Nancy is now convinced that you are a mental case, and damned if I'm not about ready to agree with her. Where in hell did you get the idea that somebody was stealing your money?"

"Henry, I got the idea from what the accounts showed me: two million dollars, give or take a few bucks, was missing from my accounts. The code and password had been changed. So what was I to think, that somebody had put it in the petty cash fund by mistake?"

"Well, it's all there now. Nothing is missing, except the time we wasted and my patience with you. And, I'm afraid, a chunk of our firm's reputation."

"I find all this hard to believe, but I'll check on it and apologize in advance if it's like you say."

"Walter, you know that in business apologies don't cut it. If you can't handle your affairs anymore, my advice is to turn them over to somebody who can. We'll bill you for every dime we can squeeze out of you for the court order fiasco, but no charge for the advice I just gave you. And make damn sure you have serious business if you contact me again."

At the bank Costa came out beaming after a short wait. "Mr. Patterson, I'm happy to tell you that everything is in order. Your money is safe, and has been all along. I was swamped the other day and in a bad temper when we talked. Sorry about that. I neglected to remind you that our computer experts were installing the next generation security technology. There was a recorded message about it, but if you're like me you get so used to hearing it you tune it out."

At the end of the day, Walter was exhausted by all the cross currents, but relieved that at last things seemed to be getting back to normal. He still planned to transfer his money ASAP just in case. Vivian was in a better mood when he got home.

"You seem a lot happier than you have lately. You must have had a good afternoon."

"It was great, Walt. Relaxing and low stress. Just what I needed to unwind. How about you?"

"I took care of some problems and things are looking up. Best I've felt in a long time."

It was their last peaceful day together. The next day Walter's world came crashing down. His accounts were empty. He called Costa in a panic, and when he didn't answer he raced down to the bank, getting a speeding ticket on the way. "When it rains, it pours," he muttered, pounding the steering wheel in frustration.

Josh Farley told him that Costa had taken vacation time and would be in England for ten days.

"Is there anyone I can talk with about my account? We have a disaster on our hands. My accounts have been wiped out."

The look on Farley's face told Walter that the assistant had been forewarned. "No sir, I'll let Mr. Costa know there's a problem, but as you can understand, I'm not authorized to act in matters of this magnitude."

Henry Freeman, still angry over the court order and probably convinced that Walter was losing it, refused to talk to him. Nancy Steadman came on the line and tried to calm Walter down, but it was obvious from her tone—the kind, empty, condescending talk one would use with an angry child—that she was convinced she was dealing with a man in some stage of dementia.

That night, exhausted with impotent rage, he went to his study, his voice shaky with the excuse that he wanted to look at some investments and make some notes. He barely slept. He realized that the first withdrawal had amounted to a cybernetic feint to set him up to be discredited later. And it had worked like a charm. Now he could cry wolf and nobody would listen. He spent most of night wondering what he should do, but no clear strategy came to mind. His finances were a train wreck and he did not know where to turn.

It was the start of an avalanche of bad luck. The next day he had a fainting spell and ran his car over a curb. Luckily no one, including himself, was hurt, but for several minutes he didn't remember where he was going and couldn't give the investigating policeman directions to his house.

It was the first of several blackouts and memory lapses. He stoutly insisted that he would be fine if people would get off his case and give him some time and space. It was worse the next day when he ran a red light and caused a four-car wreck that left a woman with moderate whiplash. "One more incident of this magnitude and you'll probably lose your insurance," agent Mac Burns warned him. "Mr. Patterson, it might be time to think about giving up driving."

Walter thought about it, as he promised Mac, but it only strengthened his determination to keep driving and get to the bottom of his troubles. But his confidence was rattled that same afternoon when he went out for his daily walk and ended up disoriented and uncoordinated. He had a couple of embarrassing falls that left him with scratches and a gash on his forehead. He saw streets he recognized by name, but they ran the wrong way and the cardinal points were misplaced. He found his way back home finally by pretending to be a stranger in town trying to find directions to a friend's house. He went out again the next day just to prove he had things under control, but became hopelessly disoriented and had to hold on to a bench to keep from falling again. After several hours and two stops at the same convenience store to ask directions, an employee hailed a passing police patrol.

"Sir, I would advise you not to go out alone anymore," the young policewoman told him as she dropped him off at his address. "Ma'am," she added, turning to Vivian, "you should make sure someone is with him. We're glad to help, but we're not always around."

He spent the next two days in futile efforts to trace his money and clear his mind. To make matters worse, the next morning his daughter Helen and husband Carl Strasburg, son Bob and his wife Betty, and Vivian came in with a uniformed constable.

"Walter dear," Vivian said, draping a slender arm around his neck, "I'll get right to the point. We think—everybody here thinks—that you need professional help. There have been several incidents—the wreck, the speeding ticket you got a while back—which I paid, by the way— the falling and lack of coordination, several close shaves in traffic, and getting lost the other day right here in our neighborhood. Several of us have had distressing calls from your lawyer and banker. That combined with your erratic behavior in recent months tells us that something is wrong and we're worried about you. You remember that I have asked you several times to go see Dr. Morgan for a general checkup."

"I recall just once, a few days ago."

"Well, see there? You forgot the other times. These past weeks you've been very . . . absentminded, Walter, forgetting what you went out to do and where you were supposed to do it."

"There's nothing wrong with me, just concerned with some financial matters, and as I told you, I'm not going to the doctor if I'm not sick."

"Dad," Helen said in a worried voice, "for everybody's peace of mind, why not put the money concerns temporarily on hold and agree at least to a general checkup? I know you don't like to go to the doctor, but you are getting older, and what you could ignore twenty or thirty years ago in your prime, might need attention now. We love you, Dad, and want the best for you. Doctors are there to help people, not to harm them."

"Dad, Helen's right," Bob said hopefully. "We're all on your side. We

197

want you to know that. But you also have to know that it's a family decision. That's why we're all here. We insist that you get the checkup."

"Is that why you brought along this gentleman?"

They looked at one another, waiting for someone to explain.

"I'm also here to help you, Mr. Patterson" the Constable said, stepping forward to shake his hand and introduce himself as Nate Hill. The Probate Court sent me. Sorry we have to be a little firm with you, sir, but it's for your own welfare. The Probate Judge has taken the position that the family has produced enough evidence to warrant a comprehensive examination of your case."

"So now I'm a case. I feel like I'm being arrested."

"Oh no, sir, not at all. It's a protective procedure to see that no harm comes to you or others. Now I'll ask you to turn your car keys over to your wife or family member, as you choose. Then we'll go to the approved clinic so the medical panel can begin the checkup. The court will make its decision based on expert medical and legal opinion. And I believe all your family members will come along to back and support you in all the sessions."

"Carl, what have you got to say in all this?" Walter asked. "Everybody has an opinion, I assume you do too."

"Walter, like everybody else in the family, I want what's best for you."

"I see," Walter said. But really he didn't. There were dark areas of Carl's character that he had never figured out.

"And you, Betty, what do you think of all this?"

"Oh, Daddy Walter, I don't like it at all. I want you back home to be a grandfather to Tim and Abigail and a second Dad to me, like you have been since I married Bob. If it's something that has to be done for your own good, then I can't really object. But right now you seem the same as you've always been. Whatever it is, I want you to get over with it and be the same strong man we all love and respect."

"Lord bless you, honey. 'Great shall be your reward in Heaven' for those words, as my mother used to say."

Then came the shocker after the panel convened. It turned out that Vivian had compiled a log of her conversations and problems with Walter dating back over a two-year period. It included references, real or—in Walter's mind—invented, to his memory lapses, disorientation, angry flare-ups, and most of all, his absurd belief that people were stealing his money. It was written to show progressive deterioration.

Walter was stunned when she produced it. Objectively he knew that her log described many of the classic symptoms of dementia. But on a level of painful illumination he suddenly realized that an enemy—maybe his main one—had been living in his house and sleeping in his bed. Of course! Of course!

Why hadn't he seen it sooner? I've been as blind as a bat. Almost from the start of their marriage Vivian must have planned his demise. What a moron I've been: just another dreary story of an old man duped by a younger woman for his money. And much cleverer than he could have ever imagined. Now she spoke so convincingly and had amassed so much anecdotal evidence against him that even before the panel of doctors and legal advisor had made their recommendation and the court issued its formal decision, he knew the ruling would go against him. Restriction at some level was a foregone conclusion. He had lost the battle. But his familiar refrain came to mind: he was not dead yet. There was still a war to fight and maybe to lose, but he would go down swinging.

2. Missing Elderly

Walter seemed surprisingly resigned and content, even happy, at Lakeside Haven. The personnel were delighted at the ease with which he made friends and complied with the rules. Being newly arrived from the outside world, he had a fresh perspective and many entertaining stories to tell. At first Helen, Bob, and Betty visited him nearly every day, but then seeing that he seemed happier and sharper than they could have imagined, their visits became less frequent. Walter assured them that he was fine and urged them to get on with their lives. Carl visited only once.

Inside, Walter was seething and scheming, but he went out of his way to be jovial and friendly to everyone at Lakeside Haven. It was a ploy to get them to relax their vigilance and allow greater freedom of movement. "I'm not dead yet," he said to himself.

"I know you have families and things to do, including taking care of my grandkids," he said to Helen and Bob. "You don't have to run out here every day."

Now that her mask was off and the pretense over, Vivian came by only twice, the second time a week later to vent her fury on Walter.

"Walter, you squirrelly old bastard! What in hell did you do with all the money, gold, and bonds that were in the safe? Where's the gold and cash? It's not in the bank where you said."

"I moved them."

"Where to?"

"Well, Vivian, you know my problem. I put them somewhere, but now I can't remember exactly where it was."

"You lying son-of-a-bitch! You know exactly where they are, and I want to know!"

"My, my, how vulgar you've become, my dear. Whatever happened to the sweet little Panhandle girl I married?"

"She got tired of an old, worn-out excuse for a husband. Now you tell me what you did with the stuff in that safe or . . ."

"Or what? You'll kill me, is that it? Well, my dear, you need to rethink that option. For if you do away with me, my love, you sure as hell will never find out, will you? Anyway, you've made off with millions in the main account. That's a lot more money than the little bit I took out of the safe. Can't you make do on that little tad of cash? You think maybe if you took in house cleaning and laundry you could make ends meet?"

"I'll find out one way or another, you dumb bastard. I've outsmarted you for years, and I'll outsmart you again. Just you wait and see. When we're finished with you, Walter Patterson, you won't have a cracked pot to piss in."

Walter picked up on the "we" but said nothing. To himself he thought, somewhere in that remark is the missing piece in this scam. Who else is involved? How can I find out? If and when I do, maybe I can see some light at the end of the tunnel.

But to Vivian he commented lamely, "Well, love, I'll have to say that so far you've had just about everything your own way."

"Yeah, and how does that make you feel, big boy?"

"Not too good at the moment, but tomorrow's another day."

"Is that some kind of a weak threat?"

"No, ma'am, just a fact. I'm sitting here cut off from everything and this place is under surveillance 24/7. I'm in no position to make threats."

"That's the only sensible thing you've said all day."

That night Walter dreamed that shadowy people were forcing him to drink a vile-tasting liquid. He tried to run but they were closing in on him and he could not get away. He awoke from the nightmare relieved that it was only a dream. But the meaning of the dream was stunningly clear and even more horrifying: Vivian—surely it was Vivian—had been drugging him. He had already noticed that his thinking cleared soon after he moved into Lakeside and began flushing a prescription down the toilet. How had she done it? Probably something in his coffee or food. Hadn't he commented recently about the coffee having a different taste? A different brand, she explained. But without giving it any importance he happened to notice that it was the same coffee they always bought. That little slip, or was it a lie, told him more than he could prove. But it was something.

The first round was over and he had lost. But now he was planning the details of his escape. He had stashed the cash and gold in a gated building on property he owned only a few miles from Lakeside Haven. And he had much more in Ardmore. Most of his money was gone, but he still had enough assets to defend himself for a while if he could find a way to slip out of his fancy prison. Vivian had taken his wallet and checkbook, but he still had a hundred-dollar bill in his shoe. As his father had told him, "Always have some money on you." As soon as he could get his hands on his hidden funds, his main strategy would kick in. It was true that Vivian had outsmarted him, but her overconfidence could still prove to be her undoing. There is no such thing as a small enemy, he had read somewhere. The wild card in the whole affair was her accomplice, or maybe accomplices, that made up the "we" she had dropped in her boastful tirade.

It took two weeks to learn the security schedules and alarm systems. His cordiality paid off; the staff paid only minimal attention to his movements around the Lakeside.

Then on a Tuesday he had enough pieces in place to begin to act. He started by spraying smoke alarms with a mosquito fumigator he found and concealed in a janitorial closet. There was panic as the alarm sounded. In the confusion he walked calmly out an emergency exit and toward a service gate. He left his books, clothes, and pocket possessions in the room so the staff would think he had run out in panic with the other residents.

On the way he yelled to a milling group of dazed residents, "You need to get as far from the building as you can! I just heard somebody say there's a fire around the propane tanks and they can explode at any minute! Get as far away as you can from the building! And be quick about it! This whole place could go down!"

Word quickly spread and panic turned into pandemonium. Residents ran, hobbled, or rolled their wheelchairs toward the street exits, heedless of staff members trying to restore order. Walter regretted the inconvenience and hoped no permanent injury would come from it. If he could open the gate, he would be long gone by the time the staff calmed the residents and ushered them all back—minus one—to their rooms. The incident would probably make the 10 o'clock local news, but he was betting the Lakeside Haven administration would not call family members until everybody was safe and accounted for. The fact that at least one resident would still be missing would delay the media calls even more. He was in a race against time, but if his luck and logic held it might be time enough.

"Damn!" he said aloud as he tried the gate and found it padlocked. Looking around he spotted four cinder blocks by a drainage installation and stacked them against the fence. "My legs may not be as good as they used to be," he thought, "but, hell, I can still climb over and jump down without killing myself!"

He stumbled and fell belly flat, but no harm done, picked himself up, brushed off the debris, and took a wide circle out to the avenue. He lucked out and flagged down a taxi a few blocks from Lakeside that dropped him a block from his house. He punched in the gate code, hoping that Vivian had not changed it, and watched with relief as it swung open. The motion light came on but he was not alarmed. Night-prowling cats and possums triggered it so often that no one noticed it anymore.

The old garage code still worked too. Apparently, she has changed none of the locks or codes, he thought. And why would she? He was not supposed to be back here. Besides, despite her cleverness, she was technologically challenged and barely knew how to turn on a computer. Her car was gone, but his was in its familiar spot. The house was dark. Vivian must be at one of her events, he thought. But as he reached the top of the stairs he heard voices. He froze, then tiptoed quietly toward the bedroom. She had left the TV on, as she usually did. "Fantastic!" he said as he expelled a breath of relief. If my luck holds, he thought, I'll be in and out before she gets home.

In a few seconds he had the safe open and was delighted to recover his cash-empty billfold and dead cell phone next to it. Remember to find a charger, he reminded himself. I may have important messages and I need to call some people I can trust—if there are any left. There were assorted keys to doors and his car, but now he had no use for them. But on top of them was the best discovery of all; there in her handwriting were the transfer codes and passwords for his accounts. "God is good! God is good!" he repeated as he copied them and stuffed them in his flat billfold. Then to thwart the thieves and buy more time, he reset the combination and put the numbers in his pocket. It would take them a long time and a lot of trouble to open the safe. He thought of grabbing some fresh clothes but he sensed that time was running out. He closed the safe, made his way in the familiar darkness down the stairs, past his car—giving it a fond pat—and out to the street. It was 9 p.m. Time was running out, he reminded himself again. The evening news would come on in an hour. He walked briskly to a hotel with Wi-Fi several blocks away and registered. No luggage, he explained. It's been delayed. He gave a credit card, then in the business room started working hurriedly on the transfer codes and passwords. By 9:50 p.m. the transactions were finished and his funds safely in Eloise Hardaman's Ardmore State Bank. At least he hoped they were. A deposit of that magnitude would be a coup for Eloise's modest bank.

At 9:55 he took a taxi out to his old property and asked the driver to wait for him.

"I'll have to leave the meter running, sir," the driver told him apologetically.

"No problem. I'll be back out here in ten minutes."

Walter retrieved his stash of money and gold, then asked the driver to take him to a suburban hotel on the north side, giving him a healthy tip. It was now 10:40 and the news was over. There was only a slim probability that any of the indifferent employees would know or connect him to the missing Lakeside elderly, even if they had given out his name on the news. It was a chance he had to take. He was more likely to be spotted on the street than in the hotel at this hour.

"God, it was almost too easy!" he said aloud to himself. There were still some logistical problems, and he had not figured out a way to annul the court order and resolve his family's misconceptions. But one thing at a time, he said with rising confidence.

He was mystified when he examined the transfers more closely and realized that there was fifty thousand dollars more than he remembered. Where had it come from? There were still some unexplained mysteries about this whole sordid business with Vivian. Well, he thought with a grin, better more than less. Anyway, it was not something he could figure out today. He was too tired to think anymore. It had been a killer day.

The next morning he faced several immediate problems. For one thing, his frumpy clothing and appearance did not fit the environment. For another, a lot of Dallas people knew him and he risked being spotted at any moment. By now Vivian was surely aware that he was a "missing elderly." He had to get away as soon as possible. "Damn!" he said. "This is more of a mess than it seemed last night in the dark. Now what should I do?"

He checked out and lugged his bags to the taxi stand, taking care not to jingle the gold coins. Several taxis were lined up. A slow day, he thought, good, good.

"Can you take me up to Ardmore?" he asked the first driver in line. "You know where it is, about seventy miles north of here? I need to get there as soon as possible."

"We're not supposed to leave the urban area."

"Just think of it as the greater Dallas area, and you're already on the north side. I'll make it worth your while."

"How much?"

"How about $400 and a bonus if you can get me there in an hour and a half? Here, I'll give you the first hundred now. How does that sound?"

"Sir, I say we're talking when we could be traveling."

They passed a marquee on Interstate 35 that read: Missing Elderly. There was the usual request to call an official number but no description of the person.

"Poor guy," said the driver, shaking his head. "At least he's not driving. Sometimes when they get like that, they drive off and can't get back home again. I've heard of cases where they find them hundreds of miles away."

"So have I. When you get to my age you run across people in that condition."

"Well, sir, you're obviously one of the lucky ones that has it all together."

"There've been a few bumps in my road and on my head but I have to say that things are going along pretty well."

"And where are we going, sir?" the driver asked as they entered the Ardmore city limits.

"Drop me off at the department store ahead. I'll show you where. Take the next exit and stay on that same street until I tell you."

It was another deceptive maneuver. After the taxi drove away, Walter walked to the bank three blocks away. Eloise was startled when she came out of her office to greet him.

"There's a long story behind the way I look, Eloise, and I'll tell you about it later. But right now I need someone to drive me to a men's store and then to a decent motel."

"Consider me your chauffeur for the rest of the day, and the evening too if you need me."

"You saw the transfer? The funds came through okay?"

"Everything is perfect, Walter. And let me tell you how happy and pleased we are that you are going with us. But you understand that we don't do anything that would alarm the bank examiners."

"Of course not. Don't worry, Eloise, it's my money. I haven't made off with stolen funds. It's all mine and I can verify it."

Two hours later, scrubbed, shaven, and decently dressed, Walter stood as Eloise came into the lobby.

"Walter, you look great in your new duds. Handsome tie!"

"Thanks. I feel better, that's for sure. I must have looked like a street person when I walked in the bank this morning."

"Well, let's just say you looked . . . interesting," she laughed. "And how are the accommodations?"

"Excellent. I'll be comfortable here."

"May I ask if you'll be staying in town long?"

"That depends, but long enough to sort out some things."

"You know that if I or my associates can help in any way, we're here, ready and willing."

"Eloise, I asked you to come by to tell you how much I appreciate not only your professional courtesy but also the personal attention. You know, of course, that you were always Evelyn's favorite cousin."

"We were like sisters, Walter. I miss her so much."

"I do too, Eloise. But I know you have other obligations, so I won't keep you long. I do feel, however, that I should tell you a bit—without going into the gritty details—about what has been going on. So you won't be blindsided. If you have the time to listen."

"All the time in the world."

He explained that he planned to stay in Ardmore for a time, at least until circumstances settled down at home. He hinted at changes in his family and personal life, but went no further.

"Bottom line and end of the chapter, Eloise, I have to ask you for another favor: that you not spread the word that I'm here. I'm not exactly in hiding, and I have certainly done nothing incriminating. I just need time to clear up some things that got out of control because I was not paying enough attention to them."

"Walter, you can count on me. And I'll tell Ed Eddleman to be as circumspect as possible in any dealings of his that have to do with you. And if anybody happens to come around asking, we don't know a thing."

The next day Walter found a well-appointed apartment. He had Ed rent him a car, bought some basic items and a charger, and contracted to have a computer installed. Later when the battery was up enough to listen to his messages, he found only one that really interested him: a call from Bill Osman several days old.

"Walter, it's Bill Osman. I was hoping I could talk to you face to face, because what I have to tell you is serious stuff. But they tell me you've disappeared. I hope it's not your health. As for me, I'm doing a lot better. The doctors were pleased with my quick recovery, although I'm sure you can hear the slur in my words. Sounds like I've had a couple too many drinks. Call me as soon as you hear this. This is something you need to know."

Something I need to know, Bill said. Well let me see what it is.

"Bill, this is Walter. I just got your message. So glad you're getting back to normal. Really great news! I had planned on coming by the hospital to see you again, but things fell apart on me. What's going on?"

"First tell me what's wrong. Are you ailing?"

"No, I was, but not anymore."

"Can you get over to my house?"

"No, I'm not in Dallas, and won't be for the foreseeable."

"Where are you, for God's sake? I can't get a straight answer from anybody about you except that nobody knows where you are."

"Bill, I'd rather not say where I am for the time being. I have my reasons. But I will tell you that I'm well and not in any immediate danger that I know of."

"My God, Walt, 'that you know of'? It sounds creepy. What in hell have you been up to?"

"You said it right, in hell. You wouldn't believe me if I told you, but tell me what's on your mind. It could be related to what's going on with me. Have you talked to Vivian about it?"

There was a pause. Bill cleared his throat and said, "Bill, it involves Vivian, and no, I haven't spoken to her. I'm not a gossip, but this is something you really need to know. I say that as your friend."

"Well, just go ahead and tell me. Anything you tell me about her won't surprise me."

"You know?"

"Know what?"

"About her . . . liaison?"

"If that's a fancy word for an affair, no, but I'm not surprised. She's pretty much tossed me out with the garbage anyway. So you don't have to spare my feelings. What's she up to?"

"It's not only what she's up to but, more importantly, who she's up to it with."

"And that unfortunate guy is . . . ?"

"Walter, I'm not comfortable talking about this, especially over the phone, but it's too urgent to keep silent about. The guy is . . . your son-in-law, Carl. Sally and I saw them together down in Los Cabos. We went down there to celebrate my quick recovery. Neither of them knows me, although it's possible we shook hands once at a reception. But Sally knows Vivian pretty well. They're in some of the same clubs. Luckily, Vivian didn't see us, and we got out of that hotel before she could spot us. Walter, I'm sorry to tell you this, and you may not take it kindly, but I felt you had to know. I—"

"Bill, say no more, and don't apologize for being my loyal friend. I was getting to a point where I felt I didn't have many left. You have just provided me with a missing piece of a puzzle that almost cost me a few million dollars and possibly my life. I've been away from home for a long time, so they could come and go as they please. So slimy Carl has been her partner in more ways than one. But my poor Helen. This is going to devastate her when she finds out."

"What are you going to do?"

"What has to be done, Bill, what has to be done, that you can count on."

"Walter, there's one more thing."

"Tell me."

"I have pictures. Sally was upset with me and said it was creepy, but I was too angry to let them just parade around and get away with it. So I hired a local guy to follow them and get the proof."

"How revealing are they?"

"Enough so that there can be no doubt about the relationship."

"Bill, if you can send them to me, it will make my day. Can you do that?"

"No problem. I'll send them right over. But what else can you tell me?"

"Just one thing but it's serious. I believe you have a problem at the bank and I suggest that you quietly investigate your Vice President with the initials GC. I have reason to believe he may have been involved with Vivian and Carl in a scheme to defraud me. I don't have solid proof, only circumstantial evidence and my gut."

The pictures were unmistakably intimate and revealing, but Walter was already emotionally detached from Vivian. His main concern now was Helen. He recalibrated his plans and called Bob.

"Dad! Where are you? We've been worried sick. What happened to you? Are you all right?"

"I'm fine, son, better than I've been in a long time. Don't tell anyone that I called. I won't tell you where I'm staying, only that I'm not in Dallas. But I need to see you. Drop whatever you're doing and meet me in Muenster this afternoon, say around 3 p.m. Can you do that? Son, I'm asking you to trust me."

"Sure, Dad. Where in Muenster? In high school we kids used to go up there to a place called Trader Dave's Café. I think it's still there, but the name may have changed. Want to try that?"

"No, it's too public. There's a little roadside park just east of town. Let's meet there. And, Bob, you have to come alone. We have a serious family situation on our hands—two of them as a matter of fact—and this time it's not me. So do exactly as I say. If you tell or bring anybody with you, it could screw up everything, me most of all."

"I'll see you at three, alone. Promise."

"Good man," Walter said but not without a nagging doubt. It was hard to trust anyone, even Bob. There was concern about calling on the phone, but he could not imagine that anyone would bother tracing the calls of a "missing elderly." There was an advantage in being dismissed as a demented old coot out wandering the streets in a daze somewhere.

Bob showed up on schedule and Walter showed him the pictures and explained what had been going on.

"Dad, Helen is going to be devastated by all this. It's probably the end of her marriage. We have to give her, Anne, and Tim all the love and support we can. I feel like starting by beating the crap of that bastard of a husband she has. I've never told you, but he always gave me bad vibes. Now I know why. And what about Vivian? What are you going to do about her?"

"Don't do anything to Carl, not yet anyway. As for Vivian, she may not know it yet, but I have pulled the financial rug from under her by stealing back my money, and I may be able put a legal scare into her, too. The details still have to play out and she'll probably have some kicking and screaming to do before she goes down."

"What can I do?"

"Son, I need for you, or it might be easier for Betty, to look for a little bottle of clear liquid next to the kitchen coffee bag or maybe the coffee maker. If not there, look in her medicine closet if you get a chance, but I think it's probably still in the kitchen."

"What is the stuff?"

"I don't know exactly, but I'm guessing some kind of toxin she was putting into my coffee that was causing my disorientation and blackouts. She used to be a nurse in a forensics laboratory in Dallas and probably knows a lot more about mind-altering substances than any of us—and where to get them. I know this: my mind and balance cleared up just days after I moved out of Lakeside Haven and flushed the prescription they had me on down the toilet."

"You mean she was trying to poison you, maybe even kill you?"

"I don't know about killing me, but tampering with my rationality and motor controls, yes, I think so. Whether I can prove it remains to be seen. That's why I need the bottle. And be careful, or tell Betty to if she goes."

"We saw the news about Lakeside. Did you have anything to do with it?"

"No comment, but tell me, did anyone get hurt?"

"I don't think so. One old couple wandered off into a neighborhood for a couple of hours, but they found them unharmed."

"That was it?"

"Well," Bob grinned, "it seems that another disoriented man wandered off in the confusion."

"And did they find him?"

"Not the last we heard. They had half the city looking for him. The police were looking for a man seen walking along the railroad. Helen and Betty were worried that it might be you."

"And what about you?"

"A little worried, I have to admit."

"Did they give the name of the man they were looking for?"

"Yeah, but you know I forgot what it was. But come to think of it, seems like it was similar to ours," Bob said with a knowing grin.

"That so? Well, the world is full of coincidences, they say."

3. Bottom Line

Still skittish about returning to Dallas, Walter asked Helen, Bob, and Betty to meet him at a steakhouse in Muenster. Trader Dave's was long gone. They took an outside table and lingered to talk after the meal.

Helen surprised the family by taking the news about Carl and Vivian better than they could have imagined. "I knew something was wrong. Things have been tense in our marriage for over two years and just kept getting worse. To be honest about it, I was ready to divorce him before all this came out in the open. In a way this makes it easier emotionally. As for Vivian, if I never hear her name again, it will be too soon."

"I want you to know, honey, that we— I know I speak for Bob and Betty—back you and the children all the way," Walter assured her with a hug.

"Dad does speak for all of us, Sis," Bob said, "We've got your back."

"Helen, we stand with you, Anne, and Tim," Betty said, teary-eyed.

"You all are precious to me. Daddy Walter is the father I never had, and you and Bob the family I lost when I was a child."

"Betty, you are as dear to me as my own flesh and blood," Walter said with a voice quivering in a rare display of emotion.

"Dad, with apologies to Helen for mentioning the name, but what has happened to Vivian?" Bob asked.

"Gone as far as I know. She threatened to put up a fight at first, but the pictures destroyed any chance she might have had for a favorable divorce settlement. Not only that, but the little vial of 'medicine' as she called it, that Betty found right there by the coffee bag, convinced her that she was lucky to get out of town without being charged with a crime. It probably would not have proved anything in court, but by that time she was too addled and scared to know it. I don't know and really don't care where she'll end up just as long as she's out of our life."

"Dad, actually, you were pretty lenient with her," Helen observed. "Didn't you let her walk away with a tidy sum of money?"

"A modest sum, but a lot less than she meant to take with her. I'm willing to pay it to be rid of her. By the way, honey, I found fifty thousand dollars extra in the transferred account. Apparently, Carl put his money in with mine because the account was doing so well. But now he can't get it back without incriminating himself. That money goes to you, plus accrued growth and interest."

"Not to pain you, Sis," Bob said, "but what about Carl? Does it bother you, or you, Dad, that they left town together?"

"I guess you didn't hear the latest, Bob. Vivian dropped him when Dad pulled the financial rug from under them. Without money, neither was very appealing to the other anymore. I guess they reminded each other of their failed scheme. Carl has tried to call me a couple of times, but the less I have to say to him, the better."

"What's the status of the Probate Court order, Daddy Walter?" Betty wanted to know. "Is all that cleared up?"

"Not yet, Betty, but with a clean bill of health from the new panel, the testimony of credible associates, and the now discredited narrative that Vivian had concocted, they assure me that a favorable new ruling is a certainty. At least that's what my new lawyer, Gil Tramonte, tells me."

"Tramonte?" Bob asked. "I thought Henry Freeman was your lawyer."

"He was for many years, but he let me down when I needed him most.

My old dad warned me that I would meet up with people like that."

"Lately, Dad," laughed Bob, "it seems that everything you get close to blows up. I heard yesterday that Bill Osman had fired his vice president, Gerald Costa. The rumor is for irregularities. You know anything about that?"

"I'm sure it was just an internal bank matter, Bob. As I told you not long ago, the world is full of coincidences. But there is one more person that may have been in on the scam."

"Who?" Bob asked.

"Dr. Morgan. He may have been a dupe or a medical dolt, but he signed off on the phony medical report. I plan to look into it, though I'm not very hopeful anything will come of it. And he may be totally innocent."

"Does all this mean you'll be coming home to us soon?" asked Betty.

"Real soon I hope, Betty, just as soon as the probate thing is cleared up and I can come back to my home county without any cloud over my head. I do have some items I need to take care of where I am now. As a matter of fact, I'm having dinner tonight with the bank president to discuss them."

"Do we know him?" asked Helen. "What's his name?"

"Hardaman, President Hardaman, a first-class person your mother knew and somebody I'd like you all to meet one of these days."

"Is he related to Momma's cousin up in Oklahoma?" Helen said. "I think she was a Hardaman."

"Could be, come to think of it. The name is not all that common, is it?" Walter replied.

As Malcolm always told Walter, never tell anybody all your business, not even family.

CPSIA information can be obtained
at www.ICGtesting.com
Printed in the USA
FFOW02n2138050517
35219FF